Sarah Lotz is a screenwriter and novelist who pens novels under the name S.L Grey with author Louis Greenberg; YA novels with her daughter, as Lily Herne; and is one third of pseudonymous author Helena S. Paige. Lauren Beukes calls her 'a natural-born storyteller. Like the hand reaching up from the dark well, she'll drag you into her thrall. You'll come up gasping.'

Pompidou Posse was Sarah's first novel. It has never before been published outside South Africa.

Also by Sarah Lotz

The Three
Day Four

For Savannah

For Savannah

First published in South Africa in 2008 by Penguin Books

First published in Great Britain by Hodder & Stoughton

An Hachette UK company

First published in paperback in 2016

1

A CIP catalogue record for this title is available from the British Library

Trade Paperback ISBN 978 1 473 61399 7

Printed and bound by Clays Ltd, St Ives plc

Hodder & Stoughton policy is to use papers that are natural, renewable
and recyclable products and made from wood grown in sustainable
forests. The logging and manufacturing processes are expected to
conform to the environmental regulations of the country of origin.

Hodder & Stoughton Ltd
Carmelite House
50 Victoria Embankment
London EC4Y 0DZ

www.hodder.co.uk

SARAH LOTZ

Pompidou Posse

HODDER

Pompidou Posse

VICKI:

The Bobby Experience

'Hey! Engleesh!'

Then again, this time louder: 'Hey! Engleesh! Over here!'

The voice cuts through the roar of the traffic blurring up and down the Boulevard Montmartre, and I immediately suspect it's targeted at us. Sage is obviously thinking the same thing.

'Christ,' she mutters. 'What the fuck's that about?'

'Dunno,' I say, trying to catch a glimpse of whoever's shouting at us.

'Why do nutters always bleeding well pick on us?'

'Who knows?'

'What do you think he wants?'

'I'm buggered if I know, Sage.'

But it looks like we're about to find out. We're being swept along by a crowd of British and German tourists, and we're nearing the source of the voice: a stone building that floats like the prow of a cross-channel ferry between two intersections. The crowd dribbles away and we're left on the pavement, an island of two.

'Fuck me,' says Sage under her breath, taking the words out of my mouth. The owner of the voice is frantically motioning us to join him, and my first thought is that he resembles a bath toy my brother had when he was a baby. Named Mr Ballso, the toy was impossible to tip over due to its bulbous shape and the weight at the base of its plastic blue arse.

'Ah. *Bonjour!* You are Engleesh, am I right?' Mr Ballso says when we get within a couple of feet of him.

I nod. His stumpy legs are clad in sausage-skin jodhpurs and his barrelled stomach strains at the fabric of a bright blue polyester shirt. A red cravat is tied jauntily around his neck. The icing on the cake is a black top hat that teeters on his ball of a head.

'I am always right! In fact you are Engleesh punks, *non?*' The fact that Sage and I are still staring at him, gobsmacked, doesn't seem to faze him in the slightest. He's probably used to it.

'Er, I'm not quite sure what we are,' I say.

He throws back his head and laughs like I've said something hilarious. Sage rolls her eyes at me and mouths 'wanker'.

'Ah. But I can see you are artistic. Am I right?'

Again I nod.

Sage leans over and whispers, 'Just tell him to fuck off, and let's go.'

I ignore her. Right now I'm willing to clutch at any straw, even one offered by someone who looks like an extra from *The Wizard of Oz.*

'You see, I can tell you are artists by the way that you dress.'

He has a point, I suppose. Sage spent twenty minutes twisting my dreads into a complicated design speared with porcupine quills, and I'm wearing my Scully Jack painted leather jacket, a floor-length Victorian velvet dress and an embroidered waistcoat. Sage also looks fairly dapper. After only a week of growth, her head is peppered with greyish stubble and she's decked out in red silk Persian trousers and a pea-green leather jacket I found for her at one of my nan's jumble sales.

Mr Ballso pops a fag into his mouth and I glance greedily

at it. He eagerly offers a crumpled pack of Marlboros. 'You need cigarettes? Here, *voilà*, take.'

I take two and pass one to Sage.

'*Merci*,' I smile, and Sage mumbles a nearly inaudible 'ta'.

As he lights my cigarette, I'm hit by a waft of industrial-strength aftershave, and now he's up close I realise he's a right short-arse. He's only a couple of inches taller than Sage, in fact.

I inhale. Beautiful. The smoke helps calm the demanding hole where my stomach used to be. How can it be possible to feel so hungry? I mean, it actually *hurts*. Since we left Natalie's place, where we ate our last reasonable meal, it's like my stomach has morphed from the innocent pink organ we had to draw in biology class into an insatiable, gaping maw – a bit like the Sarlacc monster that almost scoffs Han Solo in *Return of the Jedi*. God, I hope it isn't true that your stomach starts digesting itself if you haven't eaten for ages.

Mr Ballso's been saying something, and as Sage is still blasting fuck-off vibes at him, it's up to me to attempt to be polite. '*Pardon*,' I say. 'I didn't hear you.'

'I said, you are artists? That is what you do?'

'Yes, I mean *oui*,' I say. 'Well, students really . . . kind of.'

'You speak French?'

'*Oui, mais pas bien.*'

'No problem! I like to practise my Engleesh.' He pauses expectantly.

'And you speak it very well,' I say, which is what he wants to hear. Although his accent sounds typically French, there's something different about the way he draws out the word *Engleesh*: I imagine it stretching out of his mouth like chewing gum.

'You sell these?' Sage motions at a wall of paintings on display behind us. I've been so entranced by Mr Ballso's appearance that I haven't noticed them until now.

'*Oui*,' he says proudly. 'You like?'

We feign an interest in the artwork. It's the sort of paint-by-numbers crap you see in really old people's houses. My nan has a similar one next to her sunburst wall-clock. Hers is of a stag staring pensively over a forest. God knows why she has it, she hates nature and animals. Who the hell buys shit like this in Paris, though?

'Well? You like?'

'Um . . . Very good. You do these yourself?' I ask before Sage can say something sarcastic.

He laughs again. 'No, no! I am an agent. I sell the others' work.'

Sage and I exchange glances. *Interesting* . . .

'So, you are on holiday in Paris?' he asks.

'Not exactly.'

'What do you mean, "not exactly"? You come here to work? You are *au pairs?*'

'Kind of.'

'We're trying to find work, actually,' Sage says, managing to make even this harmless sentence sound like a threat.

'Ah. What work are you looking for? I know people, many people. It is possible I can help.'

'We're on our way to Montmartre actually. We were told it might be a good place for artists,' I say.

'Ah, you have something to sell?'

'We were really just going to check out the scene.'

'It is not easy to find a place there. There is a lot of competition.'

I smoke my cigarette right down to the filter. The last drag tastes bitter and burnt, but I don't care. I crush the butt under my boot.

'I cannot believe it!' Mr Ballso almost shrieks. 'You are artists, I am an artist, but we have not been properly introduced!'

4

'Oh, right.' I hold out my hand, but this is France. I try not to flinch as he leans forward and kisses me on both cheeks. Although his lips feel dry, I have to clench my fists to stop myself wiping my face free of imaginary Mr Ballso spit.

'*Bien*. I am Bobby.'

'Vicki.'

'Vicki, like Queen Victoria?'

'Yeah. But everyone calls me Vicki.'

'It is a good name for you.' Bobby grabs one of my hands and theatrically bows down to kiss it. 'You are indeed a queen.'

Fortunately he doesn't see Sage pointing a finger down her throat. 'And this is Sage.' I try not to smirk as Sage submits to the same cheek-kissing ritual. This should be good. Apart from the odd fight, I've never seen her share any kind of intimate contact with anyone before.

'Sage?' Bobby says, 'That is unusual, *non?* What does it mean?'

'It's a herb,' I say, a tad maliciously. 'Sage's folks were flower children in the sixties.'

'Ah. You are a . . . hippy, Sage? A punk and a hippy?'

'No I'm not a fucking hippy,' she deadpans. 'And I'm not a fucking skinhead or whatever label you want to put on me.'

Shit. At the very least I'd been hoping to hit Bobby for another couple of fags, but it looks like Sage has blown it again. I rack my brain for something to say, but he jumps in before I can speak.

'I like you!' he says to Sage. 'You have attitude, *n'est-ce pas?*'

Sage gives him a death stare. 'You taking the piss?'

'What is this: taking the piss?'

'Are you fucking with me?' she says, drawing each word out slowly.

Bobby doesn't get it. 'I am not sure what you mean, but I understand you in a way.' He turns to me. 'You are the soft one, and your friend, the herb, she is the strong one. That is why you are friends. Tell me I am right.'

'Wow, Bobby, you've figured us out.' Sage smirks. 'Any chance of another cig?'

He hands her the pack.

'So, tell me more about Vicki and Sage,' Bobby says, as he lights our fags.

'What do you want to know?' I ask.

'Why it was that you decided to leave home.'

Sage shakes her head warningly at me.

I ignore her. 'A friend of mine – Natalie – said she could find us a job as *au pairs* here. So we left home, came out here and stayed with her in her flat just outside Paris where she's working. But it turned out there wasn't any work for us after all. You know, no job, nothing. So we had to leave her place and come to the city.'

'She basically told us to fuck off,' Sage adds. She never misses an opportunity to slag off Natalie.

'*Pourquoi?*' Bobby asks. 'Why did she do that?'

'I'm not sure,' I say. 'There wasn't much room where she was staying, I guess. She didn't *exactly* tell us to fuck off.' I glance at Sage and receive a scowl in return. 'I reckon the people she worked for didn't like us being there. And maybe she didn't realise I was really serious about getting a job.'

'She knew,' Sage says. 'She knew we were serious all right.'

'Ah, so you were . . . stranded,' Bobby says.

'Yeah, that's right, stranded,' Sage says, actually smiling at him.

'With no job.'

'That's right.'

'And how long have you been in this country?'

I look at Sage. It feels like forever. 'About two weeks,' I say.

'So, why do you not go home?' Bobby asks, as I knew he would. This one isn't so easy to answer. I mumble something about always wanting to move to Paris and live the artistic dream, which I suppose is half true. I don't mention the fire, the cops, the shit we're in with the folks. I'm not stupid. It looks like this guy may help us out and I'm not going to ruin our chances with the truth.

'We'd better get going, Vicks,' Sage says. 'We've got to get our stuff soon.'

'Stuff?' Bobby asks.

'Our luggage. We left it at the hotel. We can only keep it there till four,' I explain.

Bobby frowns. 'You are not staying there tonight?'

'No.'

'So where will you stay?'

'Er . . . we hadn't really thought about it.'

'What do you mean?'

We don't really have an answer for that. I wait for Sage to speak, but she's inspecting the end of her cigarette.

Bobby puts a hand on my arm and looks at me seriously. For a horrible second I think he's going to lean in and kiss me. 'Are you in trouble? Do you need money?'

I glance at Sage. She shrugs. It's up to me. 'We're in deep *merde*,' I say.

Bobby beams as if we've given him fantastic news. 'Then it is a wonderful thing that you have met me! I will help you!' He roots around in his polyester shirt, retrieves a wallet, opens it and triumphantly whips out a crisp 200-franc note. 'Take it,' he says to me.

I hesitate.

Sage's eyes narrow. 'What are you playing at, mate?'

Bobby's grin doesn't waver. 'It is for you, of course.'

For a panicky second I'm sure Sage is going to tell him to stick it up his arse. 'Bobby, *je ne comprends pas . . .*' I say, before she can ruin everything.

'What is there to understand? I have decided I will help

7

you. This money is for another night in the hotel where you are staying. Tomorrow I will have somewhere else for you to live until you find work.'

'You serious?' Sage jumps in. 'And what *exactly* do you want in exchange?'

'Nothing.' Bobby shrugs expansively. 'You need help. I am here to give.'

Taking her time, Sage drops her cigarette on the pavement and grinds it under her boot. 'You married, Bobby?' she asks, managing to make the question sound less barbed than I know it is.

For the first time, Bobby looks ill at ease. '*Pourquoi?* Why do you ask?'

'Just wondering. Are you?'

'My wife and I are . . . separated.'

'Any kids?'

'*Non.* Again, why do you ask?'

'No reason. Just getting-to-know-you stuff.' She pauses. 'Like friends do, you know?'

'Ah, *bon.*' Bobby looks older when he's not smiling.

I watch Sage carefully, willing her not to screw up our only hope of a roof over our heads. After a brief mental struggle, she makes her decision. 'Ta very much like, Bobby,' she says, and the note disappears into one of her waistcoat pockets. 'We'll pay you back. Where's this place you think we can stay?'

Bobby's grin returns. 'I have a friend who likes the people who are . . . bohemian, artistic . . . *interesting*. You know, like you. Like me.' He shrugs modestly. 'He will be happy for you to stay with him for a couple of days, I am sure.'

'What does he do?'

'He is a student. He is about your age, I think?' He looks me up and down. It could be my imagination, but his eyes seem to linger a little too long on my chest. 'What is your age, in fact?'

'I've just turned eighteen,' I say. Sage scowls.

Bobby claps his hands. '*Bien,* my new friends, now business is done we must eat! Come, help me to pack away the paintings and I will take you for lunch! You are hungry?'

Without thinking I accept. I look over at Sage and give her the thumbs up sign. I get no response. As soon as Bobby's back is turned she pulls me aside. 'Vicki, what are you doing? We can't just go off with some vile pervert.'

I sigh. 'You don't know he's a perv. Anyway, you got any better ideas?'

Sage shakes her head. 'All I'm saying is – what sort of a man gives complete strangers a bunch of money for free?'

'Maybe he's just a nice guy. How should I know?'

Sage snorts. 'Let's just take the money and leg it, okay?'

'Think about it, Sage. We're fucked. If this guy wants to help us out, let's let him. We haven't really got a choice, have we? I mean, do you want to go back home? You know what'll happen if we do.'

'This is as dodgy as fuck.'

'Right now, Sage, I couldn't give a shit,' I say, and I mean it. Right now there isn't much I wouldn't do for even a fried egg on toast. 'Let's just go eat. We'll have time to get our stuff afterwards. Anyway, we've got to do *something*, haven't we?'

Sage doesn't reply and I turn my back on her to help Bobby load the paintings into a metal container next to the wall of the bank.

SAGE

The words to 'Wish You Were Here' by bastard Pink Floyd keep running through my head for some reason. I mean, I don't even have any Pink Floyd here with me, thank God, because it's basically shite anyway. Okay, let me get something straight here. I am NOT writing this because bastard Doctor Wankenstein Walton said I should. 'Try and work through your feelings, Sharon, by putting pen to paper. It could help you deal with your anger issues.' Yeah, right. As if writing stuff down would have stopped me from calling him a shit-head. He deserved it for ignoring me when I told him to call me by my Proper Name. Total bastard.

Speaking of names, I'm not going to do the crappy Anne Frank 'Dear diary' bollocks. From this day on I hereby name this book Gladys. That sounds better.

So. Dear Gladys . . .

I did mean to write stuff down when we were at Natalie-the-Bitch's, but this is the first time I've been on my own for fucking weeks. I know you're supposed to start diaries and shit with dates and stuff, but I'm not sure of the exact date. It's sometime in February 1988. That'll do.

So. We're back in another crappy old hotel room that stinks of other people's BO and old fags, and Vicks is out buying food for us with the money we had left over from that pervert's stash. I told her to take her time, which probably wasn't a nice thing to say, but then, who cares??

But I have a huge confession to tell you, which is one of the reasons I wanted to write this. It's not like I'm a Catholic or anything. But I do feel bad.

First things first. Me and Vicks have met this vile pervert called Bobby who says he wants to help us, but I want you to know, Gladys, that I do not trust him at all. I mean, nobody just gives money away for free. I know he wants something, and it makes me sick that Vicks can't see the way he looks at her. I should never have helped her look so good this morning. Anyway, after he gave us some cash he said he'd take us to get something to eat. I was dead suspicious and didn't want to go, but I went anyway for Vicks's sake only.

So we help the pervert load up his rubbish paintings and follow him for hours through this maze of streets. All the time he's talking non-stop to Vicks about himself and about how well known he is. He goes on and on and I'm surprised he can find a hat big enough for his big fat head. Just as I'm about to say, 'Oi, where the fuck are we going?' he finally shuts his trap and we stop outside this building that doesn't look like a restaurant at all. I mean it didn't have a sign on it or anything. I wanted to drag Vicks away right then, but she just followed him in like a lamb, so of course I had to go in there as well.

The place was bloody massive, with a glass ceiling and lots of different floors. There were hundreds of tables (I'm not exaggerating, honest, Gladys), and it was heaving with Frogs babbling in their Frog language. It was a far cry from Kath's Caff where we used to go when we were skiving from fart college, I can tell you.

And this was weird: Over in the corner there was this little brown bird flitting around the pot plants, and everyone ignored it as if it was normal to see birds inside places where you eat. Okay, so maybe then I started to feel less suspicious, as the pervert couldn't really do much with all the people around, could he?

So. We were shown to a table near the back. The head waiter bloke looked really happy to see Bobby (why????), but looked at me and Vicks as if we were dog shit. Snooty. But I didn't really care, Gladys, because the smell of the food was so immense and I've never been so hungry, ever. We sat down, and the waiter plonked down a basket of cut-up French bread. Well obviously me and Vicks fell on it like zombies on a corpse, and I didn't even bother putting butter on mine (which is weird because I normally hate dry bread). Then, just as we were both going for the last piece, bowls of boiling soup appeared in front of us. At first I didn't know what to do with mine as there was something floating in it which turned out to be a huge piece of bread and melted cheese. Frogs have bizarre ideas about food and stuff obviously. Even though the soup was as hot as fuck, I slurped it down (I've still got juicy bub-bled blisters on the roof of my mouth) and because I wasn't sure what to do with the big cheesy bread dollop, I shoved it into my gob in one go!!! You should have seen the pervert's face!! He almost shat himself.

Anyway, I'm getting to the bad part, Gladys . . .

The second we finish our onion soup, our bowls are whisked away and on comes the next course. Both Vicks and me just stare at our plates, and the pervert is dead confused. 'There is a problem?' he says, and Vicks says, 'We're vegetarians.' And he goes: 'You mean you do not eat meat?' And I'm like, 'Duh, that is what being a vegetarian means, arseface'. And then he says something like, 'Oh, this is a real pity, because this is no ordinary meat it's (guess what, Gladys??) VEAL'.

You should have seen our faces. Everyone knows that veal is the cruellest of meat. Me and Vicks had been on an anti-veal protest just before all the shit hit the fan at home.

So the pervert goes: 'You want that I order you something different?' But thing is, Gladys, it just smelled so amazing. It was like it was calling to me, going, Saaage, Saaage, no one will eveeer know if you eat me. And Vicks goes, 'I suppose we could just eat the potatoes'. Bollocks to the potatoes. We ate the lot – inhaled it really. 'Slow down, you will be sick!' the perv kept saying. We ignored him.

So that's why I feel so guilty, Gladys. And I feel even worse because I didn't actually get sick or anything after I ate it. Quite the opposite. I want more. If you brought a cow to me right now, I swear I would just sink my teeth into it, eat the whole fucking thing raw.

Vicks has promised the vile perv that we'll meet him tomorrow morning so that we can meet his friend who might put us up for a while. I could tell he was scamming for an invite to our hotel room, but no such fucking luck. Okay, I can hear someone coming down the corridor.

REMIND ME TO CHECK ON THE TABLET SITUATION

VICKI:

The Hervé Experience

'Pardon,' I mumble as the door slips out of my fingers, bangs against my rucksack and almost brains a woman behind me. Sage and I are struggling to squeeze our luggage through the slim glass exit doors at the Opera metro station. We decided to use the last of Bobby's handout on train tickets. The thought of lugging our stuff on foot from the hotel to Bobby's corner was too much to bear.

'Our bags weren't this heavy when we left home, were they?' I say, trying to break the tension.

Sage just shrugs. She's spent the morning maintaining an aloof expression and we've barely said a word to each other, even when I managed to get us lost. As we struggle up the stairs I try again to brighten the mood. 'You know what I feel like?'

She feigns a yawn. 'What?'

'You know that movie, *Labyrinth*?'

'No.'

'Yeah, you do. The one with the puppets and David Bowie in tights.'

Sage looks blank. 'No, I really don't.'

'Well, anyway. In the movie there's this character that carries all her shit on her back. I mean like everything – her whole life, history, everything she's ever owned.'

'Yeah, so?'

'Well, what I'm saying is I feel like her.'

'Really.'

I give up.

We'd had one of our massive fights that had erupted out of nowhere last night. I'm never sure how or why they start. I mean, we'd had a great afternoon, despite the fact that she was still pissed off about the Bobby situation. I'd even agreed to go and fetch some food and fags by myself, and she was in a good mood when I left. When I got back to the hotel we spent a few minutes doing impressions of Bobby and having a laugh before Sage decided to go down the corridor for a shower. I'd just made myself comfortable on the lumpy bed when she returned. She didn't look charmed.

'Just look,' she said.

'At what?'

'My feet.'

I looked down. Her favourite pair of hiking boots were soaking wet. 'What the hell?'

'You don't want to know.'

'You been outside or something? Is it raining?'

'Course I haven't been outside. Is my head wet?'

'Well, what then?'

'The bloody toilet.'

'What, you fall in?'

'It's one of those funny fucking French ones. Those ones that are just holes in the ground with nothing to sit on like normal toilets. I couldn't figure out how to flush it, and when I did—'

I collapsed into giggles. Big mistake.

'It's not funny,' she snapped. 'My socks are soaked!'

'I hate those loos,' I said, trying to defuse the situation. 'They creep me out. I'm positive that one day I'll look down and a large blue eye will blink up at me.'

'If I have to go again I'll use the one on the other floor. And the state of the shower! Jesus. You never told me French people were such fucking slobs, Vicks.'

She sat down on the bed and hurled the sodden hiking boots into the corner. Then she unpeeled the offending socks and chucked them into the bin. 'That's my last clean pair.'

'You're lucky, I haven't worn clean underwear since we were at Nat's,' I said, still trying to keep the tone of the conversation above danger-zone level.

Ignoring me, she rummaged in her rucksack.

'I suppose I'd better phone Natalie,' I said. Second big mistake.

'What the fuck for? We don't owe that bitch anything. She screwed us, remember?'

'Look, the folks have her number. If they're trying to get hold of us, we need to let her know we're fine.'

'So, just phone your dad and say you're okay.'

'You know I can't do that.'

'Just leave it. Fucking hell. When we get sorted at the place Bobby the Bastard's got for us you can phone her then, 'kay?'

'Sage, don't call him that.'

'Why the fuck not?'

'Because he's helping us out. It's not right. Besides, he's not that bad.'

Sage turned her back on me and started stuffing clothes into her bag. There was a pause. I knew what was coming. 'Obviously you know he just wants to fuck you.'

'C'mon, you don't know that.'

'Don't be so stupid. His eyes didn't leave your tits for one second.'

'Yeah? Well he spoke to you most of the time. Anyway, what does it matter?'

'It matters.'

'So what do you suggest we fucking do? We've got no fucking choice in the matter. Even if we *could* go home we haven't got any fucking money.'

16

'Do you have to swear so much?' She pulled on her dry socks. 'We'll make a plan, we always do.'

'Jesus, I don't believe you.'

'Yeah, well I hope Bobby's friend isn't as weird as he is.'

'Even if Bobby does want to – you know – what does it matter? Anyway, he's bloody old. He must be at least forty or something.'

'He's a creepy old perv.'

'Look at us. We're getting a place to stay, maybe a job, we're sorted. What's your problem?'

'It matters,' she repeated. She threw herself down on the other end of the bed and turned her face to the wall. Seconds later I heard the tinny sound of Led Zeppelin's *The Song Remains the Same* ghosting out of her Walkman's headphones.

Fuck you too, I thought. I fished out *Pet Semetary*, but couldn't concentrate on it. I tried my best to shut out the faint bass track and let myself spiral down into a delicious daydream: Bobby's friend turned out to be a cross between River Phoenix and Jean-Hugues Anglade in *Subway*, and his apartment was huge and lined with books and antique writing desks. Best of all, the guest rooms were lovely and comfy, with double beds and patchwork quilts. My room had ruched curtains that partially obscured a tantalising glimpse of the Paris skyline and was the only one with a view (fuck Sage, she didn't deserve one). I was fantasising about River/Jean-Hugues entering my room carrying a tray piled high with *pain au chocolat* when Sage nudged me with her foot and snarled: 'Just don't fucking blame me when it all turns to *shit.*'

We emerge into the winter sun. Even from the island that houses the metro exit I can make out Bobby's round blue shape working the crowd on the other side of the boulevard. I've tried to look less noticeable today, opting for a green-spotted 1940s dress and my red overcoat. Unfortunately the coat's not very warm, and I can feel the cold bite of the air through the fabric. Sage also looks like she hasn't given much thought to the day's outfit, which is unusual for her. She hardly makes a fashion statement at all in her long grey jumper and matching crocheted hat.

But there's no hope of sneaking up on Bobby.

'Hey! Engleesh!' He waves his arms over his head. Several people turn to look at him curiously.

'What a fuckhead,' Sage mutters.

'For fuck's sake, Sage. He's trying to help us out! Can you at least *try* not to be such a bitch?'

Third big mistake. It only takes a second for Sage's face to shut down completely. My stomach sinks. I'm in for another round of the silent treatment.

We hobble across the last intersection and into Bobby's waiting 'hello' embrace. I've barely put down my rucksack before he's grabbed me and planted three violent kisses on my cheeks. He does the same to Sage. Without waiting to be asked, he takes out his cigarettes and offers the pack. Sage grins at him. Obviously Bobby isn't so much of a fuckhead when he's handing out freebies.

'So, Bobby,' Sage says cheerily. 'How *are* you this morning?'

She's taken him off-guard. 'Er, I am well, and how did you sleep?'

'Fine, thank you for asking. I had a lovely night.' I know exactly what she's doing: deliberately being sugary sweet to Bobby to try and wind me up.

'*Bien*,' Bobby says, still confused at her overnight change of personality. He turns to me. 'And how is the queen today?'

'Great,' I say.

'*Bon*. Now, Hervé – my friend – will arrive in a few minutes to take you to your new home.'

'Hervé? What kind of a name is that?' Sage snorts, before she can stop herself.

Bobby ignores her. I smirk. 'Where does this . . . Hervé live, then?' she asks hurriedly, voice dripping with sugar. 'Far away, is it?'

Bobby laughs. '*Non*. Five minutes from here.'

'And you're sure it's all right by him, Bobby? This is so very kind of you,' I say. Two can play at this game.

'But of course! He is my friend. And as you are my friends, he is more than happy to help. You see, Hervé is very nice.' 'Like me', I can tell he wants to add. 'After you went to your hotel, I go to his place and tell him all about you. He is very excited.'

'That's great!' I chirp. 'We're excited too!'

Sage pretends to spot something fascinating in the distance.

'You have a lot of clothes I see?' He looks down at the pile of bags at our feet.

'A girl can't have too many clothes, eh Bobby?' I say.

'Especially when she is a queen!' he exclaims. I force a laugh. Sage looks as if she's about to throw up.

'*Bien*. Now. Do you mind waiting? I must do some work until Hervé arrives.'

'No problem,' I gush. 'I'm looking forward to seeing how you operate.'

Bobby beams, and Sage turns her back on both of us and fiddles with the strap on her rucksack.

While we wait, luggage stacked against our legs, Bobby continues to attract the attention of passers-by. '*Hola*!' greets anyone with an olive skin, '*Buongiorno*!' is directed at anyone who could conceivably be Italian, and he even throws in the odd '*Aloha*' or two. He's shameless. I try to and clock Sage's reaction to Bobby's mortifying antics, but she's staring stolidly at the pavement.

Then I spy something that's bound to snap her out of her self-inflicted sulk. I try to catch her eye. Finally she peers at me from under dark eyelashes. 'Carpet leg alert,' I say.

I point to where an old lady is hobbling past. She's not the best example of carpet leg syndrome I've ever seen. Old French ladies obviously don't have as much talent for developing a really good carpet leg as their English equivalent. This is a mediocre example: puffy ankles, dark tan tights, no noticeable break where the calf stops and the ankle begins. The faintest promise of a serious case of varicose veins. Sage's mouth twitches. The knot in my stomach loosens.

'Surprised you noticed that,' she says.

'Eh?'

'Aren't you more interested in watching Bobby *operate?*'

'You've got to admit, that was good.'

She cracks a smile. 'Yeah. Fair play, *Queenie.*'

'When you're good, you're good.'

Sage rolls her eyes. She sneaks a couple of cigarettes out of her pocket and passes me one without Bobby seeing. We're friends again. Simple as that.

We watch Bobby again in silence. He's tireless. No one is safe. 'You like art? All originals ... Ah! *Guten tag,* my friends!'

We seem to be the only people on the crowded pavement unaffected by the movement of the jostling crowd. In fact, we appear to have created an invisible two-metre perimeter around us. Thankfully, Bobby's enthusiastic attempt to attract the attention of a throng of Japanese tourists ('*Konitchiwa!* Paintings, you want paintings?') is mercifully cut short.

'Hervé! My friend! You are here!' he shrieks, as a tallish figure approaches.

Hervé immediately reminds me of the faun in *The Lion, the Witch and the Wardrobe.* His tightly curled hair is perm perfect, and his goatee does nothing to disguise an unfortunate, overlarge chin. I can't wait to discuss this with Sage. The faun had always given me the creeps when I was little, benevolent character or not. I've always liked the witch best. But what was his name? It's on the tip of my tongue. Mr Tufnall. No. Mr Tumnut. Mr Tumtum?

'Sage,' I hiss, while Hervé and Bobby are kissing each other 'hello'.

'Yeah?' She's also busy checking Hervé out.

'What's the name of the the faun in *The Lion, the Witch and the Wardrobe*?'

'Buggered if I know. Begins with a "T", doesn't it? Why?'

'Don't you think Hervé looks just like—'

Before I can finish, Bobby interrupts, introduces Hervé, and Sage and I uncomfortably kiss the faun. His beard tickles.

'This is very kind of you,' I say.

'Nonsense!' Bobby guffaws. 'You need help? We are there to give! Am I right, Hervé?'

Hervé nods shyly.

Suddenly I remember. 'Mr Tumnus!' It slips out before I can stop it.

'*Pardon?*' Hervé stares at me, confused.

Sage snorts with laughter.

'Er . . . nothing.' Heat rushes to my cheeks.

Bobby's in his element. 'Hervé will take you now to his home, where you will live until you are able to find a job. *N'est-ce pas?*'

'*Oui,*' the faun replies.

Bobby rubs his hands together.

'Can I help?' Hervé gestures at the third bag Sage and I carry between us. It's the heaviest as it contains my books, odd bits of clothing, our collection of 2000AD comics and the sculptures we couldn't bear to part with when we made our hasty getaway from England.

'Nah. We'll manage. Thanks, though,' Sage says.

Hervé looks relieved. My bright pink lacy knickers are peeking out of a split seam.

Hervé and Bobby march off down the boulevard,

chatting non-stop. Sage and I struggle to keep up. We're bent double under our rucksacks like babushkas and are desperately trying to keep the third bag balanced as it yaws and pitches.

'So, what d'you think of Hervé?' I murmur to Sage.

'Looks all right. Well, he's a wanker, obviously.'

'Obviously.'

Bobby whirls around and points at me. 'Hey! Foxy Lady!'

To his credit, Hervé looks embarrassed.

'Eh?' I say, as Sage rolls her eyes.

Bobby laughs. 'You know Hendrix?'

'Not personally,' Sage says, without bothering to keep the contempt out of her voice.

'You know the song, "Foxy Lady?"' Bobby points at me. 'That is your name!'

He's practically dancing down the street. Oh God. It's more mortifying than the time my nan fetched me from school without remembering to put her teeth in first.

We cut down a narrow alleyway and follow Hervé and Bobby down a smartish-looking road. When they reach a pair of ornate green doors set into a large stone apartment block they stop and wait for us to catch up. The building shares a corner with a black-fronted Irish pub. I can hardly believe our luck.

'Nice neighbourhood,' Sage says out of the corner of her mouth. 'At least we won't have to go far for a pint.'

Hervé taps a code into the keypad stuck on the wall next to the door. The door opens with a clunk and we follow Hervé and Bobby into a dark hallway dominated by a wide scuffed staircase.

'You sure you manage? With the bags?' Hervé asks again. 'We must go up the stairs, quite far.'

'Yes. We're *absolutely* sure, thanks,' Sage says and I shift the weight on my back again to make it more comfortable. As usual it doesn't help. Bobby motions us forward. He doesn't offer to carry anything.

I can hear the muted strains of Duran Duran floating out, presumably from the Irish pub, but there is nothing muted about the hallway's smell. At first I think it's just the odour of cooking and stale beer from the pub's kitchen, but as we follow Hervé up to the second floor and 'Rio' fades away, the over-cooked cabbage and old alcohol odour is replaced with something else.

'Is that what I think it is?' Sage whispers.

I nod. It's the unmistakable stench of hashish.

Hervé strides ahead. The staircase spirals upwards, breaking on each floor with a narrow landing which fronts a pair of posh-looking double doors. He isn't even slightly out of breath. Sage and I are gasping like we've just chain-smoked forty Woodbines. The rucksack has turned into a gorilla that's squeezing my shoulders, and my thigh muscles are shaking. Even though Bobby's far behind us, we can still hear him clearly: 'Hey, Foxy Lady. You know you're a heartbreaker, duh-duh duh-duh . . .'

'Jimi Hendrix rest in peace,' Sage mutters.

'Hervé?' I gasp.

He turns around. '*Oui?*'

'What's behind these doors?'

He looks bemused. 'Apartments.'

'Of course. Sorry. And where do you live?'

'I live on the top floor. Do not worry, it is not much further.'

We peer upwards. The stairs seem to go on forever like an optical illusion.

'Great,' Sage mutters.

The hashy smell gets stronger with every step. No prizes for guessing from which floor it originates.

There's an uncomfortable moment as the three of us hover

on the top-floor landing waiting for Bobby. It's narrow and poorly lit by an interrogation room bare bulb on a wire. No grand double-door entrances here.

'The toilet is here,' Hervé says abruptly, motioning towards a wooden door that looks exactly like the other five or six on the floor.

'Right,' Sage says. 'That's good to know.'

'You want to see it?'

'*Definitely*,' she grins.

We peer into the gloom. With a click and a faint hissing sound the toilet's light sputters on. A sad-looking lavatory is shadowed within. It's bare and stained and has no toilet seat. A ragged wedge of newspaper is speared on a hook next to it. It appears to be the only space unoccupied by the aura of stale hash, mainly because it has its own marshy shitty smell. I need to pee, but I'm too embarrassed to say so with Hervé standing there. It can wait.

'Great,' Sage mutters, nodding at the newspaper. But at least it's not one of those stand-up jobbies.

From behind one of the doors I make out the muffled strains of the Doors' 'People are Strange'.

'How apt,' Sage says in her pseudo-intellectual voice.

'All the people on this floor use this toilet, so we must try to keep it clean.' Hervé smiles at us nervously. His teeth are very white, although the bottom ones overlap.

'I see,' Sage says solemnly. To me she murmurs: 'What does he think we're going to do? Shit on the floor or something?' I quickly turn my snort of laughter into a cough.

Bobby finally makes it. He's taken off his cravat and is using it to wipe his brow. Wiry Brillo pad hairs peep through the top of his shirt.

Hervé strides down the corridor and hesitates outside the door at the end. We clump along behind him. '*Et . . . Voilà!*'

Fuck. What a let-down. It's just a room, a single room. It's gloomy and hazy with dope smoke. There's a large mattress covered with clothes against one wall; opposite it is a narrow bed on which two bodies are sprawled. As Sage and I follow Hervé in, the bodies sit up and wobble to their feet. A blond heavyset twentyish man and a skinnier dark-haired bloke greet Hervé with a gabble of French. They don't seem to notice us until Hervé points us out to them. I immediately forget their names as we're introduced. As usual, I'm uncomfortable with the whole French greeting thing. Do I kiss first? Allow myself to be kissed? Just make kissy noises in the direction of the recipients' faces? Despite practising with Bobby, this doesn't come naturally to me. I almost butt noses with the smaller of the two. As they're kissing Sage, I check them out. Like Hervé they're dressed in narrow-legged jeans and yachting shoes. Bugger. They're definitely not my type.

And they both reek of dope.

'Take a seat, please.' Hervé motions us towards the mattress. Sage and I plop down, discarding our luggage on the floor. Hervé and the two guys flop back down on the bed directly opposite us. One of them starts rolling a joint. Bobby's hovering in between the two camps. His face is bright crimson, and he's still using his cravat to wipe away the beads of sweat that keep peppering his forehead.

'*Bien*!' he says. 'I must go back to work. You be okay here?'

'Yep,' Sage says, leaning her back against the wall and crossing her legs. I push aside a bundle of musty clothes and do the same.

'That is good. I see you tomorrow?' Bobby says to me.

'Sure,' I say. Bugger. He's waiting for us to kiss him *au revoir.* I get up, and with a sigh, Sage does the same. As he kisses me goodbye, Bobby squeezes my waist. I pretend not to notice. He shoots a *salut!* at the other guys in the room, and is gone. Sage immediately bounces back onto the mattress.

'You smoke?' Hervé's balancing a *Time* magazine on his

knees and twisting tobacco from a cigarette into a jumbo-sized Rizla.

'Of course,' Sage says. 'That's quite a stash you got there, Hervé.'

Using the flame from his lighter, he's burning pieces of hash off a block as long and thick as his thumb.

'How much did that set you back?' Sage asks.

I nudge her. 'You can't ask something like that!'

'Why not? It's drugs. No one gives a shit.'

Hervé isn't listening anyway. Blondie has finished making his joint and he lights it and takes a deep drag with relish. After two hits he gets up and passes it to me.

'*Merci*,' I say. I don't really want it, but take a drag anyway. It's way stronger than I'm used to, and I almost gag as I suck the smoke into my lungs. I pass it to Sage.

Blondie's staring at us, a fixed grin on his face. 'You like?' he says.

'Great. Thanks,' I say.

'Don't you worry about the police, like?' Sage says to him, letting the smoke curl slowly from her mouth.

'*Pardon*?' he peers politely at her.

'Cos it stinks in here. Don't your neighbours complain?'

Blondie looks over at Hervé and shrugs. There's a quick babbled conversation in French, followed by giggling.

'Ah! The hash!' Blondie says. '*Non.* No complaints.'

'Lucky.' Sage shrugs. 'Where we come from you'd be locked up for that.'

'Not lucky. On this floor, most of the people, they smoke.'

'Ah.'

Hervé passes me the joint he's just made. I take another hit. I'm beginning to feel a bit disorientated. I'd better slow down, but I don't want to look like I can't handle myself. I take another, shallower hit, trying not to inhale so deeply.

Sage's voice helps break up the fug in my head.

'So how do you know Bobby?' she's asking Hervé.

'He is someone that I see every day,' Hervé says in between drags. 'One day we start talking. He is . . . *très intéressant* – very different.'

'Yeah. You can say that again,' Sage says, which everyone seems to find hilarious. She nods at the other guys on the bed.

'And you guys. Sorry – I forgot your names.'

'Michel and Claude,' Blondie says.

'You live here as well?' She looks dubiously around the tiny room.

'Of course not!' Hervé giggles. 'They are just my friends. They cannot smoke where they stay.'

Thank God for that, at least. But it looks like we've ended up in some sort of yuppies' drug den. There are now three joints making the rounds and Claude, the dark-haired guy, is continuously and expertly skinning up.

I'm hit with a wave of dizziness. I try and concentrate on the room to ground myself. There's not much to look at. It's just a box with no windows and a single door. There are a few textbooks in amongst the piles of discarded clothes, but they look as if they've never been opened. I can't see any other reading material: no novels, comics or anything I'd be interested in. Next to us stands a camping stove, a crusty pot and a large bag of rice. There's a small, stained sink wedged into a corner.

Sage follows my gaze. 'Jesus, Vicks. Aren't there any fucking clean sinks in France? The one in our hotel was almost as bad.'

Although there are no visible radiators, it's uncomfortably warm in here. Apart from the hash fog, it also smells quite a bit like my brother's room – it's got that particular man pong about it: old farts and dirty socks.

The room isn't doing much for me, so I concentrate on the faces of the others. The blond has an oblong head which looks too big for his body. The other one has bad skin, slightly uptilted eyes and pointy teeth. 'Potato Head and Dracula,' I whisper to Sage. She giggles and sets me off.

'What is so funny?' Hervé asks.

'Everything,' Sage says.

Hervé and Potato Head/Michel nod their heads sagely as if she's said something profound.

Dark-haired Dracula speaks for the first time. 'You are from London?' Dracula really is an excellent name for him. The rims of his eyes are scarlet, like Christopher Lee's.

'Nah. Wolverhampton,' Sage says.

All three look blank.

'I have been to London,' Potato Head says. 'Very interesting. Is it near to you?'

'Nah. We're near Birmingham.'

'Birmingham. And what are you doing in Paris?' Potato Head says to me. I open my mouth to answer, but can't seem to form the words.

'We're escaping,' says Sage, dramatically.

'You are escaping from Birmingham? *Pourquoi?* Why is that?'

'It's a right shit-hole,' Sage says.

'Ah. What sort of place is it? It is industrial?'

'Yeah. Guess so. Not surprised you don't know it. Practically no one famous comes from there. Except crap bands like UB40.'

'Ah. I know them!' Dracula starts singing 'Red Red Wine'. The other guys join in.

Everyone, including Sage, giggles. With a jolt I realise that I'm giggling as well. The room moves again, and I go from buzzing to nauseous instantly. I clamp my mouth shut and concentrate on the wall in front of me.

'You got music here, Hervé?' Sage asks.

'*Non.* Sorry.'

'What music you like?' Dracula asks.

'Mostly retro. You know, late sixties stuff. Incredible String Band, Gong, that kind of thing.' Everyone looks blank again. I hadn't heard of Gong either, till Sage. 'But Vicki loves Jimi Hendrix, don't you, Chuck?' She starts humming 'Foxy Lady'.

Potato Head and Dracula both wear headphones around their necks. Maybe we can score some batteries off them. This time when I'm handed a joint, I pass it straight to Sage. No one seems to notice. I'm now at the stage where if I had something in my stomach to puke up, I know I probably would. I'm trying to will myself to leave the room for air that's less thick with smoke, when Dracula passes me a packet of M&Ms. I scarf down a handful. The blast of sweetness helps stem my out of control feeling, but for a scary second I can't swallow. Oh crap on toast. If this passes soon, I will never smoke again, *I promise*. Sage doesn't pass the packet back, but sneaks it into her waistcoat pocket. She hands me a cigarette. Why didn't I think of this before? This way I can legitimately pass the joint without having a hit. Sage surreptitiously palms me some more sweets and I cram them into my mouth.

Potato Head is saying something to me. I try to respond, but all that comes out is a croak. Luckily, Sage appears to be in control. 'We're cousins,' she's saying.

'And your parents?' Potato Head asks.

'Dead.'

For a moment, I'm shocked, but I should be used to this by now. Sage's motto: why tell the truth when a lie will do?

'Oh. I am sorry.'

Sage shrugs. 'Yeah. Children's home and all that, you know.'

I feel a stab of shame. The two boys look genuinely sympathetic.

There's a gap in the conversation. But as hash is involved it isn't one of those awkward ones. Hervé is still grinning inanely and keeps looking from Sage and me to his two friends. I concentrate all my energy on getting myself under control.

When I tune back in Sage appears to be trying to teach the Frenchies English/American slang.

'Wicked,' she says.

'Ah. So if I say that something is wicked, it means that I think it is rather good?' Potato Head looks as if he's taking this very seriously, as if he's at a lecture or something.

'No. "Wicked" means something's fucking excellent. You know, really cool, like.'

'*D'accord*,' Potato Head says. Hervé and Dracula start giggling again. Thank God there doesn't seem to be a joint on the go.

'And you can also say, "crucial" if you don't mind sounding like a twat. That means the same sort of thing. So does "def"'.

'Ah, I understand.'

Sage leans in to me. 'You okay, Vicks?'

'Yeah. Bit bombed, is all.'

'Listen to this,' she whispers. 'Okay.' She claps her hands. 'Now. If you say someone is a "right tosser", it means you think they are a great bloke.'

'Sage!' I start.

'Sssssh. I'm just having a bit of fun.' She turns her attention back to the others. 'Right, Michel, you go first.'

I shut my eyes, ignoring the fact that I've needed to pee for what feels like weeks. But on the whole I'm feeling much better. I mean, all things considered, Sage and I are doing okay. From the sounds of things she's got them eating out of her hand.

SAGE

Things I miss about crappy old England:

Pints
Good old English fags
Kath at the caff
Kath's mushroom on toast
Cadbury's Creme Eggs
Star's newsagents
PRIVACY!!!!!!
Money
Easy access to batteries for music listening purposes.
Crappy old pubs full of nutters
Showers
Normal toilets
Clean sinks

Things I don't miss:

Being arrested
Coronation Street and *EastEnders*
Reg Varney
Art College
Art College lecturers
Being thrown out of pubs
Fights on buses

Bonjour, Gladys, comment sa va (or however the fuck you spell it, I mean, how should I know?)

Vicks has been sleeping all morning and Hervey the pervey is out somewhere. Probably out scoring more black. I have never been so stoned so often. Hervey and his cronies smoke all the time. It's almost like a job. I still haven't figured out where Hervey gets his money. He hardly ever seems to leave the room. At first I thought it was because he didn't want me and Vicks pawing through his stuff, but I reckon it's actually because he's too stoned to walk down the fucking stairs most of the time. He must go to university even less than me and Vicks went to fart college. Just what me and Vicks need, another professional waster in our lives. And he's like twenty-five or something, which is basically quite old to be doing nothing, isn't it? Vicks isn't into the whole smoking thing. She keeps coming up with excuses not to take drags on the joints. Like she's got tonsillitus (can't spell it soz) and stuff. No one seems to notice that it doesn't stop her smoking everyone's fags.

Dracula and Potato Head slept over last night and left (thank God) with Hervey this morning. Vicks says she doesn't fancy either of them. Actually, if you scrunch your eyes up and make your sight blurry, Dracula isn't that bad. Weirdly, neither of them has tried it on with Vicks, although when Hervey was shit-faced the other night he said to her (and I quote) 'One day I will fuck you like King Arthur'. Can you believe it? What a tosser. Vicks says Dracula asked her where we go to wash ourselves. Well, where does he think? What are we supposed to do? We're hardly ever alone here, so we can't very well strip off and wash in the (gross vile) sink while everyone's sitting around, can we? So insensitive. Vicks says that there's a place we can go and pay for a shower, but she's not too sure where it is. Tomorrow Hervey says he'll take us to the laundromat. THANK GOD. All of my clothes stink like a tramp's. What else can I whinge about? Lots, actually. Like the food situation.

All Hervey gives us to eat is this sloppy rice gunk. The chopped-up veggies that he adds to it look far too bright to be real. Like bits of plastic or the carroty bits you always find in sick. Prison food. And you know what rice does to your bowels, don't you, Gladys? Yeah, but that's a good thing considering what the toilet paper situation is at the moment.

One good thing is that the tablet situation is still quite good. I think I have about two months left if I halve them. Dr Wankenstein didn't say what would happen if I stop taking them. Maybe I'll turn into even more of a freak.

He did say that I shouldn't:

Drink alcohol (excessively) and take drugs. Yeah right. Shows how much he knows. Me and Vicks drank a sixth of whisky a day at least, as well as lots of pints in good old England and I was utterly fine. Fuck him.

I've just remembered that my sister Karen calls the tablets 'medicine for a broken heart'. Which is a bit crap but sounds better than their real name.

Oh, almost forgot. Bobby the Bastard introduced us to another wankerish friend of his yesterday, whose name is Jules and who's also about a hundred years old. Supposed to be another artist or some crap. Anyway, he couldn't take his eyes off Vicki as per usual. He looks like a reject from Jethro Tull, like he should be on the cover of *Songs from the Wood* or something. He was all dressed in leather and had long grey hair that almost came down to his waist. Pathetic. Him and Bobby started having some gross conversation about who'd be first to paint Vicki in the nude.

I hate them.

Vicks gets pissed off when I sulk with Bobby, so I'm careful not to do it around her. And when it's my turn to help Bobby the Bastard with the paintings we don't say much to each other. He never offers to buy me any food. I *hate* him. I tried to talk to Vicks about the new bastard Jules but she didn't seem to want to discuss him. I think she fancies him, which sucks. Especially as he was trying so hard to be cool and aloof.

The work situation is dire at the moment. Vicks and I pretend to go off and look for work, but really all we do is wander around a bit. We're getting to know the area quite well. My favourite place to walk is Sacré-Coeur by Montmartre. Long lines of steps like railway tracks that go up and up. Vicks keeps getting me to run up them like in *Rocky*, but I get too out of breath. Also, don't want tachycardia to visit again. Not telling Vicks this though. But I do need to resume old exercise habits at some stage. Also, really love Pigalle. Crazy place full of lovely trannies.

Everyone here either thinks I'm a skinhead or a bloke unless I wear one of my floppy hats. I like that. It keeps them away. But the art they sell in Montmartre is crap! Almost as bad as the dire paintings Bobby sells. Even the tossers at fart college could do better. Me and Vicks keep talking about maybe setting up there. We'll have to do it soon, before Hervey gets fed up with us eating all his rice.

Got to stop now, but TO BE CONTINUED . . .

Dear Gladys,

Okay, so I'm back. Soz to keep you hanging. How are you?
I'm very well, thank you. Sorry I haven't been in touch for a
few days, but I found out the date! Today is Valentine's Day, as
if you didn't know. I have loads to tell you and luckily managed to nick a new pen from Dracula.

Yesterday, Potato Head came to the flat and said he was going
to take us to his place for a shower. That's when I realised that
me and Vicks were stinkier than we thought.

   Potato Head lives so far from Hervey's dump that we had to
go on the bus, which was quite an experience. French buses are
totally different from good old English buses. They're weird
and long and stuck together with tubing. The journey was
excellent though, because I got to see all the things I haven't yet,
like the Eiffel Tower close up, and Potato Head was dead nice
and acted like some sort of tour guide. As we were walking
from the bus stop to his apartment (through this posh area) he
starts saying things like, 'When do you think you'll be able to
leave Hervey's place? It's quite small for so many people, don't
you think,' etc. Etc. He was really nice about it though, so me
and Vicks lied to him and said we'd be gone soon.

You wouldn't believe the place Potato Head lives in. Potato Head's parents must be millionaires or something. Huge apartment full of antiques, African masks and white sofas. Me and Vicks were scared to sit down in case we fucked things up. Potato Head looked a bit embarrassed when we said how posh we thought the place was and then he left us to make some coffee. Then the front door opened and this amazing woman came in. She was dressed in this Jackie O suit and was the thinnest person I have ever seen. She had bright red lipstick and long red nails and her short black hair looked as if it was painted on her head. She looked dead surprised to see us, but then Potato Head came in and spoke to her and introduced us to her, saying she was his mother. She was chain-smoking these long black cigarettes and she offered them to me and Vicks. They were dead strong, like Woodbines or something, and I saved half of mine for later. She spoke to us for a bit, but although she was polite she had this superior look on her face all the time. One good thing about this, though, was she told us about a place called the American Church where they advertise for *au pairs*. Then she sort of dismissed us and went to talk on the phone, which was a relief, as Vicks had spilled some of her coffee on the sofa, and we needed to smear it in without her seeing.

The shower was fantastic. My hair needs work though. It would be rubbish if it grew out too long. I was good and didn't nick anything from there, just in case we're ever invited back.

Anyway, after that, Potato Head and his scary mum waved goodbye to us and Vicks and me found our way back to the bus stop. I told Vicks we didn't need to buy a ticket, we could just use the old ones on the floor and pretend to push them in the slot. She wasn't too keen, but guess what – it worked! Now we can travel around for free!

But back to Valentine's Day . . .

So this morning, Vicks and me were eating breakfast (cold yesterday's rice again) as per usual. Hervey had gone on one of his mysterious errands. Me and Vicks joke that he's some sort of spy for the government because he's always sneaking off without saying where he's going. He carries round this pathetic satchel thing which looks like the one I had at school. He never leaves it alone for a second, so I haven't had a chance to see what's in it (yet). Anyway, Bobby the Bastard knocks on the door. He's holding a big bunch of flowers for Vicks for Valentine's Day. Ha Ha. Vicks didn't know what to do with them. She had to stuff them in empty wine bottles. Stupid arsehole, did he think we'd have a vase or something in this dump? He could have at least bought chocolates or fags or something useful. While Vicks was doing this I said to him, 'Did you get the same for your wife?' And he went a bit red, but as he's Moroccan or something it wasn't really obvious. Then he says he wants to take Vicks for dinner at this Vietnamese place in the evening, but Vicks says no, she's not leaving me alone on Valentine's Day, so B the B says something like, 'But I meant both of you'. *Liar.* At that moment Hervey arrived back. But guess what??? He had a girl with him!

Amazing! Me and Vicks were dead excited. We've never seen him with anyone except Potato Head and Dracula. We've been having these long discussions about whether or not he's gay (the only evidence we've got that he isn't is that King Arthur thing he said to Vicks, but a) he was pissed then and b) it was such a crap thing to say, we reckon it doesn't count.)

The girl was very good looking which was more of a surprise. She looked very French and thin and was almost as tall as Hervey. Vicks said, 'Do you want us to leave, Hervey?' but the girl said, '*Non*, we are not boyfriend and girlfriend, just friends,' and poor old Pervey looked very sad. Bobby said he would take us for breakfast, but I said 'No thanks, we've eaten', so he just left, and we didn't kiss him!!! Hurrah!

Anyway, Hervey's non-girlfriend's name is Genevieve, which is probably French for Guinevere, very funny considering Hervey thinks he's King Arthur reincarnated. (Not sure if he knows that Guinevere fucked off with one of Arthur's best mates, but I don't think there's much chance of Genevieve screwing around with Potato Head or Dracula, because she's beautiful and they're ugly).

We had a lovely chat with her and she seemed to really like us and be interested in the fact that we're artists etc. She said that lots of people sell small drawings and paintings outside the Pompidou Centre for like ten francs a go (about a quid), and that we should do a whole bunch of sketches and sell them. Me and Vicks were dead excited about this although neither of us have even been to this Pompidou place. We'll go there next time we're 'looking for work' , for a recce. She smoked a joint with us (even Vicks had some this time), and then she left.

Obviously we were full of questions for the old perv. He is such a soppy git though, and he said straight away that he was in love with Genevieve and had been for ages. So we sat him down and gave him some dating advice. Hilarious!!! Especially as Vicks has never had a proper boyfriend and you know what I'm like.

The rest of the day was dead boring, but then Bobby the Bastard turned up and talked Vicks into going to supper with him and that vile Jules guy. Vicks just can't say no to anyone.

I said I wasn't going to go and Vicks and me had a bit of an argument without anyone else really knowing we were fighting. When they left, Hervey asked me what me and Vicks were doing about work. I think he wants us to leave soon, but is too polite to say anything. So ungrateful especially after all the help we'd just given him about his love life and stuff. I don't think he'll just throw us out, but me and Vicks must make some sort of a plan soon. It's not our fault though. Most of the time we're too stoned to do anything except cook a bit of rice etc.

Then Hervey went out with his school bag and I searched through all his clothes but didn't find any money at all worse luck.

Oh – forgot. We've been totally confused about Hervey's neighbours. We've lived here forever and we've never even seen one. It's like they don't exist, except for the music you hear sometimes. Me and Vicks have been dead keen to meet whoever lives next to the Toilet of Death because their music taste's quite good (apart from the Beatles which is crap, obviously). We've been daring each other to knock on the door, but no one ever answers. Anyway, after Hervey left I was on my way to the Toilet of Death when I bumped into the guy who lives there! He's about a million years old and looks like a tramp! I said 'bonjour' and he just nodded and slammed his door behind him. Rude or what?? Cannot wait to tell Vicks this when she gets back from going out with the horrible Bastards, but I'm supposed to be sulking. If she brings me some food I'll tell her. If she doesn't, I won't.

VICKI:

The Jules Experience

Where the fuck am I?

One thing I know for sure – this is not Hervé's room. There's no telltale hash smell for a start, and although the room is dark, I can sense that it's bigger than Hervé's poky dump. It's freezing in here, even though there's some kind of heavy duvet on top of me.

Shit. No wonder I'm cold – I'm fucking naked. I peek under the duvet. My skin is puckered with goose pimples.

'Hello?' I call out tentatively.

No answer.

My mouth's dry and bitter tasting and my tongue feels like it's coated with fag ash. What was I drinking last night? I make myself burp, and taste the familiar chemical after-effects of too much whisky. That explains my woolly head. Whisky hangovers are always the worst.

By some miracle there's a glass of water next to the bed. I drink it down in one go, even though it's stale and brackish. My head clears a bit, and I feel ready to sit up. My fingers brush against the cord that's connected to the bedside light. I fumble for the switch, and wait while my eyes adjust to the light. Bloody hell. The ceiling is swathed in swooping sheets of brightly coloured fabric which makes the room seem exotic, like a harem or something. Stacks of records are piled along one of the walls, their multicoloured sleeves adding to the closed-in atmosphere. Christ. How can I not remember any of this?

And where the hell are my clothes? I kick the duvet away and stumble to the end of the bed, catching a glimpse of myself in a full-length mirror in the corner. Blimey. There's no doubt I've lost weight. My hip bones point rudely at me, and I can trace hollow arcs in between my ribs. It looks like I've lost about a stone. In three weeks? That can't be good. I turn round. There's a purple and yellow bruise about the size of a fist on the back of my thigh. Where the hell did I get that?

My clothes and boots aren't on the floor, and nor are they under the duvet. There's a door which presumably leads to the rest of the apartment, but I don't want to walk through it naked. I drag the sheet off the bed, wrap it around me like a toga and tiptoe through the door.

It's like entering another universe, but at least it's familiar. I was definitely here last night, although I don't remember it being so filthy. I recognise the battered green armchair and the murky glass table in the middle of the room, and take note of a nearly empty bottle of whisky and two glasses on the floor next to the table leg. There are cigarette butts everywhere: on the floor, scattered on the table and even stubbed out on the arm of the chair. No wonder my mouth feels like an ashtray. I stand the bottle upright, and the waft of alcohol makes me gag.

Thank God – my clothes and Docs are piled next to a chest of drawers.

'Jules?' I call out, my voice sounding rusty. 'Are you here?'

No answer. Of course there's no answer. I'd know if he was here. I'd sense it. Stupid.

I have a hazy recollection of stumbling down a corridor to a filthy toilet – one of the French hole-in-the-floor ones Sage hates – last night, so maybe that's where he is.

I drop the sheet on the floor and pick up my clothes.

Everything goes black as I bend down, and I fight a surge of nausea. I can't remember ever being so thirsty, but thankfully I spot a kitchenette half-hidden behind a tattered curtain. I'll feel better after I've had more water. Clutching my clothes to me I push the curtain aside.

It's even filthier in here. The sink is piled with mouldy plates and dirty mugs and the countertops are spattered with grease. There's an overflowing plastic bin in the corner that stinks like rotten meat, and I'm forced to breathe through my mouth. Sticking my head under the tap (there's no way I'm using one of those mugs) I gulp down mouthful after mouthful of luke-warm water. Something skitters over my foot and I jump back, knocking my knee on a half-open cupboard door. Oh gross. A gargantuan cockroach is blindly feeling its way along the bottom of the kitchen cupboards. Jules's vile kitchen must be a magnet for creepy-crawlies.

There's an old rag next to the sink. It doesn't smell too bad, so I decide to use it. I rinse it out as best I can, then wipe myself all over as quickly as possible; I'm pretty sure Jules will be back at any moment and I don't want him to catch me doing this in his kitchen. Did we do it? I don't feel sore or . . . used. Even after wiping myself with the cloth I can still smell my body: stale sweat tinged with the alcohol seeping out of my pores. There's no hope of getting properly clean though – I can't see a cake of soap or even a bottle of washing-up liquid anywhere. There's nothing in the cupboard under the sink except for a carpet of black mould and a length of rusty metal chain.

Chilled by my damp skin, I throw my clothes on as fast as possible. My dress is ruined: there's a large tear under one of the arms.

As I wander back into the living room I attempt to piece together last night's events, but it's like trying to remember someone else's life. I have a vague memory of knocking over a clay pot containing the soupy stuff that was supposed to go with the couscous Jules had ordered for us in the restaurant. I can still smell its garlicky odour on my clothes. By that time Jules, Bobby and I had gone through at least three carafes of wine (or was it four?) They'd laughed and said something about not being able to take punks anywhere. We had coffee – I think – and then Jules and I walked Bobby to his van.

Then Jules and I came back here. Yes. It's coming back to me now. I remember following him up flights of stairs. We came in here and as I entered the room his little dog started growling at me. It didn't stop until he shouted at it. He sat down on the green armchair and opened the bottle of whisky. I think at first I sat at his feet. I'd had no choice. There's only one chair in the room.

Jules started stroking my head, gently at first, then harder, his fingers tangling painfully in my dreadlocks. And then I realised he was trying to push my head down into his lap. I remember thinking, *when the fuck had he taken his kit off?* I hadn't even noticed he was sitting there half naked until it was too late. Had I tried to say '*non*' or something? *Had I?* I know he said 'Don't worry, just catch your breath,' although he was the one who sounded out of breath. Then he grabbed the back of my head again and pushed me down on him. Unable to help it, I'd retched. The room was whirling, my eyes were streaming, and I tried to lurch to my feet. I think Jules was laughing – I'm sure of it in fact – and then he said, 'You okay?' and I think I said something like 'sure' and he said, 'Good. You can't start something and not finish it . . .'

Bile surges in my throat and I barely make it to the tiny sink in time. I turn on both taps as far as they'll go and watch as the vomit squirls away, mingling with the old food on the plates.

Don't think about it.

What now? I'd better sort out the bedroom before he gets

43

back. Put the sheet back on the bed, put the eiderdown in place. Then get the fuck out of here. Even though all I want to do is scarper, I can't resist checking out the records in the bedroom. There's a lot of sixties stuff and tons of jazz LPs I've never heard of. The record on the turntable is a Nona Hendryx album. Weird fucking coincidence, but for all I know the Hendrix family is huge in France.

'Allo? Vicki? You are awake?'

Shit. I take a deep breath, scrabble my hands through my hair and walk stiffly through to the lounge.

His face is covered with grey stubble, which makes him look way older than he did last night. He's tied his hair in a ponytail, but it still reaches almost halfway down his back. There are deep furrows on either side of his mouth. His little dog growls at me and he jerks its lead. It yelps. Good. I hope he hurt it.

'You want *café?* Before you go?'

I do, but not in one of the mugs in the sink. 'No thanks, Jules.'

'You sleep well?'

'*Oui, merci.*' The little dog starts yapping. It hurts my head.

'Brigitte – shhh! *Arret!*' Jules snaps at it. He smiles at me. For the first time I notice that his front teeth are discoloured and nubbly. 'You'll come again.' It isn't a question. 'I see you next to the cafe? The big one, across from the metro. At nine. On Wednesday.'

'Yes,' I say.

'*Bon.* I will say goodbye, then. You find your way home? It is not far, I think, to where you stay. Five minutes.'

'Sure. I'll be fine.'

I want to ask how come I ended up in his bed last night. Had I taken my clothes off? Had he done that? But I don't want him to think I'm some kind of fucked-up alcoholic who's prone to blackouts, so I just leave.

∗   ∗   ∗

The sun ricochets off the white stone of the buildings, and it's far brighter outside than I expected. Why is winter sun always brighter than summer sun? The streets, as always, are packed with tourists, and for a disorientating second I can't figure out which way to turn to get home. Then I see the reassuring shape of the opera house in the distance, and I get my bearings.

As I make my way back and the buildings become more familiar – *friendlier* somehow – I start to feel more connected. I cross the Boulevard des Italiens and stroll down the narrow alleyway towards Hervé's street, passing the cosy restaurant which always taunts me with its smoky windows and expensive smells as if it knows I'll never be rich enough to eat there. As I wait to cross the road, a string of gleaming black chauffeur-driven cars glides serenely round the corner. I peer into the blacked-out windows but get nothing but my own reflection thrown back at me.

The Irish pub next to Hervé's building is dead at this time of day, and I don't meet anyone as I tap in the door code and start the long climb up the stairs. As usual, the posh-looking double doors on every floor are shut. I creep up close to the ones on the third floor and listen for a sign of life from within. Nothing. Not even the murmur of a radio or television. In the three weeks Sage and I've been crashing at Hervé's place I've never met anyone who lives behind the doors, or caught a glimpse inside one of the apartments. Come to think of it, we've hardly seen any of the occupants who share the top floor with Hervé, although we often hear snatches of their music.

Whoever lives in the flat next to the Toilet of Death is playing 'Sympathy for the Devil' again. I'm reluctant to knock on Hervé's door, in case he and Sage are still sleeping, so I slip out my useless Barclays bank card, slide it in the gap between the door and the frame and click up the latch. I sneak in as quietly as I can. At first I think the room is empty – the lights are off and it's swathed in shadows. Then I hear: 'Where've you been?' I turn on the light. Sage is sitting cross-legged on the mattress. She's moistening the edge of a roll-up with her tongue and doesn't look charmed. I'd better tread carefully.

'At Jules's,' I say.

'Oh. I was dead worried.' She says this lightly, but there's an edge to her voice.

'Sorry. It wasn't planned or anything. I kind of . . . forgot the time.'

'Have fun?'

'Yeah, it was all right. What did you do?'

'Usual. Got stoned with Hervé. Potato Head and Dracula were asking after you.'

'Really? That's nice.'

I lie back on the mattress and close my eyes.

'Isn't it your turn to help Bobby the Bastard with the paintings?' Sage says.

Shit. She's right. 'Can't you go? I'm knackered.'

'No fucking way, Chuck.'

'Please, Sage. I feel like shite.'

There's a calculated Sage pause. 'Are you going to tell Bobby you spent the night with Jules?'

'Why should I? It's none of his business. Anyway, we had dinner with Bobby last night.' I prop myself up on my elbows.

Sage shrugs and blows smoke rings. They break apart in front of my face. 'Dunno why you want to hang around with those *wankers*.'

'Fucking hell, Sage, for the thousandth time, if it wasn't for Bobby, where the fuck would we be?'

'Well, I don't want to burst your bubble, Chuck, but we're going to be back to square one soon.'

'What do you mean?'

'Hervey the Pervy keeps asking if we've found a place to stay.'

'Yeah, so? He's always doing that.'

'But this morning he said he was going to give us a deadline for when we have to fuck off. "Zee place is too small, Sage, for you and Vick-ee and me as vell."'

'Bugger.'

'Bugger is right, Chuck. I'm pretty sure we're not going to bump into anyone else on the street who's going to help us out like Bobby the Bastard did. And I can't see him pulling his finger out to help us again now that you've shagged his bosom buddy.'

SAGE

Okay, Gladys, I'm a bit pissed at the moment, so I'll try not to fuck this up too badly. But today was too brilliant not to write down. Vicks and Hervey have passed out and Hervey's snoring like a pig again. Which is good because it means I have peace to write this.

   I am so chuffed!!

But I'll start at the beginning . . .

The morning was the usual shite, eating old rice, waiting for Pervy to leave the room so we could brush our teeth etc, but I could tell something was up as Vicks was acting dead nervous as if she was scared to tell me something.

At first I thought she had some vile secret to tell me about Bobby the B or Jules, so I kept bugging her to tell me what was up. Eventually she sighs and goes: 'I spoke to Natalie yesterday, I phoned her.' I was pissed off obviously, but relieved at the same time that she wasn't hiding something gross about the bastards. But then she says: 'She's coming to Paris today, and I said we'd meet up with her.'

Okay, Gladys, that was a bit of a shocker, and we had a big fight and didn't talk to each other for a bit. Vicks and I can do this on and off for days sometimes. Like the time we decided to eat morning glory seeds from the garden centre because they're supposed to be hallucinogenic. They weren't though, so we got very pissed instead, and as always happens when we get badly drunk, we had a big fight, missed the last bus and had to walk home from Stourbridge. We ended up spending hours with this security guard and his dog on a building site in Wombourne, which was an adventure. So the fact we had a fight was good in the end.

Anyway, eventually we started speaking again, and Vicki said that Natalie wanted to stay the night with us. This was out of the question on account of all the lies I've told Hervey, so I had to come up with a plan and fast as we were due to meet her at the Gallery Laffy-whatever shop in a couple of hours. Then Hervey gets back and it comes to me. (It took me ages to convince him to help us).

We were a bit late to meet her, but that was tough shite as she'd invited herself, and for all she knew we had busy exciting lives now.

The first thing she says to Vicks is, 'You look so thin, what happened?' But I could tell she was saying this in a jealous way, not in a concerned way. And then she goes, 'I can't wait to see where you're staying.' Vicks looks all worried at this, but I'm like, 'I'm afraid you can't stay after all. The guy we're living with won't allow strangers.' And I tell her it's because Hervey's involved in this dead secret work for the government and only me and Vicks know about it.

I can tell she doesn't believe me, but then I say, 'You'd better be careful, he could be watching us right now.' She looks at Vicks as if to say 'what is this crap?', but Vicks is brilliant and looks all serious and says, 'Sorry Natalie, we really can't tell you much about it.'

Natalie says that the least we can do is go for a coffee with her, and I'm like, 'Sure, but it will have to be fast.' By now she's dead pissed off of course.

So we go to this posh café (her choice) and she tells us about her job, how crap it's getting, and how sorry she is that she couldn't find us work. Usual Natalie crap. But then she says: 'Vicki, you had better phone your dad.' Vicks goes: 'Did you speak to him?' and she says, 'Yes, he's worried about you, and the police have been round to your house.' And Vicks is like, 'Well, you did tell him we were all right, didn't you?' And Natalie looks all superior and says, 'How could I? I didn't know where you were either.' Bitch!!! I could see Vicks was getting dead worried and I asked Natalie if she knew what the police wanted in more detail. I could see she wanted to string it out and make it more dramatic, but I gave her a dead-eye so she said they needed to interview us as we were seen in the vicinity just after the art college pottery shed burned down. She didn't know who grassed on us.

Then she started asking us about Hervey, but she didn't get very far as with brilliant timing he walked in. He was excellent!! He was wearing dark glasses and he'd brought his satchel along like I'd asked him to. He comes up to our table and says to me and Vicks in this dead good put-on spy voice, 'I think it's time you left. We have work to do.' And Natalie goes bright red and says, 'Who are you?' And Hervey says in a scary serious voice, 'If I tell you I'll have to kill you,' and me and Vicks almost killed ourselves trying not to laugh. Then he left.

★　　★　　★

Natalie (for once) didn't know what to say, and Vicks said she wished she could tell her more about the situation, but it wouldn't be safe. I told Natalie that Hervey was happy for us to join his organisation because we'd told him how we'd burned down the pottery shed as an act of rebellion and he needed people like me and Vicks to help him.

We walked Natalie to the metro station and she made Vicks promise to call her and let her know we were all right. I made sure she knew that Hervey was following us.

As soon as she'd gone, Vicks ran up to Hervey and gave him a big hug for being so fantastic!! He wanted to know more about why we needed to get rid of Natalie, and I made something up about her being a bully and a stalker, which wasn't very nice as she's not that bad, but fuck it, aye? Then I said we should all go and have drinks to celebrate, and Vicks said, 'with what?' And I pulled out a fifty franc note that I'd nicked out of Natalie's wallet.

Vicki hadn't even seen me doing this, which is a sign I'm getting better at nicking stuff.

So it's all good apart from I have to get Vicks away from Vile Jules. The trick is not to be too obvious about this or let her know how much this bothers me.

VICKI:

The Jules Experience #2

I'm still feeling shaky as I let the entrance door slam behind me. Even though I'm expecting it, the loud bang makes me jump. Hervé's street is unusually busy this evening, traffic roars up and down the road, and the Irish woman who owns the pub next door is crooning 'Danny Boy' in her horrible pub-singer voice. I can't believe Sage and I still haven't been in there for a pint – maybe it's because we know it will remind us too much of home.

My breath curls out in white wisps and I shiver. I've stupidly come out without my jacket, but I can't face going back in to fetch it. Everything had been fine a few minutes ago. I was feeling quite chipper, actually. Thanks to the Natalie experience, Sage had forgiven me for staying out all night with Jules the other evening, and when I plucked up the courage to tell her that I was seeing him again, she just shrugged and said: 'It's your funeral.'

I was on my way back from the Toilet of Death when the neighbour Sage had bumped into the other day stuck his head round his door. He immediately gave me the creeps: His raggedy hair was matted and grey, and his crow's feet looked like they'd been inked into his skin by a heavy-handed Marvel artist. As I passed him he mumbled something at me.

'*Pardon?*' I said politely.

'*Putain!*' he hissed, his voice pure poison.

'You what?'

'Whore!' he hissed again, before disappearing into his room and slamming the door behind him.

'Fuck you!' I shouted, but it sounded pathetic.

Sage flew out of Hervé's room. 'What the fuck's going on, Chuck?'

'Bastard shilling next door just called me a whore.' A lump was forming in my throat. For some reason – and I still don't know why – I felt violated and raw; as if the guy had hit me.

Sage blinked. Then she walked up to the old man's door, looked at it for a few contemplative seconds, then aimed a sideways karate kick at it. 'Mother*fucker*. Next time I see you, you're dead.' She raised her voice: 'You hear me, you old fuck?' She lashed out again, her boot thunking against the wood.

'Just leave it, Sage,' I said.

'Don't worry, Chuck. Next time that fucker sticks his head out of the door, he's dead meat.'

'Yeah.' I tried to shrug it off, but I was still rattled. 'I think I'm just going to split.'

'I thought you were only going out later?'

'Yeah, but I need some fresh air.'

'Don't let him get to you,' she sniffed. Then, in a different, softer, unSage-like tone of voice she said: 'You don't have to go, you know.'

'What do you mean?'

'To meet that bastard tonight. Why don't you just stay here with me and Hervé? Genevieve's popping round later for some blow.'

'I said I would, Sage. It would be rude not to.'

She shrugged. "Kay. It's all going to end in tears though. That Jules is a right bastard. Don't do anything I wouldn't do.' As she returned to Hervé's room, she aimed another bent-kneed kick at the old man's door.

* * *

53

I usually love the area around the opera house. If it's not raining, Sage and I sometimes spend a couple of hours sitting on the steps checking out the tourists and daring each other to bum ciggies from passers-by. We've long since given up trying to spot carpet legs though. There just aren't enough in Paris to make the game worthwhile.

But I'm not feeling at all comfortable here tonight, hovering outside the fancy schmantzy cafe where I'm to meet Jules. I don't think I've ever been this cold. My teeth chatter and the skin on my face is tight. Across the boulevard, Bobby's spot looks bereft without his little blue figure bustling around. Suddenly all I want is to be at home in England in my bedroom, surrounded by the comforting posters of the Dead Kennedys and the Violent Femmes, listening to Sunday night John Peel and deciding which outfit to wear to college.

'*Bonsoir,* Vicki!' Jules calls. My stomach twists when I see him. At least he hasn't brought his vile little dog along. He kisses me three times. He smells of soap and Gitanes. 'I am sorry I am late. I have been working all day.'

'Painting?'

His eyes slide to the left. 'Ah, *oui.* Of course.'

It strikes me that for someone who says he makes a living as a painter, there was a distinct lack of artwork in his flat. 'I'd love to see your studio.'

'*Pardon?*'

'Your studio. Where you work. Where you paint.'

'Ah. *Oui. D'accord.* Any time you want.'

'Now?'

'*Non.* It is not possible. We are to meet someone. A friend of mine.'

'Who?'

'Just a friend, you will see. I think you will like her.'

'It's not your dog, is it?'

There's a beat and then he throws his head back and laughs,

giving me a good look at his little worn-down teeth. '*Non*. We are in for quite an evening, Vicki. You will see.'

It's getting late. We're in one of those brightly lit *tabacs*, slotted down a side street off the Boulevard des Italiens. It's all Formica tables and linoleum floors. Pubs should be places where you can get pissed in muted lighting, sitting on a comfy upholstered booth stained with years of spilled bitter and fag ash, and not these bare, bland places where the tables are too tiny and the plastic chairs stick to your bum. I squirm in my seat, and glance at the Japanese woman slumped opposite me. She's the "friend" Jules wanted me to meet. I've tried to talk to her, but her English is as crap as my French. Her fringe hides her eyes and she's wearing high black heels and a cheap-looking skintight lacy dress. She's fatter and shorter than I am, and thick foundation two shades darker than her natural skin tone cakes the join-the dot bumps of bad skin.

Jules has left us to 'get to know each other' while he sits with his back to us in a darkened corner of the *tabac*, chatting to a guy in a terrible leather cap. Every so often Jules turns and instructs the barman to bring us another round of shots. We're drinking pastis, which tastes like the aniseed balls my brother and I used to nick from the corner shop.

The Japanese woman downs her drink and starts swaying out of time to the background music – 'Love Plus One' by Haircut One Hundred. 'Jules!' she slurs.

He ignores her.

'Jules!' She turns the volume up.

'*Oui*?' he snaps.

She waves her empty glass above her head and laughs a *One Flew Over The Cuckoo's Nest* laugh. She's either completely cooked or off her head on drugs. Or both. Jules instructs the bartender to refill our glasses.

Nodding my head to 'Fantastic Day', I surreptitiously

watch what Jules is up to. A few minutes ago, he took a shoebox out of his bag and placed it on the table, and now he and Leather Cap appear to be haggling over it. Is Jules some sort of dodgy drug dealer? I'm dying to see what's in the box, but I can't get a clear view of it.

The Japanese woman bites off the tip of one of her false nails and uses it to pick her teeth. When she catches me watching her she grins slyly. 'Jules!' she wails.

This time when he turns around I get a glimpse of the contents of the parcel – a pile of cassette tapes, still wrapped in shiny cellophane. I recognise the cover of Blondie's *Parallel Lines* amongst them. I have it at home. It looks like Jules is just a bootlegger. *Boring*.

The room's spinning. I bite the inside of my cheek, an old trick I use to sober myself up. I bite harder, tasting blood, and the room steadies.

We're in Jules's scummy living room, but for the life of me I can't remember walking here from the *tabac*. The Japanese woman is lying stretched out on the tatty green armchair. She's tapping her heels crazily on the carpet, and her jitter-bugging stilettos are perilously close to where I'm sitting cross-legged. She flicks her fringe away from her forehead, revealing unfocussed eyes ringed in smudged kohl. Jules is clattering about in the kitchen, his horrid yappy dog puttering at his heels.

The woman wriggles in the chair, and my stomach lurches as I realise what she's up to. Ugh. She's pulling up her tight black dress, revealing a pair of almost see-through black lace pants. She's not wearing tights and her pitted thighs are clearly on show. I try to look anywhere but there, but my eyes keep being drawn back. Staring up at the ceiling, she idly strokes the tops of her thighs. I reach for the pack of fags on the table, and quick as a flash, she leans down, grabs my hand and thrusts it into her crotch. I'm too shocked to snatch my hand back. She closes her eyes and arches her back. Her tongue peeks between her tiny white teeth.

I don't want to be here, doing this. It's like I'm on the ceiling watching myself; watching as my hand is squirmed around in the woman's lap as if it no longer belongs to me.

A shadow falls over us. Jules is standing behind her chair and has his hands down the front of her dress. 'I see you two are now good friends, eh, Vicki?' he murmurs, his voice thick as if he's speaking through treacle.

I rip my hand out of the woman's clammy grasp. Her breath hisses out from between her teeth.

'I've got to go,' I say, struggling to get to my feet.

'*Pourquoi?*' Jules murmurs hoarsely. 'We are all friends here.'

I manage to get to my haunches but my body doesn't want to do what I'm telling it to. The room lurches and I lose my balance.

'At least stay for tonight,' Jules croons. 'We don't have to do anything. Just rest.'

'*Oui,*' the Japanese woman murmurs, arching her back again. She looks straight at me and beckons me closer. '*Viens ici.*'

I kick back with my legs and wriggle away from her. She shrugs and then flops back into the armchair again. Jules whispers something in her ear and she looks at me and smiles coldly.

Get out, get out, get out. Get out right this fucking second.

A spurt of adrenalin helps propel me to my feet, and I lunge for the door, nearly tripping over Jules's little dog. I kick it out of the way with more force than necessary and fumble for the handle. For an instant I'm certain it's locked and I'm trapped, but then it gives. I fall into the corridor. I hear Jules's voice behind me but I daren't turn around. I head for the stairs to my left, but my body isn't cooperating and I have to cling to the bannister to stop myself from careening down the stairs. As I reach the next landing, the corridor roller-coasters and my legs buckle. Shit. I'll never make it down the next flight before Jules catches up to me. What now? I check out the shadows bleeding out of the corridor to my left. It's a similar set-up to Jules's floor – could I hide in the bogs at the end?

'Vicki! Where are you?' Jules's voice sounds like it's right behind me. I stumble on blindly, ricocheting off the corridor walls, and biting back a scream as the passageway is blasted with light – I must have bashed into the timer switch. *Stupid, stupid, stupid.* I spy a shallow alcove carved into the wall to the right of me and I throw myself into it, squashing my body sideways and drawing my knees up to my chin.

The timer switch dies, blinking the corridor back into darkness. I hear the thunk of boots on wood – the footsteps are definitely heading in my direction.

'Vicki?' Jules calls again. He's close. Oh God. I squeeze my eyes shut. 'Vicki! Come! What is the matter?' And then, *'Merde.'*

I hold my breath and now I can hear him clumping back up to the floor above. Thank fuck. I only allow myself to relax when I hear the muffled bark of his dog as he opens the door to his apartment. But I'm buggered if I'm going to poke my head out to check that he's really gone. I've seen enough horror movies to know that it might be a trick and he's just biding his time, waiting for me to let my guard down. And even if I could escape the building, I don't want to go back to Hervé's in this state. Sage would have a field day. Fair play to her, though. She was right about Jules. I should have listened to her.

Sage and I are in the Swedish Chef's kitchen, which is set up in the centre of the stage. The Muppet Show theatre in front of us is silent, and the seats are sinisterly shadowed. We're helping the chef make spaghetti, but it keeps escaping from our grasp and wrapping itself around our legs and arms. 'Look at this, Chuck!' Sage is laughing as she allows herself to be wrapped into a pasta version of a roly-poly pudding. I try to smile at her, but truth is I'm beginning to panic as the spaghetti snakes itself around me. The Swedish Chef is ignoring us and is banging his pots and pans around singing 'Do de do de do' in his Swedish Chef voice. 'Please help me,' I say to him, but he acts like he can't hear me, as if I'm not there. 'I'm stuck!' I plead. 'I can't move my arms!' The spaghetti feels like twine and is digging into me and cutting off my circulation. It climbs up my body and begins writhing and twisting around my neck, trying to force its way into my mouth. 'Sage!' I yell before it finally gets me.

I wake up gasping for air, squeamishly aware that there's no feeling in my right arm. I jump up and shake it wildly, but it doesn't help. I slam it into a wall and finally my fingers start tingling. Light filters through from the other end of the corridor. Daylight. *Thank fuck.*

I take stock. My body feels as if it's coated in plaster of Paris. My legs ache from being in such an awkward position for God knows how long and my mouth is foul and gummy, as if I've spent the evening licking envelopes.

Time to go.

I count to ten and then leg it down the corridor, praying that I don't bump into Jules or the freakish Japanese woman, but I don't meet anyone as I fly down the stairs. Within seconds I blunder out into the safety of the street. God knows what the time is. I don't really care. I concentrate on putting one foot in front of the other, staring down at the pavement, counting the cracks in the concrete. I'm pretty sure I'm going in the opposite direction to Hervé's flat, but I carry on walking regardless. I find myself trailing up a narrow side street and follow it higher and higher, ignoring the ache in my thighs. It must be really early: I don't meet anyone, and the shuttered shops and apartments have an air of drowsiness about them.

The walk is warming me up and loosening my stiff leg muscles. I hesitate at the top of a skinny cobbled street, but decide not to turn back yet. As I make my way to the top of a steepish hill peppered with tiny boulangeries, I make out the Moulin Rouge's distinctive windmill sign. Even Pigalle is deserted at this time of day, but then I spy a diehard transvestite snuggled in a doorway and swathed in a blond fur coat.

'*Bonjour, mignon,*' she greets me as I pass. I stop. What have I go to lose?

'*Avez-vous une cigarette s'il vous plait, madame?*' I say.

'Ah, *Anglais,*' She smiles and hands me a packet of Marlboros. She's got lipstick on her teeth.

'*Merci!*'

A guy dressed in a crumpled business suit scurries out of one of the sidestreets and appears to be making his way towards us. I take out two cigarettes and pass the packet back. She lights my cigarette for me without taking her eyes off the approaching man. I nod my thanks, and move on. Pulling the smoke into my lungs, I let my feet take me where they will, which seems to be in the direction of Montmartre. I don't meet a soul as I climb up the stairs to Sacré-Coeur.

I sit on one of the tourist benches and look out over Paris. Smog and mist shroud the city, and bizarrely, I'm suddenly homesick for crap utilitarian architecture. For the Wolverhampton Mander Centre, a piss-stinking abomination of concrete and seventies-style glass. For buses that reek of fags and old ladies. For the perfumery warmth of the Beatties department store. For cold, milky tea at the British Home Stores's coffee bar.

I have to stop this pathetic, whiny behaviour. I'm getting sick of myself. *Enough.*

★   ★   ★

As I plod down the stairs back to Pigalle, it starts to drizzle. The rain doesn't bother me; I'm already freezing. I look out for the transvestite as I cross the road but she's gone. Maybe she got lucky with the businessman.

I lose my way and find myself outside a gloomy old church I've never seen before. There's a green tarpaulin strung up to the side of one of the eaves, and a bunch of scruffy tramps are sitting outside it, smoking and looking impervious to the rain.

'*Bonjour*,' one of them leers.

Head down, I stalk past them, and cross the road in front of the church without waiting for the green man 'walk' signal. A horn parps and I jump back, narrowly avoiding being swiped by a moped. The driver shouts an obscenity and the tramps laugh. Bastards. I take another side street at random and pass a *boulangerie*. The warm smell of fresh-baked *pain au chocolat* wraps itself around me. I'm starving as usual, and the sick pulse of the pastis hangover beats at the back of my head.

Finally I make out the comforting female shapes of the sculptures that surround the opera house. There are more people around now and nobody gives me a second glance.

Everyone's comfortably wrapped in overcoats and carrying umbrellas. Even the tourists look like they have a purpose today. Nearly home, thank fuck.

'Vicki!' Bobby is waving his arms over his head like someone demonstrating semaphore. His face is tinged a dark red and he's out of breath. He's clearly been trying to grab my attention for a while. I hadn't even glanced at his corner as I joined the crowd crossing the boulevard.

I'm absurdly pleased to see him, and I hug him back when he greets me. As usual he reeks of aftershave, and as I pull back his stubble scratches my face.

'Vicki, you are okay?'

'I'm fine.'

'You do not look too good, Foxy Lady, ah? Where is your coat? You must be very cold.'

'Nah. I'm fine, really.'

'*Bon*! I have fantastic news for you. I have been up to Hervé's house to find you, but Sage said you were not there. He pauses and looks at me quizzically. 'Where were you?'

In a stinking freezing corridor escaping from a pervert. 'Nowhere,' I say.

He's not really listening; it's clear he's bursting to tell me something. '*Bon*! Let us go and get some coffee. All your troubles are now over, thanks to me!'

SAGE

5 horrible (but fitting) ways to kill Bobby

1. Sneak poisonous spider eggs under his skin so that they hatch and eat him alive.
2. Peel his skin off slowly then cover him with rancid butter and fry him in a jumbo-sized pan.
3. Pop his eyes out with a rusty spoon and lock him in a dark room for two weeks with no food or water.
4. Make him drink drain cleaner while listening to Barry Manilow records.
5. Bury him alive in a damp grave after filling it with stink bombs and those ants that sting when they bite you.

DARK, DARK, DARK DAY. WORST DAY EVER IN FACT!!!!

Okay, Gladys. I'm so fucking angry my hands are shaking like an old alky's.

Hervey has taken Vicks off somewhere. He was totally freaked out by what happened and just ushered her out of the door. So I'm here alone. Except for you, Gladys, of course. And a spliff that Hervey left 'to calm me down'.

63

Today was worse than when me and Vicks were arrested by the police in Stourbridge after we were stopped in the underpass because they thought we were carrying a body. It was actually a rolled-up piece of carpet that we found outside a shop and were going to use to sleep on in the Abandoned Church. But we lied about our names and they made us spend the night in the holding cells because they said we were indigent. And the cell smelled of old sick and the next day we were in deep trouble because everyone was worried about us.

But that situation is nothing compared with this one.

The whole thing started yesterday. Vicks arrived back home after spending another night with vile Jules. She looked like shite. I had to give her a right bollocking as she'd gone out without her coat, and it would be crap if one of us got flu or something now. She didn't say fuck all about what she'd been up to with Jules, but I could guess obviously as he's a fucking pervert. One good thing is that she said she wasn't going to see him again, and I think she meant it. She didn't say why.

Anyway, Vicks was dead excited about something else and said that Bobby had found her a job working in a shop, and that he was coming round to tell her all the details.

So he comes over later, and I'm quite nice to him because of the job thing (big mistake). I ask him about it, and he says the shop is owned by one of his mates and Vicki doesn't even need to go for an interview and can start the next day.

I'm like: 'Great, I'll go with Vicks tomorrow, where is this place?' And he's like, 'No, it's fine, I'll take her myself.' And he looks dead superior in a totally smug bastard sort of way.

64

Anyway, he says it pays really well, about five hundred francs a day!!!

Here's where I'm stupid. Fifty quid a day for working in a shop??? I should have known something was up. But all I could think about was finally having some cash. We had a lovely afternoon talking about what we were going to buy with the money. Fags and batteries and books and hair stuff and mostly food. And when Hervey arrived later with Dracula and Potato Head, they were really excited as well, and we had a little party, although Vicks didn't drink or smoke as she wanted to look her best for the job. (This, Gladys, is very very ironic).

So Vicks gets up dead early in the morning and asks me to do her hair and stuff. It takes ages, as I do this wicked complicated arrangement, with it all piled on top of her head. What a waste!!! Anyway, Vicks leaves to meet B the B and I carry on sleeping for a bit. I'm woken by Genevieve knocking on the door, and as usual Hervey is all smarmy with her and acts like a total wanker. When he goes out to get some fags, I tell Genevieve about Vicki's job, and she's like, 'How much does it pay?' I don't really want to tell her in case she grasses to Hervey and he starts asking for rent money or something. But then I think, what the hell, so I say 'five hundred francs' and she looks dead surprised. Then she says 'That sounds weird, what sort of shop is it?' And I say maybe it's one of those dead posh ones round the corner near Concorde or something. And fuck, Gladys, I'm feeling really stupid now because what sort of shop hires a complete stranger and pays them a fortune? Genevieve is like, 'It's not likely to be those shops because Vicks doesn't speak very good French and loads of people want to work there.'

*   *   *

By this stage I'm really worried, Gladys. All kinds of things are running through my head, like what if the bastard has sold her into slavery or something stupid like that, which it turns out isn't too far from the truth. And as you know, Vicks is dead naive when it comes to shit like this.

So I leave Hervey's room and storm up to Bobby, who's trying to flog his crap to this bunch of English tourists, and I'm like, 'Where the *fuck* is Vicks???' and one of the tourists says, 'Steady on, chick,' in a Birmingham accent and I tell him to fuck off as well. Bobby's face is all red and puffy and gross-looking and he says, 'Vicki is working,' and I say, 'I know she's working you *bastard,* but where?' And he says, 'Why should I tell you?' And I'm like 'Because if you don't you're fucking *dead.*' And he says Vicks is a big girl, blah, blah, blah, and she doesn't need me to hold her hand. I'm getting angrier and angrier and all the people in the street and the bank behind us are stopping to see what's going on. I know that the last thing the bastard wants is a scene, so he's eventually forced to tell me where she is.

Before I left to find her, I punched one of his crap paintings and it crashed to the ground. That felt dead good, Gladys, although it should have been the bastard's face.

It took me ages to find the shop, as it's in this side street near to where me and Vicks used to hang out in Pigalle. I had to ask loads of people where the street was and most of them didn't understand me being Frogs and all, and I only found it by accident in the end.

Fuck, Gladys. It was fucking *horrible.*

Hang on, I'm just going to light the pathetic joint Hervey left me.

Anyway, so I get to the shop, but it doesn't have a name or anything on it, just a number. The windows are all dirty and grimy with these cheap-looking dayglo labels that say 'toys' and 'cinema' and 'booths' on the outside and one window has this gross display of bondage gear and stuff, which makes me feel sick. There's no door, just this dirty beige-coloured curtain. It's like something out of Soho. Even the shops in Pigalle aren't that bad.

I push open the curtain. The place is full of dildos and porn photos and racks of dirty videos with pictures on the front of naked women sucking guys' dicks, and at first I don't see Vicks. She's sitting behind a counter in front of this corridor which looks dead creepy and grimy. I can hear deep breathing sounds and crap seventies porno music coming from there. And all Vicks is wearing, although it's cold, is this leather bra thing which doesn't cover much, I can tell you. She's looking dead embarrassed as there's this old perv in the shop who's pretending to look through the racks of porn, but actually he's looking at her and I swear he has his hand down his trousers and is playing with himself.

Then Vicks looks up and sees me and I'm like, 'Get the fuck out!' and she bursts into tears, and says, 'I can't!' and I shout, '*Now*, Vicks!'

And this *huge* fat guy comes out of the back and says something like, 'What's going on?' And I say, 'Fuck you!' Vicks is still crying, but she's getting her stuff together, and I grab her arm and start pulling her out of the shop. Then Bobby the Bastard appears and he's sweating and out of breath and looks like he's about to have a heart attack (which he doesn't, worse luck). Fatty starts shouting at him, but by now me and Vicks are running away. I check to see if Fatty is going to chase us, but he's too gross and slow. (I feel bad now because I didn't think fast enough to nick some of his money out of the till.)

We run all the way into Opera and we're both out of breath, and Vicks keeps trying to speak to me and explain stuff, but I just ignore her and walk dead fast all the way to Hervey's without saying anything because I'm *that* angry.

When we get back to the room I'm glad Genevieve's gone, but Hervey's lying on his back on the bed. He looks dead surprised when we walk in and quickly pulls his jumper down over his trousers, like we've caught him having a wank or something.

I'm still seething and Hervey reads this on my face. Vicks has stopped crying but her mascara's halfway down her cheeks. 'What's going on?' he asks, but before I can say anything Vicks says, 'I did it for us, Sage.' Like I'd *really* want her to prostitute herself.

Then she says something that I will never forget and is basically UNFORGIVABLE: 'If you weren't so fucking *useless* then I wouldn't have had to take the job in the first place, Sage.' Then she went on and on about how much pressure she's under to find us work blah, blah, blah, which is totally unfair because it's much harder for me to find work here on account of I don't speak Frog. So naturally I lose my temper again and I have to punch the door so that I don't hit her, and it really hurts.

Then we hear a banging on the door and Hervey opens it.

Guess who it is? Yes, the bastard himself.

He says to Vicks, 'Can we talk outside?' and I say, 'Of course you can't you fat *fuck*, you'll never talk to her again.' And Vicki goes, 'Sage!' in a warning way, and that really sets me off.

Something weird happens to me when I'm angry, Gladys. I suppose I'm a bit like Bruce Banner. It's like a force takes over my body, which would be quite cool and magical if I could fucking well control it. Anyway, I launched myself at Bobby, and he looked like he was going to crap in his horrible jodhpurs. It wouldn't have taken much for me to seriously fuck him up. I've had loads of practice fighting hard bastards from Gornal, so compared to them it was like hitting a little girl. He's a coward with a podgy weak stomach. When I punched him in the gut he made a sound like one of those whoopee fart cushions. Then Vicks tried to grab my arm and I elbowed her in the mouth by mistake. Okay. I felt a bit bad about that, Gladys, it was B the B I was after, not Vicks, but it was a genuine accident.

Then Hervey starts yelling '*Arret*!', which means 'stop' in French, and Bobby slinks out holding his stomach. Vicks's face is covered in blood and she hobbles over to the sink. You should have seen Hervey, Gladys! He was angrier than I've ever seen him (well, we've never seen him anywhere close to anger). His eyes were as jittery as a nutter's and he looked quite hard, actually. I didn't think he had it in him, to be honest.

Then Hervey says that he's going to take Vicks away for a while to give us both space to calm down. And Vicks is still sobbing and says she has to get changed first. She grabs some clothes and heads for the Toilet of Death and me and Hervey just sit there in silence and staring at nothing until she gets back.

Then he hands me a joint and takes Vicks out.

And that's what I'm smoking now, Gladys. I keep wondering if I should just fuck off out of it now. If I shouldn't just leave and go somewhere else. But I haven't got much choice have I, Gladys? I'm stuck here. Vicks and me have had some shit-hot fights in the past but nothing like this.

I'm not sure it's going to be all right with Vicks and me after this, Gladys. I'm not sure of that at all.

And then what the *fuck* am I going to do?

VICKI:

The Pompidou Police Experience

I gingerly prod the inside of my mouth with my tongue. My top lip feels enormous, as if there's a tractor tyre stuck to the side of my face. I probably look like the Elephant Man. No wonder Hervé's stalking down the pavement without checking to see if I'm still following him.

So much for Foxy fucking Lady.

'Hervé?' I call. 'Where are we going?'

'You need time away from your friend. And I need to talk to you,' he says without turning around. I fix my gaze to the lipstick-stained cigarette butts that lie discarded in the gutter, and almost crash into Hervé's back when he stops abruptly.

'*Un moment*,' he snaps and disappears into a corner shop next to us. It's starting to drizzle, and it's getting dark. The day's slipped away sneakily, as if it's popped out for a packet of fags and is never going to come back. Tears are threatening again and I distract myself by checking out the notices stuck to the shop's grubby glass window. I can read French better than I can speak it, so I learn that someone's lost their dog, massages are available at a very reasonable 200ff a pop, and someone else is looking for a place to live. Join the club, I think. A plump, overcoated guy with a Yorkshire terrier dancing round his heels stares at my face as he passes. I mouth 'fuck off' at him and he drops his eyes.

When Hervé finally emerges with a clinking carrier bag, he

doesn't look quite so pissed off. 'Let us walk. And then we will sit and have a drink. Where would you like to go?' He says this kindly and a lump forms in my throat again. Shit, I'm getting sick of this. I must have overactive tear ducts or something. I take a deep breath. I almost say the first thing that pops into my head, which is: home. Not his crap flat, but *proper* home. England. My parents' house. My nan's comfy, cluttered fag-smelling flat. Even the Abandoned Church Sage and I used to sleep in when we missed the last bus home from Stourbridge. Anywhere but here, in fact.

Instead I say: 'The Pompidou Centre?'

Hervé looks at me quizzically. '*Pourquoi?*'

Good question. 'Because Sage and I haven't seen it yet.'

'*D'accord.* It is far though.'

'The further the better,' I mumble.

Again I follow him mutely. As I weave around the other pedestrians, I keep replaying the afternoon's horrible incident over and over again in my head. How could I have been so fucking stupid? Admittedly, when Bobby steered me into the sex-shop, I thought he was joking at first. But when I realised what was happening I should have put an end to it. Certainly I shouldn't have just stood behind the counter like a stuffed toy while the vile guy showed me how to use the till, his hand snaking round my waist and down to my bum, his breath hot and heavy with garlic. ('*After work today, you and me go for a drink?*') I shouldn't have got changed in front of him and Bobby, trying to squash myself into the uncomfortable leather bra that smelled of another woman's sweat and was meant for someone at least two sizes smaller. I shouldn't have just sat there behind that stinking counter while that putrid old man wanked in front of the magazine stand.

I deserve everything Sage threw at me. Calling her useless was unforgivable. I knew it would strike a nerve; I knew it would hurt.

I don't look up from where my feet are mechanically following Hervé's lanky stride until he grabs my arm to lead me down a slipway to the riverbank. I stare at the gently bobbing streetlight reflections on the river's surface. It's colder down here, but it's not unbearable, and the sound of the traffic above us is strangely muted. The buildings that flank the river look other-worldly and far away in the orangey evening light. It's the first time I've walked along the banks of the Seine and I'm pleasantly surprised. It doesn't smell nearly as bad as the Thames or the canals in Birmingham, and unlike them it's not skimmed with rainbow swirls of spilled diesel or littered with Walkers Crisps packets, floating turds and condoms.

'Bloody hell,' I say. 'This is one freaky fucking building.'

We're the only two people on the massive sloping forecourt of the Pompidou Centre.

Even though I've seen pictures of it, it's still quite a shock taking it all in. It's the kind of building Willy Wonka would create if he'd been let loose with a box of Meccano after dropping a tab of bad acid. I'm about to ask Hervé what he thinks of it, but all his attention's concentrated on trying to relight the soggy joint he's been failing to fire up since we left the relative shelter of the river. The drizzle is still deciding whether or not to turn into full-blown rain, and behind us the tourist shops and cafes are shuttered and silent. Despite its size, the Pompidou Centre reminds me of a discarded children's toy left out in the rain.

'Sage will freak when she sees this,' I say without thinking.

'It will be all right, between you and Sage?' Hervé asks, giving up on the spliff and pointlessly grinding it under his trainer.

I shrug. I try and get my head around the fact that Sage may never want to see or speak to me again. I've got no idea what it would be like not to have her lurking somewhere in my life. I take a swig of wine from the bottle we've been sharing since we left the river. Unsurprisingly, there's not much left – I've been knocking it back like a wino. I drain the last drop, trying not to gag at the thought of Hervé's spit mixed in with the dregs. I close one eye to focus and lob the bottle into a metal bin ten yards in front of us. It lands with a satisfyingly loud smash. 'She shoots, she scores,' I say under my breath without much enthusiasm. Hervé unscrews the top of the second bottle (only the best for Hervé) and hands it to me. He walks over to a low wall to the right of the forecourt and sits down. I do the same with some relief – my legs are aching like buggery. He begins to roll another joint on his knees, his hands shaking slightly from the chill in the air. I shiver, but not from the cold. The desolate atmosphere's still getting to me. In the distance I can just about make out the murmur of traffic, but there's another louder, metallic screeching sound I can't place at all. A couple sharing an umbrella run past the building without glancing at it or us. Tucking his head in the collar of his jacket, Hervé manages to light the joint. He takes a deep drag, but it doesn't seem to calm him down. He's fidgeting like a schoolboy who needs the loo but is too afraid to ask the teacher. I know he wants to say something to me, and I know what it is. I toy with letting him squirm a bit, but then decide to put him out of his misery.

'Hervé?'

'*Oui?*'

'Just say it.' I take another long pull of the wine and pass it to him. He hands me a cigarette.

'*Merci.*'

His eyes dart everywhere and anywhere that's not my face. His curly hair is jewelled with drizzle droplets and his eyes are bloodshot and saggy-looking. Without looking at me he begins to speak. 'Okay, Vicki. It has been fun. But you and Sage must leave now. And very soon.' The words come out in a rush. 'It has been three weeks, Vicki. It's too long now.'

I take a drag of my cigarette and blow a smoke ring that fizzles out lamely. 'I know, Hervé.'

'You do? You will leave? No hard feelings?'

'Absolutely.' I turn to face him and he reluctantly meets my eyes. 'Look, Hervé. I realise what you've done for us. I'm not stupid. Neither is Sage. If you want us to leave, we'll leave. Just give us twenty-four hours, and we'll be out of your hair.'

'My hair? *Je ne comprends pas.*' He shakes his head to under-line this and I'm splattered with raindrops that I squeamishly imagine are coated with hair oil.

'Fuck it.' I sigh, taking another swig of wine. 'We'll go, Hervé. Me and Sage will leave your flat.'

'That is excellent! *Bien!* We must celebrate, Vicki! As Sage says, you are a "right tosser", *n'est-ce pas?*' He takes a huge relieved gob-full of wine, which leaks out of the corners of his mouth and spills down the front of his denim jacket. He's stopped looking shaky, but I can see there's something else on his mind. 'Vicki? May I ask you another question?'

'Sure,' I say. 'As long as it's personal.' It's a line from a crap Molly Ringwald movie I've been dying to use for ages. It falls flat. Hervé just looks confused again.

'You and Sage,' he begins. 'I was wondering. Why is it that you do not wash? Especially down there?' He points at my crotch.

'You what?' I hadn't expected him to take the weak 'per-sonal question' joke so seriously. Now I'm the one squirming with embarrassment, whereas Hervé is completely at ease, as if he's just asked me what book I'm currently reading.

'Because Michel and Claude have also noticed that you guys are . . .'

'Stinky?' I say.

'*Oui.*'

'It's not out of choice, Hervé,' I snap. 'It's too bloody hard to wash ourselves in the flat, and we don't have the money to pay for a shower.'

'Ah, I see,' Hervé nods. 'That's cool.'

What a question! But hadn't the faun in *The Lion the Witch and the Wardrobe* also ended up being a bit of a dead loss in the end? 'Doesn't really matter now, Hervé,' I say, pulling him to his feet. 'You won't have to smell our stinkiness much longer. Come on. I want to see what's making that funny fucking noise.'

The second bottle of wine is almost empty, and I'm feeling warmer and less freaked out. Hervé and I are sitting on the slippery metal wall that surrounds a pond full of arty-farty sculptures. They're surreal and more than a little creepy, but they also remind me of the pretentious crap the other students at fart college used to cobble together. One of them is the source of the sinister metallic sound: every so often it shrieks as it's tickled by the breeze.

With no warning, I'm hit with a familiar but curious sensation. It's what Sage terms a 'random money shot life moment' where, 'just for a second, everything is brighter, sharper, clearer, as if it's caught in a camera's flash. I'm simultaneously aware of the eerie, gravelly sound of the sculpture, the feel of the cold metal on my bum, the vomity taste of the cheap wine, the ache in my legs from the long walk here and the peaty smell of Hervé's dope. According to Sage, this means all these tastes, smells and feelings will be caught in my memory forever, as crystal-clear as if I'd just felt them.

Or, I could just be very, very pissed.

I'm about to ask Hervé if this has ever happened to him, but he speaks first.

'There is an art gallery up there.' He points to the top of the building.

'No shit?'

'Yes shit.'

He drains the dregs of the wine and turns the bottle upside down. 'All gone, *finis*.'

He hands it to me and I pitch it expertly into a nearby bin. This time there's no satisfying crash of breaking glass. I look up at the metal fence directly in front of where we're sitting. It's criss-crossed with fat metal pipes, and through the chain-link I can make out a stairwell.

'There's seriously an art gallery up there?' I say.

'*Oui*.'

'I'd love to see it.'

'*Moi aussi*. I have never been.'

I stand up. 'Well today is your lucky day, Hervé.'

'*Non*, Vicki. It is very late. The place is closed up long ago. Anyway it is time we were getting home.'

But I'm not ready to face Sage just yet. 'Come on, Hervé. Where's your sense of adventure?'

I do a quick recce: there's not a soul to be seen. It would be a crime not to, wouldn't it?

Before Hervé can stop me, I take a deep breath, clamp my fag between my teeth and run at the fence. The metal is slippery but I force my stiff fingers around the freezing metal and heave myself up, using the thoughtfully placed pipes as leverage and throwing one leg over the metal pole at the top. Suddenly I get one of those uncontrollable giggling fits you can't stop. I'm stuck half over the fence, one leg flapping like a cod on Hervé's side. If I fall now I'll be in serious trouble. This thought doesn't sober me up. I'm forced to spit out my cigarette. It narrowly misses Hervé's head.

'Hervé! Help! I'm stuck! Give me a boost!'

'Vicki!' he hisses. 'What are you doing? Get down!'

'Push my other leg up and over, will you?'

He takes a feverish look around, climbs onto the lowest pole and pushes my dangling leg upwards. I swing my body over and land with a *clang* behind the fence. It's quite a drop, but somehow I manage to land on both feet. Easy-peasy, as things always are when I'm a bit pissed. On the other side of the mesh, Hervé's wringing his hands like a character out of a BBC Dickens miniseries.

'Come on!'

'I'm not sure, Vicki . . .'

'What are you, a chicken?' I start doing a chicken impression, flapping my arms and clucking my tongue. But what is chicken in French? *Lapin*? No, that's rabbit. Then I have it. *'Poulet, poulet,* Hervé is a *poulet!'*

Hervé sighs. 'Okay,' he says. *'Un moment.'* He backs up as far as he can go (narrowly avoiding tumbling backwards into the sculpture pond), fixes a determined expression onto his face and takes a running jump. The sound of him crashing into the fence is immense. I'm expecting a legion of cops to come running, but when the chain-link has stopped shuddering the place is still as silent as before. Hervé throws himself up and over the top with a complete lack of grace, and lands with a *whoomp* beside me. We glance at each other and crack up.

'I cannot believe that I am doing this!' he gasps.

'Come on,' I whisper. 'Let's go.' We start up the steps, our boots clattering on the metal rungs. For some reason I start humming 'Teddy Bears' Picnic'. I don't bother to keep the noise down. We're invincible. Maybe I'm cut out for this sort of work. Vicki Evans: cat burglar.

'Meow!' I say, setting Hervé off again.

We clatter up until we reach a pair of glass doors. I grab hold of the handles and shake them roughly. 'Let us in!' I yell. 'We are tourists lost in Paris, heeeellp usss!'

'Vicki! Do not shout so loudly!' Hervé splutters.

The stairwell continues upwards to our right, ending at a

low-ceilinged concreted room that looks as if it could be a parking lot for cars belonging to midgets. We head up into the gloom. It's pitch black and it takes a few seconds for my eyes to adjust. The room seems to stretch on forever and appears to be empty. It smells of dust and that uriney damp concrete stench.

'Boooring,' I sigh. I motion Hervé to follow me deeper into the space, but then my heart plummets.

Oh fuck. There's a bright light creeping closer to where we're hovering, and I'm sure it's the glow of a torch.

'Get down!' I hiss, pushing Hervé back towards the steps. Shit! There's no chance we'll be able to leg it back to the fence and throw ourselves over before the light catches up to us.

'Vicki? What is happening?'

'Ssssh!' I pull him down so that we're crouching just below the end of the stairwell. The torch's eye sweeps our way, and now we're not moving around I can hear the *clop clop* sound of its owner's footsteps. The steps falter, hesitate and then move on.

'Oh, *merde*,' Hervé whispers mournfully, and before I can tell him to shut up again, he lets off a fart that sounds like a shotgun blast.

'Fuck,' I say, no longer bothering to keep my voice down. There's no point.

We're in a room as bland and uninspiring as those in British cop shops. Same peppermint-coloured walls and posters depicting men with squinty eyes and stubbled faces. For some reason I thought French police stations would be more *chic*. I try and catch Hervé's eye to give him a reassuring grin, but he's in full panic mode. I don't really blame him. The cop shops may be the same, but the cops certainly aren't. Sage and I tend to treat British police people as Mr Plod figures of fun. It was always a piece of piss talking our way out of tricky situations that were the normal result of drunken jaunts in Birmingham or Stourbridge. But French policemen and women mean business. They wear guns at their hips and avoid eye contact.

A podgy moustachioed policewoman motions for me to empty my pockets onto a steel table in front of us. Next to me, Hervé is doing the same. It doesn't take me long as all I'm carrying is my passport, a chewed Rizla paper, an eczema-ridden M&M and a tampon that's swollen and bulging out of its cellophane wrapper.

'*Tu est Anglais?*' The policewoman flicks through my passport and curls her lip at my photograph. She pushes my stuff around the table using the end of a biro, loudly snapping her chewing gum. If I'm headed for a strip search I hope she won't be the one doing it. She points to my swollen lip. 'What is this?' she nods at Hervé. 'He do this? You 'ave a fight?'

'Nah,' I say, trying to look innocent. 'I walked into a door.'

She snorts in disbelief then disappears with my passport.

I check out Hervé's side of the table. His policeman could be my one's twin. He has the same steely-eyed stare, sensible haircut and moustache. Hervé's pockets seem to contain a never-ending stream of crap and he's nervously fumbling and dropping his stuff on the floor. The cop's eyes are beginning to glaze over. Just when it looks as if he's done, Hervé brings out another object for inspection, as if his pockets are like those clown cars in circuses. In addition to the pile of stuff already littering the table, he hauls out a money clip wadded with cash, (I file this information for later); two packets of Camel cigarettes; a plastic lighter; an ID document; a brand new pack of XXX strong mints; a huge bunch of keys; a notebook; a purse bizarrely embroidered with ladybirds; a breath freshener spray; a packet of Rizla that the policeman picks up and inspects knowingly, and then something quite unexpected. The policeman contorts his mouth into an expression that could possibly be a smile.

'*C'est pour elle?*' He picks up the last item – a jumbo packet of condoms – and waves them suggestively in my direction. 'Ahhhh,' the policeman says, reading the label out loud, '*Avec ribbing.*'

Hervé turns the colour of Heinz tomato ketchup.

The cop leaves the room with Hervé's ID, sniggering the ha ha ha laugh of a cartoon villain. The minute he's out of the door, Hervé starts piling the stuff back into his pockets. I don't bother with mine. They can keep it.

'Hervé,' I say. 'It'll be fine.'

He ignores me.

'We'll just get a caution or something, you'll see.'

Still no response.

I reach over and grab his cigarettes and lighter before he can sweep them back into the black hole masquerading as his jacket pocket and swing myself up onto the table. Legs dangling, I light two cigarettes and pass one to Hervé. He takes it wordlessly. Both of us ignore the 'no smoking' signs.

Oh shit. How could I be so fucking stupid? They've got my passport! Fuck! What if I'm wanted by Interpol? Will I be deported? The police aren't that organised are they? Am I being paranoid? I glance over at the door – they've left it open and I consider making a run for it. But where would I go? I can see the *SUN* headlines now: *Busty businessman's daughter in fugitive flight.* I'd better tell Hervé the situation in case the shit hits the fan.

'Hervé, there's something I need to—'

The policewoman slams back into the room, tapping my passport on her hand. I stub the fag on the underside of my boot and wait for her to slap the handcuffs on and wheel me down to the cells. But she simply hands me my passport, looks over at Hervé and babbles something in French. I don't understand any of it but recognise the word 'general'. Hervé goes limp with relief.

'What did she say, Hervé?'

'We can go,' he says.

'Eh? How come?'

He doesn't answer. I know I shouldn't push my luck (what if they change their minds?), but I can't help myself. I turn to the policewoman. '*Pourquoi libre?*' I say to her in my rubbish French.

'Why are we letting you go?' She nods curtly at Hervé. 'Ask your boyfriend. He has a very famous father.' She chuckles humourlessly. 'Very well known here.'

As we leave the station the two cops wave us away with a cheery *au revoir*, as if we've been there for tea instead of breaking and entering. Weird.

Outside it's stopped raining and the morning light is seeping through the cloud cover. I take a lungful of fresh air, then hare after Hervé who's striding away from the police station at a cracking pace.

'Hervé, what's going on? Why the fuck did they let us go?'

He stops and turns to face me, but he doesn't meet my eyes. 'They realised we were only having fun,' he says, but I can tell he's lying. I consider prying further, but decide to leave it. Like Potato Head, it seems Hervé also comes from money and influence. I can't wait to tell Sage about this, but then I remember – we're not talking.

As we walk on I check our surroundings. I don't recognise where we are at all. Luckily, Hervé seems to know where we're going. He pauses and hands me a cigarette. I stop dead as something occurs to me. I can't believe I didn't think of it before – especially after we were arrested.

'Hervé! Shit, what did you do with your dope?'

'Eh?'

'Your hash! When the police got us, did you dump it?'

Hervé turns around and grins at me for the first time since we left the cop shop. He holds up his tightly clenched fist, swivels it like a magician doing a trick and opens it up. The pound coin-sized block of black sits on his palm.

'You were holding this all the time?'

'*Oui.*'

'Fucking hell, Hervé, you have serious balls! No wonder you looked so shit-scared!'

Hervé shrugs modestly and offers me his arm. We stroll companionably through a series of cobbled streets, again the only people in a deserted city.

My legs are really killing me as we pass the *tabac* at the end of Hervé's street. The city is coming to life now, and a squat green street-sweeping machine hums past us, spraying the pavement with water. I breathe in the smell of wet concrete only to be hit with another 'random money shot life moment'. Two in one night – a personal record. And another thing I can't tell Sage.

Hervé stops me as we reach the Irish pub. 'Vicki, I do not think it is a good idea for you to come to the flat,' he says seriously. 'You wait somewhere and I will bring Sage. *D'accord?*'

He's obviously shitting his pants at the thought of another Sage versus Vicki bout. I don't blame him though. 'Yeah. Good thinking. I'll wait by the opera house steps. Okay?'

Hervé nods his agreement. Just before he keys in the door code he turns round and kisses me gently on the cheek.

'What was that for?' I say, resisting the urge to wipe my face.

He shrugs. '*Merci*, Vicki, it was a good night.'

I wonder if this is French sarcasm, or if he really means it.

★   ★   ★

I shift my bum around a bit to try and get the feeling back into it. My nan's always going on about how sitting on concrete gives you piles, but this is the least of my worries right now. I look up at the naked sculptures surrounding me. I'm fond of them. They're the size and shape of real women – not false Barbie bodies with thin legs and fake tits.

My heart lurches as I make out the familiar shapes of Hervé and Sage rounding the corner over by the posh cafe. Sage seems to be lagging behind.

There's another shock as a figure that resembles Jules crosses the road next to the Metro. I can't be absolutely sure it's him, but it's certainly the same long hair little dog combination. I try to make myself smaller, less noticeable, but thankfully the figure disappears into the bowels of the Metro station.

Hervé takes his time walking towards me. Even from here I can see the dark circles under his eyes: he's obviously coming down from last night's surreal experiences. Sage is a little quicker, but she doesn't look at me directly. There's a slight cut above her eye. I can't remember if I did that, or if it's a casualty of her scuffle with Bobby.

"Allo, Vicki,' Hervé says, eyes darting all over the place. The poor bugger is completely out of his depth.

'Don't worry, Hervé,' Sage sighs. 'We're not going to cause a scene.' She pauses. 'Are we, Vicks?'

I shake my head.

'Go back to the flat, Hervé,' she continues. 'We'll be along later.' She's paler than usual. We both know this is a make-or-break situation. Especially after what I promised Hervé last night. I wonder if he's told her?

He looks at me. 'You are sure?'

'Absolutely,' I say.

He nods and smiles with relief.

Sage sits stiffly next to me and we watch Hervé retracing

his steps, throwing a last nervous glance over his shoulder. Sage takes out a box of Camels and passes me one. She lights it with Hervé's Zippo, which she no doubt thinks of as hers by now.

'Thanks,' I mumble.

'Pleasure.'

'Where did you get the fags?'

'Nicked them from Pervey, of course.'

'Of course. Nice one.'

We smoke in silence for a bit.

'You all right, then?' she says, before the silence has stretched into a place of no return awkwardness.

I shrug. 'Yeah. You?'

A shrug. 'You know. Sorry about your lip, like.'

Sage never apologises. 'No worries.' I touch the tender swelling with my tongue. 'It's quite cool, actually.'

'Yeah. Makes you look hard.'

I smile. I can't help it. Sage grins crookedly. 'Sorry for what I said about you being . . . you know. I didn't mean it, Sage.'

'Yeah you did.' But she smiles again and hands me another cigarette. This time the Zippo refuses to spark into life. Without getting up or asking in French, Sage cadges a light from a bemused passer-by, who is forced to climb up several steps to light our cigarettes.

Sage sighs. 'Look, Chuck, we've got to get another place to live. Hervé's had enough.'

'Yeah, I know. He told me last night.'

'We need a plan.'

I'm encouraged. At least she's said 'we'. 'Time to do what we should have done ages ago, I suppose.'

'What's that?'

'Go to the American Church. Get some sort of naff *au pair* job like Potato Head's mum said.'

'Herve's given us twenty-four hours. That's only one day.'

'We'd best get cracking then, hadn't we?' Even though I've had no sleep I'm suddenly energised. 'Look. Let's get cleaned up. Head over there right now. You never know.'

'Yeah,' Sage grins. 'We've done all right up to now, haven't we, Chuck?'

'Course.'

We have a plan. We're always okay when we have a plan.

Both of us get to our feet. My legs are still stiff, but I couldn't care less. As we walk down the steps, Sage nods towards Bobby's corner. 'I see Bobby hasn't got the balls to show up today.'

The knot in my stomach threatens to reappear. I don't want to talk about Bobby or Jules right now. But Sage grins wolfishly and cracks her knuckles. She winces proudly and I notice her hands are bruised and swollen. 'I don't think he'll be bothering us again, do you?'

'I don't think so, no.'

'What the fuck did you and Hervé get up to last night, then, Vicks? He wouldn't say.'

'You wouldn't believe me if I told you.'

'Try me.'

By the time I've finished there are tears of laughter streaming down her face. She's laughing so hard she can barely make it up the stairs to the flat.

SAGE

Bobby Poem

Bobby is an ugly git,
Who made my best mate cry,
He looks just like a pig's arsehole,
I wish he'd bloody die.

His tummy's fat, he's such a twat,
His eyes are small and brown,
But one day soon, I'll get him back
And bring the fucker down.

What do you think? I wrote that last night, Gladys. Thought it was quite good myself, although Vicks said I didn't get the 'scansion' right (whatever the fuck that is when it's at home). Just shows she went to a posh girls' school to know boring stuff like that.

Anyway, best news ever. Vicki's got a job!!!! I know, I know, I can hardly believe it myself!!!

And I'm writing this in our NEW HOME!!! Sitting on our NEW BED!!! which is a thousand times better than Hervey's stinking mattress.

Talk about cutting it fine. We were about to be thrown out on our arses. Anyway, I'll fill you in on the details as I've got fuck all else to do at the moment. After the big fight day (also known as the Beating Up Bobby Experience), me and Vicks had to get seriously sorted and fast because Hervey had given us twenty-four hours before we were history at his place. I helped Vicki smarten up a bit, which wasn't easy, let me tell you. I tied her dreadlocks up in this dead neat bun, and we did our best with make-up. Luckily her big fat lip had gone down a bit.

The main problem we had was clothes, as Vicks's wardrobe isn't exactly kosher for a job interview, consisting as it does of mostly skintight 1950s dresses and leather stuff. And mine's not a lot better (and obviously I never wear dresses). Anyway, we ended up 'borrowing' one of Hervey's very stiff suit jackets, which Vicks wore over a long velvet Victorian dress, and she actually looked quite square. A bit like Mary Poppins would look if she ever joined The Cure or something.

There wasn't much we could do about the shoe situation, but we polished Vicks's Docs using spit. Next, we cadged some cash from Hervey (the bugger couldn't say 'non' could he? Vicks saw how much cash he had on him after the police thing, and anyway, he owes us for leaving when he asked us to) and got going. Sure, we did get a bit lost and had to ask people where the fuck to go, but eventually we ended up at this American Church place. Although, God knows why it's called that, cos it looked like it had fuck all to do with America. Anyway, this miserable looking woman (who turned out to be French and not American) eventually pointed us towards the noticeboard. And hurrah! There were tons of jobs on offer. Vicks wanted to write down the details, but I told her to pick three and then ripped the notices off the board when no one was looking. Most of them advertised a room in exchange for babysitting, which was what we wanted.

So, blah blah blah, to cut a long story short, Vicks called the numbers up and two of the three said they could see her for an interview in the afternoon. By this stage we were running out of cash (well we had to buy essentials, didn't we?: fags, matches, slices of pizza etc) and it took us ages to get to the first place – a big old white stone apartment block (I noticed today that nearly all the buildings in Frog land are the same fucking colour!!!) Anyway, I waited outside while Vicks went in. She was dead nervous but I could see she was trying not to show it. She came out almost straight away shaking her head. The job was a dead loss as the room was actually in the apartment, which meant I wouldn't be able to sneak in there without being busted, and Vicks said the woman was a carbon copy of Potato Head's scary mother.

We sat down for a fag break, then headed for the next one, which was like a hundred Metro stops away. Vicks and I are getting dead good at finding our way around though. The place is in this area called 'Saint German' or something, which sounds dead posh. Luckily the people on the phone had given Vicks spot-on directions (which was a good sign). This time Vicks was ages and when she came out she wasn't by herself. This oldish fat lady wearing glasses and crap hair was with her. Vicks gave me a look which meant 'pretend you don't know me', so I followed her at a distance. They went into another block of flats down the road (not as posh, but with the same James Bond coded door key thing as in Hervey's building).

When they came out, Vicks waved goodbye to the woman and started walking in the opposite direction to draw attention away from me in case I'd been noticed. I caught up with her and she was wearing this dead excited grin on her face. 'So?' I said, and Vicks paused and then said, 'They're fucking desperate!' All she has to do is look after this kid for like two hours a day and we get our own private room away from the bosses. Vicks says she's going to pick up the keys the following day and we can move in. They're not going to pay us or anything, but what the hell.

Anyway, Hervey let us stay another night at his place on account of the fact he knew we were leaving for deffo, and told us he was going to throw us a wicked big goodbye party. Vicks said, 'We'll still be friends though, eh Hervey?' But both me and her were thinking the same thing, which was: Like fuck!

Everyone was invited (except B the B of course, although part of me wished he was there so I could smack him one again). Me and Vicks got a bit drunk and when Genevieve arrived we told her quietly that Hervey was in love with her but was too scared to do anything about it. She was like: 'I already have a boyfriend and he's coming just now!' Poor old Pervey. You should have seen his face when her shag turned up. He's this dead rich guy with a yellow sweater draped over his shoulders. He looks like a bloke you'd see in an advert or something. Square face, a bit like Rob Lowe, but with dark caterpillar eyebrows that meet in the middle of his forehead. Anyway, turns out he's not a Frog but Italian!! Me and Vicks felt a bit sorry for the old perv, as he looked dead sad. Luckily Genevieve and her boyfriend (who's got a Porsche) didn't stay long. Later on, Potato Head arrived with a bottle of champagne (funny ay it, Gladys, how the good booze always comes out when you're saying goodbye to someone). And we all got pissed and Dracula tried it on with Vicks like he knew it was his last chance. She snogged him a bit but that was all. Even Vicks has better taste than that. We were very careful not to let Hervey or any of the other Frogs know where our new home is though (for obvious reasons).

Oh, and on the way out the next morning I kicked that mad bastard neighbour shilling's door hard for good luck.

So Vicks goes and fetches the keys the next day and I wait round the corner with our bags. They were extra difficult to carry as we didn't have time to pack properly on account of both having stinking hangovers. And I didn't manage to nick as much cash from Hervey as I'd have liked. It was all a bit of an anticlimax actually as when we left, Hervey, Potato Head and Dracula were out buying coffee for their hangovers and we sort of snuck away. But at least we didn't have to kiss them goodbye.

GOOD THINGS ABOUT THE NEW ROOM:

1. It has a real bed (we'll have to share, but so what? I'm not complaining).
2. It's miles away from Hervey and Bobby the Bastard.
3. We don't ever have to listen to Hervey farting in his sleep again.
4. The sink in the room is almost clean with only a few stains.
5. It also has a dressing table and a mirror, which makes Vicks very happy.
6. There's an electric frying pan in the corner, which would be ace if we somehow managed to get any fucking food to cook in it.
7. Most importantly: IT DOESN'T SMELL OF HERVEY, HIS HASH OR HIS DIRTY CLOTHES!!!!

BAD THINGS:

1. Surprise surprise it's on the very top floor.
2. It's only a one room jobby with a sink in it, but no toilet (although, at least the communal one down the corridor is a normal one, thank fuckery).
3. Yet again there's no shower anywhere (all I can say is there must be thousands of stinking Frogs in this country. Gross).

Oh shit. I forgot to put one very important thing on the bad things list. The building has this caretaker woman who is supposed to keep tabs on who lives in the building etc (like a spy although not as dangerous or as much fun). Vicks has named her 'Mrs Danvers', which is the name of this total bitch in a book called *Rebecca*.

Anyway, as we were lugging our stuff up the staircase, Mrs Danvers glides out of her dark cubicle thing, which is tucked away like an upright coffin next to the front door, and looks at me with dead suspicious eyes. I could tell straight away that she hated me, because I'm basically a squatter. Only Vicks is allowed to use the room.

Vicks keeps panicking that she'll lose her job because of Mrs D's beady eyes and then we'd be back to square one. I'm not worried though. Mrs Danvers has a moustache as thick and lush as Tom Selleck's and she only wears black clothes, which shows a lack of imagination. She's no match for me.

Better sign off now, Gladys, as Vicks will be back from work and I want to do a quick tablet recce before she gets back.

PS – you won't believe the name of the kid Vicks is looking after. When she first told me I thought she'd said: 'The kid is called Nausea' !!!, but it's actually Nausicaa or something. Seriously. Vicks said she almost died when she heard this. But apparently the kid's named after this Greek mythology person (you know, like Hercules but a woman) as its parents are professors of antiquity or something.

How fucked up is that?? I mean, my folks wouldn't win 'Parents of the Year' or anything, but that's fucking cruel.

VICKI:

The Job Experience

'Sage! Holy shit! What the fuck's the time?'

There's a grunt from beneath her sleeping bag, but that's it.

Shit and buggeration, I was only supposed to be having a brief 'hangover helper' nap before getting ready for work. I yank my legs out from where Sage has been using them as a pillow. She makes a sound like water gurgling out of a drain, but doesn't get up. Hands shaking, I scrabble around the slippery fabric of my sleeping bag for the watch Sage nicked from *Hervé*. Then I remember – I tucked it into my boot before I passed out this morning so I wouldn't lose it.

Fuck! Ten minutes to get changed and walk up the hill to Nausicaa's flat. I'll never make it. I throw myself out of bed and realise too late that my leg is pins and needles dead (thanks to Sage's head), and it won't take my weight. There's a sharp jarring pain as I keel over, and for an instant I'm sure I've broken my ankle. I clench my teeth to stop myself crying out and carefully try to put my weight on it. It hurts like buggery, but I think I can manage to hobble on it.

Okay, next mission. I slept in my clothes last night: can I get away without changing? I do the armpit test (bad) then notice that my dress is spotted with vomit specks (very bad).

Sage is fast asleep again and for a second I envy her so much I could hit her. It's not fair: She can sleep all morning if she likes, whereas I have to walk half a mile up the hill on an ankle that feels like it's been dipped in fire. As I stumble over to the sink and hopelessly try to lather up our cake of soap, I try to come up with a believeable excuse for why I'm going to be late.

I grab the first dress that comes to hand (I don't bother to change my underwear or leggings). It smells of old socks and stale deodorant, but it's better than the BO and vomit option. Then I remember something. I root around in the stuff Sage nicked from the guy last night and unearth a can of Old Spice. Better to smell like a bloke than an alky, surely?

'Bonjour, ça va?' Nausicaa's mother greets me unsmilingly as she lets me into the apartment.

I've never seen her smile at anyone (not even her daughter), so I don't take it personally. She's what Nan would call a 'hard-faced cow'. I check my watch. I'm only fifteen minutes late. The walk up the hill was bloody murder, but I've made quite good time, all things considered.

'Oui. Tres bien, merci!' I lie.

Nausicaa's mother looks at me dubiously. 'You are sure? You do not look very well.'

'Just a touch of flu.' I pretend to cough, but she's not convinced. For the life of me I can't remember her name and I've left it too late to ask – I've been working for her for two weeks now. 'Sorry I'm late, by the way,' I babble on. 'Just couldn't get out of bed – you know how it is when you're feeling under the weather!'

She narrows her eyes and looks meaningfully at my dress. Typical, I've put it on inside out. I pull my cardigan tighter to hide the telltale outside seams and 'dry clean only' label. We've reached an impasse. I hover in the narrow hallway, wondering how to sneak past her without getting too close (I'm sure I need to keep a good three-foot radius to pass the alcohol/sweat/fag smell-test). Luckily Nausicaa saves the day. With impeccable timing she hares down the corridor and jumps up into my arms. Her mother is forced to retreat into the kitchen to avoid being hit by chubby flying legs as I whirl Nausicaa around. My hangover shifts into fourth gear, and for a scary second I think my ankle will snap.

'Airplane, Vicki!' Nausicaa laughs. '*Vite! Vite!*'

'*Parle Anglais!*' her mother snaps at her. One of my jobs is to improve Nausicaa's English, which is a bit harsh in my opinion as she's only two or so. I put Nausicaa down and allow her to drag me into the sitting room. Thankfully the mother stays put.

'And today, we go to the park?' I say.

'*Oui!* The park!' Nausicaa squeals, as if we don't go there four times a week. I plonk myself down on the couch, and my ankle breathes a sigh of relief. I imagine it swelling and turning black inside my boot. Oh fuck it. It can't be that bad, can it? I send Nausicaa to her room to fetch her anorak, and I enjoy a few precious moments of peace. The first time I walked into the apartment it felt like I'd stumbled into the Tardis. The modest front door and entrance hall imply that the flat will be about the same size as a British council house, but there's a bewildering number of rooms. Although it's as massive as Potato Head's apartment, it's nowhere near as clean or shiny. The carpets are a scummy beige colour and are dotted with mysterious swooping stains, and I'm yet to come across a television. Even the thousands of books that coat the walls and lurk in piles waiting to be tripped over look battered and dull. It's as if Nausicaa's parents have never heard of Stephen King or Philip K. Dick. And while Nausicaa is blonde and bubbly and ripples and sparkles with two-year-old energy, her parents are as tired and baggy as Bagpuss. Her dad is the sort of guy who wears corduroy trousers and the mother has an endless supply of 1970s polo-necked jumpers. They're nice enough I suppose, but I'm glad they're not my fucking parents.

'Come, Nausicaa, let's go!' The flat always smells of damp washing and old milk and it's making me feel sick again.

As usual, everything for our little excursion has already been obsessively organised. The pushchair is waiting in the hall, and Nausicaa's snack box is packed with precision and waiting on the kitchen counter. The mother peers at me gloomily through her bottle-bottom glasses as I strap Nausicaa into the chair and wheel her out of the apartment. I'm already knackered and I haven't even started the day's chores.

By the time we arrive at the park my ankle is so sore I'm forced to shuffle along like Quasimodo, leaning my weight on the pushchair. As usual, the other nannies are clustered around the benches next to the swings, like the vultures in *Jungle Book*. They all stop chattering as soon as I arrive and look at me as if they can't understand what the fuck I'm doing daring to gatecrash their world.

On my first day here, a couple of the Canadian ones tried to be friendly, but the appearance of Sage soon put paid to that. They could just about handle me, but Sage's skulking presence totally threw them. Still, I'm relieved in a way. They're not my sort of people. They all wear variations on the same outfit: sensible woolly two-pieces or high-waisted Mum jeans. Some even wear little wispy scarves around their necks like they're trying to be Audrey Hepburn.

I sink down onto a shady bench as far away from them as possible. I free Nausicaa from her pushchair prison and she makes a beeline for the sandpit. The other kids scatter when she approaches. I wave at her conspiratorially. Like me, she doesn't seem to give a shit that she's an outcast in nanny park world. My stomach moans, and I battle with the usual desire to rip open Nausicaa's lunchbox and gobble down the two tiny yoghurts, the apple and the slices of delicious processed cheese. I usually have to content myself with cadging spoonfuls of yoghurt from Nausicaa, pretending it's some sort of game. Since we blew the last of Hervé's cash on fags and a six-pack of crème caramels, I've been supporting us with the loose change from the Nausicaa family daily shop, and what I can smuggle out of their fridge.

An old man appears at the outskirts of the park. He looks like he's taking the piss out of being French, which is kind of cool. He totally looks the part, right down to the black beret, his little black moustache and the brown ciggy drooping out of his mouth. I smile at him as he passes, but the nannies stare at him accusingly until he gets the message and wanders off. My stomach grumbles again. The food Sage and I managed to con out of the guy last night would normally have kept me going, but I had to stupidly puke it up, didn't I? To stop myself dozing off, I try to gauge whether last night's adventure was worth suffering today's hangover. It's a difficult call.

Yesterday, Sage and I had wandered down to Notre Dame to do some 'work'. We still have a half-baked notion about selling some sketches, and God knows we need to make some cash somehow. We found an empty bench opposite the cathedral by the bank of the river, made ourselves comfortable, and had just started to scribble when Sage nudged me.

'Tosser alert, Vicks.'

A man on the bench next to ours was staring at us and smiling. He wasn't much to look at: big Potato Head moonish face, little piggy eyes and squashy stomach. All the sexy Frenchmen who look like movie stars with slip-on shoes and scarves flung nonchalantly around their necks never flirt with me or Sage. I suppose it's because they're too busy hanging out in trendy coffee bars with girls that look and dress like Genevieve.

Sure enough, he wandered over with the excuse of cadging a light. I immediately liberated two of his Gitanes, and he took this as an invitation to plonk himself next to me. There was the typical, 'What are you doing? I see you are artists,' conversation, as Sage blasted out her usual 'fuck off' vibes and I did my best to explain that we were *literally* starving artists. It wasn't easy as his English was minimal and my O-level French hasn't improved, even though we've been in exile here for ages. I was hoping he'd offer to buy us some takeout, but instead, after ten minutes of unintelligible babble, I clocked that he was inviting us back to his place for a meal. Without consulting Sage I agreed.

'Vicks,' she hissed. 'Are you off your fucking head?'

She was right of course, but I was desperate to eat something that wasn't stale baguette or stolen Nausicaa family groceries. I tried a new strategy to convince her. 'What if there's a shower at his place? I'm sure he wouldn't mind if we used it.' I knew Sage would probably sell her soul for a proper wash, and I was right. She agreed to the plan reluctantly, making me swear that we'd scarper straight afterwards.

His place wasn't a palace, but it was better than our garret: a dining room furnished in dark brown wood, one boxy bedroom, a tiny kitchen full of grimy spices and a largish bathroom that smelled of aftershave and urine. We'd barely walked through the door when Sage asked him if she could use the shower. It took me a while to figure out that he was telling me it was out of order.

'Typical,' she said. 'No wonder the ozone layer's fucked, the amount of deodorant you lot must use instead of washing.' She knew he wouldn't understand her, but he got the gist. I think it was then that he twigged he wasn't headed for a torrid night of shagging and threesomes and that we were probably going to be using him more than he'd planned to use us.

Shower or not, this didn't stop Sage locking herself in the bathroom for ages while the guy struggled to flirt with me. When Sage finally reappeared she stank like the shampoo section of Boots. While we waited for him to prepare us some smelly cheese sandwiches, Sage flicked through his record collection. 'Toto? Chicago? Bon Jovi? You've got to be fucking kidding, we're in soft rock hell.'

She unearthed *Sticky Fingers* by the Stones and put it on, which reminded me of the horrible old bastard in Hervé's building. But apart from these minor fuck-ups the night was quite a good laugh. Eventually the guy gave up trying to get into my pants and, sensibly realising he wasn't going to get rid of us before the booze dried up, got into the swing of it. We'd flattened two bottles of wine when Sage noticed a sticky bottle of peppermint liqueur hidden behind a pile of *National Geographics*. I can't remember much else after that. One minute I was head-banging to Joan Jett and the Blackhearts, and the next Sage and I were running full pelt past the closed cafes of St Germain, toilet rolls and nicked shampoo spilling out of Sage's pockets. We passed out at around four, after I'd been copiously and horribly sick under the oak tree outside our building. I'd woken at seven, desperate to pee, but had to use the Toilet of Death#2 without flushing, because it makes a noise like a train passing through the building when you pull the chain. I hadn't wanted to risk pissing off the other inhabitants of the floor more than we already had. I was confident our earlier drunken entrance wasn't the quietest. Mind you, our neighbour situation is a weird state of affairs. As in Hervé's flat, we haven't encountered a single fellow occupant. I'm beginning to think that Paris must be full of agoraphobics like my great-aunt Vera, who hasn't set foot outside her Kent bungalow since before I was born.

I take a furtive sip out of Nausicaa's juice bottle. It doesn't erase the putrid taste in my mouth, but I'm so thirsty I'd drink Birmingham canal water if it was on offer. Although I scrubbed my teeth and tongue this morning I'm positive I can still taste

peppermint liqueur. I stick my tongue out as far as I can to see
if it's green. One of the nannies sees me doing this and nudges
a clone next to her. Both giggle girlishly, their hands covering
their mouths. I shoot them a dead eye.

It's time to leave. I grab Nausicaa's attention and lure her
over to me with the temptation of her lunchbox, steeling
myself for our exit. Most of the time, Nausicaa's a happy little
kid, always eager for hugs and 'airplane' rides, but when it's
time to leave the park she becomes Regan from *The Exorcist*.
Everyday I have to set my face in a stony expression and carry
her out of there. This isn't easy as she somehow makes her
body go as rigid as an ironing board. The nanny mafia eye me
smugly. I'm pretty sure the spectacle of me and Nausicaa
leaving the park is the highlight of their day. They never offer
to help. Mind you, Sage is a dead loss when it comes to kids
as well. She treats Nausicaa and the other kids in the park as
if they're alien beings that can't be trusted. But today I have a
plan. Distracting Nausicaa with her lunchbox and juice bottle,
I strap her into her pushchair, and by the time she's realised
what's happened, I've wheeled her past the disappointed
nanny brigade and out of the park. This triumph doesn't blunt
the misery yet to come. It's chore time. Today's shopping list
is monstrous and will involve navigating three different stores.
Fuck.

When I let myself into our room after hobbling up the stairs
like a broken android, Sage is still fast asleep, her head barely
visible beneath the roll of her sleeping bag. Again I feel a surge
of irritation. The least she could have done was get her lazy
arse out of bed and meet me at the park. I don't bother keeping
the noise down as I slam my way around the room, but I'd
have more luck waking the dead. I sit down heavily on my end
of the bed, and bracing myself for a horrible sight, take off my
boot. Not fair! My ankle looks exactly the same. I was hoping

to use the injury as an excuse to guilt Sage into cleaning up the room or something.

I'm dying to lie down and pass out, but there's something else I have to take care of first. It's Sage's birthday tomorrow. I would never have known if she hadn't let it slip last night when we were pissed. I've no idea how she keeps track of the date, I'd be hard pressed to say what month it is. I was hoping to nick some cash out of the Nausicaa grocery fund, but the bastards had cunningly given me almost the exact change. My last resort was to attempt to nick a bottle of vodka from the miserly liquor cabinet (and then fill it with water and replace the bottle) but the mother had shadowed me like a clingon when I'd returned to the flat. All I could manage food-wise was two yoghurts that I slicked out of the fridge while I was rinsing out Nausicaa's juice bottle. Although the temptation to scarf them down immediately is enormous, I push them under the bed. Bugger. I have to get Sage a gift even if she doesn't deserve one for being an inconsiderate bitch-face. But what do you get the girl who has nothing? At home, Sage was always making stuff: painting jackets, customising waistcoats, sewing the funny little colourful pixie hats she likes to wear.

I glance around the room for inspiration. Could I wrap up one of the items Sage nicked last night, and pass it off as something I've bought? Doubtful. She has a good memory for stuff like that. I look over to where my sketch pad lies open and crumpled beneath my vomity dress. I could always do a drawing for her. No. I have a better idea.

SAGE

Mrs Danvers Poem

She lurks on the stair
Trespassers beware
She has lots of hair
On her top lip.

Maybe I should be a poet or writer or something instead of being a sculptor, or my latest idea – joining the FBI. Vicks says the Mrs Danvers poem is a bit like a 'haiku', which sounds quite intellectual and intelligent.

Anyway . . . Happy Birthday to me . . .
For two days ago actually.

So I know you're wondering: What's happened since then, Sage? Well, the answer is a *lot*, actually, Gladys!!

Okay, it's official. Me and Vicks (especially me) are now bonafide B & E experts and drug dealers. And although I really want to get straight to the juicy bits, I'll start at the beginning . . .

So the last time I wrote to you, Gladys, I was age seventeen.

Now I'm officially an adult, which means absolutely nothing as I've been drinking in pubs since I was fourteen.

Normally I hate birthdays, it's usually the folks and my good sister Karen and her crap perv of a husband Pete all going out for a shit meal which always ends in me and Pete fighting about something stupid like Enoch Powell. This year was totally different. Vicks had nicked two of Nausicaa's yoghurts (the ones that taste like sweetened snot), so we had a small but touching birthday breakfast in bed. Then, with a flourish, she whipped out my present. Which was a story she'd written for me!! Well, obviously I'd have preferred a packet of Rothmans and a pint, but it was pretty cool. Fucking cool, actually. It was called 'The Apartments of Death', and was about these two girls who were obviously supposed to be me and Vicks, who lived in this building in Paris. In the story all the girls' neighbours ended up dying horribly, and the killer ended up being the character based on me (so it was quite true to life ha ha). By the end of the story I was almost crying with laughter. (Vicks looked a bit pissed off, though. I'm not sure she meant it to be funny.)

Vicks had the day off, so after brekkie we decided to go for a birthday walk to the Pompidou Centre so that she could show me the sculptures she's always going on about. She was right, they are crap. The Pompidou Centre is cool though. And guess what??? We found out that anyone can go in and use the music library there for free! Guess what I listened to? Ha ha, Pink Floyd of all things.

Then we explored for a bit.

It was torture walking around the Latin Quarter. Everywhere you look there are these booths selling big shiny kebabs and with these huge blown-up photos of their food outside. It was like they were saying 'Look at all this food that you can't buy and eat, Vicki and Sage.'

We ended up on a bench outside this Chinese takeaway place. It wasn't proper Chinese takeaway obviously as it was French and just looked like a shop selling upside down old dried-looking ducks. To torture ourselves we made a list of what we'd like to eat if we ever got our hands on some cash. This was quite fun and interesting, especially as most of the things we chose contained meat items, and we'd only stopped being vegetarian because of Bobby the Bastard.

Vicki's food list:

Marks & Spencer microwave Chicken Tikka Masala.
Pancakes on Pancake Day.
Big family roast lunch (with Yorkshire pudding and NO family arguments).
Treacle tart and double cream.
Baked sausages (so the skin goes all hard and chewy).
Jellied eels (yuk!!).

Me:

Egg on toast.
Fish and chips.
Takeout curry of ANY sort from ANY curry house (except the one near Wolverhampton train station, as the health inspectors apparently found traces of sperm in their chicken korma).
Kentucky thighs and drumsticks and a side order of coleslaw.

As we were torturing ourselves with the list of stuff we couldn't have, this guy and his girlfriend came out of the Chinese take-away. He was a fat-arse and was shoving this dumpling thing into his mouth. His girlfriend was just nibbling hers, on account of she was anorexic. She had arms like sticks and those bandy bendy legs anorexics always have (Why??? Do they really think it looks nice??) Anyway, I really hope me and Vicks don't end up looking like her.

I could tell that fat-arse and his skeleton weren't really enjoying their food and I nudged Vicks. She knew immediately what was up, and both of us just stared at them willing them to put their leftovers in the bin next to our bench. It worked! They threw their dumpling things away and as soon as they'd walked away a bit, I dived into the bin and grabbed the food. But the guy turned round just as I was doing this and looked at us with this dead superior and disgusted look on his fat face. I'm like, 'What the fuck you looking at??' so he just shook his head and left. Even though me and Vicks were starving, I could see why they'd ditched the dumplings. They were cold and woolly-tasting. Not very pleasant, Gladys, but better than a kick up the arse.

We decided to go back to the room. As usual, we tried to sneak in to avoid Mrs Danvers, but no such luck. The bitch was there in her coffin knitting something with rough brown wool. She gave me her usual glare as we walked past. I said I hoped she was knitting a balaclava to hide her ugly fucking face, and Vicks laughed. But I could tell that Vicks was quite depressed that we hadn't scored any food or booze for my birthday. I wasn't that bothered to be honest, but I knew a plan had to be made RE the food situation.

And guess what, Gladys, I made one. By myself.

I waited till Vicks was fast asleep (this took ages, as she always reads for like hours before she goes to sleep). Then, careful not to wake her, I snuck out of the apartment building and started walking.

Can you guess where I was going?

All right, I did get a bit lost, but not too badly as I'm dead good at directions and Paris is only about the size of Birmingham (probably). It only took me about two hours or so (not really sure as I forgot to take the stolen watch) to get to Opera. Luckily the place was deserted, which was dead weird, because this is a city isn't it? There are more people milling about Stourbridge town centre at 3 a.m (hooligans and pissheads and stuff) than in Paris. Vicks had told me how quiet it was when she and Hervey broke into the Pompidou Centre, but I hadn't believed her to be honest.

So obviously you now know I was going to Hervey's place, Gladys . . .

I couldn't get the door to Hervey's building to open at first, and then I realised I'd tapped in the wrong code! (I'd used the code for our new dump). When I got inside the hash smell was as strong as ever. I could hear every step I took on the stairs as it was dead quiet, what with the Irish pub being closed and the non-existent other inhabitants doing whatever the fuck it is they do early in the morning, polishing their antiques or whatever. It was so fucking weird being back. I didn't dare turn on any lights. Even though we'd only left there a few weeks ago, it felt like for ever, and I expected everything to have changed. Like maybe Hervey had left and run off with Genevieve or some shite (although I doubted it, him being such a limp dick tosser and Genevieve having a very rich and sexy boyfriend).

My heart was beating fast as fuck as I reached Hervey's door, especially as I hadn't thought of a cover story (which you always need in these sorts of situations). It's not as if I could say we'd forgotten something and I'd come to collect it (yeah right at 3 a.m ha ha!!!). In any case, we'd 'borrowed' quite a few things when we left (Hervey's knife, watch, lighter, interview jacket, some clean socks, some Rizla papers etc.) Anyway, I carefully slid Vicks's bank card in the door crack and unlocked the latch. It sounded like the noisiest thing in the world, but there was no going back, Gladys. I stepped into the room and there they were, the three fuckateers, Dracula, Potato Head and Hervey, having a snoring and farting sleepover.

And did I feel guilty about what I was about to do, Gladys?

Did I *fuck*.

It was dark in the room but my eyes adjusted pretty quickly, and I knew where everything was. I grabbed Hervey's lump of hash off the floor next to his bed, but I couldn't see his wallet anywhere. Then, guess what?! Potato Head sat up, opened his eyes and looked straight at me!! I almost had a heart attack; but then he grunted, turned over and went back to sleep. He must have thought I was a fucking dream or something! Hilarious!!!! I was about to leave, but then I saw Hervey's satchel over by the door. I was going to take it but decided not to. He loves that satchel and it would be cruel. But I couldn't resist having a look inside it. Wish I hadn't now. There were three porno mags with pics of huge fat women doing vile stuff to each other, and four packets of condoms. (IS EVERYONE IN FRANCE A PERVERT????)

As I was sneaking out, the mad old shilling from next door poked his head out of his door. We looked at each other for a few seconds and then I did something fucking hilarious. I put my finger to my lips and did like a slicing motion across my throat – you know, meaning 'if you say anything you're dead,' but I did it in a very cool Bruce Lee or Mafia type of fashion. His eyes almost popped out of his skull and he shrank back into his room, like a turtle going back into its shell.

By this stage I didn't think there was any point in being quiet, so I ran down the stairs as fast as I could.

Anyway, I was just thinking how cool it was that there wouldn't be any witnesses when a van pulled up outside the Irish pub. A guy got out and unloaded a cardboard box of fruit and veg and left it outside the pub door. I hid in the doorway, and when he left, I thought 'what the hell' and took the box with me (ditching most of the 'tatoes on account of the weight factor.)

On the way back there were a few more people about, and some were dead polite and nodded and said *'Bonjour'* when I passed them. They probably thought I was a fruit delivery person!!

Hold on, need a break – my hand's hurting.

Okay, where was I?

Vicks was still asleep when I got in so I had to wake her up. She was so impressed when I told her what I'd done that she gave me a big hug!! (Not so useless NOW am I???) Anyway, she never does that and it kind of made the whole trip worth it. Anyway, we just fell on the fruit and ate it in about three seconds and then we even scoffed the vegetables (even the potatoes) without cooking them (which was a bit of a thick thing to do). But there's a nasty twist to this tale I'm afraid, Gladys. Normally I'd try to save your sensibilities, but I can't this time. You see both me and Vicks had been horribly constipated on account of mostly eating rice and crap at Hervey's, and after we scoffed all that fruit, things started to happen. Vicks was in the loo for like an hour, and when she came out she was dead white. It wasn't pretty I can tell you. I hope we didn't block it up. Luckily we still had some of the nicked toilet paper handy.

Anyway, after Vicks finished babysitting the brat the next day, we walked down to the Latin Quarter to sell Hervey's black. I'd cut it into tiny pieces that we were going to say were eighths, and wrapped them in little swatches of silver foil (from the stolen yoghurts) so that they looked professional. Obviously both of us were shitting ourselves. We've never been drug dealers, believe it or not. And we had no idea what we were supposed to do. I mean you can't just walk up to someone on the street and say, 'Hey you want to buy some drugs?' (even if we did know how to say that in French). But big surprise – it was a piece of piss!!! Vicks spotted this group of posh yar yar English schoolboys sitting at this outside cafe and we wandered past them a couple of times. Then Vicks said, 'Oh fuck it', walked up to one of them and said, 'Hey, you want to buy some black?' And the kid almost fell off his chair with eagerness. It was that easy after all.

They were dead loaded. We sold them nearly half our stash (as well as the three 'eighths' that were actually just empty pieces of foil). We made 300 francs! Fucking wicked!!!

On the way home we stopped at the little cafe and bought:

1 packet of fags (Lucky Strikes, Vicks's favourites)
1 packet of crème caramels (mostly for Vicks)
1 loaf of bread (not a baguette, a sliced white loaf!!!)
1 packet of Babybel cheeses.
1 packet of strawberry jelly powder (this was free – I nicked it).

Hurrah!

RESULT!!!

VICKI:
The Sid and Nancy Experience

I crane my neck to try and spot Sage in the crowd around the Pompidou Centre, but she's nowhere to be seen. The bench on which she normally waits for me after I've finished work is occupied by a couple of podgy tourists wrestling with a fold-out map. She's probably just popped to the loo or something.

I decide to head down to the centre and meet her outside the toilets on the ground floor. The Pompidou forecourt is teeming with tourists and I have to bob and weave around the groups clustered round the crap clown and mime shows.

Finally I see her. She's standing on the outskirts of a group watching a badly made-up Pierrot creating phallic-shaped balloon animals. She's talking animatedly with two scruffy guys and seems to be laughing her head off at something one of them is saying. Weird. Sage never does this. She's so afraid of encountering 'Bobby the Bastard clones' that most people who approach us get the silent treatment.

She clocks me before I can call out to her, and waves me over. 'Vicks! Come and meet two travelling musicians!'

That explains it. For some reason, Sage has a soft spot for musicians. But it's still a major U-turn from her usual anti-social behaviour. I check out the guys as I wander down the slope. They look like polar opposites. The shorter one has blond dreads and a massive stainless steel ring through his nose. The other guy is a full head taller, has close-cropped hair (like Paul Weller's) and is swathed in an outsize army parka, despite the fact that it's warm today. Two battered guitar cases lie at their feet and they're bouncing a bottle of red wine between them.

'All right?' I say, nodding to the two guys. They both give me the once-over. This normally annoys Sage, but she simply grabs the bottle from the tall one and passes it to me. I take a large gulp, trying not to gag. The wine is as foul as the cheap gut-rot Hervé used to feed us.

'Vicks, this is Scotty and Irish,' Sage says.

'No prizes for guessing where you two come from then,' I say.

'Yep,' Sage says before they can speak. 'They really do come from Scotland and Ireland. *Seriously.*' She rolls her eyes. I'm relieved to see she hasn't changed everything about her personality.

The blond one grins at me. I try not to stare. His teeth look like they've never seen a toothbrush. They're coated with gungy yellowish moss.

'Pleased to meet yer,' he says in a thick Irish accent, holding out a grubby hand and squeezing mine limply. His fingernails are lined with dirt. The tall guy nods at me without changing his expression, and doesn't offer to shake hands.

'I said we'd do some bottling for them,' says Sage.

'Ah,' I say. 'What the fuck is bottling?'

The Irish guy grins at me again and I get another view of the world's most disgusting teeth. 'You know, collectin' the money like, when we play.'

'Okay. Sounds good.' I shrug and take another slug of gag-inducing wine. 'What kind of music do you play then?' I direct this at Scotty to see if he'll answer.

'Wait and see.' Irish winks at me. 'I think yer gonna like it.'

I'm about to ask what they're doing in Paris when a harsh yelping sound grabs my attention. It's coming from a bench a few feet away from the one Sage and I think of as our own. Several scary French cops are approaching a group of tramps, and a little dog attached to its tramp owner by a raggedy piece of string is having what Nan calls a 'conniption fit' – barking its head off and straining at its makeshift lead. The tramps are always hanging around the benches opposite the centre, sharing bottles of wine and lounging around. Sage and I generally give them a wide berth, but they've never approached us for fags or freebies, so we tend to ignore them. But today, an older, plump-looking tramp standing on the outskirts of the group catches my eye and waves a greeting at me. I find myself waving back.

'Know them, do yer?' Irish asks.

'Nah. Just seen them around.'

'Best be moving on.' Scotty nods towards the police. His voice is as gravelly and mournful as his expression.

'Aye, let's find us a spot,' Irish says, picking up his guitar.

'Where?' Scotty asks.

'What about the Metro?' I suggest. 'There are usually tons of buskers down there.'

'Yeah, well that's the fookin' problem. There's a rota.' Irish screws a soggy roll-up into the corner of his mouth.

'A what?'

'Like in the Underground. Yer get allocated a spot. If yer play in someone else's pitch when you're not supposed to, yer get the fookin' shite knocked out of yer.'

'Fuck. Seriously?'

'Aye, they've practically got a fookin' union for fookin' buskers, haven't they Scotty?'

'Aye. Same as in the Undergound,' Scotty says, voice dripping with deep sadness. He sounds like a Scottish version of

Eeyore the depressed donkey in *Winnie the Pooh*. God, I hope he isn't the vocalist.

'Best we find a nice busy cafe around here, and you goirls can collect the money,' Irish says, and the two of them stride off ahead.

'What the fuck's going on, Sage?' I whisper once the buskers are out of earshot. I'm secretly delighted not to be the one in the wrong for once.

'Bummed a fag off them and got talking. They seem all right.'

'Yeah, but did you see the Irish guy's teeth?'

'Fuck, yeah. He won't be doing any Colgate adverts, that's for sure.' Sage and I snigger and catch up to them.

'Let's try here, then,' Irish says. He's settled on a cafe-lined side street, parallel to the centre. They plonk their guitars down in front of an ornamental pond with a burping fountain in the middle. The tourists sitting on the pond wall near to us immediately gather their stuff and wander off.

'What do you want us to do?' I ask Irish.

Scotty pulls a moth-eaten black trilby out of his case and passes it to me. 'Use this, while we're playing, like.'

'Eh?'

Sage rolls her eyes. 'Duh. Use it to collect the cash, thicko.'

'Fuck off, Sage.'

'Now, now, goirls.' Irish winks at us.

As they only have one 'buskers' hat', Sage reluctantly removes her pixie hat. I'm always amazed how naked she looks without her headgear. Her thick black hair has grown out a fair bit since we were at Hervé's, and she no longer looks like an androgynous skinhead. I like her hair longer, but would never dare say so to her. She's proud of what she calls her 'lack of vanity issues'.

Sage and I hover nervously while Scotty and Irish make a bit of a show of tuning up. The people sitting in the cafe opposite start to take an interest; craning their necks and peering over.

'Fuck, Sage, I don't think I can do this,' I whisper.

'Me neither,' she says and then hiccoughs. It looks as if she's had more wine than just the few odd sips. She's got the right idea – alcohol will probably make the whole asking-people-for-money thing easier. I grab the bottle of wine and take three large gulps. A group of old German tourists glance at me in disgust as they pass. Fuck them. Who are they to judge me? At least I've got the decency not to wear fucking socks under sandals.

Scotty and Irish launch into a barely recognisable Velvet Underground and Nico number. I've always thought a bag of hammers could sing better then Nico, but Scotty (who is the vocalist, after all) makes her sound like Debbie Harry. His voice is lifeless and, as far as I can tell, out of tune. Every word sounds like doom personified. Sage looks at me and opens her eyes wide.

'Shall we scarper?' I whisper. 'This is dire beyond belief!'

'Nah. Come on. I dare you to ask that fat fuck over there for cash.' She nods over to where a touristy type man is approaching, his face buried in a ginormous ice cream. Thank God for the wine I've just glugged back. The fat guy doesn't look up as I approach him, his ice-cream absorbing all his attention.

'*Monnaie pour la music monsieur!*' I trot out, smiling as sweetly as I can. He blinks at me in shock, fumbles wordlessly in his pockets, thrusts a fistful of coins into the hat and stalks off at top speed. He's probably never walked so fast in his life. I grin in triumph and hold the hat aloft. Irish catches my eye and winks again.

Sage shakes her head and snorts. 'Fair play, Vicks!'

'Now it's my turn,' I say, scanning the passers-by for a suitable victim for her.

The whole bottling experience is embarrassing and exhilarating at the same time. Although Sage and I have no problem bumming fags from strangers, this is a whole different ball game. Asking a stranger for cash (especially when it's for such utterly crap music) is almost like going out in public without any clothes on. And after the fat guy's reluctant bunch of centimes, our luck seems to have dried up. The people I approach refuse to meet my eyes, shake their heads in irritation, or shrug, grin ruefully and wander past. Sage seems to be getting much the same response and looks more self-conscious than I've ever seen her.

Then, just as I'm thinking we're done, I have a run of three ten franc coins. This coincides with Scotty pausing to tune up before segueing into a painfully flat rendition of 'Sweet Jane'. Maybe if they *stop* playing, people will give us money.

I don't say this out loud.

The song's verses seem to go on endlessly, and as Scotty's Lou Reed impersonation drones to its nasally end, a couple of scabby old tramps sitting nearby on the pond wall clap and whoop. 'Giz another one, mate,' one of the tramps slurs in a Manchester accent. English tramps: that explains the lack of musical taste. I silently will the buskers to call it a day. The owner of the rapidly emptying cafe opposite isn't looking too charmed, and I haven't yet dared to approach anyone sitting outside it, although Irish keeps nodding at them meaningfully.

Sage and I give up and sit on the wall as far away from the rowdy tramps as we can manage. No one else gives us any cash, apart from a furtively hurrying tone-deaf passer-by, who apologetically plops a bunch of centimes into the hat. Probably getting rid of loose change. Finally, Irish and Scotty run out of steam without bringing a heart-rendingly awful rendition of 'Hotel California' to its rightful (or wrongful) conclusion.

The remaining cafe customers palpably relax.

'Wotcha think then goirls?' Irish asks as he packs away his guitar. 'Not bad, eh?'

'Great!' I lie. I nudge Sage. 'What did *you* think, Sage?'

'Can I have one of your roll-ups?' she says to Scotty, cannily avoiding answering the question.

With our meagre earnings (fifty francs and some brown coins), the four of us make a beeline for the nearest corner cafe and buy a couple of baguettes, some cheese that smells like my brother's trainers and more crappy wine. I'm disappointed that no one suggests splurging on a packet of fags, but there's always Scotty's roll-ups. The tramps and their furious little dog are nowhere to be seen as we flop down on the bench in front of the centre. I scan the area for any sign of the cops, but they've also disappeared. Sage makes a show of sharing out the food equally.

'Where are you staying?' I ask Irish, realising my mistake too late. Shit. I don't dare look at Sage.

The buskers look at each other and shrug. 'Dunno.' Irish shrugs. 'Can we crash at your place the night?'

I get up the gumption to see how Sage is taking this. She's doing her usual peering-off-into-the-distance face.

'Sure,' I say, trying not to sound as reluctant as I'm feeling. 'But just for the night. Even Sage isn't supposed to be staying with me.'

'Ta,' Irish says, unscrewing the wine to seal the deal.

'Fuck knows how we're going to get these two past Mrs Danvers,' Sage whispers irritably. 'What were you thinking?'

She may have hooked up with the buskers in the first place, but I knew it would end up being my fault in the end.

*　　*　　*

The wine's nearly finished, and we've made serious inroads into the piece of Hervé's black Sage held back for a 'rainy day'. Our room is swirling with smoke, and the dope and booze is helping numb the anxiety caused by our encounter with Mrs Danvers. I'd tried to be smart about it, feeding everyone into the building one at a time, with reasonable delays between us, but when it was my turn she was waiting for me, outside her coffin-booth, arms crossed and face like a smacked bottom. I grinned at her, but she didn't smile back (I'm not sure she even knows how) and she barked something sarcastic about 'more *visiteurs*.'

I'm certain she's going to grass me up to Mr and Mrs Nausicaa.

Irish is stretched on the floor, and Scotty is crouching on his rucksack, dirty-jeaned legs folded up to his ears like a bony-legged spider. He tips the last of the wine into his gob. 'Shall we get another bottle?' he says.

'Course,' Sage slurs. She's smashed. 'Scotty, you know who you remind me of?'

'Nah,' he replies. I'm assuming Sage is going to say something really insulting, like Gollum from *Lord of the Rings* or Lurch from *The Addams Family*. Far as I'm concerned he could be the love child of Herman Munster and Ichabod Crane. But Sage has someone else in mind.

'Sid Vicious,' she says.

Scotty perks up. It's the most animated I've seen him all day. 'Seriously? Sid's all right, so he is.'

'Yeah, with a bit of eyeliner and some lipstick you'd be a dead ringer. What do you think, Vicks? Want to play dress-up?'

The skinny guy wielding the vicious-looking flick knife has wide staring eyes and looks like he means business. I freeze, and I can sense Scotty withering next to me. The man doesn't change his expression. This time, the *SUN* headline is: *British Babe in Paris Bloodbath* (picture page four). The guy shakes the knife in our faces again and Scotty rears back, lifting his hands up in a 'whoa, man' gesture. Then, without warning, a torrent of (almost) perfect French squeaks out of my mouth:

'*Non! Desole, Monsieur! Ce n'est pas necessaire! C'est seulement une folle! Nous sommes tranquille!*' Even though the situation is as dodgy as fuck, I'm still amazed that I've managed to dredge up these words. Where did they come from? I didn't even know that I knew the word for 'joke' in French. Our whipcord-thin would-be assailant immediately backs off and his eyes lose their crazy edge. He gives us the once-over and snorts in disgust. I don't blame him. Then he backs into and is swallowed by the crowd clogging up the Latin Quarter alleyway. As soon as I'm sure he's gone I breathe again. My legs are shaking and my heart's roaring in my ears. Scotty looks over at me and shrugs nervously.

'Fuck, that was close,' he says in his usual monotone, but I can tell he's rattled. He almost drops his pouch of tobacco as he pulls it out of his pocket. 'Shall we knock this on the head for a bit?'

'Yeah,' I agree nonchalantly, as if being threatened by a knife-wielding psychopath happens to me every day. I shake my head when he offers me the Rizla packet and tobacco. I don't want him to see my fingers trembling when I try to roll a cigarette.

Fuck. Sage's idea for me and Scotty to dress as Sid Vicious and his junkie girlfriend Nancy Spungen while we went on a wine run had seemed like a brilliant idea half an hour ago. Now I feel like a complete moron. I'm in ripped fishnets, a tiny pink minidress and Irish's cheap leather motorcycle jacket, and I've got a fake beauty spot gored on my cheek (which Sage said looked like a splattered fly). Scotty looks as ridiculous as I feel. The black eyeliner I'd carefully applied is now smeared down his face, and his Sid Vicious trademark red lipstick makes the rash of acne scored over his too-white skin look vivid and painful. The spikes Sage and I had gelled into his short hair are now drooping pathetically, and are flecked with large pieces of dandruff. I cringe at the thought that only a few moments ago we'd been striding through the crowd, 'don't fuck with us' expressions on our faces. It had worked until Scotty had bumped shoulders with the skinny guy and tried to do a Sid Vicious on him.

'Fuck awrf!' Scotty had sneered à la Sid, but instead of giving him a wide berth, the guy had whipped out a knife so fast it was a blur.

'Shit, man, I need a drink,' says Scotty. 'Shall we open the bottle?'

I've almost forgotten the clinking plastic bag I'm holding. More red wine is the last thing I'm craving. 'Nah, let's wait till we get back home.'

Scotty nods mournfully.

I'm desperate to get back to the room. I want to give Sage a bollocking for encouraging us go out looking like this. I mean, she knew we were completely pissed. Something bad was bound to happen. And she was supposed to come with us. Mind you, it's probably for the best. If she'd been with us she'd have challenged the guy to a knife fight.

'Shall we tell them, like? You know, about what happened?' Scotty asks while trying and failing to scatter tobacco onto a tatty roll-up paper. His hands are still unsteady.

I shrug. 'Yeah, why not?'

'It was close all right, eh?' He finally manages to cobble together a cigarette. I light it for him.

'I can't wait to see Sage's face.'

'Yeah, it was quite a good laugh when you think about it, eh?' He straightens his back as if he hadn't been shitting in his pants a few moments earlier. I'm pretty sure that if we get round to telling Sage and Irish, they'll get a hugely exaggerated version. And even though I'm looking forward to this, I'm still rattled. Nutters scare the shit out of me at the best of times. At home, there were several who'd taken up office outside Top Shop in the Wolverhampton Mander Centre. There was one headcase who marched up and down the centre dressed in cowboy gear. Even if he hadn't dressed in his mad outfit, it would have been obvious he wasn't holding a full deck. His eyes rolled around in his head like veined marbles, and he always had flecks of bubbly spit balled in the corners of his mouth. He carried around this enormous ghetto blaster blaring out country music, and you never knew when he'd appear over your shoulder and try and convince you to sing along with Dolly Parton, while the other shoppers sniggered smugly, glad they weren't the ones being accosted.

I wonder if the guy who threatened us was an actual psychopath, or just a guy having a bad day who hated punks and rudeness. Weird, I'd kind of assumed that Paris, unlike Wolverhampton, was a place where you didn't need to watch your back.

Returning to the room after our run-in with the knife-wielding maniac is a bit of an anticlimax. Mrs Danvers wasn't at her coffin-post for once, and Sage and Irish are fast asleep, Sage on her back on the bed, mouth open; Irish cocooned on the floor in his tatty sleeping bag, dreadlocks poking out of its end like a dirty mop head.

'Pussies,' Scotty growls, forgetting that mere minutes ago he'd been a bit of a pussy himself.

I climb over Irish to get to the sink and wipe off the beauty spot with one of Sage's discarded socks. I'm about to suggest to Scotty that we wake the sleeping beauties, when there's a banging at the door. *Shit*. What if it's Mrs Danvers or even worse – Nausicaa's parents? They've never shown up here before, but if Mrs Danvers has been squealing on me, it's entirely possible they'd pay me a visit.

'Oh shit,' I hiss at Scotty. 'What the fuck am I going to do?' He looks at me uncomprehendingly and goes as if to open the door.

'No!' I almost yell. 'Leave it.'

There's a pause and then the banging starts up again. This time it's more insistent and Sage sits up and wipes a hand over her face. Irish doesn't move.

'Wha' the fuck?' she says.

Whoever's outside isn't going away. I grab the can of Old Spice and spray it liberally around the room, desperately trying to mask the stubborn hashy smell. 'Hide!' I hiss at Scotty and Sage, but they look at me blankly. Obviously there's nowhere *to* hide.

I take a deep breath and open the door a crack, so that whoever's out here can't see in, motioning Scotty and Sage to keep out of sight behind me. I'm expecting to see Mrs Danvers's miserable face scowling at me as I peer out, but instead a strange man is staring back at me.

'Er . . .Yeah?' I say, not sure whether to be relieved or annoyed.

'*Bonjour,*' he replies. He's creepy looking: skeletally thin with parchment skin and sunken eyes.

'Can I help you?'

He clears his throat. 'Someone dropped this in the *toilette,*' he says in accented but perfect English. He's holding a lump of hash in his hand. I'm dumbfounded. How in the hell did he know it was ours? Could he be a cop testing us? The silence stretches and I'm just about to deny it's mine when Sage elbows me out of the way.

'Christ!' she yells, snatching the black out of the guy's hand. 'I thought that was gone for good. Thanks mate.'

'*De rien.*' He nods curtly and disappears down the corridor.

Sage shuts the door, leans on it and rolls her eyes. 'Fuck, that'll teach me not to put things in their proper places.'

I flump on the bed and close my eyes.

SAGE

People and characters who are more attractive than Mrs Danvers:

Quasimodo (from Notre Dame)
Ian Dury (from Ian Dury and the Blockheads)
Shaggy (from Scooby Doo)
Shane snaggletooth what's-his-face (from the Pogues)
Vile brother-in-law Pete (can't believe I just wrote that)
Kath's husband Eric – fat, greasy and smelly, but we still ate
    his food (from Kath's caff)
Irish's teeth (from Irish's head)
My new friend Bob (from the Pompidou Posse)

People and characters who are less attractive than Mrs Danvers:

Bobby the Bastard (from wherever arseholes like him spring
    from)

It's been difficult to write etc what with the buskers around all
the time. It's not as if I've been lazy or anything, so take that
angry look off your face, Gladys (ha ha).

Well, it's been a weird few days, but there's been some fabness
all the same.

The best news is that: My and Vicks's days of being hungry are over!!!! And it's all thanks to a tramp named Bob (how ironic that he has the same fucking name as the Bastard).

Scary Scotty and Tatty Irish stayed with us for two nights. I'm proud of Vicks, she didn't shag either of them. Anyway, after the kind (but freakish) neighbour returned our black, Vicks had a hissy fit and said that the buskers had to leave as they were 'jeopardising our position.' They were nice about it though and said they'd head off to the Riviera. Fuck, I hope the people there don't have any taste in music otherwise they'll go seriously hungry.

Anyway, when Vicks headed off to work the next day, I walked with them to the Pompidou to say bye. While we were there I had to sneak off to the toilet in the centre as we can't use the Toilet of Death #2 at the moment. I'm not pointing fingers, but one of the buskers has fucking well blocked it up. They'd used newspaper instead of toilet paper (well, I'd hidden our stash for Vicks and my personal use, but still). Gross. I hope Mrs Danvers is handy with a toilet brush and a plunger, otherwise Vicks and me will be in deep shit (but seriously, Gladys, it's not funny is it?)

I get back from the toilet (where I'd also had a sneaky wash) and they're talking to this podgy old tramp guy. I recognised him straight off – he'd waved to Vicks the other day as if they were old friends. Scotty and Irish introduced us and that was the first time I learned Bob's creepy name. But I got a right shock when I heard his voice. I mean, he looks like a saggy stubbly slightly smelly tramp guy (you wouldn't look twice at him on the street), but the voice that comes out of him is dead posh. Even posher than Vicks, who doesn't have so much of a Wolverhampton accent as me on account of her going to a posh school in Birmingham and me having to make do in the stinking comprehensive.

Anyway, Irish and Scotty go to hug me goodbye, but luckily I manage to squirm away before they can do so, and then Irish says, 'Ye will take care of them goirls, eh, Bob?' Oh. My. God. What was Irish thinking?! Anyway, off the buskers go, leaving me and Bob standing there staring at each other.

I didn't trust Bob at first. I mean, how much of a coincidence is it that he's got the same name as B the B?? And he has these strange bulgy watery blue eyes that look like they're about to pop straight out of his head. If he ever gets a slap on the back of the head, I reckon they'd plop out of their sockets like snooker balls. I was about to bugger off as I was feeling dead uncomfortable (it was like the smelly version of when you meet someone new and there's that weird pause when no one knows what to say), when Bob goes, 'Where's your friend?' I'm like: 'Why do you want to know?' (dead suspicious).

And he's like, 'Because you always seem to be together, that's why.'

I was about to tell him to go fuck himself, when I caught him looking at the arse of a Frog boy who was walking past us. Ha! So I decided to give Bob another chance, because he was probably not interested in girls and wouldn't try it on with Vicks.

So I asked him what he was doing being a tramp when he talks so posh and he said he'd decided to 'opt out of society for a while', but didn't say why. I didn't pry. I wasn't in the mood to ask personal questions.

Anyway, he had a pack of those vile Frog Gitanes cigarettes and we sat on a bench while he asked me loads of questions about me and Vicks. At first I didn't want to say anything, but he was a really good listener, and suddenly I found myself telling him a bunch of stuff. It just poured out, Gladys, about me and Vicks not having money and Mrs Danvers and the whole story about B the B. Bob nodded and smoked and looked quite sympathetic. Then I asked him what he did for money and he said he was a beggar (but he didn't look ashamed about this or anything, which I quite respected actually) and showed me the cardboard sign he uses for begging. It was a piece of shite, and I drew him another one with a flower on it, although he did the writing as it's in French. I couldn't really do a good job, because he only had a tatty old biro, but he was dead impressed and asked me why me and Vicks didn't do chalk drawings for money.

I was like, 'Yeah, duh, where?' And he said that in the summer, loads of art students do chalk drawings all over Paris. He took me to the spot near to where me and Vicks did the bottling for Irish and Scotty. Then he said he'd show me around the area a bit as he's been here forever and knows it like the back of his (dirty) hand. But first, he said, he was going to get us some wine from his bag in the left luggage room in the centre. I thought about scarpering when he left. I hate it when other people just assume you should trust them, but for some reason I stayed. Which, as you will see, Gladys, was a good thing in the end.

He came back and we walked down this dead long creepy street that was lined with shady doorways, and he said it was the Rue St Denis where the prozzies hang out. And sure enough, there were loads of prozzies there. Most of them were black and all of them were fat, and they ignored me and Bob completely. Then we cut down an alley and through another street towards this old church. And he said, 'But you must know this one,' and I was like, 'Why?' And he said, 'Don't you and your friend come here for food?'

Guess what, Gladys! There's a FUCKING SOUP KITCHEN in Paris, and I never even knew. Bob was dead surprised when I told him that me and Vicks have been starving like Ethiopians!! Anyway, he said that we can just come to this St Eustache place and sign up to get the soup kitchen grub.

Then he had to leave on account of having to go to 'work' (ha ha), but he said he'd meet up with us later at the soup kitchen (probably). He wasn't sure as he doesn't eat there often any more.

I couldn't wait for Vicks to get back from work. Soon as she'd finished I took her straight there, and we found our way to the church's office thingy to sign up for the free food. This quite nice and friendly woman said to us 'Can you cook?' and Vicks was like, 'Of course we can cook!' And the woman smiled and handed us a big bag full of packets of couscous. Vicks took it and we walked out. But then I said, 'What the fuck are we going to do with that then?' And Vicks was like, 'Fuck, I'm so stupid.'

The woman hadn't meant 'can you cook' but have you got the facilities to cook. DUH!!! Vicks felt like a total spazz!

So we went back inside and Vicks explained her fuck-up and the woman gave us this form to fill in saying we were skint and hungry and couldn't afford to buy food and all that shite. We would have given false names like we used to with the cops back home, but the woman needed to see our passports.

Anyway, so eventually it was time to go and wait outside the church to collect our food, but bloody hell it was like a tramps' conference there! There was a huge snaking queue of all kinds of tramps (but not many young ones). But the worst thing was the smell of some of them!! Fuck, it was seriously bad. And a few of them looked like the lepers in those old Bible movies. They were draped in rags and I expected them to start saying 'Alms for the poor' and to have missing fingers and big gaping sores. I didn't want to get too near them. If I hadn't been so hungry I reckon they'd have put me off my food. As we were waiting in line, trying not to vomit, this guy with a Mohican and one leg came hobbling up on his crutches, and totally perved at Vicki. She didn't take much notice as it was her turn to get food, but I didn't miss it.

Okay, so this is what you get:

1 cup vegetable soup (not bad)
1 tin butter beans in tomato sauce (gross)
1 Babybel cheese (out of date, but still yum my favourite)
1 Tin John West tuna in curry sauce (yeah, I know, obviously no one bought this shit from the supermarkets, so they give it free to the tramps, because beggars can't be choosers, eh?)
Half a baguette.
1 orange

Hurray!!!

We didn't wait for Bob, but moved as far away from the others as possible and sat down and scoffed the lot. It was the best thing ever.

The only bad news I have is that I still haven't figured out what to do if I run out of tablets. I've still got shitloads at the moment. Thank God I had the foresight to bring the ones that were out of date as well. And I lied to Karen and said that I'd lost a whole lot so she had to go and refill my prescription. I mean, when we left home I wasn't sure how long we'd be away, was I? I can't remember exactly what it was like before vile Doctor Wankenstein put me on them. Vicks didn't know the old me. I can't tell her. I just can't. I couldn't bear it if she started treating me like some kind of freak.

Poem for Bob

Some say he's quite soppy
His eyes are all poppy
They bulge from his head
Like a corpse that is dead
He's not a big spender
I think he's a bender
His name could be 'Slob'
But it's not. 'Cos it's 'Bob'.

I don't think I'll show this one to Vicks.

VICKI:

The Banana Hold-up Experience

'This is a banana hold-up. Give us yer money or a bottle of whisky, or I'll shoot yer.'

The guy standing splay-legged in front of us is holding a banana in each hand, like a fruit-wielding stick-up artist. He looks deadly serious.

For once, Sage has lost control of her features, and she's gaping at him. We both start giggling nervously.

'Did yer hear me, lassies?' he growls.

'Er, yeah,' I say carefully. I'm not sure how to respond to this guy. What if he's an unhinged nutter like that scary knife-toting guy or something? Those bananas could be dangerous in the wrong hands.

'Sorry, mate.' I shrug as if I mean it. 'We're fresh out of cash and alcohol.'

He doesn't respond or drop his 'guns'. His hollow cheeks yawn in deeply, and his skin is the calloused leather that I've come to recognise as typical of street people, especially the old ones. I reckon it's because they're outside so much of the time, but their eyes also seem to sink lower and lower into their faces, as if the whole structure is subsiding from over-exposure to booze and sunlight. He reminds me of the old alkys you sometimes see drinking the day away in naff Wolverhampton town centre pubs.

Out of the corner of my eye I notice Bob approaching. I

breathe a sigh of relief. I hope he knows how to deal with this obvious nutcase. Sage and I had been waiting for Bob next to the crap sculpture pond when the banana stick-up artist sneaked up behind us. We're normally on high nutter alert, especially around this area, but he'd taken us completely by surprise.

'Hello, girls,' Bob says in his posh voice. 'I see you've met Alex?'

'You *know* this guy?' Sage says. I'm also a tad shocked. Although Bob is unapologetic about his tramp status, he's always struck me as remarkably normal. Plus, he speaks like one of my folks' stockbroker friends. I'm dying to know the story behind his exile here, but I'm used to leaving the prying up to Sage. Strangely, unless there's something she hasn't told me yet, so far she hasn't bothered to pry. It's probably because she's convinced he's in the closet, which in her eyes makes him 'safe' and unlikely to 'do a Bobby' on us. And maybe she doesn't think it's fair to be nosy. Without Bob, we'd still be surviving on stolen Nausicaa yoghurts.

'Alex is an institution around here. Aren't you, Alex?'

'Aye.' Alex nods proudly.

'Now, let me introduce you properly,' Bob says as if he's at a cocktail party, 'Alex, this is Sage and Vicki.'

Alex grins. His remaining teeth are little brown pebbles. His eyes are bright blue stones that gleam wetly from their dark sockets. I wouldn't call it an evil face though. He nods at us. 'Is a pleasure,' he drawls in an accent even broader than Scotty's. 'A *clochard de luxe* at your service.'

'A what?' Sage scrunches up her face.

'*A clochard de luxe,*' Bob says. 'A luxury tramp.'

'I'll not be havin' ye callin' me a tramp now, Bob.' Alex winks at us. He reminds me of those rugged characters that always play the ex-con baddies on *Taggart*. 'Now young lassies, will ye join me for a wee walk aboot the toon?' He offers us a crooked arm each. Sage looks horrified. I shrug: It doesn't look like we've got much of a choice. Trying not to flinch at the feel of his dust-caked donkey jacket, I hook my arm through his. Scowling, Sage does the same. Neither of us wants to offend Bob by telling his friend to fuck off. Still, I can't help but feel a pang of annoyance as Bob sits down on the pond wall and waves us cheerfully on our way as if he's doing us a favour.

The three of us hobble towards the smattering of tourist shops in front of the centre's entrance. It's not an easy feat. Alex walks with a bow-legged gait as if he's spent far too long in the saddle or has that rickets disease we learnt about in school. Waves of alcohol and ancient sweat radiate off his body. The tam o' shanter perched sideways on his head is so filthy the dirt has made its own tartan pattern in the material. His trousers flap a good two inches above his Doc Martens.

Mind you, it's not as if Sage or I look any great shakes at the moment, either. I can't remember what it was like to have clean clothes. My underwear is scratchy after hasty washes in the sink with hand soap. It almost seems to creak when I move, as if I'm wearing cardboard pants. My dresses have failed the sniff test so many times I now just rotate them in order of least stinky. I noticed Nausicaa's mother wincing the other day when I'd mistakenly allowed her within smelling distance. It's doing Sage's head in; she hates being dirty, and she's had to wear the same sweatshirt for the last three days.

We cut a swathe through the tourist traffic as people naturally give the three of us a wide berth. I'm pretty sure everyone thinks we're some kind of bizarre sideshow, or perhaps they assume Sage and I are taking our mad uncle for an outing. We're the tramp version of the *Wizard of Oz* characters, with Alex as a scabby Scottish Dorothy, leading us down the Yellow Brick Pompidou Road.

From the way Alex's eyes are predatorily scanning the

passers-by, I'm getting the impression that a 'walk aboot the toon' isn't quite what it's cracked up to be. Alex stops dead in front of a queue of people waiting outside the cinema. Quick as a flash, he drops our arms, pulls the bananas out of the waistband of his scrofulous trousers and aims the fruit guns at a middle-aged couple, who are doing their best to make themselves less noticeable. The other members of the queue titter nervously.

'This is a banana hold-up, giz yer money or a bottle of whisky or I'll shoot yer.'

Unbelievable! The couple start laughing and the smartly suited man pulls out a fifty-franc note and passes it to Alex. Sage looks at me and mouths 'Oh my God.' Alex nods curtly to the couple, as if it is they who should be thanking him for the privilege of being accosted, and not the other way around, then crooks his arms again, signalling that we're off.

'Bloody hell, Alex, nice one,' I say, no longer feeling quite so self-conscious.

'Aye,' he sniffs, 'Bloody Frogs. Easy marks, all of 'em.'

I catch sight of Sage's face. She's grinning. It looks like she's met a kindred spirit.

We've walked a full circle and are back outside the sculpture pond with Bob. On our short walk, Alex held up two more people. I can't figure how he susses out which ones to pick on. They're all completely different. The second guy was a handsome African guy, draped in one of those dress-like robes, the third victim a middle-aged French matron who reminded me of Mrs Danvers.

'Right, lassies, time for a wee break. Let's go off and eat something, what do you say?'

Alex has made over one hundred francs in less than ten minutes.

*　　*　　*

Sage, Bob, Alex and I are sitting in Formica hell, eating couscous. The restaurant is a do-it-yourself affair, similar to
motorway service centres. You slide your tray round a long
metal rail, helping yourself to bowls of couscous and
grease-peppered meat, while above you garish fantasy pictures let you know what the food is supposed to look like. I
compare the sad mess on my plate to its glossy picture. Instead
of the promised plump juicy meat, the curl of sausage next to
my bright yellow couscous looks like an anorexic dog turd.

Sage's brother-in-law is a cookery book photographer and
she's telling Bob and Alex how he uses mashed potato instead
of ice-cream when photographing it, because otherwise it
melts under the camera lights. I've heard this one before.

'Is that right, lassie?' Alex says.

'Yeah. Can you imagine what would happen if someone ate
that by accident, though. Think about it. It's a hot day and all
you want is a cool mouthful of ice-cream topped with cher-
ries . . .' Sage stares off into the distance. She hates her
brother-in-law. Her sister's okay though.

'Eat up, lassie!' Alex grins at me, spitting food everywhere.
I've never seen anyone eat quite like Alex. He shovels far too
much food into his mouth and then gummily chews it, open-
mouthed. The gooey excess seeps out of the corners of his
mouth like spit from a rabid dog. He takes a long draught of
his beer and belches noisily. 'Hits the spot!' he says and then
loses himself in a coughing fit. The remaining pieces of couscous in his mouth are ejected like shrapnel all over the table.

Sage is picking at her food. This would never have happened a few days ago. We would have jumped at the chance of
a free meal. But now, since food is no longer an issue, it's
stopped being the centre of our universe. I don't feel like mine.
Couscous still reminds me of the first night I slept at Jules's. I
shudder. Sage raises an eyebrow at me. I shake my head in an
'it's nothing' gesture. I still haven't told her the gory details

about my two vile nights with Jules. Curiously, Sage hasn't reacted to Alex's disgusting table manners. Normally she's quick to pop out a sarky comment or pull a face whenever someone does something even slightly annoying. In fact, she seems totally at home in the company of Alex, who reeks like a sweaty brewery, and Bob, who might well be a nice guy, but is still a middle-aged beggar with weird bulging eyes. I can't understand why she's so happy to hang around with these losers but gave Hervé such a hard time. Perhaps it's because she found them and not me.

'So, Alex, what are you doing in Paris?' I say, taking a sip of my 7-Up.

Alex taps the side of his nose. 'Ask no questions and I'll tell yer no lies, lassie.'

'Sorry. Didn't mean to be nosy.' Maybe there's some tramp code about never asking about people's previous lives.

'Nah, don't be ridiculous.' Alex flaps his arms about like an epileptic. 'Me and Bob here had to get away. Right Bob?'

Bob squirms in his seat. I'd assumed they'd met here, in Paris. I can't imagine what might have connected them before trampdom. Alex is almost a parody of a drunk hobo, whereas Bob looks like he washed up on the streets by accident. Although he's always in dire need of a shave, I can tell by his posh accent and the cut of his crumpled suit jacket that he probably once had some kind of profession.

Again I'm surprised Sage doesn't call him out on this. She's normally quick to pick up on evasive behaviour. God knows I can never get away with it. She merely snorts and says: 'Sounds like our story.'

'Oh, aye?' Alex says, but it isn't really a question. I can tell he doesn't really care what the fuck we're doing here. He lets out a sneeze. I'm beginning to suspect that his eyes are rheumy because he's got the flu and not because he's had too much whisky.

'How did you two meet then?' I ask.

'Ah now, lassie, that's the question,' Alex says, making a sound like a foghorn into the large tartan handkerchief he's pulled from the pocket of his donkey jacket. 'That's the question, so it is.' Tucking his handkerchief back into his trouser pocket, he looks off into the distance. Without any warning he croons, 'Walk on, walk on—'

'You what?' I say.

'—with ho-ooope in yer heart . . .' His voice rises with every word. I look at Sage, expecting her to be horrified, but she merely shrugs.

Alex stands up, his voice getting louder and louder. 'And you'll neiveeeer walk alo—' He coughs, sneezes, and carries on singing as if the interruption hadn't happened mid-syllable.

The other patrons in the restaurant are staring and grinning.

Alex gets up and heads for the exit, all the time blaring nasally: 'Waaaalk ooon, walk oooo-ah ah ooon, with hoooope in yer heart . . .' Bob, Sage and I mutely follow him out.

He throws open the glass doors and stands, arms outstretched, belting out the song's finale.

Then he spins around and whips off his tam o' shanter. His grey hair is greasily plastered to his scalp in rat tails. He bows to us theatrically. 'Right now, lassies, Bob. I'll bid yer good day.'

And he's off.

We watch as he struts into the crowd, pausing to accost an Arabic-looking businessman. The man reaches into his jacket and removes his wallet.

'Amazing,' Sage says.

'Yep,' says Bob proudly. 'That's Alex for you. Now, girls. I have a favour to ask you.'

★   ★   ★

The bus is silent except for the stomach-turning 'crunch crunch crunch' noise: the sound of a pissed Scottish man with few teeth gnashing his way through a whole crab. Bits of pink shell fly everywhere, and the usual rubbery old shoe bus smell is swamped by the odour of fish. My face burns and I don't know where to look. I try not to flinch as a hairy crab claw bounces off the tip of my boot. Sage has squirrelled herself into a window seat. She's staring out of the window as if her life depends on it.

Alex is sitting in the middle of the back seat, blithely crunching, spitting, slobbering and sucking. A cluster of French workaday people are hunched together like refugees as far from the three of us as they can get. A couple of them are tutting and shaking their heads, but most are just staring.

Alex offers me a dripping claw. I shake my head.

'Yer sure, lassie?' Or at least I think that's what he's saying through the avalanche of crabmeat tumbling out of his mouth. Shell flecks coat his donkey jacket like dandruff and his gnarled hands are glistening with fishy threads. I silently curse whoever thought it was a good idea to give Alex the bag of crabs. It was obviously someone who's never shared a meal with him.

He pauses from his work to cough into his sleeve. This is why he's coming home with us. He's got some kind of nasty chest infection. Bob took us aside earlier to ask if Alex could stay with us for a night to give him a chance to get better. He's been passed around various friends and acquaintances, and tonight it's our turn.

How could we say no? If it wasn't for Bob, we'd never have found out about St Eustache and the food. But I'm not sure my little room can stand any more guests. I still haven't been able to kill the hash stench from the buskers' sleepover. That, and a blocked toilet, are all our last guests left behind. I'm finding it impossible to picture Mrs Danvers's face when she catches sight of my latest *visiteur*. It was hard enough sneaking Scotty and Irish past her Nazi commandant stare, and they were relatively normal. Christ knows how she'll react when I try and smuggle a loud, pissed, fish-coated Scottish beggar into my room.

I rummage in my boot and pull out the watch. Five a.m and Sage and I have had absolutely no sleep.

By some miracle, Mrs Danvers wasn't at her post when we ushered Alex up the stairs. The minute he entered the room he flopped down on our bed and dropped off, leaving me and Sage to sleep on the floor. Eventually we gave up trying to get any shut-eye. Alex is no less noisy and inconsiderate in his sleep. We've spent the last few hours listening to a chorus of trombone farts, shuddering snores, incoherent mumbling and rackety, scary coughs. Half an hour ago, Alex jerked awake and staggered out of the room without a word. Sage and I are now huddled in our sleeping bags desperately trying to block out the awful noises emanating from the communal Toilet of Death#2. The sounds must be sending shock waves through the entire building.

'Fookin' 'ell!' his voice reverberates down the corridor.

I wince as it's followed by the splash and groan of what sounds like an enormous amount of vomit. We listen with bated breath for the train whoosh of the toilet flushing. It doesn't come. Oh God, Sage and I will have to draw lots to see who goes in there to assess the damage. I don't think I'll be able to stomach it. I have a vile image of one of Alex's knack-ered lungs draped over the toilet seat.

Mercifully there's a few seconds of silence. The building feels quieter than usual, as if its occupants are collectively holding their breath, waiting to hear what the next audible horror will be. It can't get any worse, can it?

It can. Another lung-shattering coughing fit is followed by, 'Guaaaaaaaaahhhhhhhh!'

It doesn't even sound human.

I fully expect to hear the clump of Mrs Danvers's sensible shoes heading up the stairs. Sage sighs and scowls at me as if it's my fault we haven't had any sleep. She throws off her sleeping bag, stalks over to the sink and sticks her head under the tap.

'Christ! What a fucking tosser!' she says. Even though Sage in a foul mood is nothing to be sniffed at, I'm relieved. For a while there, I'd thought a body-snatcher had taken over her habitual 'take no shit' personality. I'm glad things are back to normal. This I can handle.

She turns to me, face like thunder. 'Why the fuck did you let him sleep on our bed? It fucking stinks!'

I hold my tongue. The last thing we need right now is a blazing row, although I suppose it might act as diversion from the grue-some liquid noises floating down the corridor. Anyway, she's right about the stench. Even though Alex has left the room, his particular ripe body odour hasn't. The place reeks like a hot day in a fishmonger's. At least it's buried the hash pong.

Sage almost trips over Alex's tatty rucksack as she makes her way back to her sleeping bag. She pauses. I know she won't be able to resist. She bends down, unclips the belt that holds the bag together and starts rooting around in it. I pre-tend not to see what she's doing, but I notice her pocketing something she's slicked out of an old cigar tin wrapped in a shirt. The toilet door slams and she jumps guiltily and hastily buckles the belt.

Heavy footsteps thunk down the hall towards our room. But Alex isn't content to shatter the silence using only one method: now he's also singing a raucous football song.

'And we'll really shake them up, when we win the World Cup, 'cos Scotland's the greatest football team!' He throws open the door as he belts out the last line. Sage glares at him, but he's oblivious.

'Ach, girls, I'd best be getting back. Thanks for letting me kip here the night.'

He collects his bag from the floor and is almost out the door when he turns back to us. 'I almost forgot. I wanted to give yous something to say ta, like.'

Sage perks up. We both know how much cash Alex is capable of making. He sticks his hand in the pocket of his donkey jacket and pulls out a bulky plastic bag. He chucks it over to Sage, who catches it neatly, realises what it is and flings it away from her, as if it's red hot. It's the crab bag, slimy and stinking with day-old crab juices.

'Ta again, girls.' He winks and nods to where the bag's now lying under the sink, its contents spilling over the floor like the remains of a crustacean massacre. 'Enjoy it, eh?'

And then he's gone.

Neither of us speaks as he sings and coughs his way down the stairs. We're both holding our breath. I'm about to give Sage the 'A-Okay' sign when we hear the rumble of raised voices.

At first I think it's our neighbours coming to lynch us for the desecration of their toilet, but then I realise it isn't coming from our floor. I creep over to the door and open it a crack. I can hear a French accent pitched louder than a normal speaking voice, but can't decipher any actual words or tell for sure if it's Mrs Danvers. But then there's a clear Scottish 'Fuck awrf!' followed by an ear-splitting bang as the front door is slammed.

Oh shit.

'Think she'll come up here?' I whisper to Sage, as if the concierge has superhero hearing.

'What if she does? She can't prove he was staying in our room can she?'

But I'm thinking, yes she can, unless she's lost her sense of smell.

The building is silent once more.

Neither of us are tempted to climb onto the bed, which still bears the imprint of Alex's body, right down to two scuff marks on the sheets from his filthy booted feet. Even though I'm totally wiped, I daren't snooze in case I wake up late for work. I decide to read *The Shining* for the fourth time until it's time to get ready.

But Sage has other ideas. She bends down and rummages under the bed, then looks at me and grins. 'Hey, Vicks, how do you feel about going for a whole new look?'

'What do you mean?'

She waves something in my face. It's a cut-throat razor – the item she nicked from Alex's bag.

I can't stop staring at the patch of dried egg on Nausicaa's dad's brown jumper. Nausicaa's parents can't take their eyes off my new hairstyle. Sage went ape-shit with the razor. She shaved all the hair off both sides of my head, and I now have a perfect Mohican. The parents aren't too charmed by my new look. Their daughter took one look at me and immediately demanded the same drastic action to be taken on her own blonde curls.

But my makeover isn't the reason I'm sitting on an uncomfortable chair in front of them instead of pushing Nausicaa to the park. When I knocked on the door (ironically on time for once), it was opened by the bland corduroyed father instead of the hard-faced cow of a mother. I knew immediately something was up. He didn't return my breezy, '*Bonjour!*' and it was only the second time I'd seen him since the day of my interview. He was normally off boring university students to death while I took his daughter for her daily outing.

With barely a word he ushered me into the living room and

sat me down on the wooden chair he'd obviously placed there for the purpose (I'm not stupid).

'Victoria,' he begins, 'You have had a month's trial, which is what we discussed before, *n'est-ce pas?*'

'*Oui,*' I say, thinking, here it comes . . .

'But we have decided not to keep you on. You will have a week to vacate the room. Leave the keys with Madame le Clerc'.

I'm about to ask him who the hell Madame le Clerc is, when the penny drops. He means Mrs Danvers. The name we've given her fits her so well, it hasn't occurred to me she might have a *real* one. I decide not to ask him why I'm being fired. I'm pretty sure it's got something to do with a Scotsman with poor toilet hygiene and a small, scowling, cropped-haired sidekick.

Instead I say '*D'accord*!' which pops out sounding far too cheerful for the circumstances. The mother frowns. 'May I say goodbye to Nausicaa?' I say, trying to sound contrite.

'*Oui,*' the father shrugs. He's barely shown a flicker of emotion.

'Does she know what's happening?'

'*Oui, bien sur.*'

I get down on my knees in front of Nausicaa, who's still staring at my patchy head, entranced.

'Sorry, Nausicaa, I'm going to have to go now. Thanks for being such a good girl for me.'

'We go to the park?' she asks hopefully. I turn to look at her parents, who are still impassive.

'No, I'm sorry, Nausicaa, but another nanny will be taking you. I have to leave.'

At first I think she hasn't understood, but then juicy tears start welling in her eyes. She clenches her fists and plants her feet apart. I know what's coming next. '*Nooooon!*' she shrieks, taking in great shuddering breaths. '*Nooooon*, Vicki!'

I'm not sure what to do, but as the parents are still sitting stiffly on the couch and are making no attempt to comfort their daughter, I pick her up and give her a hug. She wraps her arms around me, clinging on like a baby chimp.

'*Noooon*!' she screams again, and I can feel her hot snotty face on my neck.

Sighing irritably, the mother gets up and wrestles Nausicaa's stiff body from me.

Nausicaa grips a clump of my remaining hair, but the mother bats her hand away and stalks out of the room with her writhing and screaming cargo. When she wasn't doing her Linda Blair imitation, Nausicaa and I had been pretty good friends. She was okay. A lump forms in my throat as I listen to her howls becoming muffled as her mother shuts her in her room.

'*Au revoir,* Nausicaa,' I call as I follow her father to the door. He ushers me out as if he's a bouncer evicting an undesirable from the premises. He doesn't say goodbye, merely snaps that he expects the room to be clean when I leave. Then he shuts the door in my face. *Bastard*. I gulp down a swallow of salty tears and head out of the building.

But the second I'm out into the sunlight, a lightness takes over, and my tears are forgotten. It's as if everything vaguely shite about my life has just floated away inside a giant helium balloon. I can't remember when I last felt this relieved or this free. I skip along the pavement: I can't wait to get back to tell Sage. And we've still got another week left in the room! That's plenty of time to make another plan. But in the meantime I'll be able to spend as much time as I like at the Pompidou Centre and Les Halles without having to tromp my way to the park or fetch the bastards their groceries. Even though I've had no sleep I practically fly down the road, that annoying Katrina and the Waves song running through my head.

I only realise I'm singing it out loud when I pass one of the foul Canadian nannies and register her shocked expression.

'I'm walking on sunshine, wooo-hooo!' I croon to her stiff, disgusted back.

Alex would be proud.

SAGE

Farewell Mrs Danvers Poem

Farewell to our toilet,
Our sink and our bed,
Farewell Mrs Danvers
I wish you were dead.

Farewell to our cupboard,
Our mirror as well,
Farewell, Mrs Danvers
May you rot down in hell.

Sorry I haven't written for a while again, Gladys. Tons and tons has happened, and as we don't have our own room any more, it's dead hard to write this where I won't be disturbed. This is the first time I've been alone since we had to leave our room after Vicks got fired. As she didn't have to go to work for the last week, we spent nearly all our time together. And, as you know, Gladys, you are one of my secrets.

Anyway, I'm writing this in the biggest fuck-off church you've ever seen. I love it in here. I'm not turning into a God-botherer or anything, but bloody hell it's great. I've seen it from the outside like a hundred million times, but it's the first time I've been inside it. As you've probably guessed it's called Notre Dame, like in the hunchback, Quasimodo, and it's dead quiet and solemn even though tons of tourists come through here all the time. The lights are all creepy and low and all you can hear is whispering and the shuffling of feet. Like someone turned the sound down on the world. I'm sitting in the middle of the rows and rows of uncomfortable chairs. The tourists stick to chairs near the aisle, if they bother to stay long enough to sit down, which most of them don't. The best thing is it's free!! If anyone who looks churchy wanders over and dead-eyes me, I just bow my head and pretend to look prayerful and sombre and they go away. Ha ha.

Vicks hasn't bothered to find another job. Can't say I blame her. I mean, now we can eat whenever we like there doesn't seem much point, eh? I'm fucking sick of tinned butter beans in tomato sauce and the same old shite from St Eustache, but there's not much I can do about that, worse luck.

So, the last week in our room was very quiet. Me and Vicks think that everyone in the building probably got up a petition to get us kicked out, like they do with hard-bastard families in council estates. Anyway, we weren't really panicking or anything about leaving as Bob had said he'd help us out, as long as we didn't mind sleeping 'Al Fresco'. Typical, innit, Gladys, that me and Vicks make friends with the ponciest tramp in Frog land.

The worst thing about leaving our room was that we had to dump a load of our shite. It was very traumatic even though we knew we couldn't keep it cos it would be too tricksy to carry it all the time. One bad thing about this was that we had a massive fight about what should stay and what should be sacrificed. It was weird, because we haven't had a fight about anything since we left Hervey's, which was an all-time record. Take us back to crappy old Stourbridge and I bet we'd still be fighting like bastards every day.

Anyway, this is a list of what we decided to dump and leave behind in the room:

1 large ceramic skull Vicks made at fart college (60% sulk factor VICKS)
All of Vicks's books (90% Sulk Factor VICKS)
All of our 2000AD comics except for the first issue. No way was that going to be left (70% Sulk Factor VICKS and SAGE)
3 leather jackets (2% SF – we hadn't worn them as they were second-hand and smelled of old man's skin).
7 pixie hats (160% SF SAGE under duress).
1 hairdryer (0% SF, never used and tramps don't have electricity).
1 Ladyshaver (2% SF, used once)
17 cassette tapes (100% SF and huge fights. FAREWELL CAMEMBERT ELECTRIC MY OLD FRIEND).
Big pile of assorted stinky clothes (0% SF – big relief).

Ha ha!! Nausicaa's crusty old parents are going to think that we're satanists or something when they see the skull and smell the room.

In the end all we had was one rucksack each and our sleeping bags. But they were still as heavy as fuck. We said goodbye to our room, and it was dead weird shutting the door behind us that last time. It made me feel a bit sad actually, Gladys.

On the way down Vicks dropped off our key with Mrs Danvers. The bitch didn't say goodbye or anything of course and just took the key with a creepy smirky expression on her cat-arse face. When Vicks was heading out the door, I turned round and spat at Mrs Danvers and burbled some crap like I was putting a gypsy hex on her. She just gave me this secret nasty smile, so I knew it was her who grassed us up for deffo.

We were staying that night with the tramps, but we had no fucking idea where. We met Bob at the usual Pompidou place after me and Vicks had picked up our supplies so he could show us where we were going to kip.

It was very exciting. Bit like a sleepover. Thing is, Gladys, me and Vicks had done a fair bit of sleeping rough. There was the old faithful Abandoned Church at home in Stourbridge (that sometimes had tramp relics lying around it) and once we slept out in a construction site after we missed the last bus home after the Ramones concert in Birmingham. So it wasn't as scary as it would be for most people.

It was getting dark as we followed Bob down to the river. We walked for ages under these long dark bridges, and there were these strange noises coming from the back of one of them. We couldn't see what was going on and I didn't want to look to be honest. 'What the fuck's that?' Vicks says to Bob, and he's like, 'Oh, that's where the gays meet up.' Hmmm, typical that he would know that, eh, Gladys? But I didn't say anything and I haven't let on that I know he's a woofter.

Vicks looked dead scared, but not because of the gay sex, obviously, it just looked like the kind of place where muggers and serial killers hang out waiting for victims. Like those underpasses you take from the Bullring in Birmingham to get to the market. Dead unsafe.

And talking about unsafe, it turns out that Bob and Alex are ex-cons. Surprise, surprise, eh, Gladys? NOT. I found out some of this by eavesdropping, and then I asked Bob face to face if it was true.

Turns out Bob and Alex met in Wormwood Scrubs, which would be dead exciting and interesting except that we were going to be sleeping two feet away from them. But I don't think they were in for like GBH or murder or anything. Bob won't say what they were in for. Anyway, he says they skipped out on their probation and ended up here. He says there are loads of Brits over here. He says they're like the cons that run away to the Costa del Sol, except they don't have any money or homes or anything. And Alex hasn't even both-ered to learn any French. But what I want to know is how come we still have to kiss them 'hello' in the French way every time we meet them even though they're English???? Cheeky bastards. Alex does his begging with bananas thing and Bob just begs for cash. I can't get my head round that though. Begging? Fuck. At least me and Vicks haven't stooped that low.

Anyway, so we head to this other bridge that had this grassy slope next to it. There were three other tramps there as well. They were:

Richard: Frog, blond, always wears tight blue trousers and an anorak. He has floppy blond hair and a big moustache. He fancies Vicks a lot, worse luck.

Alex: who you know, scammy old Scottish coughing bas-tard etc.

Norbert: he's very old and has one of those bumpy faces. Luckily we don't have to kiss him though as he's not normally part of the tramp posse. He has this huge lump on his neck, like a second head, which Vicks says is called a goitre. Gross.

There was a bottle of wine going round and me and Vicks had some. I had to keep wiping the top of it without anyone seeing so that I didn't get any tramp germs. And we sat around for a bit just talking shite. Then these two really scruffy, dirty old tramps came up to us and Bob's like, 'Sorry, mate, this is our place,' and they didn't want to go, but Richard was like 'Fuck off' but in French, so eventually they went.

Bob said we should use our bags as pillows so that no one could nick them in the middle of the night and Vicks was like, 'Is it safe to be doing this?' and everyone laughed and Alex said, 'We're the people everyone is afraid of, lassie', so Vicks seemed to be okay after that.

Then everyone just got into their sleeping bags and crashed even though it could only have been about nine or something. I made sure no one else was too close to me and Vicks. It was quite fun at first like when we used to sleep in the Abandoned Church. Soon the others started snoring. It was the strangest feeling, we were outside in a city, sleeping under a fucking bridge, for fuck's sake! The river's dead loud at night, Gladys. And the odd thing was, even though Alex kept making his coughy snorting sounds in his sleep, they didn't sound too bad outside. As if they fitted in. Can't explain it better than that. And although we were right by the river it wasn't that cold, which really surprised me. I could hear that Vicks was sleeping and the next thing I knew it was morning. I woke up and my eyes were dead gritty and my head felt all dirty. It was as if someone had sprinkled dirt all over us in the middle of the night. When I woke up my arms were wrapped around Vicks. I left them there for a while (I couldn't move because of pins and needles) and anyway it couldn't have bothered her as she never said anything about it.

When everyone had woken up and stowed away their shit, we all went to the McShite near the Latin Quarter and Bob bought us all a coffee with these voucher things that one of his 'punters' gave him while he was begging.

Then, Richard, Norbert and Alex buggered off to do whatever it was they did in the morning, and Bob took us to the Pompidou where he said we could stash our bags in the left luggage place so that we didn't have to carry them everywhere.

There are loads of things you need to know if you want to be a good tramp, Gladys. I think I should write an SAS survival book about it or something.

Tricks so far:

Leave luggage at the Pompidou, although it's closed on Tuesdays!!! WHY???

Always get to the soup kitchen first before all the soup is gone and before the queue starts.

Bum fags early from the people on their way to work – they are too hassled to say no. (Yesterday Vicks got a whole pack of neatly rolled joints from this dead stiff-looking guy!!! Bonus).

Never buy a Metro ticket, just jump over the turnstiles, although you have to be careful of cops. (Slight problem as haven't yet figured out how to sneak through the slidy doors in the Metro down at Les Halles. They automatically swing shut behind you when you put in your ticket and walk through, and they are too high to jump over. I know there's a way to do it though, as Bob always uses that station when he goes off begging and that.)

Use the toilets at the Pompidou early before people come in and complain that we're brushing our teeth in there. Big fucking deal. You'd think the public would be glad to see others looking after their hygiene, wouldn't you?

Poem About Gay Sex

There's a noise in the night,
I think it's a fight,
But it's only the gays
Having their way
Under the bridge.

I'm getting better, aren't I, Gladys?

VICKI:

The *Clochard* Experience

How many cops does it take to search a tramp? There are four clustered around me and Richard. Two are checking out our passports, a policewoman is efficiently patting me down, and a male cop is doing the same to Richard. It's the third time I've been stopped and searched by the police now. It's a routine all *clochards* have to go through. They don't give us any undue hassle and we don't bitch about it too much. It's like we have an understanding with them. They do their job and we do ours.

Thank God I remembered to stash the penknife we nicked from Hervé in my rucksack, and that the fingernail-sized piece of black is safely stashed in the matted mass of hair at the back of my head. Even though I know the chances of it being discovered are slim, I still breathe a sigh of relief when the meaty policewoman finishes the job. I don't miss that she wipes her hands on her tree-trunk thighs when she's done. When the cops approached us, I thought for a stomach-dropping second that she was the same one I'd encountered after the Pompidou Break-in Experience, but this one is nicer and hasn't got such an obvious moustache.

The cops hand us our documents and amble off. They're probably heading to the Pompidou bench where Sage is waiting for me. Shit. She'll be in an even fouler mood if she's searched without me around. She hates the cop routine with a passion. 'At least buy me a drink first,' she'd grumbled to the first policewoman who'd patted her down.

But I'm buggered if I'm going to worry about Sage right now. Richard and I make our way into the Quartier de l'Horloge and sit on the wide concrete steps opposite the garish gold clock. I edge closer to him until our legs are almost touching. Sage and I discovered the area a couple of days ago. It's a hop, skip and a jump from the Pompidou, but it feels like a different world. We like it because its concrete and uneven paving stones remind us of the arcade near Waitrose in the Stourbridge Town Centre. It's a great place to smoke and take time out from the other members of what Sage calls the Pompidou Posse. Apart from the clock on the side of one of the buildings (which Sage thinks is kitsch shite), it's so dull it doesn't 'feel' like it's part of Paris at all. And it's nearly always deserted.

Richard flaps his hand in front of his face. 'I can smell something that is *mal, n'est-ce pas?*'

He's right. There's a blocked-drain stench wafting around from somewhere. I really hope it's not coming from me. I didn't have time for even a cursory wash in the Pompidou toilets this morning before I was due to meet him. I quickly light one of the fags I cadged off a passer-by this morning and offer the pack to Richard. Christ. I hope the smoke masks the smell. If I don't shower soon I'm scared I'll spontaneously combust. We've been sleeping under our bridge for over a week now and I haven't changed my clothes for three days. The tiny cut on the middle finger of my right hand is gooey with yellow pus. It's the first time I've ever had anything go septic. I ball my hand into a fist. Every pore is visible between my fingers; dirt has squirmed its way into the creases. My hands only seem to stay clean for seconds after I've washed them. My hair is heavy with grease and my scalp is continually gritty as if I've been rolling around on a beach. And horror of horrors, my teeth are beginning to feel furry. What if they end up looking like Irish's mossy gnashers? Apart from the Pompidou Centre you have to pay to use the public loos, and as per usual, Sage and I are broke.

Richard and I smoke in silence. We learned early on that it's generally too much work trying to have a conversation. I've tried to ask him how old he is, but he never seems to understand, even though it's one of the few questions I know I've got right. He must be at least in his twenties, I reckon. I take a peek at him without him noticing. His yellow hair flops silkily over his eyes and I can't see any lines on his face. I've never gone out with a guy with a moustache before. My nan says only men with something to hide wear hair on their faces, but Hervé didn't try to screw us over and he had that vile goatee thing.

Last night while Sage was arguing with Bob about Margaret Thatcher or some stupid political thing, Richard and I sneaked away for a joint down by the river. He took my hand as soon as we left the others, but didn't try to snog me or anything, even though I thought the whole rambling next to the river thing was quite romantic. Weird. What was the point of sneaking away from the others if he wasn't trying to get off with me? We'd also had quite a good laugh that afternoon in Les Halles, but I still can't work out whether he likes me in that way. He's a bit of a mystery. He's only slept outside with us for two nights, and I've no idea where he goes on the others. Perhaps I should ask Bob to do some snooping for me.

'*On y va?*' he says as we stomp out our fag butts.

'*Oui,*' I say, hiding my disappointment that we're leaving so soon. We climb down the steps and make our way to the front of the Pompidou. The usual suspects, Bob, Alex and Norbert, are gathered around the bench, but today I can make out a few new faces. I spot Sage immediately. She's crouched on the cobblestones to the right of the bench, trying to stroke a little dog. I can't be certain, but it looks like the one that went mental at the police when we were with Scotty and Irish. Sage isn't having much luck making friends with it; it's yipping and barking like it's really angry with her.

'Ralphie, shhhh!' An unfamiliar voice floats out of the cluster of *clochards*.

Something's going on. There's no early morning bottle of wine doing the rounds and the new arrivals are in deep conversation with Bob, who's looking deadly serious. Without acknowledging me he waves Richard over to him and they start rattling away in French.

I amble over to Sage. 'What's happening?'

'Dunno,' she snaps. I'd left her to dump the bags in the Pompidou while I went off with Richard and she's still sulking about it. I decide to give her a few more minutes to cool off and edge closer to where Richard and Bob are deep in conversation. I can't get the gist of what they're saying but I hear Alex's name mentioned.

I wait for Bob to draw breath before diving in. 'What's going on, Bob?'

He keeps rasping his hand over his unshaven cheeks and pulling at his chin as if he's trying to stretch it. 'Alex has been taken.'

'You what?'

Sage wanders over.

'The Blues got him,' Bob says.

Sage and I exchange confused glances. What the fuck are 'the Blues'? An image of the scammy old Scotsman being carried away by Lightnin' Hawkins and B.B King pops into my head. Perhaps he means that Alex is seriously depressed or something. I don't want to ask though, in case I lose street cred. It's obviously some tramp code word.

'What the fuck you on about, Bob?' Sage pipes up. 'What do you mean "the Blues got him"?' Bob drags his attention away from Richard. Both look at Sage in exasperation, but she obviously doesn't give a shit. 'Well?'

Bob sighs. 'The Blues are this special band of police who go round collecting tramps in their vans. It's high tourist season and they don't want their city looking messy.' He shakes his head wearily.

Oh shit. How come we didn't know about this before?

'How do you know what these "Blues" look like?' I say. I have a picture in my head of the creepy child snatcher in *Chitty Chitty Bang Bang*.

'They dress in bright blue uniforms and overalls. You can't miss them.'

'So they're not like the cops who search us every day?' My voice sounds small and scared. So much for street cred.

Bob chuckles. 'No, you don't have to worry about them. But if the Blues arrive, you have to run, and fast.'

'But how do they know if you're a tramp or not? I mean, you could just be a tourist, couldn't you?' Sage asks belligerently, as if the existence of the tramp police is entirely Bob's fault.

Bob rubs his hands over his stubble again. His chin is red from too much yanking. 'They keep an eye out for those of us who are here on a regular basis. If you don't hang around or beg in the upmarket arrondissements you should be fine.' He gives me a reassuring smile.

'Huh?' Sage says.

'You know, St Germain, Opera, places like that.'

Sage snorts. 'Not much fucking chance of that.'

'What are they going to do with Alex?' I ask.

Bob shrugs. 'Depends. Sometimes they just take your shoes and dump you on the outskirts of Paris.'

'And the other times?' Sage asks.

'They lock you up, delouse you and shave your head.'

'Fuck,' Sage breathes. But I don't know why she's

complaining. She's always whingeing on about her hair being too long.

'It's not all bad though, girls.' Bob winks. 'They always feed you a plate of couscous if they keep you overnight.'

'Great,' I say. I'm not sure which would be the worst punishment.

'But what if you don't have any lice?' asks Sage.

'You will when they let you out. The *clochard* cells are crawling with pestilence.'

Sage shudders. It's her worst nightmare. Bob's warned us that it's extremely difficult to get rid of head and body lice when 'you live outside normal society'. Both Sage and I had nits at school, so we're not that bothered about them (although I haven't got a clue how I'd get them out of my dreadlocks), but until Bob, neither of us had known that something as vile as body lice existed. According to Bob they're just like nits except they feed off your skin and breed in your clothes. He says they're almost see-through and are dead difficult to spot. Sage finds the thought of this terrifying. On more than one occasion I've seen her frantically checking the inside seams of her sweatshirts for any sign of their tiny transparent bodies. I hope she's not going to get paranoid about this.

'So will Alex be all right?' I ask.

Bob's face clouds over again. 'We're on our way out to look for him, in case they've dumped him and he's stuck. It's not good though, girls. You know how sick he is.'

'Shall we come with you? Maybe we can help.' Although I'm buggered if I know what we could actually do.

'No, girls. It's best if you stay here. I'll meet you at St Eustache later.'

'Okay,' Sage says quickly, obviously relieved. She turns to me. 'Anyway, we've got work to do, Vicks.'

She's right. Today we're going to try out our pavement drawing skills.

Bob and Richard head off. Although Bob turns and gives us the thumbs up, Richard just stalks off without a backward glance. My stomach drops. Was it the smell? Maybe he's too worried about Alex to think about me.

Something's snuffling around my boot. It's the little dog Sage was trying to stroke earlier. It's by itself, its string lead trailing on the ground. I bend down to stroke it and it snaps at my hand, making me jump. I try and nudge it away with my boot. What's with these vicious little French dogs who hate me? This one's got the same snappy temperament as Jules's nasty dog.

'You like? *Mon chien* – the dog?' I can't see who's spoken as the sun's too bright and the speaker's in silhouette.

'Er . . . *oui*,' I lie. 'Very nice. What's his name?' Then I remember – Ralphie. I shield my eyes against the glare.

'*Pardon?*' says the guy. His English is obviously crap. A cloud shifts across the sun and I'm able to check him out. There's not a single patch of skin on his face that's not pitted and scarred with acne. His eyes are wide slits in his face like snips in brown paper. His hair hangs down his back in ragged dreads, but they're way scruffier than mine – the result of hours of dedicated work with beeswax.

'Bob Marley, yeah!' He points to his head. I swear there's something crawling in there. His jeans are caked with grime and there's a studded belt slung round his hips. 'Ralphie, *viens!*' he shouts at the dog, which is now attacking Sage's laces. Another tramp I haven't seen before ambles over to us. He looks like an older version of Ralphie's owner: same dark, weather-beaten skin and sun-creased eyes. Instead of dreads, he's wearing what looks like a filthy tea cosy on his head.

'*Bonjour,*' Tea Cosy says to us. 'What is your names?'

'Sage and Vicki.'

'Ah. My name is Danny and this is Stefan.'

Stefan nods and smiles. In startling contrast to the rest of him, his teeth are beautifully white and straight.

Next to me I can sense Sage fidgeting. She moves subtly away from the two tramps, no doubt in case they try and kiss us 'hello'. I quickly bend down to pat the little dog to avoid any opportunity of this and it snaps at my hand again. I pretend not to be bothered. The older guy's saying something.

'Stefan, he is a . . . *gitan*. Ah, a traveller. Me, I was a *restaurateur*. A cookeur.'

'A chef?' I say.

'*Oui. C'est vrai.*'

I don't want to ask what happened to his restaurant, it can't be good considering how he's turned out.

'What's happened to your restaurant, then?' Sage asks.

'*Non* money,' he shrugs. '*Et ma femme,* my husband, *non,* my wife, she is gone.'

'I'm sorry,' I say. He seems like a nice guy. Although I'm a little taken aback at how forthcoming he is about his life story. Getting information about Bob and Alex's background is like getting blood from a stone.

'He's your son?' Sage asks, nodding at Stefan.

'Stefan?' He translates this to the dreadlocked guy. They both burst out laughing.

'*Non! Il est mon ami.*'

'Nah, they're just friends,' I say to Sage.

'Hmmm. That's what they all say,' she says under her breath.

Stefan gathers up Ralphie's lead.

'*Bon.* We must be leaving you now,' Danny says, adjusting his tea cosy hat. 'We have the work to do.'

'Nice to meet you,' I say. With a wave they head off in the direction of the Rambuteau Metro stop.

Sage looks at me askance. 'Fuck, Vicks. We're like creepy-old-perv magnets or something.'

I don't say anything. Apart from the acne, there's something about the younger guy I quite like.

'It's shite, isn't it?' Sage sighs.

'Yep, utter, utter, utter shite.'

I cock my head to one side and make my eyes go blurry in a vain attempt to make our chalk pavement drawing look better. It doesn't help.

We've made seven francs. The coins sit in Sage's hat, which is placed next to the drawing. Pity coins. If we were in England some wit would have said, ''Ere you go love, go and get yerself some art lessons.'

'We haven't even made enough for a fucking packet of fags.' Sage scuffs her boot over the drawing, smearing it into an even worse mess.

'I know. Total cock-up.' I'm gutted. We'd planned on using the money we made today on washing our clothes and going for a shower. But there's no hope of that now.

Last night, before the light had died, Sage had made a rough sketch of what was to have been our masterpiece. It was a complex mass of interlocking spirals that looked totally cool and Escher-like. But translated into a chalk drawing it looks like the work of a blind man with too much time on his hands.

'We should've done what Bob said and done a copy of the Mona Lisa or some shite.' Sage sighs and wipes her hands over her head. She looks like a skin-headed clown. Her face is almost entirely blue and pink. Our hands are so covered in chalk we look like we're wearing colourful gloves. And our art supplies are now nearly non-existent. There are only tiny crumbs of chalk left in the box. Bugger, I'm not sure what the chances are of us scoring some more.

Sage reads my mind. 'Think there's any chance of getting Richard the git to get us another box, Vicks?'

'Dunno.' For once I don't bother asking her to give the 'git' stuff a rest.

After his dismissive behaviour this morning, the whole Richard thing is doing my head in. It's all I thought about while I was making bad art this afternoon. Maybe he's got a split personality or something. Yesterday evening he seemed to be totally into me and the afternoon we'd spent together had been a good laugh. After breakfast yesterday Bob asked him if he'd take us 'shopping' for art supplies, and he appeared to be dead chuffed with the idea, especially when Sage announced she wasn't going to come with us.

Richard and I rambled companionably around Les Halles for a bit before heading into the bowels of this creepy little shopping centre I hadn't encountered before. It was dark and echoey and its walls were covered with grubby white tiles. Richard waved me into a store with a dusty easel plonked in its window, then stood next to a magazine rack and gestured for me to indicate what stuff Sage and I needed. The shelves were randomly piled with a mass of paint tubes and brushes and it took me ages to find a box of chalk. I wasn't sure what I was supposed to do with it, so I left it where it was and pointed it out to Richard.

He said something to the woman behind the counter, then took my arm and ushered me out of the shop. I followed him meekly out of the arcade and into the sunlight, confused as to what was going on. Actually, I was a bit pissed off. I'd been counting on getting hold of something that would enable me and Sage to make some cash. Then, as we made our way back to the Pompidou Centre, he whirled round to face me and whipped the box of chalk out from the inside of his jacket.

'How the fuck did you do that?' I spluttered. I hadn't seen him go anywhere near the shelf where the box was displayed. He'd even waved '*au revoir*' to the woman behind the counter as if we'd just been innocently browsing in the shop.

Richard shrugged modestly. '*Magique*?'

Even Sage looked impressed when I told her what had happened, although she still calls Richard a 'floppy haired Frog
git' at every opportunity.

It's supper time. We made it back just in time to wash our
hands and faces in the Pompidou loos and collect our bags
from the left luggage counter. I slog my rucksack over my
shoulder and follow Sage up the centre's sloping forecourt.
I'm beginning to really loathe my bag. I thought I was being
really cool buying a rucksack from the army surplus store, but
I'm buggered if I can figure out how the hell the squaddies
manage to carry those bags on their backs for more than ten
minutes without throwing them down in despair and kicking
the shit out of them. The leather straps cut like razor blades
into my shoulders and it never keeps its shape. It was fine
when we had a place to dump our stuff on a regular basis, but
now we have to carry them with us most of the time it's
becoming unbearable. I think of it as a monkey on my back,
even though I know the saying actually means you're an alky
or something. And my sleeping bag never stays rolled in a
neat little tube like Sage's. It always manages to free itself from
the bundle I tie to the base of the rucksack and ends up trailing
along the floor like a polyester bride's train. It's becoming
frayed and utterly filthy. Sage smugly has no trouble with her
rucksack. It's a modern nylon one with thoughtfully padded
shoulder straps.

I'm in a seriously grumpy mood when we join the queue
outside St Eustache. My back's aching and my palm is stinging
from where I scrubbed away the chalk dust. A couple of
tramps grunt in recognition as we arrive. They all seem to
keep to their 'types'. Bottom of the barrel are the raggedy old
stinking guys with gummy toothless mouths who dress in rags
(they seem to be mostly French and mostly white); then there

are the middle-class tramps like Alex and Norbert, who have found themselves washed up in hobo land for whatever reason; then there are the ones like us and Bob, the aristocrats who still have our own teeth and who could rejoin the human race if we wanted.

Sage and I haven't spoken since we collected our bags. Both of us are smarting from our spectacular failure in the pavement art stakes. As we move nearer to the front of the queue I pull off my rucksack, throw it on the steps and kick it vicously. Sage looks at me and raises an eyebrow.

'Fucking thing,' I mutter.

Someone taps my shoulder. At first I think it's one of the tramps about to complain that my bag's in the way. I open my mouth to tell whoever it is to fuck off, but the words die in my throat as I'm confronted by a familiar, widely grinning face. It's the ginger-haired, one-legged guy with the Mohican who always leers at Sage and me whenever we see him around Les Halles. He's squashed himself into the queue behind us, but the raggedy tramps he's shoved out of the way don't look annoyed. This would never happen at home. On the few occasions I've been in the pick 'n mix section at Woolworths, even the slightest indication that anyone was thinking of pushing her way to the front had the surrounding old ladies seething and tutting for all they were worth.

'All right, girls?' the guy says in a Tom Jones accent.

'Er, yeah, thanks,' I reply. 'You?'

'I'm Taffy,' he says.

I tell him our names, and the shutters come down on Sage's face.

'I know who you are,' he says, then, almost as an afterthought, he nods to a lanky guy hovering next to him. 'This here is Hippy.'

Hippy glares at a space above our shoulders and doesn't say a word. He looks almost as pissed off as Sage. God knows where he got his nickname; he looks nothing like a hippy. In fact, apart from the tatty trilby perched on his head and his mangy Hitler moustache, he's a dead ringer for Del Boy's brother Rodney in *Only Fools and Horses*. But what's with these unimaginative nicknames? Everyone seems to have one. Scotty, Irish and Taffy: all the British Isles represented. Maybe Sage and I should change our names to 'English' and 'Wulfrunian' so that we fit in.

'Seen yer around.' Taffy winks lasciviously at me. 'You hang out with Bob's crowd, don't you?'

'Yeah,' I reply.

'I think you're gorgeous,' he says, eyes travelling shamelessly up and down my body. Blood rushes to my cheeks and I pull my cardigan tighter around my front.

'Thanks,' I mumble, while Sage yawns ostentatiously. It's impossible for me to return his compliment. Whoever cut Taffy's hair into a Mohican must have been totally pissed. It's asymmetrical and leans drunkenly to one side. He also has a patchy goatee that would resemble Hervé's if it wasn't so unkempt. If Hervé's a faun, this guy's a ginger, one-legged version of Satan. To make matters worse, small red sores bloom around his mouth. His almost non-existent eyebrows frame his only good features: piercing bright blue eyes.

'You feel like coming with us after? We've got some blow.'

'Come with you where?'

He shrugs. 'You tell me, beautiful.'

I glance at Sage to see how she's taking this blatant flirting, and surprise, surprise she's concentrating on the back of the *clochard* in front of us.

'We've got to wait for Bob,' I say, wondering why Sage hasn't told him to fuck off yet. Maybe she's tempted by the offer of a spliff.

'I'll take you back to Bob after we've had some fun.'

Sage remains tight-lipped. Taffy taps her shoulder. 'Don't say much, do you?'

'What happened to your leg?' she asks, snippily.

'Car accident,' he says almost proudly. 'Boosted a car, rolled it, got me leg trapped under. Didn't even get done for taking and driving away. Magistrate said I'd suffered enough.' He hefts the stump upwards and opens the folded trouser leg that covers it. I don't want to look, but can't seem to tear my eyes away. A vicious, raw-looking scab zigzags across the lumpy end of his thigh where his knee once was, standing out against the ragged mess of pink scar tissue that seals the stump. Surprisingly, Sage looks impressed and leans down to peer at it. She's normally squeamish.

'Hasn't it healed properly?' she asks, forgetting for a second to be rude.

Taffy shrugs. 'Keep bashing it.'

Sage opens her mouth to ask something else, but then I catch sight of Bob's portly figure jogging up to us and I nudge her.

'All right, Bob?' Taffy says.

'Yes,' Bob says, throwing Taffy a slightly confused glance as if he's trying to place him. He turns to us. 'Alex is in the hospital.'

'Shit,' I say. 'That sounds bad.'

'Pneumonia.' He shakes his head wearily. 'Apparently he collapsed when they put him in the cell.'

'Christ.' Poor old Alex. I think back to the night he stayed with us. I can't imagine anyone being sicker than that.

'Listen, girls, I've got to go back there, check he's got everything he needs. I'll meet you by the bridge later.' His eyes flick to Taffy and Hippy. 'You'll be okay?'

'Sure,' I say. 'Give our love to Alex.'

With a nod and another glance at Taffy and Hippy, Bob hurries off.

'We'll look after them, Bob!' Taffy calls.

'Cheers!' Bob shouts without turning around.

'We don't need looking after,' Sage says through clenched teeth.

Taffy winks. 'Steady on there, tiger.'

'Don't fucking tell me what to do.'

Taffy bursts out laughing. 'Calm *down*, sister.'

Sage narrows her eyes and stares at a point over Taffy's shoulder, as if he's beneath her contempt.

Despite the Sage–Taffy fireworks, I'm beginning to feel reassured. If Taffy was dodgy then Bob would have warned us, surely?

Taffy and Hippy wait while we collect our food, but don't get any for themselves. They follow us over to our normal spot on the wide stone steps opposite the church.

'Not hungry?' I say to Taffy.

'Not for food,' he leers.

Sage shakes her head in disgust. 'She's got a fucking boy-friend.' I glance at her in surprise.

'Oh yeah?' says Taffy, but he doesn't look as if he gives a toss.

'So why don't you leave us the fuck alone?'

'Just trying to be friendly.' Taffy winks at me. I can't help it, I smile back.

'Go and try that somewhere else,' Sage says, scowling at me.

'Jesus, your mate's quite protective, isn't she? We're only offering some blow and a few laughs, nothing else, honest.' Taffy hitches his crutches under his arms and spreads his hands in an 'I'm innocent' gesture. He wobbles unsteadily on one army-booted foot.

Sage snorts but doesn't say anything else.

It's weird trying to eat while someone is staring at you. I'm so self-conscious I almost forget to give Sage my Babybel.

She's already passed me her tin of butter beans, but I'm not sure I can manage two tins tonight. There are advantages to sleeping outdoors though. *Beans, beans, they're good for your heart . . .*

'You don't eat here?' I ask Taffy. I'm curious to see if it's possible to have a normal conversation with him.

'Nah. Never eat that shite.' Taffy looks at our food with distaste. Without waiting for an invite he chucks his crutches onto the floor and with a sinuous but creepy hopping movement plonks himself down next to me. Hippy immediately sits down next to Taffy, but gets up straight away as if the stone has burned his bum. He hasn't stopped fidgeting since we sat down. In contrast to Taffy's ruddy complexion, his skin is so pale that the spots on his face stand out as if they're coated in fluorescent paint.

'Taffy,' he says.

'What?' Taffy barks, dragging his eyes away from me. Hippy seems to shrink.

'It'll be closed soon,' he whines. He has a thick *EastEnders* accent.

'Fuck you. I told you I wanted to check out this woman, didn't I?'

'Yeah, but—'

'*Fuck*, Hippy.'

Sage and I exchange glances. There's obviously no confusion about who wears the trousers in the Taffy/Hippy relationship. Taffy turns to us and sighs as if he's got the weight of the world on his shoulders. 'You wanna come with us to the chemist to get Hippy here his medicine? Then we'll go somewhere after. It won't take long.'

'You sick, Hippy?' I say, trying to sound concerned.

Hippy looks at me as if I'm mad. 'Yeah right, look sick do I?'

I want to say, well yeah, you look fucking terrible *actually*. He's clenching his fists and his face is slimy with sweat.

Sage says, 'No. We don't want to go with you to get your fucking medicine.'

'Ah, c'mon,' Taffy says in a wheedling voice that's a world away from the harsh tone of voice he used with Hippy. 'I was only mucking around with your friend. What else you going to do?'

It'll probably be hours before we meet up with Bob and the others. And it's been ages since Sage and I spent any time with anyone our own age. Everyone we hang around with these days seems to be older than our own parents. I shrug. 'What do you think, Sage?'

'What's wrong with him?' Sage asks Taffy through a mouthful of Babybel and baguette.

'Nothing. Needs his codeine fix is all.'

'His what?'

'Codeine. You know, what they put in cough medicine. Gives you a buzz.' Despite herself, Sage looks interested.

Hippy scowls and starts picking at a yellow-headed spot on his chin that's the size of a large bluebottle. I'm suddenly no longer hungry.

'Got any fags, then?' Sage says, dumping the remains of her baguette and soup cup on the floor.

'Here you go, love,' Taffy says, ignoring Sage's black look at the 'love'. She snatches his pack of JPs without even a nod of thanks and passes me one.

'So we're off then?' says Taffy. Before we can respond he grabs my rucksack and effortlessly slings it over his shoulder on top of his smaller and more convenient bag. Now we've got no choice but to follow him. He clatters down the road parallel to the church like a heavily laden three-legged spider, his folded-over trouser leg swinging with every lurch of the crutches. Hippy trots after him eagerly. Sage and I have to scramble to gather our stuff together and catch him up.

Sage nudges me as we leg it after them. 'I don't like this, Vicks.'

'Come on, Sage,' I say, already out of breath. 'Bob would have said if they were dodgy.'

But deep down, I don't like it either.

SAGE

Code names for tramps who are members of the Pompidou Posse:

Richard: Git (because he is one)
Bob: Poppy (cos of his eyes)
Stefan: Stig (from *Stig of the Dump*, that series that was on telly about the caveman boy)
Danny: Benny (from the old *Crossroads* programme: the nutter who always wore a crap woolly hat)
Taffy: Doris (I'm not sure why, it just seems to fit). Vicks wanted to call him Jake the Peg, but that's too obvious ay it, Gladys?
Hippy: George (from the telly programme *Rainbow*: the stuffed hippo who's as thick as shit and is always sad and brings everyone down)
Norbert: Lumpy (because he is)
Alex: Smelly (because he is)

As you see there are quite a few of us now, Gladys. Quite a little crew.

And we've found a new place to sleep!!! And a new way to make money!!! Only, not very much money, to be fair.

The other day, Stefan and Danny, who are now Posse members, showed us a very cool spot to kip: Right in front of lovely Notre Dame, in the gardens! The bushes there are so thick and overgrown that no one from outside can see in, and Bob reckons that the Blues won't suspect that tramps would be brave enough to sleep in such an obvious place. Stefan never seems to wash and Danny is always pissed as a fart, but fair play to them for sussing it out. We're the first tramp posse to use this place and so it is ours. It's also dead convenient because it's just across the bridge from St Michel and close to the Pompidou Centre where we dump our bags.

It's much better than sleeping under the Bridge of Gays, Gladys. It's quieter and the floor is comfier. Bob gave me and Vicks a bunch of flattened cardboard boxes to use as a mattress so that our sleeping bags wouldn't get too dirty. It's amazing how quickly you get used to not sleeping in a bed. Looking up at night and seeing the stars as your ceiling eventually becomes a normal thing that you take for granted. What's also good is this: Vicks and I always sleep close together. Her sleeping bag is far comfier than mine, so I think we're going to use hers as another mattress layer and mine as a blanket.

Anyway, the money situation has improved slightly. Wait till you hear, Gladys, it's hilarious!!!

Yesterday, Vicks and I were hanging around the St Michel fountain with vile Taffy, when this fat American woman comes up to me and Vicks and asks if she can take our photograph. I'm about to say, 'No, fuck off,' when Vicks says, 'Sure, but it'll cost you ten francs.' And the woman paid! Vicks looked dead surprised that she'd thought of saying that, and I was really proud of her for thinking so quickly. And then another bloke who saw what we were doing asked us the same thing, and we made twenty francs for doing fuck all!!! Although I think it was mainly my doing as Vicks had asked me to use the rest of the gel that day to do her hair up in a Mohican, so she looked dead nice, and I'd just shaved my head again in the loos at the Pompidou, so both of us looked quite cool.

We should have used the money for cleaning up a bit, but we decided to buy food instead. I'm sick of the soup kitchen shite and we needed a break. Vicks says if we could only get our act together and make some cash on a daily basis we'd have it made.

Because what's weird is this: although Bob acts as if we're like his daughters or something, he almost never buys us anything or even offers to lend us any money. Tramps are tight-arses obviously, and it's impossible for me to nick anything from them. They don't mind sharing their wine, though, which is a bonus, although Vicks was worried that they'd think we were takers, so she said we should share the rest of our black with them. And now it's all gone, worse luck. It was my insurance in case we ever needed cash in a hurry.

Bob says he can show us a couple of good begging spots where we're sure to make tons of cash. But, fuck it, Gladys, I'm not sure I can stoop that low. Vicks says she'll give it a go, but I reckon if we keep hanging round the fountain at St Michel every day for photo opportunities, we'll be fine.

Mind you, the other day me and Vicks decided to spy on Taffy. He's always going on about how much dosh he makes as a beggar, but neither of us believed him on account of how dire he looks and is. After we'd all had our morning coffee at the McShite we followed him through the Latin Quarter and down towards the main boulevard in St Germain. (Dead dangerous because of the Blues). He propped himself against a wall outside a swish-looking cafe as if he was just hanging out, and pulled out a cardboard sign. I couldn't read what it said from our hideout behind a bus shelter on the other side of the road, but it seemed to work like a charm!! Vicks said Taffy played his punters like a violin. He appeared to be cracking jokes with them and chatting with several who treated him like an old mate. One of them even bought him a cup of coffee!

Vicki says that Taffy is like the taxman for guilty consciences or something. Ha ha! And talking of Taffy, it finally looks like the Welsh git has given up trying to shag Vicks. But there was never any real chance for the ginger bastard. Vicks says she'll only get off with Taffy 'when there's no longer a hole in my arse', which is one of her nan's sayings.

I mean, even a dumb fuckhead like him can see that she's still got the hots for vile Richard. (Why oh WHY has Vicks got such bad taste in men?) We have much more fun when we're on our own together without anyone else interfering, but she doesn't seem to realise this. And who'll have to pick up the pieces when Richard fucks her around again? Guess who, Gladys. Yep. ME, of course. It's so obvious that she likes him because he's not always panting after her like most of the blokes she knows, but when I tell her this she just denies it.

So the other day Taffy says to me, 'Yeah, well, Vicki's not that nice anyway, and I reckon she's got black blood in her.' Ha! Stupid racist arsehole. Bad thing is though, I think he's thinking of trying it on with me next. Why are blokes so thick? Like I'm really going to be interested in a one-legged, drug-addicted, ginger Welsh fuckhead who spouts racist crap. And he was showing us his tattoos the other day, and one of them is a swastika! Vicks didn't say anything about it, but she did look a bit sick. He's done most of them himself and they were shite, Gladys, like prison tats. And Hippy's not much better. He's like Taffy's servant or something and is either moping around stoned out of his head or whining at Taffy to go with him to get the eight million bottles of medicine he chugs down every day. He's dead rude to me and Vicks, but treats Taffy like he's a god or something. I reckon he's in love with Taffy and hates girls who interfere in their relationship.

What else can I tell you about our new fun-filled exciting tramp lifestyle? Oh yeah . . .

I hate Richard, but he did do something quite cool last week. One morning, Bob said he was going to take us 'Tramp Shopping' (which is not where you go off and buy tramps or anything, Gladys, ha ha.) So me, Vicks, Bob, Richard and Norbert all took the RER (which is much posher and bigger than the Metro, but quite similar) to this supermarket place somewhere outside the city. It was much bigger than Waitrose or Sainsbury's and it had a thousand aisles that just went on forever. Tramp Shopping is a piece of piss and a really good laugh. What you do is go up to the deli counters and choose what slices of meat, cheese or whatever you want, which you're supposed to pay for when you leave. But as you walk round pretending to shop for other stuff, you eat the deli stuff and drink whatever you fancy and no one bothers to stop you!! Vicks and I stuffed ourselves with pastrami and this funny cheese with holes in like you see on cartoons.

Anyway, while me, Vicks and Bob were Tramp Shopping and wandering round making rude comments about all the arbitrary stuff in the other parts of the supermarket, we saw Richard piling a trolley high with food and all sorts of other stuff. And we're all thinking, 'What the fuck's he up to?' I mean, he's dead good at nicking stuff, but no matter how big his pockets he could never fit all that stuff in. All of us follow him, dead confused, but instead of going to the check-out places he just walks out with the trolley, right past the security guard! He didn't even rush or anything. He just strolled out as if he was completely innocent!! As soon as we joined him outside he said we could have anything we wanted out of the trolley, but all he took was a metal bar that looked like a crowbar or something. Typical though, Gladys, the stuff he'd shoved in the trolley was mostly crap. Tea towels and kitchen equipment. WHY?? Although we did get some soap and a few cans of Coke. Better than nothing I suppose.

But then, when we were walking through the car parking lot back to the RER station, Richard smashed the back windscreen of a car with the crowbar and nicked a jacket and handbag off the back seat!!! Of course Vicks looked dead impressed and thought he was really brave to take such a chance, dozy cow. I mean, how clever do you have to be to smash a car window? Duh.

I was dead angry as he could have got all of us into shit. He was lucky the place was so quiet.

Oh God, with all the tramp excitement I almost forgot – you'll never guess who we saw on the metro the other day!!!

Me and Vicks were practising sneaking through the slide doors at Les Halles Metro without paying. They're quite narrow and only open for a few seconds after you've slotted in your ticket. I'm fucked if I know what fat people do, though. Maybe they just get stuck.

Mind you, there aren't that many fat-arses in Paris. Anyway, I digress, as Bob's always saying. So, to get through these slidey door things, you have to wait for someone to go through first, stay really close to them and slip yourself through. So

I'm following this guy through, but I don't quite time it right and end up bumping into his back. The guy turns round, and guess who it is? Only fucking Potato Head!!! Vicks nearly wet her knickers when she saw him!!

Anyway, Potato Head looks like he's really pleased to see us (ha ha, hope he's forgotten about the great hash robbery) and kisses us 'hello', although I can tell he's not keen as we must be even stinkier than when we lived with Hervey. He asks us all about how we are etc. and we're going 'great yeah blah blah blah' when one of the old leper tramps we know from the soup kitchen, and who's begging in the Metro corridor, waves and shouts '*Bonjour*' to us like we're old friends!!!

Potato Head scarpered after that, so we didn't get the chance to pick his brains about Hervey and the rest.

Why it's better to be a tramp:

We have the power of freedom.
We never pay for the Metro.
We never pay for food.
We never pay rent.
We can do what we like all day, every day.

Why it's crap:

Tablets are running out (although this isn't really a tramp-related problem, is it?) From now on I'm only taking half a tablet a day to stretch them out.
    Need money to go and have a shower.
    Nowhere to permanently keep our bags.
    Scary threat of the Blues and lice and couscous.

Have to kiss other smelly tramps 'hello' all the time, which is gross.

Dirty all the time.

Food can get a bit samey.

No money ever.

Okay, okay, I know there are more bad things on the list than good things, but the good outweighs the bad on the whole. HONEST!!

VICKI:

The Begging Experience

Oh God.

I have absolutely no idea where to put my eyes. I finally decide to drop my head as if I'm praying and let them hover on a piece of chewing gum stuck to the pavement in front of where I'm sitting. I'm gripping my sign so tightly my hands are starting to ache, and small circles of sweat are blossoming around my fingers and darkening the cardboard. Through my fringe I can make out the different kinds of shoes traipsing back and forth in front of me, and it's murder resisting the urge to look up at their owners. On the couple of occasions I've caught someone's eye, they've looked straight through me as if I don't exist.

I'm gasping for a fag, but according to Bob one of the golden rules is never to smoke when we're 'on the job'. This is one of the few nuggets of wisdom he shared with us during our brief begging tutorial this morning as we made our way here on the RER. After our disastrous attempt at street painting, we've bitten the bullet and decided to give begging a go. After all, if Bob and Taffy the Welsh tosser can do it, so can we. As Sage said this morning as we were psyching ourselves up, we're much better-looking than them *and* we've got all our limbs.

We'd approached Bob yesterday afternoon and he promised to show us a couple of good begging spots out in the

Paris suburbs. Apparently the Blues don't bother picking up *clochards* who work outside the city.

But I hadn't realised it would be so hard. Taffy had made it seem like a piece of piss. I keep trying to convince myself that it's much easier than getting a job. It's not as though begging is actual work is it? But truth be told it's a thousand times worse than when Sage and I collected money for the buskers. I'm feeling just like I do in those dreams where I realise I've forgotten to put on any trousers and I'm wandering around the Mander Centre naked from the waist down.

I'm constantly aware of every movement of my body as I fidget around to make myself more comfortable. Risking a quick peek upwards, I accidentally catch the eye of a passing man. He frowns at me as if I'm a piece of dog shit he's just avoided stepping in and disappears through the hissing supermarket doors a few feet from where I'm huddled.

Bastard.

I concentrate on the pavement again and count the passing feet. A pair of scuffed stilettos approaches and hesitates. I hold my breath. There's the telltale clink of a few coins dropping into the hat placed in front of my crossed legs. I mumble a barely audible *'merci'* and the stilettos clip clop away. Result! I wait until there's a gap in the shoe traffic, lean forward and peer into the hat to count the coins. Ten francs! It's nearly enough to pay for a shower. Making sure no one's looking, I take out the only silver coin and sneak it into my pocket. That way the scattering of centimes will look all the more pathetic (another Bob tip). I need much more than this though. Maybe I don't look hungry and desperate enough. I try my best to look meek and mournful, but I can't hold it for long without my cheeks hurting. Hopefully Sage is having better luck. And *Christ,* it's boring. Mind you, my nails could do with some attention. I have to keep them short otherwise the dirt creeps underneath them and I have to winnow it out with a matchstick.

I'm busy gnawing on the nail of my little finger when a pair of tasselled loafers stops in front of me. Goody. I wait for the clink of coins. It doesn't come and the loafers don't move.

'Oh, you poor thang!'

I can't help but look up. There's a youngish woman staring down at me. Her face is framed in an unflattering bowl haircut and there's no mistaking the pitying look in her eyes. She abandons her trolley and squats down on her haunches, inches in front of me. *Shit.* Willing her to move on, I stare fixedly at the rigid creases in her jeans.

'How terrible for you!' she says in an American or Canadian accent. Canadian, I decide: she sounds similar to the nannies who hung around Nausicaa's park. '*Je suis . . .er . . . desole,*' she says in stilted French. I'm a bit relieved. If her French is crap I can pretend to be a Frog and that way avoid having to chat to her. She reads the words on my begging notice slowly, like a kid learning to read. '*Aidez-mois, s'il vous plaît. J'ai faim*'. Help me, please, I'm hungry. Oh, I *bet* you are!' At first I think she's being sarcastic, but then she stands up and starts rummaging in her over-laden trolley. 'Here, take these.' She places a pile of groceries next to me. Out of the corner of my eye I check them out. A punnet of those vile yoghurts I used to feed Nausicaa (in some weird flavour I don't recognise), a loaf of sandwich bread and two tins. My heart sinks when I see that they're fucking butter beans in tomato sauce. Typical. As if I don't get enough from the soup kitchen.

'*Merci,*' I say, but what the hell am I going to do with these bloody things? No one will give me any cash if I'm sitting next to a kilo of yoghurt.

'Is there anything else I can do to help?' she drawls slowly, as if she's speaking to a mentally deficient child.

Yeah, give me some cash you daffy Canadian sod.

'*Non, merci bien,*' I say, ladling on a thick French accent and willing her away. She stares intently at my face. For a second I think she's going to pat my head. 'How you must suffer.'

Oh. My. fucking. Christ. She takes one of my hands in hers, and her eyes fill with tears. I resist the urge to snatch my hand back. Hasn't she ever seen a beggar before?

Don't they have them in Canada? A few shoppers wander past and I can sense them starting at us.

'*Comment appellez-vous?*' she asks.

Oh crap. I'll have to think of a French name. I search my brain, but strike out. She asks me again, slower this time. Then I have it. 'Emmanuelle,' I say, silently thanking my brother for unearthing my dad's secret porn stash last year.

'*Je m'appelle* Stacey,' she says.

Who gives a shit? I think. Am I turning into Sage? No, Sage would have told her to fuck off by now. I make an attempt to smile gratefully at her. I know it's the kind of look do-gooders live for. Stacey reminds me of the couple of hardcore Bible bashers who occasionally helped Nan with her jumble sales.

'I have to go now,' she says slowly, as if she's scared the news will upset me. 'The family I work for will be expecting me.' Her face screws up as she concentrates on translating this into French for me. 'Er . . . I hope life treats you better soon, I really do.'

I nod again meekly. '*Merci,*' I mumble in what I hope is a starving beggar voice.

With a last simpering look she wheels her trolley away.

I wait for her to disappear round the corner before I jump up and dump the bread in the nearest bin. An old lady sees me doing this and tuts and shakes her head. I decide to keep the yoghurts and tins. I roll up my sign and slip it inside my jacket and collect the hat and the change. I've had enough.

Better check the time. Blimey. I've only been here thirty minutes. It felt like three hours. Best go check on Sage.

It takes me a while to get my bearings. We're miles outside Paris in the suburb of Rueil Malmaison, which didn't sound too promising (*mal* meaning 'bad' after all) when Bob suggested it. The houses and apartments are plain concrete boxes and there are hardly any of those tall white Parisian apartment blocks or cobbly little streets leading nowhere. The people wandering around look fatter and tattier than in the centre of Paris.

It's a real pity that our photograph money has dried up. There's no chance of my hair forming into a proper Mohican without a good supply of spray and gel, and we've run out. No one wants a photo of a scammy tramp with floppy dirty hair, do they?

I recognise the green neon cross of a pharmacy at the end of the high street where Sage is begging, and head down there. I have no trouble spotting her cross-legged figure sitting outside a furniture store. She doesn't look up as I stop in front of her. She's obviously employing the same 'pretend I don't exist' strategy as I did. I peer down at her hat. A few centimes glimmer pathetically back at me. My heart sinks. I was counting on Sage making up the shortfall.

'*Bonjour* leetle girl,' I say in a fake French accent, making my voice as deep as possible.

Sage jumps and looks up, a ready scowl on her face. Then she sees it's me and the scowl is replaced with a look of relief. 'Hi. Ouch!' She winces as she gets to her feet and stretches her back. 'Sore arse.'

'So? How did you do?'

'Fucking awful,' she says. 'Hardly any of the bastards stopped.' She nudges the hat with her boot. It makes a faint clinking sound.

I bend down and collect the cash. Four francs. If we pool our money we'll have just enough for one load of washing.

I shrug. 'Better than nothing. I made about ten, so at least we can get our clothes done.'

'Yeah. How long have I been sitting here?'

'About forty minutes.'

'Fuck. It felt like days!'

'I know, how weird is that?'

'I'm sure this is a shit spot though. I reckon Bob keeps all the good places for himself.'

'Nah, Bob wouldn't do that.' Would he?

'Shall we knock this on the head?'

'Yeah.' I'm glad I'm not the one who made the suggestion. 'We can always come back tomorrow, can't we?'

'Yep.' She bends down and collects her hat and the jumper she was sitting on.

'Good news though, Sage,' I say as she straightens up. 'Look what some daffy bitch gave me instead of cash'. I show her the vile flavoured yoghurts and the cans of butter beans.

'Thank God for that,' she says without missing a beat. 'I was afraid the soup kitchen was going to run out of them.'

We wander down the high street towards the RER station. Sage grabs my arm as I'm about to blithely walk in and hop over the turnstiles.

'Wait, Vicks!' she hisses.

There are several cops crawling around the front of the station and hanging out by the ticket booths and turnstiles.

'Bugger, what the hell are we going to do now?'

Sage shrugs. 'Wait for them to piss off, I guess. There's no way we can pay for a fucking ticket or anything.'

'Shall we do some more work for a bit?' I suggest, immediately regretting it. It's the last thing I feel like doing.

'Up to you,' Sage says, but she doesn't look any keener than me.

'You got any fags left?'

Sage takes the battered Marlboro packet we use for our morning 'collection' out of her inside pocket. It's empty. I could have sworn there were at least two fags left in there when I headed to my pitch. My eyes stray over to the magazine stand. Sage follows my gaze. We're both thinking the same thing.

'Fuck it,' she says. 'We'll come back tomorrow. Maybe we'll have better luck then. One day won't make any difference to our clothes, eh?'

'That's the spirit.'

We buy a packet of Lucky Strikes from the stand and wander down the street until we find an empty bench. I light my cigarette and inhale deeply and greedily. Gorgeous. With a full packet of fags in my pocket I feel like the richest person in the world. Tomorrow we'll make loads of cash. Course we will.

'This is a banana hold-up. Giz us yer money (cough) or a bottle of whisky (cough) or I'll shoot yer (cough).'

Alex hobbles towards the Pompidou Posse bench where Sage and I are sitting and bends down for the usual kissy-kissy hello. I try not to show how shocked I am at his appearance. If his face was gaunt before, now it's cadaverous. His skin is egg-yolk yellow and the whites of his eyes are flecked with brown dots. It's hot today, but he's still wearing his donkey jacket. It hangs off him like a scarecrow's coat. Even his bananas look rotten.

'Fuck, Alex,' Sage says. 'Shouldn't you be in bed or something?'

'Nah.' He flaps his hands at her. 'Gotta catch up with the work, like.' He's bent double as his body convulses from the force of another coughing fit.

'Take it easy, Alex,' I say.

'Takes more than this to take me doon,' he says, trying and failing to look cheerful. 'I'll catch yer later, lassies. If yer see Bob tell him I'll meet him at Notre Dame, like.'

'Sure.'

He stumbles into the stream of tourist traffic and accosts a couple of tourists with his usual banana hold-up spiel. But he can't get his words out and he fumbles and drops his bananas. I jump up to help him, but he waves me away. The couple stares at him in disgust and I want to run up and shake them. Alex tries to shrug off this defeat and collect his dignity. With a mournful nod in our direction he ambles away.

'Jesus,' says Sage. 'He's definitely on his last legs.'

'Poor old Alex. Should we go after him?'

Sage shrugs and takes Hervé's watch out of her pocket. 'He'll be fine,' she says dismissively. 'Fuck, Vicks. It's not even lunchtime yet.'

I'm amazed. 'Bloody hell. I thought it would be about five p.m or something.'

I'm glad Bob's not around. I don't feel like discussing our lack of begging success with him and explaining why we're back so early.

'I'm off to listen to some sounds.' Sage nods at the Pompidou Centre. 'Coming?'

I'm about to say 'yes', when out of the corner of my eye I spot a familiar blue anorak. Richard. My stomach does its usual flip at the sight of him. 'Nah. Think I'll hang out here for a bit.'

Sage stares pointedly in Richard's direction. 'See you later then,' she says snippily. 'Have fun *hanging out*.' She heads off.

'Hang on, Sage!' She pauses expectantly. 'Will you shove these in my bag?' I pass her the tins of beans and the remaining yoghurts. She scowls but takes them without a word.

I lean back on the bench and try to look nonchalant. Richard is definitely heading my way. Then he stops and starts talking to a couple of *clochards* who have appeared out of nowhere. I try and catch his eye, but no luck. His eyes flick in my direction, but he doesn't return my smile. Total bastard. What now? Should I catch up with Sage? Nah. She'll only give me one of her 'told you so' faces and she's probably in a sulk. At least I have the cigarettes. I light one for something to do.

'Vicki!' I spin around eagerly, thinking maybe Richard has changed his mind. But it's Stefan, the dreadlocked scruff, and Danny Tea Cosy. There's a telltale growling yap and Ralphie races up to gnaw on my boot. I attempt to check out Richard's reaction as Stefan kisses me 'hello', but I can't tell if he's noticed or not.

'*Bien,* Vicki. We are to walk. You like to come?' Danny says. I look over at Richard again. He's still pretending not to see me. Fuck him.

'Yeah. I would actually.'

Stefan bows to me and offers me his arm, and Danny does the same. As I walk away, tramp on each arm, I can't resist looking back at Richard. Ha! He's staring and I'm sure he's looking miffed. Good. Serves him right.

'Sage!'

Maybe she hasn't seen me? I wave my arms above my head, but she doesn't acknowledge me. She's in front of the Pompidou doors, and appears to be deep in conversation with Taffy. Hippy is standing off to one side, smoking and looking as sulky as ever. I'm relieved to see my rucksack at her feet next to her own bag. I was worried I'd be too late to collect it. I race down the deserted forecourt towards where the three of them are sheltering from the rain. It's tipping down, and dribbles of water trickle down my face.

'You won't *believe* what I've been doing!' I call when I'm in earshot. 'Hey, Sage! Listen to this—'

'Fuck, Vicks,' she snaps. 'I was dead worried about you. Don't you know what's gone on?'

'Eh?'

'Alex is seriously ill, so Bob had a whip-round and got him a hotel room. Fuck, I couldn't find you anywhere and Richard Git Face said you'd gone off with a couple of strange men.'

She must be really livid if she's willing to start a fight in front of Taffy and Hippy. But what's with Richard? Trouble-making bastard. He knows full well that Stefan and Danny are members of the posse.

'Wait. You don't understand—'

'We looked everywhere for you,' Taffy pipes up. 'Sage was really worried.' He puts an arm protectively around her shoulders. Sage shrugs it off irritably.

'Sorry. I didn't mean to worry you—'

'Well, you fucking did,' Sage interrupts.

'So what's going on with Alex?' I say, hoping to deflect the conversation away from me.

'I told you. He's sick as fuck. Bob has gone off with him, and we've got to find somewhere to kip out of the rain tonight.'

'I've got a place,' Taffy says.

'Yeah. So I said we'd go with Taffy and Hippy and stop the night with them.'

'Oh. Okay.' I'm confused. Sage hates Taffy's guts. What's going on?

'But we've got a quick stop to make on the way, like,' Taffy says. Hippy perks up.

'What, the chemist again?' I say, trying to catch Sage's eye for a conspiratorial smirk. She ignores me.

'Nah. Somewhere else. Come on, we'd best get going. We can't be late.' He doesn't offer to carry my bag, and without another word the three of them start jogging up the forecourt. I follow behind, trying to heft my bag onto my shoulder. The straps are wet and slippery and it's murder trying to get a grip on them.

'Sage! Wait up!' I can tell she's pretending she can't hear me. I'm dying to tell her my news, but it doesn't look like she's going to snap out of her sulk anytime soon.

We head down into the warmth of the Rambuteau Metro station, and I fall behind as I struggle to leap over the turn-stiles with the weight of my rucksack skewing my balance. For a second I think I've lost them, but then I hear Taffy's voice blaring out of the corridor on the right. I jog down the steps and grab hold of Sage's arm. She shrugs me off, but slows enough to enable me to fall into step with her.

'What the hell's going on, Sage? I thought you hated Taffy's guts?'

'Whatever.'

'Look, I'm really sorry about going off like that.' She sniffs but doesn't even glance at me. Shit. How long is she going to milk this for? 'So, we're really going to sleep with Taffy and Hippy tonight?'

'It's fucking pouring out there, the gardens will be a dead loss and Taffy said to Bob that he'd help us out. Happy?' she snaps. 'If you'd been around, maybe we could have made another plan. But you were off doing your own thing, as per fucking usual, so it was up to me, all right?'

Sage joins Taffy and Hippy on the platform. Feeling like an outsider, I stand a few feet apart from the little group, wishing I'd stayed with Stefan and Danny. They'd offered to find me a place to stay out of the rain.

The train whooshes up with a blast of dirty air and we scramble on. It smells like wet dog and old feet and is heaving with damp commuters. As I squeeze in, my bag bashes into someone's face. I ignore the gasps of irritation and push my way to the aisle, lunging for one of the handrails. I've ended up next to Taffy.

'All right, Taffy?'

'Yeah,' he says, without a trace of his former leery behaviour.

'So where we off to first?'

'Gare du Nord, got someone we gotta see.'

'Right.' I'm absurdly pleased that at least *someone's* talking to me, even if it is the Welsh git.

My legs are killing me as I follow Hippy, Taffy and Sage through the cavernous train station.

My stomach rumbles, and I'm glad of the yoghurts and beans in my bag. It's way too late to head to the soup kitchen.

'Come and meet Dakota,' says Taffy, nodding at a dark-haired guy who's sitting languidly on a bench in front of the left-luggage lockers. The guy looks up at the sound of Taffy's click-clacking crutches and takes his time stubbing his cigarette on the floor. As we get closer I hear a growling sound and a massive black Alsatian slithers out from underneath the bench. I hang back; I don't trust French dogs. They all seem to be in a foul mood, and this one looks as if it could do some real damage.

'All right?' Taffy greets the guy. It's obvious Taffy's also wary of the dog, but Hippy doesn't seem to be bothered by it. For the first time since we met him he appears to be in a good mood and isn't fidgeting as much as usual.

'You're late!' snaps the guy, pulling out a pack of Gitanes and popping one into the corner of his mouth. He lights it without looking, flicking his eyes at me and Sage. 'Who're they?'

'Ah, sorry about that, Dakota. Got stuck on the Metro. This is Sage and Vicki. Newbies.'

'Right,' says Dakota. 'How are you, lassies?'

Sage nudges me and rolls her eyes. 'Are there any bloody Scotsmen left in Scotland?' she hisses in my ear. At least she's talking to me again.

'Er, we're fine thanks,' I say to the guy. 'Nice dog.'

He turns back to Taffy, and as they share a whispered conversation, I check him out. His hair is the same length and floppy style as Richard's and he'd be quite sexy if his eyes weren't so close together. He's a cut above top tramp calibre. His black jeans and boots are spotless.

'Shall we, gents?' he says to Taffy and Hippy, as if Sage and I don't exist. Without checking to see if anyone's following him, Dakota picks up the dog's lead and starts walking briskly through the station. Sage and I hang back as Taffy and Hippy trail him through the exit doors and out into the rainy haze.

'What's going on, Sage?'

'Fuck knows, but that guy gives me the total creeps. And what's with his stupid fucking name? Dakota, my arse,' she snorts.

We wait, huddled under the concrete overhang, while the three guys mumble conspiratorially. Taffy's eyes keep flicking from Dakota to the dog. This is a new side to him: He's deferring to Dakota like a farm worker simpering to his landlord. Sage is also watching with interest, although she's trying to assume a bored, world-weary air.

'Want anything, lassies?' Dakota calls over to us.

'Eh?' I say.

'Got some strawberries in. Or Supermen if you prefer. Good stuff. Very spicy. Give you my personal guarantee of quality.'

'You what?'

Dakota looks amused.

Sage elbows me. 'Duh. Acid, of course.' She nods at Dakota. 'How much?' she asks, deadpan.

'Fifty francs a pop. Strawberries are double-dipped but I'll give you them for the same price.'

I glance around nervously. He hasn't bothered to keep his voice down and there are quite a few people hurrying into the station. Thankfully nobody seems to be paying us any attention.

'Cool,' says Sage. 'Maybe some other time. How do we get hold of you?'

'Always here, in my office, nine to five,' Dakota winks. 'Ask Taffy.

Taffy roars with sycophantic laughter.

Dakota's all business again. 'Is that it then, gents?'

'Yeah. Ta, Dakota,' says Taffy.

'Sure I canna tempt you, lassies?' Dakota asks as he heads back into the station. His dog growls at us.

'We'll think about it,' Sage says, refusing to be intimidated by either the dealer or the dog.

'You do that'. He disappears through the sliding doors.

'Let's go, Taffy,' Hippy says eagerly.

Taffy shoots him a scowl to remind him who's boss, then follows him into the station. Once I'm certain they're out of earshot I grab Sage's arm. 'You're not serious about the acid, are you?'

'Sure, why not?' Then she stops and looks at me, eyes narrowing. 'I thought you liked taking trips?'

Oh shit, had I lied to her when we first met at college and said I was into acid? I can't remember. 'Yeah,' I try to rally. 'But mushies make me sick as a dog.' This is true. The one time my brother and I picked magic mushrooms from the field behind my parents' house, I'd puked all over the dining room carpet. I don't mind a wee bit of blow, but I don't like that out of control feeling.

'Acid is nothing like shrooms, Vicks,' Sage says patronisingly. 'As soon as we've made enough dosh we'll get some and you'll find out. It's the coolest thing ever.'

'Great,' I say. But I'm relieved. At the rate we're going we'll never have enough cash to waste on drugs. I put my hand in my pocket and wrap it protectively around the three ten-franc coins. I'm glad I haven't told Sage about my afternoon's activities, after all. If she can't be arsed to ask me what I've been up to, then tough. It will be my secret.

'Are you fucking serious?' Sage asks, looking around her in disgust.

We're in the underground car park across the road from the St Michel fountain. The too-bright strip lighting hurts my eyes after the stormy gloominess of outside, and it reeks of petrol and urine.

'Is this it?' she continues. 'A car park? I thought we were going to a squat or something.'

'Least it's dry,' Taffy says.

'So where do we sleep?' I ask.

'In between the cars,' Taffy says, as if I'm thick. Now that I'm no longer the object of his affections I've been relegated to Hippy status. He points to a stack of cardboard that's piled against the wall. 'There's your mattresses, girls.'

'Where's Hippy gone?'

When we arrived at St Michel he'd mumbled something in Taffy's ear and wandered off down the street, oblivious to the weather. Not that I care. The more Taffy treats him like shit, the ruder Hippy is to Sage and me. But talk of the devil. Just as Taffy is about to open his mouth to answer me, I catch sight of Hippy's shambolic figure gingerly making its way down the tarmac slope that connects this floor to the next level. He's weaving all over the place like a sleepwalker. With a jolt, I realise he's not alone. There's a smallish girl I've never seen before walking a few steps behind him. Her arms are tightly crossed across her stomach as if she's cold. With her straight bobbed hair and huge eyes, she reminds me of a Japanese anime character. Sage is looking a bit put out. She hates surprises.

As the girl gets closer I notice there's a huge glistening sore on her cheek that doesn't look like it's going to heal any time soon. She's also wearing more eyeliner than Jules's Japanese friend. For some reason this makes me feel self-conscious. Apart from a touch of lipstick, I haven't bothered with make-up for ages.

Taffy greets her cheerily, and she allows him to kiss her 'hello'. Suddenly her shoulder ripples and bulges and a giant black and white rat pokes its head out from underneath her jacket. Sage takes a step back and mumbles, 'Gross'.

'Nice rat,' I say.

The girl looks at me impassively, and then glances at Sage with the same lack of interest. But no one can do impassive better than Sage. Neither Taffy nor Hippy introduce us to the new arrival. The rat climbs sinuously to the top of the girl's head and she plucks it off and brings it towards her face, as if she's going to kiss it. Sage looks as if she's going to be sick.

'Right,' Taffy says, looking meaningfully at Sage. 'Shall we make ourselves comfortable?'

A thought pops into my head. 'What do we do if someone comes to collect their car when we're sleeping? We could be run over or something.' I can't imagine ever being able to sleep in the multi-storey car park in the Mander Centre. It's always busy.

'Don't worry about it. This is the long-term parking floor. Most of them only use their cars on the weekends.'

'Oh.'

'Have to be up bright and early though,' he says.

'Why?'

'Blues.'

Oh great.

Hippy sinks down on his haunches next to a silver saloon-type car. His head lolls to one side, giving him the appearance of a mannequin with a broken neck. His pupils are dense black Jelly Tots, and an uncharacteristic beatific smile dances round his lips. He's definitely on more than his usual codeine medicine. Taffy sits down next to him and Sage and I do the same. It's very cramped in between the cars and Sage flinches as Taffy's stump snuggles in next to her leg. He pulls out a large chunk of black and passes it to her to roll up. She takes the Rizlas and dope wordlessly, as if this is a routine they've been practising for ages.

There's a shuffling sound behind me. It's Rat Girl. She jumps up onto the bonnet of the silver car and lies back against the windscreen.

It's chilly down here, but it's not unbearable. There's only room for two people to sleep in the gap between the cars, so Taffy doesn't get a look in. Just before we collected our cardboard mattresses he'd said to Sage, 'Let me know if you need keeping warm, like.' I'd waited for her 'fuck off asshole' retort, but she'd simply shot him a 'you can't be serious' look, which is almost the equivalent of encouragement from Sage.

I'm already homesick for the comparatively comfortable Notre Dame gardens. The car park's strip lighting shines incessantly and I still can't get used to the stench of piss, diesel and rubber. I snuggle deeper into my sleeping bag. Sage and I are wedged in head to toe. I hope this isn't freaking her out too much, I know how she feels about being too close to people.

'Night, Sage.'

'Yeah,' she says. She still hasn't asked about my afternoon, or even who it was I'd buggered off with. The money sits in my pocket like a dirty secret. I can always add it to the cash we make tomorrow when we're begging. She'll never know, and then we can use it legitimately for a shower. It's a bummer I have to keep it to myself though, I'm dying to tell her all about it. The afternoon had been a real eye-opener. And hanging out with Danny and Stefan had been a good laugh. There was only one awkward moment when Stefan had tried to take my hand as we were wandering down the Rue St Denis. I'd tried to explain about Richard, which had caused some confusion, but Stefan seemed to accept that I wasn't interested in him quite good-naturedly. Even if Richard stops being such a weird bastard, I can't see myself ever snogging Stefan. He's just too dirty, and I have to have some standards, don't I? I've agreed to meet them tomorrow afternoon. If the morning's begging is a dead loss, at least I'll have an alternative income to keep us going. I decide to tell Sage about it tomorrow.

Probably.

'Wake the fuck up!'

'Huh?' Someone's shaking my shoulder. I open my eyes and flinch. Taffy's scrofulous face is hovering inches from mine. His eyes look as if he's edged them with blood-red eyeliner.

Sage sits up and rubs her hands over her sleep-puffed face. 'What's going on?'

'Get up,' he hisses, spattering my face with spit. 'The Blues are on their way!'

Oh fuck! We don't need to be told twice. We wriggle out of our sleeping bags and scramble to find our boots. I shove mine on my feet and haul my bag onto my shoulder. My hands are shaking and I can taste the irony tang of adrenaline. Sage and I run out from between the cars.

'Bloody hell, I really don't like this,' puffs Sage.

We race over to where Hippy, Taffy and Rat Girl are getting their stuff together.

'What now?' I whisper to Taffy.

'We get the fuck out of Dodge,' he hisses back. 'Be as quiet as you fucking can, all right, girls?'

We nod obediently. Sage's eyes are wide with fear and her hands are also shaking.

The five of us creep up the slope that leads to the next parking level. I'm desperately trying to shove my sleeping bag into my already crammed rucksack. Hopeless. I'll just have to carry it as it is.

'How do you know they're here?' I whisper to Taffy.

'Hippy went out for a slash this morning. Caught sight of their van just outside the fountain.'

'Isn't there another way out? Surely there must be an emergency pedestrian exit or something?'

Taffy narrows his eyes. I can't believe he hasn't thought of this already.

'Yeah,' he says grudgingly. 'Think there's one on the next floor. Let's go.'

We leg it up the slope and into an identical parking area. Rows of cars stretch into the shadows, but at the far end I can see sunlight glimmering teasingly through the exit ramp.

'I don't see any cops,' Sage snaps under her breath.

'They'll be here any second,' Taffy whispers. 'They always check the parking garages first thing. Fucking Hippy was supposed to get us up earlier.' Taffy glares at Hippy's back, which flinches as if Taffy had actually hit it.

'Over there,' I say, pointing to a green neon *sortie* sign above a grey metal door. It's only a few metres away from where we're hovering.

'Oh *fuck*.' Taffy nods towards the far end of the parking lot where several pairs of legs are walking purposefully down the slope. 'Come on!' he hisses. 'Fucking leg it!'

The five of us run as quietly as possible towards the narrow door. Hippy reaches it first, Rat Girl close behind him. Taffy and I bring up the rear. I feel a sharp tug on the sleeping bag trailing behind me.

'Fucking hell!' Taffy almost shouts. There's a clattering sound and something whacks me on the back of my leg. I whirl around. Taffy's lying sprawled on the ground, face contorted in pain. His crutches are out of his reach. Shit, shit, shit. Should I leave him?

Sage is almost at the door. 'Sage!' I hiss. She turns round and gasps in shock. Hippy and Rat Girl pause and then disappear into the stairwell. Sage dumps her bag by the door and scoots over to me. 'Go!' I say. 'There's no point both of us being caught. I'll help him.'

Taffy's still crawling on the ground, trying to reach his crutches. One of them has skittered under a car. Sage opens her mouth as if to protest.

'Go, Sage! Go tell Bob. He'll know what to do.' She hesitates, then grabs my sleeping bag and runs for the door.

I'm too scared to even glance in the direction of the exit ramp. It's impossible they didn't hear us. Lying on my front, I grab the elusive crutch and pass it to Taffy. With a monumental effort he pulls himself upright. His face has lost its normal ruddy look and his eyes are crazed with panic and pain. Pound coin-sized spots of blood plop out of his lacerated stump and spatter the concrete.

'What the fuck are we going to do?' I whisper. What the hell *can* we do? They must have seen us.

'Hide.'

I grab his bag and my rucksack and help him crawl behind a station wagon at the end of a row. I hold my breath. My heart feels as if it's going to explode in my chest. Taffy glances at me, eyes still glazed with pain, and puts a finger to his lips. God, I wish I was pissed. I was nowhere near this scared when Hervé and I were nabbed at the Pompidou. I hear voices coming from what sounds like right in front of where we're cowering. Stern, male, police-like voices. I squeeze my eyes shut, cross the fingers on both hands and let my breath hiss out through my teeth. Taffy taps my arm. As quietly as he can he lifts his bag over his shoulder and motions for me to do the same. The voices are fainter now.

It sounds as if they've retreated to the level where we were sleeping.

Taffy positions his crutches under his armpits and slings his bag round his neck. God knows how he thinks he's going to have time to pull himself up and head down the stairwell before the cops catch up with us.

'Ready?' he whispers.

I nod.

He points towards the front of the car park. Eh? What's he on about? 'Shouldn't we leg it down the stairs after Hippy and Sage?' I whisper.

'Nah. I'll never make it. I'm crap at stairs. After five, you ready?'

Am I? I've never tried to run with a bloody rucksack on my back before. Doesn't look like I've got much choice. I suppose I can always ditch it if the going gets too tough.

'. . . Three, two, one, go!'

Taffy heaves himself up, wobbles dangerously, and then he's off. I ignore the thump of the rucksack on my back and race after him. I've forgotten how fast he can move, and it takes all my strength to keep up with him. I'm certain I can hear feet pounding after us, but I don't dare look back. We fly through the never-ending rows of cars and hare up the slope. There's a scary second when it looks like Taffy's going to lose his balance, but he rights himself and then we're out into the sunlight.

'Don't fucking stop!' Taffy yells.

I'm too out of breath to answer, and my eyes are finding it hard to adjust to the blast of natural light. We zigzag past a couple of early morning delivery men, and without even looking, dash across the boulevard. I hear a screech of brakes and a cacophony of loud angry French, but focus all my attention on Taffy's back. When we reach the other side of the road I risk a look back. The Blues' van is parked at an angle close to the kerb near the St Michel fountain. A few policemen are gathered there, gesticulating in our direction. It's the first time I've seen a Blues policeman in the flesh. Is it my imagination, or are they bigger and fitter than the normal police?

Taffy also pauses and turns round.

'Christ, Taffy,' I breathe. 'That was close.'

'Yeah,' he says to me. Then he yells, 'Hey! Motherfuckers!' and gives the cops the finger. Bad move. They look as if they're readying themselves to chase after us. We don't stop to check.

We scream down the narrow cobbled street in front of us. I'm not looking where I'm going and slam into a man heading towards us. Both of us are spun round by the force of the impact, but I manage to extricate myself like a dancer ditching her partner, and force my legs to carry on. Taffy's now way ahead of me, but I spot him disappearing round a corner.

'Come on!' I hiss to myself, and gritting my teeth, I thrust myself forward with a last burst of speed. Taffy grabs my arms as I reach him and pulls me into an alcove outside a restaurant. We crouch down behind a pair of large green bins that reek of old fish and rot. All I can hear is the blood pumping in my ears. I don't want to move, but within seconds Taffy is pulling me to my feet.

'Taffy?' I say, unable to keep the wobble out of my voice. 'You sure it's cool?'

He doesn't answer, but hobbles to the end of the alleyway. He turns round and gives me the thumbs up signal. *Oh thank fuck.* I sink to my haunches and take in a large gulp of air.

'Fuck, that was close,' he sighs. 'And Jesus, will you look at my fucking leg?'

The bottom of his trouser leg is black with blood. He gingerly rolls the fabric over the wound. The scab at the end of his stump is hanging by a thread of crusty flesh. I'm too relieved at our narrow escape to feel sick at the sight of it. I pull a pair of tights out of my bag and use them to staunch the blood flow.

'I'm going to fucking kill Hippy,' Taffy growls. 'This is all his fucking fault. I told the bastard to wake us up before the fucking pigs searched the car parks.'

I breathe an inner sigh of relief. At least he's not blaming me. After all, it had been my sleeping bag he slipped on.

'Let's get a move on,' Taffy says, grabbing the tights out of my hand and chucking them in the bin next to us. 'I've got to teach Hippy a lesson and I need to find my girl.'

It takes me a second to realise he means Sage.

SAGE

Poem for Alex

He blocked up our bog
He loathed all things Frog
He liked to sing songs
And always he ponged
But he was our friend
And that is the end.

(Can't think of a rhyme for bananas, so had to leave that out, sorry)

Oh dear. RIP Alex, or Smelly as he was known in Tramp Code language.

Vicks is dead upset. She's never known anyone who's died before. I have. I found my granddad in his flat when I was ten. He'd died in his sleep. He looked all grey but didn't smell or anything.

Anyway, the whole Alex dying thing wasn't gross or anything (thank God), and none of us even knew he'd pegged it until Bob tried to wake him up in the morning and Alex didn't move. Me and Vicks had already left for the coffee run by then, so we didn't see any of the gory stuff. He went in his sleep (like Granddad),' which Bob said 'was how he would have wanted it'. And if you ask me, that's quite a nice way to go. Much better than drowning in your own phlegm or being murdererd or something foul like that. Like I said, Vicks was still really upset though, even when I explained this to her. I wasn't that sad. I mean, Alex was one of the posse, but he wasn't like our best friend or anything.

I asked Bob if his body was going to be sent back to Scotland, but he says no. No one can afford it, and anyway he hasn't got any family there, Bob says, except a wife who hasn't spoken to him in like twenty years. His kid lives in New Zealand or somewhere crap like that.

Poor old Bob, though. But I think part of him is sneakily relieved. I reckon Alex cramped his style a bit. Like friends do sometimes (i.e. Natalie-the-bitch for example).

I was really glad that me and Vicks had scarpered by the time they discovered he was stiff, 'cos Bob had to move his body out of the gardens, so that the normal cops or ambulance people wouldn't know we slept there and tell the Blues to put our spot on the tramp checklist.

Bob and Norbert moved him out of the bushes before the tourists started arriving and propped him on a bench in the park on the other side of the cathedral, so it looked like he'd kicked the bucket while watching the river. No wonder Bob was so freaked out. I hope Alex didn't have rigor mortis when they moved him. I didn't ask. Seemed a bit insensitive, although I was dying to know.

Just after it happened Vicks was like, 'I'll never be able to sleep in the gardens again.' But she's fine now. Mainly because that night we all had a wake for Alex in the gardens and we all got pissed and passed out there. Loads of different types of tramps came (even the scummy ones) and everyone told an Alex story. Me and Vicks told the one about the crabs on the bus, and instead of being sad, everyone laughed, although I did see Bob crying a bit.

Mind you, I could see Vicks's point in a way. I mean, imagine if Alex's spirit is still in the bushes and he becomes like the ghost of Notre Dame tramp city? You know, like 'This is a banana hold-up woooooooooo. Giz us yer money or a bottle of whisky, or I'll haunt yer, wooooooo'. (Sorry, Gladys, that wasn't very nice. Or funny.)

That's the only tragic piece of news I have. The rest is pretty positive, I think.

Let's see . . .

Oh shit, yeah!! Remember how I said that I'd never be a beggar? Ha ha! Yeah right!!

Begging is our new job. It's dead easy but it totally fucking sucks. I can see that people think I'm some kind of waster and it's horrible if they don't give you money for ages. Vicks is much better at it than me (even though I know she hates it just as much as I do) and she hasn't figured out that I don't stay at my begging post for long. Ha ha. I sneak off round the corner soon as she goes off to her own spot.

She's making quite a lot. Enough for us to buy acid from vile drug dealer Dakota and his crap Alsatian almost every day, which is our new fun!! Vicks didn't want to try it at first, but now she's totally into it. We can only afford half a tab each, but so what? It's almost becoming like a routine with us. Vicks begs until we get enough to buy food, fags and a tab, and then we head off to the Gare du Nord and it's party time.

I love taking acid with Vicks. The whole time we're tripping it's like we're on the same wavelength, and it's like this long giggling frenzy where we hardly have to say a word to each other because we already know what the other one's thinking. And we have a good laugh trying it out in all different places: inside, outside, on the escalators in the Pompidou, during the day, at night, etc, etc, etc. One time we sat knee to knee and just stared into each other's eyes and we had to keep saying what the other one was thinking. And guess what?? We were nearly always right!! It's almost like the old days before bastards started interfering with our friendship. Yesterday we dared each other to trip inside those funny space-agey public bog cubicles they have on the pavement. It's a dead weird feeling when you go in there, Gladys. The walls close in on you, and we take it in turns to see who can stand it the longest. Vicks always wins.

But night-time tripping is my favourite. Paris is dead wicked at night. I love it when the lights next to the river go all blurry and gooey. I can sit and watch them for hours. Vicks says we should walk down to the Eiffel Tower tomorrow and see what it looks like on acid. But neither of us likes going on the Metro when we're tripping. Vicks says she feels like she's being swallowed by a huge snake and the whooshing noise of the train coming into the station sounds too loud and scary, so we'll have to make sure we get there before the acid kicks in properly.

Sometimes Taffy and smack-head Hippy come with us when we head off to Dakota. Taffy's such a tosshead. He keeps trying to mess with mine and Vicks's friendship because he thinks this will give him a better chance of getting into my pants. WANKER. He's always going on about how Vicks has got something going with Stefan and Danny Tea Cosy. What he doesn't know is that when it comes to spying on people, I am the champion. He must think I'm really thick. I know full well what she gets up to when she disappears off with them. Although fuck knows why she won't tell me about it. I've decided not to sulk about it though, mostly because, like I say, me and Vicks are hanging out a lot on our own, taking acid and that, and Richard the git is completely out of the picture.

Anyway, the extra cash she makes comes in handy and she always buys me a Babybel and a packet of fags when she gets back from hanging out with them, and says stupid things like, 'Oh look, I found some extra cash at the bottom of my pocket!!' Duh! Plus, the one time I'd spied on her I'd felt quite proud of what she was up to.

Ironic to think I'd only followed her that day because I thought she was sneaking off with Richard git-face, so it was a big relief when I saw what she was actually doing. At first, I was dead confused. I was hiding behind a magazine stand when she met up with Stefan and Danny and I'd shadowed them to a cafe in Les Halles. Stefan and Danny were carrying these big long sticks and old Coke bottles filled with clear liquid, and I couldn't figure out what the fuck they were going to do with them. Then, Danny faces the cafe and starts babbling this big spiel, which obviously I couldn't understand because it was all in Frog. Then, Stefan took a big gulp out of the Coke bottle, lit the end of the stick and blew into the flame and it looked like fire was blasting out of his mouth! Meanwhile, Vicks trotted up and down in front of them with a hat, doing their bottling. Bit of a con, obviously. I mean how hard can it be to spit petrol or paraffin onto a stick and pretend it's fire-eating?!

I'm really not that bothered if she wants to go and help them out, honest, Gladys. There's no way she'd have anything to do with Stefan, Stig of the Dump. He's like the dirtiest person alive. And Danny's not bad as far as Frogs go. He's like a French version of Bob, although he does look at Vicks in an old man pervy way sometimes, which creeps me out a bit. And he's always pissed. But who isn't??

So fuck Taffy for trying to interfere in the friendship. As if I wouldn't know exactly what Vicks was up to!! What sort of a friend does he think I am? And he beat the crap out of Hippy after the Blues Experience, which shows what an utter utter bastard he is anyway.

Vicks and I are still paranoid about being picked up by the Blues. I just know that if they put us in the cells we'd end up three stones lighter and with bald heads like those concentration camp women in the photos at school. Bob says they don't arrest tramps who have dogs. Apparently it's too much trouble and the cops can't be bothered dealing with a scammy tramp and a dog at the same time. Explains why so many tramps have dogs, though.

Vicks says she's going to ask Stefan if he'll rent bad-tempered little bastard Ralphie out to us so that we can work inside Paris instead of having to head out into the crappy old suburbs. We're always getting thrown off the RER, and sometimes if we're really unlucky the ticket guy will chuck us off at every stop, so it can take bloody hours to get home. It would be dead good if we didn't have to do that any more.

Ow! Sore hand. Not used to writing so much these days. What else can I tell you??

Oh, yeah . . . Even though we're rich now and can buy a pack of fags each every day, we've got a new emergency place to bum fags if we decide to spend the cash on other things (i.e. more acid) Guess where, Gladys?: the Rue St Denis where the prozzies work! The prozzies are dead friendly now they've got to know us a bit, although most of them (except the trannie at the end of the street) can't speak English. They call Vicki '*Mignon*' or something, which Vicki says means 'cute'! Vicks said Stefan introduced her to a few of them on the first day she disappeared with him and Danny.

But what I can't figure out is this: are we lower or higher status-wise than the prostitutes? I mean, if we're bumming fags from prozzies, what does it make us?

WHO CARES!!!!

So, as you can see nothing crap to report, Gladys. Oh shit – apart from Alex dying, of course. (Whoops. Forgot for a sec, how bad is that?)

VICKI:

The Somerset Maugham Experience

If I eat another mouthful of the Royale burger in front of me I'm going to puke. The 'special sauce' has congealed into a rubbery skin over the bun, and I'd rather eat Soylent Green than bite into the ice-cold patties again. I take a sip of chemical milkshake instead and stuff a few wooden chips into my mouth. The woman sitting opposite me narrows her eyes as I bravely pick up a tiny piece of lettuce and add it to the sawdust mixture in my mouth. My eyes tear up with the effort of swallowing it down.

'You are not hungry?' she says.

'Of course I am,' I lie. 'I just like to eat slowly.'

She glances at her watch. We've been in here for twenty minutes. I don't tell her that it's the third McShite meal I've eaten in less than an hour and that there's no way I can cram any more food down unless she takes me to get my stomach pumped. Why doesn't she just sod off? My heart sank when she approached Ralphie and me outside. I knew straight away she was one of those do-gooders who wouldn't give me cash in case I spent it on drugs (which, let's face it, is exactly what I would have done).

I dip another drooping chip in a smidgen of mayonnaise and take a tiny bite. It's the last time I'll bloody well beg outside a McShite. I've practically eaten my way through the menu this morning. Although I've made a fairly good haul cash-wise, passers-by keep taking my 'me and my dog are hungry' sign literally. Ralphie and I had barely sat down this morningbefore the first do-gooder plonked down a cheese-burger meal without a word. We shared it quickly before too many punters noticed. Then, half an hour later a pervy-looking guy handed me a couple of burgers and an apple pie and hung around while I pretended to be grateful. He'd only bug-gered off when he tried to stroke Ralphie and nearly lost one of his fingers. But this do-gooder is much more persistent. She insisted on following me into the restaurant, and we've barely exchanged a word since. I don't think we have too much in common. It's impossible to miss the oversized cross peeking from underneath her blouse, and she's dressed in off-duty nun clothes: drab beige skirt and lace-up shoes.

It's not as if I was even hungry in the first place. The acid Sage and I shared last night is still making my stomach clench. In fact, I haven't felt like eating since we started our acid experiments. I've been surviving on synthetic-tasting crème caramels and Sage is sticking to her diet of Babybel cheese and the occasional Latin Quarter kebab.

The woman sighs impatiently and looks meaningfully down at my tray. I glance out of the window to check on Ralphie. Since I tied him to the railings outside he hasn't stopped barking and snarling at the passers-by. At least there's little chance of him being nicked. I don't know how I'd explain that to Stefan. In exchange for bottling for his and Danny's fire-eating show, Stefan lends me Ralphie every so often. It's made all the difference in the world to me and Sage. Not only do the French love dogs, and so are more inclined to part with their dosh, it means we can beg in Paris, which is far more lucrative than the scummy old suburbs. Sage and I have even consid-ered getting our own puppy, to 'expand our business' as Sage calls it.

But sod this for a game of soldiers. I have to get out of here.

'*Toilette,*' I say, getting up and nodding in the direction of the loos.

The woman tuts. She probably thinks I'm going to shoot up in there or something.

I push through the swing doors that lead into the ladies. There's a mirror behind the door, and as usual it's a shock catching sight of my reflection. It's one of the things I still can't get used to about living rough. I didn't realise how often I checked my appearance when I was at home (or even at Hervé's place or our Nausicaa room), so when I see myself these days it's like being confronted by a stranger. I don't look too bad, all things considered, although my pupils are dilated and my eyes are sore from lack of sleep. Sage and I have tried to be good and leave a couple of days between trips, but for the last week we've been on a bit of a binge.

I lean in closer to check my face close-up. My skin and lips still feel a tad scorched from yesterday's fire-eating experiment, but they look normal. The only thing out of place is a plop of mayonnaise lurking at the corner of my mouth like one of Hippy's zits.

I still haven't told Sage about my extra-curricular activities with Stefan and Danny, although she must suspect something's up. I keep having to come up with excuses for why I disappear for a while, but as she spends most afternoons at the music library, it hasn't been too difficult to get away with it. Fortunately, the shows Danny and Stefan put on never take long. Fuck, if anyone had told me I'd be a fire-eater one day I'd have told them they were crazy. Danny says they always make more money when I'm with them. He's come up with a bullshit story for the punters about how we're all one big happy circus family. Stefan and I are supposed to be his kids who are desperately trying to keep the family together. It works like a treat, although apart from our dreadlocks we couldn't look more different, especially as

Stefan is mixed race and all. The punters seem to love the sob story though.

Yesterday, Danny convinced me to have a go, as he said it would be a real draw if the whole family could get in on the act. I shouldn't have done it really. I could smell the alcohol on his breath and it was obvious he was more pissed than usual. Stefan hadn't looked too keen, but played along. I was terrified. But it wasn't as though I was being asked to master rocket science, was it? I mean, how hard could gobbing a mouthful of flammable liquid into the air be? Way bloody harder than I'd expected, as it turned out. The white spirit tasted awful and I'd had to hold it in my mouth for ages while Danny went through his spiel and Stefan put on his little show. The trick is to blow the liquid out of your mouth as hard as possible, but the temptation to swallow is huge. I was paranoid that I'd accidentally breathe in, and that my lungs and throat would sizzle and burn to a crisp like overdone bacon. I held the fire stick as far away from my face as possible and, after counting to ten, spat the liquid out as if I was projectile vomiting. The flame felt far too close, although I could see it was much smaller than the flourishes of fire Danny and Stefan usually manage. I obviously looked like I was shitting myself, and as soon as it was done, I grabbed a glass of Coke off someone's table and glugged it down. It was dead embarrassing. I'd had to wash my face and hands for ages in the Pompidou loos to get rid of the smell of white spirit and charcoal, and I must have drunk three litres of Orangina to get rid of the taste. Danny thought it was hilarious, but Stefan babbled something in French which I think meant 'stick to what you know.'

I leave the bathroom as quietly as I can, pushing the door gently so that its hinges don't squeal. The nun woman is still sitting at the table when I emerge, but sod her. I'm out of here. Head down, I race towards the glass doors and push my way out into the fresh air. As I untie Ralphie's lead I glance at the window. She's staring at me, and I can make out her disapproving expression. I'm tempted to give her the finger, but settle for a rueful 'what did you expect' smile and a shrug instead. She was trying to help, I suppose. Although why do people like that have to be so judgemental? Like Sage says, it's *our* business what we do with the cash people give us. We've come up with this theory that beggers are necessary because they make people feel good about themselves when they donate money.

I head round the corner to where Sage is waiting for me. She's on Blues lookout duty most of the time these days, and leaves the begging up to me on the whole. I've offered to let her have Ralphie so she can have a turn, but he still hasn't taken to her, and Stefan and I are the only two people he doesn't try and maul: Stefan because he's his owner; me, because I always have a supply of chocolate on hand.

'Fuck, Vicks,' she says irritably as soon as she catches sight of me. 'You took your bleeding time.'

'Yeah, I know. Bloody ex-nun or something made me go into McShite with her. I'm so full I could burst all over the pavement.'

Sage grimaces. 'So? How'd we do?'

'About sixty, I think,' I say, jangling the coins in my pockets. 'Maybe more.'

'Nice one,' she says. 'Home James?'

As we walk towards the Metro, Sage pauses to bum a fag off a passing, suave-looking businessman. We can afford to buy our own cigs now, but sometimes we regress back to the old ways for fun. Occasionally we even go to the soup kitchen, but it's mostly to catch up on the tramp gossip. I can't remember the last time I ate a can of butter beans. We stroll past the tourists queuing for tickets and hop over the turnstiles. I let go of Ralphie's lead and he runs between our legs. He knows the routine by now. We're in luck, a train whooshes to meet us as soon as we reach the platform. As the doors hiss closed, I spy a band of cops heading down the stairs. Excellent timing. Sage and I make ourselves comfortable on a double seat, putting our feet up on the bench opposite. Ralphie leaps up onto my lap and nuzzles the pocket where I keep his bribe chocolate. A couple of *clochards* that we know by sight get on at the next stop and nod at us. One of them starts accosting passengers for cash, all the while spouting a hard-done-by spiel. We've never dared work the Metro. It's a sure-fire way of getting Blued. You never know when a posse of cops will turn up, so it's the begging equivalent of playing Russian roulette. Sage lights a cigarette, ignoring our fellow passengers' scowls. Sage calls anyone who's not a *clochard* a 'civilian' and says they're beneath our contempt. She's got a point. They all go off to work and their boring lives, wheras we can do whatever we like, all day, every day, if we choose.

The panhandling *clochards* jump off at the next stop, and Sage passes them her half-smoked cigarette before the door closes behind them.

'What shall we do this afternoon, then?' Sage asks as we pull into St Michel. I shrug, using the excuse of collecting Ralphie's lead and ushering him onto the platform not to answer her. I haven't told her that I've promised to meet Stefan this afternoon. When I collected Ralphie this morning he'd asked me to meet him outside Notre Dame. He wouldn't say why, just that he had a surprise for me. God knows what he's planning. Since we've been working together he seems to have taken the 'circus family' bullshit literally, and acts as if I'm his little sister or something. Sage still calls him Stig, but treats him with more respect than Richard. I'll have to use the usual excuse of returning Ralphie and hope she won't want to come with me. I don't want Sage to spoil whatever Stefan's got planned with one of her sulks.

We head straight for the fountain so Ralphie can drink.

Sage lights us both a fag and we sit down for a breather on the low stone wall. A group of older *clochards* greet us, and Sage chucks them a couple of cigarettes.

'All right, girls?' a familiar voice calls.

Sage mouths 'fuck' at me as Taffy swings himself towards us, Rat Girl and Hippy sloping along behind him. Sage slips her fags into her pocket so that she won't have to offer them around. Taffy nods a cursory 'hello' to me and turns his attention to Sage.

'What's going on?' he asks.

'Nothing much. Usual.'

I smile at Rat Girl and Hippy. We still don't know Rat Girl's name, and I've hardly said a word to her except for the usual stoned mumblings when we share a joint. Thinking about it, it's the first time I've seen her in daylight. I always associate her with night-time dope smoking escapades as if she's a drugged-up vampire or something. As usual I have to will myself not to stare at the never-healing sore on her cheek. Why doesn't she do something about it? It hasn't even scabbed over yet. Maybe she picks it. Gross. Hippy's looking as maudlin as ever. There are dark circles under his eyes.

'How's your leg, Taffy?' I ask.

'Not bad,' he says, without taking his eyes off Sage. 'Wanna see?'

'No thanks,' I say quickly. I've had my fill of dealing with Taffy's war wounds. There are still traces of his blood on my rucksack from our run-in with the Blues at the car park.

'What you up to?' he says to Sage.

'What's it to you?'

'We're on our way to Dakota, wanna come?' Sage's eyes light up.

'I'd better get Ralphie back to Stefan,' I say. 'Sage, why don't you go with them?'

She glances at me suspiciously. I drop my head and pretend to untangle Ralphie's lead.

'Yeah, Sage, we'll have a laugh,' Taffy says.

'What*ever*,' Sage snorts.

How much abuse can one man take? He still hasn't given up hope, which is bizarre as he gave up on me after a couple of days. Sage has been giving him the cold shoulder for weeks, but it just seems to egg him on. He's tried to corner me on a couple of occasions for advice. All I ever tell him is 'don't call her "love".'

Ralphie spies Rat Girl's rat, which has squirmed its way out of her jacket and is nestled on her shoulder, nibbling at her hair. He starts barking and yipping and jumping at her legs and I have to yank him away.

'Here,' I say, thrusting a bunch of coins into Sage's hand. 'Go get yourself a tab, and I'll catch up with you later. I'd better get him out of here.'

'Thanks, Mum,' she snaps, but she takes the money and gets to her feet.

'I'll meet you later!' I call as she and the others head down the steps to the Metro. She doesn't look back. I'm flooded with guilty relief.

'Right, Ralphie, let's walk.'

I'm beginning to feel a tinge of excitement at the prospect of Stefan's surprise. I hope it's nothing to eat; the burgers are still sitting heavily in my stomach. We head towards the kiosk for Lucky Strikes and more Ralphie bribe chocolate. I check the watch. Still early. Should I grab a coffee or just head to the bench in front of the cathedral?

I'm dithering at the crossing when I feel someone tapping my shoulder. I whirl round and come face to face with Richard.

'*Café?*' he asks.

As both of us are stalwart members of the Pompidou Posse, it's impossible not to bump into him occasionally, and as little as a week ago I'd have jumped at the chance to go for coffee with him. But now I can't remember why I even fancied him in the first place. Nan was right about men with moustaches being weirdos.

'*Non merci.* I have to meet Stefan.' Richard's face falls as I bid him a cheery '*au revoir*,' an enormous grin spreading across my face.

I collapse on an empty bench and Ralphie immediately jumps onto my lap and snuggles into a ball. I stroke his head. I'm becoming quite fond of him. Although I'd never dare tell her this, he reminds me of Sage. It's probably the little out-of-proportion legs and snappy personality combination.

As I watch the tourists streaming in and out of the cathedral my eyelids droop. Sage and I barely slept last night. That's the other thing about the acid. It's impossible to get any kip until it's worn off.

The sound of running feet jolts me awake. I grab Ralphie's lead and tense my body, ready to leg it. The Blues often patrol this area, and although I have my dog insurance, I'm still on high alert. But it's only Danny and Bob. What are they doing here? I search the smattering of tourists around me for any sign of Stefan. Shit. I hope nothing's happened.

'What's going on?' I say as they reach my bench.

'Wait and see!' Although he's out of breath, Bob looks cheerful for a change. He's been a right miserable bastard since Alex died.

'Wait and see what?'

Danny grins and nods towards where Stefan is legging it towards us, something bulky in his arms. As he gets closer, I realise it's a cardboard box.

Ralphie yips excitedly as Stefan plonks the box down at my feet. For a second I can only stare at it.

'Bloody hell.' It's full of books. 'Where the hell did you get these from?'

Bob chuckles. 'Outside the English bookshop.'

'What, you bought them?'

Bob looks at me as if I'm crazy. 'Of course not. Stefan nicked a box from outside and just walked off with it. It's a gift for you.'

Of course. Tramp Shopping.

Danny and Stefan are looking at me expectantly. I jump up and throw my arms round Stefan. Ralphie yelps as he's dumped unceremoniously on the ground. '*Merci*!' Stefan hugs me back, and before I can do anything about it, he's pressed his mouth to mine and I can feel his tongue snaking into my mouth. I have just enough time to think: thank God Sage isn't here, before I kiss him back. His arms are incredibly strong and he squeezes my waist and lifts me off my feet. For a minute I forget all about his crap skin and dirty jeans.

When I disentangle myself, Danny and Bob are grinning at us like proud parents.

'How did you know I was desperate for books?' I ask Bob.

He shrugs. 'Sage mentioned it. I was going to ask Richard to do it, but then Stefan offered.'

I hug Bob and Danny as well, before getting on my knees and rummaging through the box. I can't wait to see what's in there.

I roll over on my back and stretch contentedly. It's been one of the best afternoons ever, full of 'money shot life moments'. Stefan, Ralphie and I had found a small empty park where we'd made ourselves comfortable on the grass. Ralphie curled himself into my side and Stefan stroked my back or dozed as I devoured the book of Somerset Maugham short stories I'd unearthed from the box. As the afternoon wore on, Stefan kissed me briefly, gestured for me to watch Ralphie and disappeared. I'd barely noticed his absence. He returned with both our bags, a couple of kebabs and a can of dog food for Ralphie.

The worst part of the afternoon had been deciding which books to keep. The box obviously contained the shop's bargain selection. Most of the books were dog-eared and many of them were dire. Not that I cared less. I was so desperate for words, I would've read a Mills & Boon if it'd been on offer. I settled on four: The Maugham short stories; a non-fiction book on serial killers for Sage; *That was Then, This is Now* by S.E Hinton; and a bizarre book of stories about haunted cats. The rest – mostly westerns and 1930s pulp fiction – I'd left regretfully in the box. I made a mental note to return it to the shop before they opened tomorrow, although they probably hadn't missed it.

I read until the light fades and I can no longer see the words on the page. For the last half an hour I've been vaguely aware that Stefan's been staring at me intently.

As I reluctantly close my book of short stories, he pulls me to my feet.

'*Viens,*' he says, leading me towards the Notre Dame gardens. What the hell. He deserves it.

'You hear that, Stefan?' I sit bolt upright, nearly braining myself on a branch.

'*Quoi?*'

There's a rustling in the bushes as if someone's fighting their way towards us. Ralphie starts barking.

'Shit!' I hiss, grabbing my clothes and yanking my dress over my head. 'Stefan, *vite!*' Christ, I hope it's not the cops. I don't want to be shoved in the back of a police van half-naked.

'Vicki! Vicki! Where the fuck are you? Are you in here?'

I'd recognise that voice anywhere. What the hell does Taffy want? His ginger head pokes through the foliage just as I'm wriggling into my leggings.

'What the fuck, Taffy?'

Stefan looks at me in confusion. He's also throwing on his clothes.

'It's Sage!' Taffy yells. 'She's totally freaking out. You gotta come before the cops nab her.'

'What do you mean, freaking out? Have you pissed her off or something?'

'No! Look, just hurry will you? I've been bleeding well looking for you everywhere!'

'*Que s'est-il passé?*' Stefan asks.

I do my best to explain that my friend is in trouble as I push my feet into my Docs. Thankfully Stefan gets the drift and motions me to follow Taffy, signalling that he'll bring my bag along with his. The bushes whip and scratch my arms as I fly out after Taffy. What the hell could have happened? Has she picked a fight with the wrong person? My heart's thudding in my chest as I leg it past the cathedral, race across the road and head through the streets that will eventually link up with the warren of alleyways surrounding the Pompidou. I have to stop for a second to catch my breath; a stitch knifes my side.

Taffy waves me down the street that leads to the sculpture pond. 'Where the fuck is she?' I gasp.

'Over there. Look.'

I make out Sage's bent-headed figure sitting with her back to us on the far side of the metal wall surrounding the pond. The streetlights from the church opposite don't provide much light, but it's unmistakably her. Someone is sitting next to her, and Hippy is fidgeting in front of them.

There's a thump of feet behind us as Stefan arrives, barely

221

breathing hard at all – impressive considering he's carrying both our bags and dragging Ralphie.

'Sage?' I call. She doesn't look up, but as I get closer I recognise Rat Girl's sleek bobbed hair next to her.

I don't know what I was expecting, but it wasn't this. There's a bunch of sticks and leaves on Sage's lap, and she's pushing them around and seems to be counting them. She's mumbling under her breath.

'Sage?' I sit next to her and gently shake her arm. 'Sage? It's me, Vicks.'

'Vicki?' She looks up at me. Fuck. Even in the dim light I can see that her pupils are wildly dilated and her skin has the unnatural pallor of a Madame Tussaud's figure. She looks as if someone has siphoned the blood out of her body.

I'm finding it hard to swallow. 'Sage, what's going on?'

'Vicki!' She grabs my hand hard enough to hurt. Her palm is clammy and cold. 'You have to help me. Where are the tablets, Vicks? Count the tablets. Quickly, quick, count the tablets, count them, how many are there, I—'

'It's okay, Sage,' I say, my voice is trembling. 'It's okay.'

'Have you got them, I can't fucking find them, where are they?'

I look over at Taffy. 'What's she talking about, Taffy?'

He shrugs. He's also wasted. He can barely hold my gaze for more than two seconds, and he's wavering on his crutches.

'She has been saying this for more than an hour now,' Rat Girl says to me in perfect English. Despite the worry about Sage, I'm surprised: I've only ever had stilted conversations with her in French.

'What's she taken?' I snap at Taffy.

He shrugs again.

'*Taffy!*'

'It is acid,' Rat Girl says. She pats Sage's hand.

'Vicki,' Sage whispers. 'I think I'm losing it, Vicks. What's happening to me?'

'Shhhh, Sage. You'll be fine. It'll wear off soon, I promise.'

'Will it? But what about my tablets? Where are they, Vicks? Where are they?'

'What tablets, Sage?'

She shakes her head and starts picking at the leaves and twigs again.

'She's had more than just acid,' I shout at Taffy. 'What's this about tablets?'

'How the fuck would I know? Far as I know, all she's taken is acid.'

'You know anything about this, Hippy?'

'Don't ask me,' he slurs. Dead loss. I turn back to Taffy.

'Look at the fucking state of her! She's never been like this before. We take the bloody stuff all the fucking time! She must have had something else.'

'*Non*, he is right,' Rat Girl says. 'I am sure that is all she has taken. She is just having a bad trip.'

I'm relieved to see she doesn't seem to have her rat with her. God knows what Sage would do if she caught sight of it in this state.

Stefan, who's been hovering a few metres away from us, says something in French to Rat Girl. She babbles at him for a bit, obviously telling him what's going on. Ralphie starts barking at her, and with a supportive nod at me, he leads him away.

'But she's usually fine,' I say to Rat Girl, the only one who appears to have her shit together.

'Perhaps she has had more than usual.'

'How many did she take, Taffy?' I'm pretty sure I only gave her enough money for one hit.

'Two, three, maybe?' he whines.

'But where'd she get the cash for that?'

Taffy's eyes slide guiltily away from mine.

'Is she going to be okay?' I ask Rat Girl.

She shrugs. 'I do not know. Perhaps. Or perhaps not.'

Fuck.

SAGE

Holy shit, Gladys!!! So much has happened I can't believe it!! Where to start?

Vicks is dead upset because Stefan (aka Stig of the Dump) has been arrested for breaking and entering and has been locked up. We only learned about it when Vicks disappeared to do her sneaky fire-eating thing, and neither Danny nor Stefan were anywhere to be seen. Danny came and found her later to tell her, and she freaked out. She finally told me about doing their bottling for them (and I had to try and look dead upset and confused about the whole thing as if I didn't know anything about it!) But I can't get my head around why Stefan being in the slammer should upset her so much. She swears nothing was going on with him. Still. Does it matter now, Gladys, seeing as he's out of the picture?

I hope she didn't fucking well sleep with him though. Gross.

Anyway, although this is good news in a way as I get Vicks all to myself again, it's also bad news, because guess who has to look after Ralphie, the miserable snappy bastard dog all the time? Yeah. Us. I was like, 'How come Danny doesn't look after him?' But apparently Vicks is the only one the little bastard doesn't try and bite and Danny doesn't want to be bothered with him, or something lazy like that. Ralphie hates me, and it's a real pain in the arse looking after him. It's as bad as having a kid around all the time. We have to keep remembering to feed him and buy fucking dog food and fetch water etc, etc. And he's like a shitting machine or something. Vicks had to dump all her new books so she could fit his fucking bowl in her bag, which at least shows she's dedicated, I suppose. Perhaps he'll be like a boyfriend substitute so she won't start falling for Richard's crap again.

Mind you, we're making shitloads of cash with Ralphie around all the time. The Frogs love dogs for some reason. God knows why.

The other major thing is this, Gladys. Never never never never never never again, will I ever take acid!!! That stuff is evil. Thank God Vicks turned up when I was zonked out on it. I have never felt so crap in my life. Even worse than when I flipped out at home and the parents sent me to see bastard Dr Wankenstein. Christ. It was like the whole world was against me, and at one stage I thought I was going mad and that it would never end. Even though it happened ages ago, Vicks still keeps looking at me as if I'm a fucking invalid or something. We've been totally clean since then (apart from getting pissed and a few spliffs, obviously).

But there have been other repercussions (is that how you spell it??) to this . . .

Apparently, when I was babbling on while I was freaking out, I said something about my tablets, and this got Taffy the bastard thinking. He's such a bloody scammy arse! So a couple of days after the Bad Trip Experience he corners me and he's like, 'What's this about tablets and stuff? Are you sick or something?' And I'm like, 'None of your fucking business.' Then he says, "Cos if you are, maybe I can help. All you need is a man in your life!!!' So I say, 'I suppose you mean you,' and he says, 'Why not?' And I'm like, 'Because I'm not blind or mental is why not.' Then his eyes go all crinkly and evil and he says, 'What do you see in her?' and I'm like, 'Who, what you on about?' and he says, 'Vicki, of course.' I'm about to tell him to go fuck himself, when he says, all sneaky, "Cos she's such a slag, isn't she? Shagging Richard and Stefan at the same time?' And I'm like, 'She never slept with either of them, you're just pissed off with her because she doesn't fancy you!' and he looks at me as if to say yeah right. Then he says, 'Are you a lezzer?' and obviously now I'm getting really angry, and I shout, 'Just because I've got short hair doesn't mean I'm gay. Just because you're a Welsh bastard doesn't mean you can sing or eat leeks or whatever it is Welsh people get up to.' And we're just about to have this huge fucking row, when Bob comes up to us, and Taffy mumbles some lame excuse about needing to find Hippy and hops off. What an arsehole!

Since then, we haven't had anything to do with him, although he still gives me funny looks whenever we bump into him.

Otherwise, apart from Stefan, Taffy and dog excitement, Vicks and me are doing really well. She did something hilarious the other day. When you get thrown off the Metro or RER (which happens a lot to us as you know, Gladys) all the ticket inspectors can do ('cos they know we don't have any cash) is write down the name and address of the 'contact in case of an emergency' person you've got written in the back of your passport, so that they can send them the bill. So Vicks has scratched out her nan's address and written, Myra

SARAH LOTZ

Hindley, c/o Holloway Prison!!! Now, every time we get done for riding the trains without a ticket the bill will get sent to evil old Myra!! Ha ha. Serves her right for killing kids and going to jail and having loads of girlfriends inside, when she should have much worse punishments (Vicks knows all about her from reading a book on serial killers that Stefan nicked for her).

Taking a quarter of a tablet a day now, Gladys, and I'm feeling fine. Maybe I'm cured. It would be typical if there was nothing wrong with me in the first place. I'm not worried though. I'm not, honest. I reckon I only flipped out because of the pressure society put on me, which is what Bob goes on about all the time. I don't agree with him about Margaret Thatcher though. He thinks she's some kind of god or something. Weird that he's a tramp, but is also a crap Conservative, ay it? Because in other ways he's the opposite of right-wing bastards like vile brother-in-law Pete. People can be dead fucked up, can't they, Gladys???

Talking of fucked up, after supper yesterday, me and Vicks tried to write limericks (her idea) about all the posse members:

Taffy limerick

There once was a Welsh git named Taffy,
Whose hair was all red and quite crappy,
He fell on his head
As he's minus a leg
And this made all the rest of us happy.

228

Hippy limerick

There once was a tosser named Hippy
Who thought he was clever and witty,
But he's actually thick
And he pongs quite a bit,
And he thinks that the Welsh git is pretty.

Then we got bored. But it's *typical* of Vicks to nick my poem idea.

VICKI:

The Axe Experience

'Yer all going to fooking die, you bastards! Gaaaaaahh!'

I can actually hear the breath whoosh out of Bob as Taffy slams his crutch down onto his curled-up figure. The light-weight sleeping bag Bob's cowering in can't provide much protection, and I wince and squeeze my eyes shut. Next to me Sage is desperately trying to wriggle out of her sleeping bag. I'm trying to do the same, but my limbs have gone numb. Plus, I'm holding onto Ralphie's collar with one hand, which makes the manoeuvre almost impossible. He's whining and wriggling and trying to reach Taffy. I clamp my hand over his muzzle to shut him up. The rest of the posse are still snuggled in their sleeping bags like giant shiny slugs, their bleary-eyed faces registering incomprehension at this unexpected wake-up call.

As I finally manage to kick the slippery fabric off my legs I catch sight of Richard and Norbert trying to ease themselves out of their own bags without attracting Taffy's attention.

Everything suddenly goes quiet – eerily so. Even Ralphie has stopped struggling and trying to nip at my hand. The dawn light is hazy and the bushes cast deep shadows, but it's not hard to see what's unfolding.

'Hippy!' Sage screams, shattering the silence. 'Where the fuck are you? Taffy's going fucking mental here!'

'Hippy,' Taffy spits out. 'Hippy, Hippy, Hippy, Hippy, Hippy, Hippy, Hippy. *Fuck* Hippy!'

Oh shit. His dead eyes fixed on us, Taffy's hopping our way, lifting his crutch as high as he can over his head. There's no way he can balance like that, surely? He wobbles but then rights himself.

'Vicks, cover your head,' Sage shouts. She's extricated herself from her own sleeping bag, but she won't have time to get to her feet before Taffy lashes out. I grab Ralphie's wriggling body as tightly as possible and curl myself into a ball, wrapping the sleeping bag around us. Ralphie writhes and squirms and nips at my arms.

'Bob! Do something!' I shout above Ralphie's whines and yelps.

'Taffy,' Bob calls half-heartedly, but it's too late.

The end of the crutch smacks into my back. The sleeping bag cushions it a little, but the force is vicious enough to make me grunt and lose my grip on Ralphie. 'Ralphie!' I yell. 'Sage! Get him!'

Ignoring the dull ache in my back, I scramble onto my hands and knees. Ralphie's trying to snap at Taffy's laces, and it's only a matter of time before he'll get whacked by the wildly swinging crutch. Then, Taffy chucks the crutch onto the ground and hurls himself past me into the bushes, his booted foot narrowly missing slamming into my stomach. Sage grabs the dog by the scruff of his neck as he tries to chase after Taffy.

'Quick!' She hauls me to my feet, and thrusts Ralphie into my arms. 'He's gone. Let's leg it out of here!'

'What do you mean, gone?'

I look to my right, catching a tantalising glimpse of orange street lights through the tree branches. They look safe and comforting and far away, and I desperately want to be there. There's a rustling sound in front of me, and I spot Richard disappearing into the gloom. Norbert and Bob are also readying themselves for a quick getaway.

'Yer all fucking dead!' Taffy shouts. It sounds like he's inches behind me, but that's impossible, isn't it? I whirl around.

'What the *fuck*?' Sage's eyes look ready to pop out of her head. Taffy's thrashing his way towards us, and instead of his crutch, he's now clutching an axe. He's perilously close to Sage, and she has to jump back to leap out of his path. Oh Christ! Where did he get that? Then I remember the maintenance shed at the end of the gardens. Some bastard must have forgotten to lock it.

'Let's get the hell out of here!' Bob yells, throwing himself into the bushes without a glance backwards. Norbert is crawling on his hands and knees as if he doesn't have the strength to stand.

It's obvious who Taffy's next target will be. Ignoring Sage and me, Taffy steels himself to throw his body in Norbert's direction. The poor bastard is now cowering on the ground, hands over his head.

Hippy crashes through the bushes behind us, his eyes wide and glassy. 'Taffy!'

Taffy stops dead and turns his blank stare back to us.

'What's he taken?' I fire at Hippy.

'Christ knows, we got a bunch of tabs from Dakota and he just started freaking out!'

It's the most I've ever heard Hippy say. 'Oh shit, oh shit, oh shit,' Hippy whines, eyes fixed to the axe that's swinging around like a demented pendulum. 'This is not happening!'

'Yes, it fucking is!' Sage says. As Taffy hops towards us, Sage drops to the ground and lashes out with her right leg. It connects with his knee and he overbalances and falls backwards. The axe lands somewhere behind him.

'Gaaaaahhhhh!' Taffy yells. 'Yer all fucking dead!' He scrabbles around behind him for his weapon.

'Bob, Richard, Norbert!' I shriek, 'Help us out here!'

There's no answer. Now Hippy is backing away.

'You fucking cowards!' Sage screams into the bushes.

Taffy's desperately trying to right himself, and with a lurch I realise he's managed to get hold of the axe again. I'm not sure I'll have time to push myself out of the bushes with the struggling Ralphie before Taffy gets to his foot. He's blocking the easiest exit route.

'Taffy! Taffy! It's me, Vicki. Taffy, Taffy! Stop it, stop it!' The words pour out of my mouth and I don't think about what I'm saying. 'Taffy, Taffy, it's us, you know us!' He stares at me with the same empty expression. 'Taffy, Taffy, we love you! We *love* you, Taffy!'

Something ignites in his eyes. He drops the axe, looks blearily at Sage, and then, almost matter-of-factly, turns over and throws up.

Sage stares at me, open-mouthed. 'Nice one, Chuck,' she murmurs, as Taffy retches and writhes. 'Let's fuck off before he goes mental again.'

'I don't think there's any danger of that, Sage,' I say. Taffy groans, flops onto his back and passes out, mouth wide open. 'Think he's okay?' I put Ralphie down, gripping his lead tightly in case he makes a run for Taffy's unconscious figure.

Sage walks over to Taffy and kicks his ribs. He makes a grunting sound. 'Yeah,' she says.

'What if he ODs or something, though?'

Sage shrugs. 'Good riddance to bad Welsh rubbish, if you ask me, Vicks.' She sighs at my shocked expression. 'He'll be fine. Look, we'll push him onto his side so that he won't choke if he pukes, but he looks to be breathing okay.' Using her foot, Sage rolls Taffy over, grimacing as his head flops into the puke with a squelch. 'I'll get Hippy to keep an eye on him when we catch up with the cowardly bastard.'

We make our way out of the bushes and into the Notre Dame forecourt for a well-earned fag. The traffic's almost non-existent, and the grass around us is still slick with dew. I can make out the Invisible Man footsteps of the axe attack escapees criss-crossing the lawn in front of our bushes.

Sage clears her throat. 'Don't get me wrong or anything, Vicks, you handled Taffy nicely, like. But what was all that "we love you" shite?'

'I have absolutely no idea.' It's true. I don't.

'Who'd have thought that would stop him in his tracks? I always thought a right good kicking would be the only way to sort the bastard out.'

I shrug, stub out my cigarette and put the butt in my pocket. Everything around us is so pristine, I can't bear the thought of soiling it.

'Right,' Sage says briskly, chucking her fag on the ground where it dies in the dew with a hiss. 'Let's catch up with the rest of the posse. They are so fucking dead. Bunch of pussies.'

'Think Taffy's all right? Maybe we should hang around a bit.'

'Who cares? Arsehole. That's what you get if you fuck around with drugs and don't know what you're doing.' She says this without a trace of irony.

'Do you mind if I catch up with you later?'

'Eh? What you going to do?'

'Feel like a walk. We hardly ever get up this early.' It's true. Although we're all early risers to avoid the seven a.m Blues round, I haven't experienced the dawn hush of the city since Hervé and I left that cop shop a million years ago after breaking into the Pompidou Centre.

Sage looks at me quizzically. 'Sure he didn't hit you on the head?'

'I'm fine, honest. I'll meet you at the Pompidou in a bit. But will you take my bag? I've got to get Ralphie his breakfast.' I rummage in my rucksack and take out the smaller bag in which I carry his bowl, water bottle and can opener.

'We working today?' Sage asks.

I check my pockets. Fifty francs. 'Nah, let's have today off. After that I think we deserve a break, don't you?'

'Cool. Catch you later.' She hefts my rucksack on top of hers and we head off in different directions.

Ralphie's as eager as I am to set off, and his lead cuts into my hand as he pulls me along. The Indian shop at St Michel won't be open at this time of the morning, so we need to kill some time before I can buy his breakfast. We trot across the bridge. The little green street-sweeping machines are still out and I have to yank his lead to stop him snapping at the brushes that polish the sides of the pavement.

The adrenaline has leached away, and my hands are only slightly shaky now. The pain in my back has virtually gone. I light a cigarette and breathe in smoke and the early morning smell of wet concrete.

Where to? Should I head down to St Germain? Even though it's fairly close to our territory, we tend to avoid it as if it's No Man's Land. But after the Taffy Axe Experience, I'm feeling invincible, as if the whole city belongs to me. The high-end cafes are still closed, and I take my time peering into the windows of the boutiques as I pass. I haven't been window-shopping in ages. That sort of thing is part of another life. To think that my favourite thing used to be swanning around Birmingham market on the hunt for vintage dresses. I don't lust after anything I see displayed in the windows: what would I do with it? I'd only have to carry it around. I want less stuff, not more. As if to underline this, Ralphie squats down and shits, right outside a boutique's front door.

'Come on, Ralphie. Breakfast for you.'

We turn round and wander back towards more familiar territory. The supermarket must be open by now.

Oh *fuck*. It can't be.

At first I think I'm hallucinating, but Sage and I haven't had any acid since her bad trip experience, and we only smoked half a joint yesterday. I walk closer to the poster-covered wall situated in between a shoe store and a poky restaurant. The poster's stuck in amongst the other notices; one of its corners is flopping down and partially obscuring the black print across the top of it. I go to rip it off the wall, and it comes off easily.

My hands start shaking again as I read it: 'Have you seen these girls? Missing since February. Victoria Evans and Sharon Watling.'

It's me, there's no doubt it's me. But what's this about a Sharon? I've asked Sage a thousand times if Sage is her real name, and she's sworn on her parents' lives that it is. Although my brain's reeling, part of me is thinking: What else has she lied about? And why lie to me? The photo on the flier is definitely her, although she looks about twelve and her hair's long. I'd recognise those dark eyes anywhere. I'm beginning to feel sick and butterflies jump and loop in my stomach.

How could my folks choose such a crap picture of me? Maybe it's a good thing. Only someone who knows us really well will identify the two black and white girls in the photographs as us. Won't they? Better check. I head back to the shop window and peer at my reflection, holding up the photo for comparison.

The grainy photograph shows a smiling teenager with long permed hair and chubby cheeks. My reflection reveals a thin-faced tramp girl with long dreadlocks and a pierced nose. Thank Christ for that.

With a jolt, something else occurs to me. Sage has been telling the posse the same sob-story she'd blabbed to Hervé about us being sad little orphans. It won't look good if they find out someone cares enough about us to print posters and stick them up all over the city.

I have to get back and warn Sage. I shove the poster in my pocket. Ralphie whines.

'Okay, okay. I'll feed you in a bit.'

And there's something else: Does this mean the parents have been here looking for us? What if they're still in Paris? But the poster doesn't look as if it's just been put up. I search the walls for a duplicate, but this appears to be the only one. And there can't be any around Les Halles or the Pompidou or we would have seen them.

Overwhelmed by a sense of urgency, I make it to the Pompidou bench in record time. There's a fair crowd of *clochards* hanging about, and I spot Sage on the outskirts. I jog towards her. The second she catches sight of me, she strides up to meet me and grabs my arm, halting my progress.

'Don't, Vicks,' she says, voice grim.

'Eh? Don't what?'

Sage nods at the bench. The group of *clochards* thins, and I make out Danny sitting there, head in his hands.

I pull myself out of her grip and approach him. 'Danny?'

He raises his head and I bite my tongue to stop the scream. It looks like he's wearing some kind of sick Halloween mask. White liquid blisters surround his lips, and ragged pieces of skin melt off his cheeks. His eyes are livid with pain.

Bob appears behind me, takes one look at Danny and drops to his knees in front of him.

'What happened?' he asks me.

'I don't know. I only just got here. I was about to ask Danny myself.'

'*Que tu est-il arrive?*' Bob asks Danny gently.

'*Le feu,*' he croaks. 'Beeg mistake.' He tries to smile at me, but only manages a grimace.

Oh shit. What if he inhaled fire? No. He'd be dead then, wouldn't he? Christ. I was supposed to be helping him yesterday, but I hadn't felt like it, and Sage and I left Ralphie with Norbert and snuck away to listen to music at the

Pompidou Centre. Would it have made any difference if I'd been there? I hadn't even noticed that he hadn't slept in the bushes with us last night. I hope he hasn't been out all night in this state.

'We'd better get him to a doctor, and fast,' Bob is saying.

'I know a chemist,' I say, thinking of Hippy's codeine supplier.

'He needs more than a fucking chemist, look at him!' Bob snaps. I've never heard Bob swear before. 'Sorry, love,' he says quickly. 'It's just with Alex and everything – you know.'

'Yeah.' I drop my head so no one can see the tears pricking my eyes.

'*Non,*' Danny croaks. 'I will be okay.'

'Danny,' I say, trying to swallow the lump in my throat. 'Bob's right. You need to get that seen to.'

Sage appears at my side. 'Christ,' she whispers. 'That must burn like fire.' Realising what she's said, she clamps a hand over her mouth.

'I will take him,' Norbert says. He's always in and out of hospital getting that goitre thing on his neck seen to. '*Viens, Danny,*' he says. '*Viens avec moi.*'

'Do you need us to do anything?' I ask Danny.

'*Non.*' He takes my hand and squeezes it. I feel a tear sliding down my cheek and wipe it away. Bob and I help him to his feet and we watch as he and Norbert walk slowly and carefully to the Metro.

'Don't worry, girls,' Bob says. 'He'll be fine. It looks worse than it is.'

'Shit,' Sage says. 'What a morning. First Taffy, now this. How can everything get so fucked up so quickly?'

'One of those things,' Bob says, shrugging.

Sage scowls at him. 'You didn't need to snap at Vicks like that though, did you, Bob?'

'Leave it, Sage,' I say quietly. Shit – with all the Danny

horror, I've forgotten about the poster. 'Let's get out of here.'
I grab her arm and yank her towards the Quartier de
l'Horloge.

'What's going on, Vicks? I wasn't going to hit Bob or
anything.'

'It's not that.'

As soon as we sit down, I shovel Ralphie's food into his
bowl and light us both a cigarette. Without a word, I hand her
the poster.

'Holy shit!' She drags deeply on her cigarette, but the smoke
goes down the wrong way and she ends up coughing violently.
'Are there any more? We have to find them.'

'I'm not sure. There must be. But I wouldn't worry too
much. Look at the photos.'

'Oh right. Shit, yeah.' She looks like she's starting to calm
down. 'You'd never say that was me, hey, would you, Vicks? I
mean, just look at my fucking hair.'

'Haven't they got a more recent photo of you?' I ask.

She shrugs.

''Cos you look about twelve or something.'

'Bloody hell,' she says. 'What a fucking bollocking mess.'

I take a deep breath. 'Sage?'

'Yeah?' she says distractedly, without taking her eyes off her
photograph.

'How come the name on the poster is Sharon?'

She starts. I look away while she collects herself. 'My stupid
parents,' she says so quietly I have to strain to hear her. 'Always
fucking things up.'

I decide not to push it. 'I think we should phone home, let
them know we're okay.'

She squints at me through her cigarette smoke. I can sense
she's relieved I'm not going to harp on about the name issue.
'You serious?'

'As a heart attack.'

She nods and sighs. 'You might be right. We'd better find out where we stand. Come on.'

We make for the bank of phones in front of the tourist tat shops. 'If Natalie-the-Bitch has been spouting crap to them, she's fucking dead meat,' she snarls as I pass her some change.

My heart shudders in my chest as I dial the number.

'Hello?' The voice sounds furry, confused. Shit, I've forgotten it's still really early. I've probably woken them up. 'Mum?' I say tentatively.

There's a pause, and I can hear a gasp in the background. 'Vicki? Is that you? Where are you? We thought we'd lost you!' She sounds tearful, out of control.

'I'm fine, Mum. Really.'

'But we thought the worst . . . we thought—'

The dial tone buzzes in my ear as the connection's lost. I listen to it for a few seconds. When I place the receiver back in its cradle it's slick with sweat. Bloody hell. Should I phone them back? I wasn't expecting that reaction. I'd barely spoken to my folks in the last year. I've convinced myself they couldn't care less where I am. I fumble in my pocket for the pack of cigarettes. Several fall on the floor as I try to take one out with trembling fingers.

Trying not to eavesdrop on her conversation, I wait for Sage to finish talking to her sister. She looks as shaken as I feel when she finally joins me.

'Well?' I say.

'Fuck. They're in a right old state.'

'Did they come over here?'

She looks at me in confusion. 'Eh? Didn't you ask your parents?'

'Nah. Got cut off.'

'Oh. Giz a fag.' I pass her one and wait impatiently while she lights up. 'Jesus, Vicks. Friend of your folks put up the posters when he came over here on business. All of them are totally freaking out.'

'Did Karen say anything about the cops?'

'Nah. Just gave me a right old bollocking about not being more responsible and letting everyone know where we were. Apparently Natalie-the-Bitch told your folks a whole load of shite.'

'Oh God, yeah. That whole Hervé spy thing.'

We look at each other and then burst into giggles. The hilarity doesn't last long. Lost in our own thoughts, we make our way back to the Pompidou bench.

'Well, at least we know now that they're not here,' Sage says.

'Is that all you can say?' Guilt is beginning to nag at me. I still can't get over how devastated my mum sounded. The only time she'd shown any kind of emotion towards me in the last year was when she was yelling at me to do something about my hair.

'I feel like getting totally wasted,' Sage sighs.

Getting slammed sounds like a plan – if nothing else it'll help smother the guilt.

'You're not going to puke again are you, Sage?'

'Nah,' she says decisively, but she still looks green about the gills. Red wine and sun – a lethal combination. She'd thrown up the first time outside the Pompidou Centre on the way to get our bags. One show the tourists hadn't been expecting, that's for sure.

I'm beginning to sober up, and a headache beats at my temples. At least the pain helps distract from the guilt about Danny and the phone call.

My stomach rumbles. 'Shall we go to the soup kitchen?'

Sage looks at me as if I'm mad. 'You what?'

'We haven't got enough dosh to buy food.'

'God. How the hell you can think about food now is beyond me, Vicks. Giz a fag.'

'Run out.'

'*Fuck*. Bob!' she calls, 'Got any fags?' He throws his packet over to us and we light up.

'*Bonjour*!' a voice says next to us. It's Rat Girl. I haven't seen her since Sage's bad trip experience.

'All right?' I say. Then I catch sight of Hippy scuffing his feet and scratching at his arms a few metres behind her. I'm not surprised he's antsy: Sage is giving him her best dead-eye.

I wave him over. 'How's Taffy?'

He grunts. 'Not good. Still sleeping it off. Moved him down to the car park, so he'd better get it together before the Blues arrive.'

Sage shakes her head slowly. 'Serves him right. By the way, thanks for all your help this morning, you useless twat.'

'Yeah. Sorry about that.'

Sage is disappointed. She was obviously spoiling for a fight. 'Yeah, whatever.'

'You want to come to a party with us?' Rat Girl asks.

'What party?' I ask.

'It is at the squat of my friend.'

'You gotta see this place, it's wicked,' Hippy chips in.

Sage and I stare at each other in bewilderment. Rat Girl, who's barely said a word to us since we met, is treating us like we're her new best friends, and we're actually having an almost normal conversation with Hippy. In fact, without the Red Peril around, he's a different person – relaxed and cheerful. Even his skin looks less putrid and pasty. Are Sage and I different people when we're not together? I don't think I'll be discussing this with her any time soon, though.

'I can't,' I say, nodding to Ralphie.

'You can bring him,' Rat Girl says.

'Bob'll look after him. He owes us for this morning, after

all,' Sage says. She's made sure she's said this loud enough to carry over to where Bob is chatting to a couple of buskers. 'Bob?' she calls. 'Will you watch Ralphie, while we head out for the night?'

'Yeah,' he smiles weakly at me. 'You girls go and enjoy yourselves.'

'You know how to feed him?' I say. 'I'll have to fetch his bowl and—'

'Of course,' Bob says. 'Off you go.'

'Great,' I say. 'Squat party it is then.'

'Christ, Vicks,' Sage says as I sort out Ralphie's gear. 'Every bloody day here is like something out of a movie.'

'Tell me about it.'

'No, I really mean it. Think about it. This morning we were attacked by an axe-wielding Welshman with one fucking leg; there are posters of us dotted around Paris, like everyone thinks we've been abducted or something; Danny almost burned his face off; and now a girl with a giant rat has invited us to a party. I mean, how much freakier can things get?'

SAGE

Reasons why this week has been crap:

1. *My best friend is a smack-head.*
2. *I have to look after a snappy little dog who hates my guts.*
3. *A one-legged Welshman who tried to kill me with an axe last week wants to be my boyfriend.*
4. *I'm rubbish at begging and the soup kitchen is closed!!!!*
5. *I have practically no fucking tablets left.*

It's been a week from hell, Gladys.

I don't even know where to bloody well start . . .

Okay, so after the whole phoning parents thing, Vicks was totally freaked out. I could tell it had done her head in and that, but that's no excuse for what she did!! Hang on, I'm getting ahead of myself, as Bob would say.

Everything started going to shit at this fucking squat party. I'd like to say I had a bad feeling about it before we even left the Pompidou that day. I mean, I've never really trusted Rat Girl, she's just too fucking weird and hardly speaks, except to her rat. And why oh why did we trust Hippy? What were we fucking thinking???

Anyway, we have to go on the RER to get to the squat, which is miles outside Paris. And all the way there Vicks is like, 'We can't stay too long because of Ralphie, blah, blah, blah,' which turns out to be dead ironic, of course.

The journey takes for fucking ever, and just when I'm thinking we're never going to get there, Rat Girl tells us to get off, and then we follow her and Hippy through this scummy area until we reach a kind of industrial estate. It's full of the sort of run-down buildings you see from the windows of the Wolverhampton to Sandwell and Dudley train. Vicks said it looked like a set from *Blade Runner*.

Me and Vicks look at each other, dead disappointed, and we're about to give Hippy a bollocking for bringing us to such a shite hole, when Rat Girl points to this old warehouse. Its walls were covered in crap graffiti and tags, and the windows were all broken. Not very promising to say the least, Gladys. Rubbish music blasted out of it. You know, boom, boom, boom, 'Pump up the Volume' shite (which I know Vicks secretly likes.)

So we walk up to this huge metal door in the side wall and Rat Girl bangs on it a few times. No one comes for ages, and I'm about to say, 'Nice one. Thanks for wasting our fucking time,' when this guy opens the door. I almost burst out laughing. He's a dead ringer for Hervey!! i.e. very tall with a crap goatee beard.

The guy says, 'Howdy, dudes,' or something equally and crappily American, and beckons us in. So we walk up loads of stairs, which are dead dark and creepy, and follow Hervey USA through this curtain that's hanging across a doorway. We go into a massive room that's only lit by candlelight, and it's empty except for a few old couches and mattresses scattered over the floor. There are a bunch of people hanging about smoking dope and drinking and shite. Okay, I admit I was impressed at first. The walls were painted with freaky psyche-delic swirls, like on the cover of *Camembert Electrique*, and canvasses were stacked up all over the place. Hervey USA says that the dopeheads scattered around the room are art students and that they're turning the building into an artwork. Pretentious as fuck, of course. But I started thinking that maybe I could nick some paint and art supplies etc. so me and Vicks could have another crack at making money out of what we're good at for a change. Then he starts introducing us to these arty-farty people, and the weirdest thing happened. They all looked at us with respect and treated us as if we were celebrities or something. This one stoned guy comes up to us and says, 'Like, you guys live on the edge, man.' And even Hippy was being treated with respect, which must have been a totally new experience for him.

There's tons of booze and stuff around and Vicks and I make a beeline for the vodka, even though I've still got a sore head from puking up wine earlier. Vicks gets talking to this American girl, who looks dead impressed with the way Vicks is dressed. Hervey USA says I should go and look at the exhibits.

Okay, Gladys. This part is freaky. By this stage I was a little bit pissed and I'd had a few drags on the spliffs doing the rounds, so I'm not sure how much of this is accurate. So Hervey USA tells me to go down the stairwell and take a look at what they've done on each floor of the place. Total mind-fuck. One room was empty except for a bath in the middle of it. And in the bath was this naked mannequin with red fabric spread under its body, like it was bathing in blood.

On another level, sand and cement had been spilled all over the entire floor in the shape of eyes and spirals. It must have taken weeks to shift all that sand and cement up there.

Then – jackpot!! In the basement I found a studio filled with art materials. Obviously these 'students' had shitloads of money. I searched for ages but couldn't find any chalk, so I collected a bag of oils and brushes and stashed them in the stairwell for easy collection purposes when we left.

So that was all good.

Then everything turned to shit.

I returned to the main room. Everyone was sitting silently in a circle and some misguided arsehole had put the Sisters of Mercy on full blast. Then I realised I couldn't see Vicks any-where. At first I thought, 'she must have gone for a piss', but then I spotted a figure lying on a mattress in the corner of the room, and I could see it had dreadlocks and boots like Vicks's. Things got dead surreal then, Gladys, as if everything was happening in slow motion. I walked past the creepy circle of spaced-out students, and as I passed them I saw Rat Girl trying to put a needle in the arm of this dead scared girl – the one who was talking to Vicks earlier. The girl's going: 'It will be okay, right? I'll be fine, won't I?' over and over again. Suddenly, I know what's happened and leg it to the corner. Vicks is just lying on the mattress, eyes wide open. At first I think she's dead, but when I shake her, she looks up at me, totally zonked, and slurs, 'Hey, Sage.'

I pull her up and yell 'We're getting the *fuck* out of here!' But when she stands up she's sick everywhere and tries to lie back down on the mattress.

247

I'm really angry now. Partly because I'm really scared Vicks is like OD'ing or something and partly, Gladys, because I CAN'T BELIEVE SHE'D TAKE IT WITHOUT ME DOING IT AS WELL!!!

I know, crap thing to say, but true.

So I go up to Rat Girl and ask her what the fuck's going on, but she's also off her face, and I can't get a word of sense out of her. Then she says to me, 'You want?' and holds up a little packet of smack. And time suddenly stopped. Would I have done it, Gladys? Yeah, I suppose. Maybe. Even just to get back at Vicks (but I'm not sure about the whole needle thing.)

But then an American over in the far corner starts shrieking, 'He's OD'ing, he's OD'ing, I can't wake him, I can't wake him!' and then everything went totally mental.

Hippy appeared from nowhere and said to me, dead serious, 'Get the fuck out of here now.'

I raced over to Vicks and yanked her to her feet. She got sick again, but I didn't take no for an answer. It was a bloody nightmare getting her down the stairs and the walk back to the RER took forever, as Vicks had to keep stopping to be sick, although there was nothing left for her to bring up.

Vicks was sick the whole of the next day and I gave her the biggest bollocking in the whole history of bollockings. *Shit*, Gladys. We've talked about trying it, I mean, who hasn't? But I always thought it would be me who took the plunge, not fucking Vicks, OR we'd do it together.

Anyway, Vicks has been feeling like shite for the whole week and can barely get up in the morning. She spends most of her time with Danny in the park next to the English bookstore. They sit on the same bench all day, every day, like two old people – Danny with his face like melted wax, Vicki barely able to string a sentence together.

So it's up to me to make all the cash. But I'm fucked if Vicks is getting her hands on any of it, in case she wants to buy more smack. I've told Hippy to keep Rat Girl out of my sight, unless she wants her head kicked in. And I'm buggered if Taffy doesn't keep trying to be really helpful and keeps bringing me Babybels and offering to dog-sit Ralphie for me. Total tosser. He's so one of those people who loves it when other people have nasty experiences. He seems to think we've all forgotten the Axe Experience, but of course we haven't, and I'm this close to telling him to fuck off away.

Of course, the worst part is the endless dog-sitting. Me and Ralphie hate each other, but I can't beg safely without him, and at the moment he isn't going to get fed without me, so we have to put up with each other. It's tough, but at least he's less smelly than vile brother-in-law Pete's slobby Labrador.

No poem today, Gladys, as I'm too fucking tired, being the breadwinner n all.

VICKI:

The German Tear Gas Experience

Gross. I look down at my feet and watch as the pool of dirty water swirls down the drain. Finally the water sloughing off my body runs clear. It feels like weeks since I last showered, and my skin is raw and tingly from the scrubbing I gave it with our last cake of hard soap. The only part of me that's not free from ingrained dirt is my hair. We've run out of shampoo. Still, I've done my best with the soap, and my scalp is less itchy than before.

I have to will myself to get out from under the delicious warm water. I've only paid for fifteen minutes and there's no money left for another round. My towel smells musty and mildewed so I rub it over my body as fast as I can. The shower's done wonders. I wish I had a screw-top head like in *The Man with Two Brains*, and then I could give my brain a good scrub as well.

I don't get dressed straight away. There's a full-length mirror in the communal changing area and I'm pretty sure I'm the only person in the shower block. I stick my head around the door, and true enough it's deserted. Taking a deep breath, I walk out and stand in front of the mirror.

Bloody hell. My arms are burned a deep nut-brown. Apart from my head and neck, the rest of me is fish-belly white in comparison, even though people are always going on about my 'olive skin'. It looks like I'm wearing muddy opera gloves.

The pinprick and bruise where the needle went in is almost gone. Thank God that didn't turn septic or anything. It's weird though. I was sure I'd lost a ton of weight, but my bum looks as plump as ever (worse luck) and my tummy still shows signs of its usual pot belly. The last time I caught sight of myself naked was in Jules's flat, and I'm sure since then I've actually put on weight. How can that be? I've barely eaten anything but a few crème caramels in the last two weeks. Nothing else stays in.

I'd better get dressed and brush my teeth. I cup my hand over my mouth and breathe into it. Rank. The Mrs Danvers-style woman who sits behind the counter in front of the shower place is mumbling to someone, so I leap back into a cubicle and pull on my clothes. Now I'm clean, they smell sweaty and smoky, almost like cured meat. I'm sure it's the same stench that emanates off the scummy *clochards* who queue up outside the soup kitchen. There's no cash left for a trip to the laundromat.

The fresh air on my damp scalp does wonders. My constant headache has retreated to a low, bearable throb. I wander over to where Sage and Ralphie are waiting for me next to the St Michel fountain. Sage nods approvingly at me. 'Wow, Vicks. Much better. You don't smell like shite any more.'

'Thanks, Sage.' Ralphie jumps up at me and I stroke him. 'Did you give him his breakfast?' I say, immediately regretting it.

'For your information, *Vicki*, while you've been a recovering smack-head, I've been carrying the can. So, yeah, the little bastard has been fed, okay?'

Typical. She's been a nightmare since the 'smack experience' as she calls it. I'm getting sick of reassuring her I'm not an addict or anything. I only tried it once, after all. Well, maybe twice. I have a blurry recollection of Rat Girl saying that I had to have another hit so that my body could get accustomed to it or something, but did I? I can only remember Rat Girl sticking the needle in once. Trying to pretend I was just getting an immunisation shot, I'd watched as my blood mixed with the brownish liquid in the syringe, but didn't yank my arm away from Rat Girl's vice-like grip. It hit me straight away, which I hadn't been expecting. It was nothing like acid, which takes ages to kick in. A floaty, woolly feeling whooshed through me, starting at my head and ghosting down to my limbs. I desperately wanted to sleep; moving wasn't an option. Whenever I shifted my position I felt like puking, and Sage said I threw up for hours that night although I don't remember that part. Anyway, she can talk. She was the one got us into the whole acid thing in the first place, and I reckon she'd have tried it if she wasn't shit-scared of needles. And it's as if she's totally forgotten her bad trip experience. I mean, I had to look after her when she was freaking out then, didn't I? I haven't brought this up; I haven't got the energy for a full-on fight. Today's the first day I feel able to work. It's not going to be easy building up the coffers again. Fair play to Sage for trying to bring in some money, but I always seem to do better than her for some reason.

I bum us a couple of fags from an American studenty type, and Sage's mood seems to improve.

A familiar portly figure emerges from the Metro.

'Bob!' I call.

He wanders over. He's looking worse for wear again. His suit jacket is rumpled and I swear his stubble is greyer than usual. I haven't seen him smile for ages and I'm pretty sure he's half-cut most of the time these days. I don't know if it's because he's still mourning Alex, or if there's something else bothering him.

'What's up? I ask.

'Bloody Germans.'

'Eh?' says Sage.

He cocks his head in the direction of the Metro, where five giant men are exiting into the sunlight. They all sport overgrown beards and studded leather motorcycle jackets, as if they're the Hells Angels of *clochard* land. Sticking close to their legs are three of the biggest dogs I've ever seen. All three are panting and drooling; their heavy black coats must be murder in this heat. The giants wander over to the opposite side of the fountain and allow their dogs to drink. Ralphie strains at the leash, and I have to wrap it round my hand several times to keep him in check. The Germans glance at us with little interest, and thankfully their ginormous dogs ignore Ralphie's growing hysteria.

'Ralphie, shhhhh!' Sage snaps. He immediately shuts up. Amazing. He's never done that with me.

'Who the hell are they, Bob?' she asks.

'German *clochards*. They normally only arrive here for the winter. God knows what they're doing here this early in the season.'

'What's with their massive bloody dog accessories?'

Bob shrugs. 'Protection?'

'Maybe they're their girlfriends or something,' I say.

'Christ, they give me the creeps, why don't they stick to their own fucking country?' Sage says without any irony.

My stomach rumbles. 'I suppose I'd better go and do some work,' I sigh.

'Watch your back,' Bob warns.

'Eh? I've got Ralphie. I'll be fine.'

'I'm not talking about the Blues, Vicki.' He nods at the Germans. 'It's them you've got to watch. Bloody Krauts. They come here and steal our best begging spots. And they don't bother to say "please".'

'You mean they're violent?'

'You want to mess with that?' Another leather-clad bloke has joined the group. He must be at least six foot five, and his boots alone look like they weigh as much as me and Sage combined.

'There aren't that many of them.'

'You haven't seen the half of it. This is the first lot. There'll be another wave arriving soon. Fuckers.'

Sage and I exchange glances. Bob rarely swears.

'Okay,' I sigh again. 'I'm really off now.' Sage readies herself to leave with me. 'It's okay, Sage. It's my turn. You need a break. Just lend me your sign, I can't find mine anywhere.'

'You sure?' I know she's dying to continue her Pink Floyd feast in the music library.

She's always going on about how much she hates them, but she can quote every line from *The Dark Side of The Moon*.

I wave goodbye to Bob and Sage, and Ralphie and I head for the Metro entrance. I decide to make for my McShite pitch. It's a bit of a slog to get to, but it's usually lucrative, and as the vague hunger pains have morphed into starvation, I'll be quite happy for punters to ply me with burgers today. I give the Germans as wide a berth as possible, but Ralphie strains at his leash and tries to take a running leap at one of their dogs. One of the bearded giants – a blond with glinting eyes – stares at me as I pass and says something to one of his companions. Their booming laughter follows me as I head down the stairs, and heat rushes to my cheeks.

'Bastards,' I hiss. Ralphie looks up at me and whines. 'Come on.' I tug him on, but he doesn't seem to want to go any further, and I have to drag him down the next few steps. 'What's the matter, Ralphie?'

Behind me I can hear the heavy clump of several sets of feet. I look back. Bugger, it's the Germans. Are they following me? Ralphie starts growling. 'Fuck it.' I give in and pick him up. It's not easy navigating the stairs as he writhes in my arms, but I'm desperate to reach the ticket foyer before they catch up to me. Bob's warning rings in my ears.

I'm nearly at the base of the stairs when I hear shouting echoing up from one of the platforms below.

Now what?

Oh shit.

There's a rumbling sound, and then a jostling crowd of men and dogs surges around the corner, heading straight for me. For a few stupefied seconds all I can do is stare. Then, through the throng I make out the telltale bright blue of the Blues' uniforms – they've obviously got wind of the Germans' arrival and I'm fucking well stuck in the middle! Fuelled by panic, I don't stop to think about the potential danger of running into the midst of the giants following me down the stairs. 'Run!' I scream at their approaching bodies. 'Police!' They don't need to be told twice. I risk a glance behind me. The mob is almost on my heels, and I still have a flight to go before I'm safely back outside. I'll never make it with Ralphie in my arms. I chuck him on the floor and drag him up the stairs. He barks and snaps at the feet surging around him. I'm shoved roughly from behind as body after body knocks into me and streams past. An elbow whacks my ear and I lash out automatically. The noise is immense: swearing and shouting and the howls of God knows how many dogs.

I'm nearly at the top of the stairs, which has formed into a bottleneck of bodies, when I feel something cool and wet splattering the side of my face. I'm practically lifted off my feet as the bodies behind push with enough force to propel me out into the sunlight. Then the pain hits. Oh fuck, the skin around my eyes is burning like acid and I can't seem to open my eyes. I no longer care about the Blues or the Germans as I'm pummelled by bodies that are only a vague blur in front of me. What the hell's happening? My face feels as if it's being attacked by a swarm of angry bees. I open my mouth to scream, but nothing comes out. Then I feel a tug on my hand. The lead! Oh, thank God. Ralphie. I haven't lost Ralphie. But my eyes. *Get to the fountain. Get to water.* I have to wash whatever's on my face away, and fast.

But where is it? How can I not see it? *Please God, don't let me go blind.*

'Sage!' I scream at the top of my voice. 'Bob! Help me. I can't see! Sage!'

Someone grips the top of my arm. I attempt to twist free, but whoever has me is way stronger than I am. I rub frantically at my eyes with my free hand, but it only makes matters worse. Everything is still blurry and I can't see who's got hold of me. Fear swallows the pain for a second – what if it's one of the Blues?

'Fuck off!' I yell. 'I've got a dog!'

'Run!' a gruff voice I don't recognise shouts in my ear.

'Let go of me!' I scream, but my voice is swallowed by the cacophony around me.

'Come on!' It's the same voice, but the urgency is turned up a notch. 'You have to run!'

I lash out blindly with my leg, trying to kick at whoever's holding me, but my foot doesn't connect. 'I can't fucking see! How can I run anywhere? I have to wash my face.' I lurch in what I hope is the direction of the fountain.

'*Nein.* That is the worst thing you can do. Come on!'

I'm almost yanked off my feet as the bloke manhandling me drags me forward.

'Ralphie!' For a horrible second I think I've lost him, then I feel another tug. The lead's wrapped so tightly around my wrist that my hand's gone numb.

I'm dragged blindly along. I try again to open my eyes wide, but the pain makes me gasp. 'Who are you?' I yell at my assailant.

'I am trying to help you. Move!'

'I'm trying my fucking best!' I don't attempt to open my eyes again. Fuck. My life is now in the hands of a complete stranger who sounds suspiciously like he's got a German accent. I bash into something solid and furry and almost go flying, but the iron grip on my arm doesn't relax for a second.

It hits me that I can no longer hear the furious mob.

'Sit down,' the voice barks.

'Where?' I feel myself being pushed backwards and something hard presses against the back of my knees. A bench! I sit down with relief and rub my eyes as hard as I can again.

'Do not do that.'

'Who the fuck *are* you?'

'Keep still.'

Cold spray peppers my face, and I scream and start batting at the air in front of me. 'Get the fuck off me!'

'Calm down. This will help.' Liquid runs down my cheeks and into my mouth. The taste is familiar, but I can't place it. Oh God, am I bleeding? My throat closes up, and my breath hitches.

'*Shiza!* Sit still,' the voice orders. Without a doubt it's a German accent. Oh crap.

'Take your fucking hands off her!' I recognise the voice at once.

'Sage?' I say, but it comes out in a whisper.

'What the hell do you think you're doing?'

'It is orange juice,' the German replies. 'It is the only thing that vill neutralise the tear gas.'

Orange juice? Is that what I tasted? But what's this about tear gas?

'Tear gas?' Sage says, shocked. 'Who the hell sprayed you with tear gas, Vicks?'

'Pepper spray or mace is perhaps the more likely,' the German continues. 'Fucking cops. Every year it is the same ting.'

'Why orange juice?' I ask, squirming as another stinging blast of liquid hits my face.

'It can help. Better than water. Try to open up your eyes now.'

I slowly lift my lids. It still hurts like buggery, but the blurriness has gone, and the more I blink, the better my vision becomes. And now I can see for sure that my saviour is one of the huge bearded Germans after all – the one who was staring at me earlier. By the looks of things, he's also taken a blast of the pepper spray. His eyes are swollen and the surrounding skin is inflamed. Bugger. Is that what I look like?

'What happened?' Sage asks.

'The cops, they must have been following the others from the Metro. This girl warned us about them.'

'So Vicks here saved your arses?'

'*Ja*. That is so.'

'Come on, Vicks. Let's get out of here. We're far too close to St Michel for my liking if the Blues are in the vicinity.'

I realise I haven't heard Ralphie for a few minutes. I must have let go of his lead. 'Where's Ralphie?'

Sage points to where a couple of other Germans – similarly red-eyed – are taking a breather on a nearby bench. Oh *shit* – Ralphie is perched on the back of one of their massive black dogs and is desperately trying to hump it.

Sage stalks over to the dogs and rips Ralphie away from his obese girlfriend (or boyfriend – I can't tell from here). 'Let's go,' she says to me. She turns to the German, who towers over her. 'Ta for helping my mate.'

'It is me that is to be grateful.'

'Thanks anyway,' I say. 'You know, for the orange juice and that.'

He shrugs. 'You are welcome. I am Gerhard. You are Vicki, is that right?'

'Yeah.'

'Okay. I hope to see you around, Vicki.'

Sage rolls her eyes and gives me a 'don't go there, Vicks,' look.

Ralphie whines as Sage drags him out of the park. His potential mate ignores him. 'Come on Ralphie,' says Sage. 'She's just not right for you. Not that that's ever stopped your owner.'

'Hey, I heard that.'

'You were supposed to.'

It's a huge relief to be back on the Pompidou bench. Sage hands me the bottle of water she bought from a kiosk so that I can bathe the sticky juice off my face. My eyes are still stinging but the pain has lessened.

'So . . . what does it feel like, Vicks?'

'What does what feel like?'

'To be tear-gassed or maced or whatever.'

'You know when you're washing your hair and shampoo gets in your eyes? Like that times a million.'

'Ouch.'

'Yeah. You can say that again. How do I look though, Sage? My eyes feel puffy – do they look bad?'

'Nah. They're just a bit swollen is all. A bit like Dracula's used to get after he smoked too much black.'

'Nice.'

'It's not that bad, Vicks. It looks better already.'

'Good. I'd hate to end up with a scarred face like Danny or something.'

A cough sounds from behind me. Shite – I hope Danny didn't overhear me. But it isn't him. He's on the other side of the bench with Norbert. Both of them are as pissed as farts.

Sage lights me a cigarette. 'Feeling better now, Chuck?'

I take a drag. I should be feeling better, I know. But then, out of nowhere, pressure starts building in my chest.

'Vicks? Vicks? What's wrong?' Sage asks with uncharacteristic gentleness.

It's the trigger I need. Tears seem to explode out of my eyes, washing away the last of the citrus on my cheeks and stinging the tender skin.

'*Vicks?*'

'I can't take this any more,' I sob. My thoughts are jumbled; I try to stem the hysteria, but it's more powerful than I am. 'I want to go home!'

'Oh shit. Come on.' Sage grabs my hand and leads me away from the bench. Danny and Norbert are staring at me with bleary concern.

'But Ralphie!' I sob.

Sage nods to Danny and he picks up Ralphie's lead. 'I've got to sort her out, Danny. Will you be okay with Ralphie for now?'

'*Oui.*' He may be pissed but he gets the gist.

'Come on, Chuck,' Sage says. 'I know exactly what you need.'

Something's pressing into the side of my face. Ouch. It's bloody sore. I lift my head and bat away the twig that's been digging into my cheek. I let my head drop back down. It's fuzzy, as if it's full of static. Have I been asleep for long? I don't remember dropping off.

'Sage?'

'*Bonsoir,*' a strange voice says from somewhere behind me.

I sit up too quickly and have to blink away stars. Christ. My head feels like it's caught in a vice. Did someone just speak to me? Did I imagine it? My stomach spasms and saliva gushes into my mouth, but I somehow manage to stop myself throwing up.

'Sage?' I call again. This time there's no answer from anyone.

It's dark here in the bushes, but they don't look like the familiar Notre Dame ones. There's a wall in front of me, and I can make out the yellow glimmer of lights in the distance. I can't figure out which bank of the Seine I'm on. Are the lights coming from St Michel? I try to stand up to get a better look, but another wave of nausea hits. I put my head on my knees, and wait for it to pass.

'*Ca va?*' the voice comes again. I jump.

'Who's there? Richard? Is that you?'

A dark figure rustles towards me and squats down beside me. It's too dark to see his face clearly, but it's definitely not Richard. Is it another *clochard*? I can't place the voice at all.

'Where's Sage?'

'Eh?'

'My friend, er, *ma amie. Ou est elle?*'

The figure shrugs and moves closer. Now I can make out that he has a large nose and short hair. He doesn't smell like a *clochard*. Cologne wafts off his clothes, and he looks to be wearing a smart anorak over a suit.

'Who are you?' My unease is now stronger than the nausea. I shift away from him.

'You are okay?' he asks softly. He starts stroking my arm. My heart's pounding; each beat thumps in my ears.

'I have to go—' I attempt to push myself up, but my balance is off.

'*Non, non,*' he says, placing a strong hand on my shoulder and pushing me back down.

Oh God, oh God, oh God, his voice sounds just like Jules's when he was trying to get me to do that vile stuff with that Japanese woman. '*Non!*' I try to say, but again all that comes out is a whisper. I can feel him panting in my ear, and suddenly the adrenaline kicks in as my detached brain starts to register what's actually happening. I squirm as hard as I can and try to shift his weight off me, but I can't move. My arms feel leaden as I push his head away from mine, and he grabs them with one of his and holds them above my head. He's tugging at my leggings with his other hand.

'Nooooo!' This time the word rips out of my throat.

'Shhh,' he says. 'Shhhh.'

His legs force mine apart and I feel his fingers scrabbling around underneath my knickers. It hurts, and his weight on me is making it hard to breathe.

'Shhhh!' he hisses in my ear.

Then he forces his tongue in my mouth. I taste halitosis and some garlicky thing. My stomach tips over and vomit explodes out of my mouth. It happens so fast I don't get a chance to turn my head to the side.

Suddenly, his weight is gone and I roll onto my side and I gag and cough. I can move again, but I can't seem to focus properly. Where is he? My eyes are streaming with tears and I desperately rub at them.

There's a violent rustling in the bushes. Blood roars in my ears as I scramble to my feet, ignoring the twigs that scratch and snatch at my clothes and hair.

Get to the lights, get to the lights. Using the wall as a guide, I rush along, not daring to look back. What if he's following me?

Smells: diesel, rubber, vomit, urine. Oh Christ. I lean over and retch, but only a weak dribble comes out. I gasp for air. How the fuck did I get here? It looks like I'm in the bloody underground car park. I'm crouching between two cars, a wheel nut pressing into the small of my back. My thighs protest as I get shakily to my feet. My neck's so stiff I can barely turn my head.

Fuck. That horrible scene with that guy in the bushes – did I just imagine it? I run my fingers through my dreads. Leaves and twigs are tangled through them. No, it happened. I must have legged it down here in my panicked state.

Breathe. Cigarette. Then get out of here. What's the time? It can't possibly be morning yet, can it? I light a cigarette and the first blast of smoke makes me gag again. I check out my reflection in a wing mirror. Apart from the small forest in my hair, I look okay. No bruises, no black eyes. He didn't hit me then. My eyes are slightly red – probably still from the tear gas, so that's okay. I don't want to investigate the rest of my body yet, but I don't have much choice: the stench of vomit is unbearable. It's splattered in a thick red mess all down the front of my dress. I'll have to get rid of it. I yank it over my head, ignoring the sound of ripping fabric. Thank goodness I'm wearing a T-shirt underneath. I use the unsoiled back of the dress to wipe away the splatters on my boots and leggings, then dump it underneath a BMW.

Christ. Where's my bag? I need more clothes. Clean clothes that he hasn't touched. Has Sage got it? Where the hell is she? And Ralphie? No. That I do remember, we left him with Danny. But was she with me when I ended up in the bushes next to the river? She can't have been. Not Sage. She wouldn't have put up with that kind of shit for a second.

I finish the cigarette and immediately light another. That's better. Now, remember. Piece it together. *Think.*

Okay, so I freaked out at the Pompidou after the tear gas thing, and Sage said we needed to get pissed. I remember thinking it was the last thing I felt like doing. We left Ralphie with Danny and headed for our favourite corner shop in Les Halles. When I asked her how we were going to buy booze when we didn't have any cash, Sage went all coy and whipped out a fifty-franc note she said she was saving for emergencies. And if this wasn't an emergency, she said, what was? Sage went into the shop by herself and I hung about outside. Then, I heard her yell, 'Vicks, run!' and she hared out of the shop, a clinking plastic bag in her arms, a Babybel wheel and a punnet of crème caramels spilling out of her pockets. The shopkeeper chased us for a few hundred metres before giving up, and I remember laughing hysterically and thinking, fuck, why am I always *running*?

We started out in the Quartier de l'Horloge, then made our way to the banks of the river. This is where it gets blurry. Sage said something about me fancying the huge German guy who'd dragged me away from the Blues, and I'm pretty sure we had a huge fight. Did we finish all three bottles of wine? Is she still speaking to me? Is she okay? I have no idea.

Christ. I'd better find out.

SAGE

Experiences we've had so far:

The Bobby Experience.
The Hervey Experience.
The Sex Shop Pervert Experience.
The Beating up Bobby Experience.
The Job Experience (aka the Mrs Danvers Experience).
The Buskers Experience.
The Alex Crab Experience.
The Bridge Experience.
The Pompidou Posse Experience.
The Begging Experience.
The Bad Trip Experience.
The Taffy Axe Experience.
The Phoning Home Experience.
The Smack-Head Friend Experience.
The German Tear Gas Experience.
The Vicks Wanting to go Home Experience.

Vicks wants to go home. And she's serious. I can tell. Like she
says, how can everything turn to shit so quickly? Vicks can't
handle our lifestyle as well as I can. I mean, she comes from
this dead posh background and everything. Her house is like

a mansion. And of course I haven't told her what Karen said on the phone when Vicks made me call her. It's my secret. Why, oh why, am I so *thick*, Gladys? I should have monitored the situation more carefully and used my brain more. And it's not as if I don't get homesick as well, is it?? I miss lots of things, even *EastEnders* and crap like that. But you never hear me complaining, do you?

Horrible Hippy says there's a priest guy in Paris who buys ferry tickets for runaways who want to go home to England. I haven't told this to Vicki though. I'll only use this information in an emergency.

I don't want to make a fanfare about this, Gladys, but I haven't had any tablets for ages now.

I feel fine! Ha! So much for Dr Wankenstein. Shows you how much he knows!! So if I can do it and try to be happy here without tablets, so can Vicks.

Vicks won't tell me what happened exactly after we got pissed and had the Big Fight. I woke up on a bench by the river and she'd disappeared. And when she came and found me later, she looked like utter, utter shite. I've never seen her look so bad, Gladys. She was covered in scratches and puke and her eyes looked even worse than just after she was tear-gassed. Obviously I have my suspicions about what happened to her, but I keep trying not to think about them. The thought of anyone hurting Vicks like I was hurt makes me shake with anger, and I can't afford to lose it, as it's up to me to get things back on track. Vicks doesn't seem to realise how important it is that everything gets sorted. I mean, if we were really smart we could be making loads of cash every day, and then we could save up and get a place or something where we could stash our stuff and have a wash every day and things. I mean, she's always going on about not wanting to sleep outside in the winter, and we don't have to if we don't want to.

So much has happened to us since we came here, we can't just throw it all away, can we??
And what about the posse? Bob, Norbert and Danny? We can't just leave them, can we? Yeah, all right. I suppose we could, but still.

I know how fucked-up Vicks was after she spoke to her folks etc., etc., but that led to her making a big error in judgement, and it's since then that things have gone downhill. Drugs are the thorn in this equation (nicked this saying from Bob). If we can't think clearly, then we're totally screwed.

Vicks and I will definitely never take drugs again. We must make a pact to seal this resolution, like when we made our Friendship and Solidarity Pact the first night we stayed out in the Abandoned Church. We even cut our palms so our blood could mingle and we'd become Blood Sisters.

It is vital that Vicks and I stay clean!!! And not get too pissed or anything or take any more drugs, even though it's dead tempting, especially when we've made loads of cash. We must turn over a new leaf.

Why Drugs are Bad

> They make your head ache
> Like a squashed chocolate cake.
> They mess with your life
> Like a thug with a knife.
> They'll screw up your head

Like a clochard who's dead (RIP Alex).
Yes it is very sad
But most drugs are dead bad.

Maybe I should sell this poem to the government for their 'Just Say No' campaign. Ha ha.

VICKI:

The Lice Experience

Unbelievable. I haven't done this badly since my first day on the job. The smattering of centimes and the solitary silver coin barely add up to ten francs. What the hell's going on? Ralphie and I have been sitting outside the supermarket for over an hour now. At our usual spot we would normally have made enough for the day after twenty minutes.

Maybe the effects of last night's acid are still etched on my face or something and it's putting the punters off. Christ, I hope I'm not turning into one of those druggy-looking *clochards* like Hippy or Rat Girl. I run my hands over my face. It feels like clammy putty. I'm dying for a cigarette. I scramble in my pocket and pull out a roach with a centimetre of spliff left on it. I light it and drag it into my lungs, ignoring the old man who glares at me in disapproval before trudging past me into the supermarket. Ralphie looks up at me and whines.

'Not you as well. It's just one hit.' Ralphie's also not himself this morning. He's curled up next to me and barely raises his head whenever someone comes within snapping distance. He doesn't like this area either. It's been ages since I've ventured to the suburbs. Even though I have my dog insurance, when I woke up this morning I'd had an uneasy feeling about today. Since the Tear Gas Experience, I'm getting paranoid. Yesterday the Blues seemed to be patrolling everywhere, even though it's getting colder and the tourist traffic is waning. It's probably because of the Germans. Without Sage as a lookout I've been feeling antsy even out here. And to make matters worse, we keep hearing horror stories about the Germans beating the shit out of local *clochards* so that they can nick their pitches. Looks like Bob was right all along. That Gerhard bloke seemed to be okay, but we haven't bumped into him again.

'Let's go, Ralphie.'

I kill the joint and get to my feet. Ralphie stretches and does the same, wagging his tail half-heartedly as we set off. This was a bad idea. I'd left Sage asleep in the park by herself. I double-checked she couldn't be seen by casual passers-by, but still. She'll never forgive me if the Blues root her out. I hadn't planned on staying out here so long. I quicken my pace.

We decided not to sleep with the posse in the Notre Dame gardens last night, partly because we needed a break from them, and partly because Bob would give us a right bollocking if he knew we've been taking acid again. He's always lecturing us about the 'evils of drugs', especially after what happened to Taffy. I do feel a bit guilty, actually. We'd only taken a half each, but I shouldn't have let Sage take it at all after the Bad Trip Experience. Not that it was a great success. We tried doing the whole daring each other to go inside the claustrophobic toilet cubicle thing, but it had felt forced and was quite depressing after a while.

I'm really regretting that joint. The sun is too bright and my eyes are watering. There's a smattering of cops on the other side of the boulevard as we make away down the high street to the RER station. I keep my head down and try to look innocent. I'm sure I can feel their eyes on me. The pavement lurches beneath my feet, although I'm sure the acid must be out of my system by now. I don't dare look back as I hurry past the ticket booth and hop over the turnstile. Ralphie's lead gets tangled in the metal bars and it seems to take a life-time to unravel it. Sweat bleeds into my palm, and my heart's juddering. Shit. I should never have smoked the bloody thing. *Stupid.*

As I make my way up from the bowels of the RER station, a crowd appears from nowhere. I'm jostled and swept along by the tide, and it suddenly feels as if my throat has shrunk to the size of a pinprick. I let Ralphie take the lead and he pulls me down a long flight of stairs to a deserted Metro platform. I need to sit down for a minute and catch my breath, but it doesn't seem to help. My hands are tingling and growing numb, and I have to bind Ralphie's lead around my wrist to keep a grip on it. The garish advertisements on the curved, tiled walls feel like they're caving in on me, and the words on the Galeries Lafayette poster right in front of me shift and shimmer. A train whooshes into the station and I jump on it without thinking.

I need fresh air.

I have to get out of here.

I fumble with the door handle as the train creaks into the next station and I blindly let Ralphie pull me across the gap onto the platform. I don't recognise it. It must be one of the few we haven't explored. It's darker and dingier than any of the familiar stops, and there aren't any *clochards* slumped in the plastic seats which line the walls, although a smashed bottle of sherry lies under a bench. I let the other departing passengers walk up the stairs ahead of me. Ralphie strains at his leash, and I bend over, hands on my knees, and try to suck in a deep breath. It must be a bad reaction from the joint. It'll pass. It *has* to pass.

As the last passenger traipses up the stairs, I follow behind and turn left into an echoey corridor. There's a small knot of people at the far end. Oh God. They're surrounding someone.

Someone who's lying down. A woman moves away from the group and puts a handkerchief to her mouth. A man wearing a leather jacket peels away to comfort the woman, and now I can see what's happening in lurid detail. The figure on the floor is dressed in a business suit. His face is grey, his eyes are rolled back in his head. His legs are twitching, yellowish foam seeps out of the corners of his mouth, and the crotch of his trousers is dark. One of the spectators bends to wipe the foam from his mouth.

I don't want to see this. I numbly drag Ralphie back the way we came. As if I've summoned it, a train arrives as I reach the platform. By some miracle I remember how to work the door handle, and I lurch inside, pulling Ralphie behind me.

That's it. I swear I will never take acid again. Just let me get through this (whatever *this* is), and I'll never do anything wicked again. It hits me that I don't have a clue where the train is heading, so I almost shout with relief as it pulls into St Michel.

I pick Ralphie up and carry him out of the train and up the stairs. There's no way I'm using the lift. The warmth and weight of his body calms me, and oxygen finally starts to reach my lungs.

It feels like we've been gone for hours, and I fight to recall which part of the park Sage and I had bedded down in last night. Then I catch a glimpse of blue through the foliage – Sage's sleeping bag. Thank God, she must still be fast asleep. I sink onto a bench a few feet from where she's snuggled in the bushes. I shake my fingers; the horrid numbness is lessening. Should I wake her? In a sec. I cross my arms and snuggle into my jacket. Ralphie jumps onto my lap. I close my eyes, but I can't allow myself to fall asleep. I can't forget that Sage and I are still in prime Blues country.

★   ★   ★

I lunge awake. Christ. How long have I been asleep? And where's Ralphie? 'Ralphie!'

He wriggles out from beneath the bench. *Thank God.* I'd better feed him. Both of us skipped breakfast this morning.

As I stand up, something tickles the side of my face. I try to brush it off, but it stubbornly clings to my cheek. I pick it off with my thumb and forefinger and it squirms in my fingers. It's a tiny black insect. Oh *shit*. My scalp's been itching like mad for the last few days, but I'd put this down to the usual gritty-head thing from sleeping outside. I scramble into the bushes and roughly shake Sage's shoulder.

'Sage!'

'Wha—?'

'Get up!'

'What is it – the Blues?'

'No. Worse – kind of.'

'Huh?'

'Don't panic. Look, just get up, okay?'

She shoots me a quizzical glance, inches out of her sleeping bag and rolls it up with typical Sage economy. I grab my ruck-sack, which looks tatty and ill-organised compared to hers. My sleeping bag's definitely on its last legs – it's now vomiting fluff – and clothes peek out through my rucksack's split seams. I collect Ralphie's bowl and water bottle.

'Well?' Sage asks. 'What's going on?'

'We might have a bit of a problem.'

'Giz a fag first.' I hand her one of our two remaining cig-arettes. 'You could have at least brought me a coffee.'

I take a deep breath. 'I think I've got head lice.'

She screws up her eyes and peers at me through the smoke. 'Don't joke, Vicks. It's not funny.'

'Do I look like I'm joking? Here. Check my hair.' I motion her over to the bench and sit down.

'Okaaaay . . . If they're anywhere they'll be at the back of your head.' She clamps the cigarette between her teeth, and I feel her picking through the dreadlocks that snake down my back.

'Christ, Vicks. We've got to do something about these clumps at the back of your head. You're beginning to look like Stig of the Dump. I can't see anything. Hold on.' She stubs out her cigarette and I wince as she tugs the matted mass apart.

'Ouch. Don't be so rough.'

'Don't be such a baby. Can't see anything. Must be your imagin— Oh shit! Oh, gross!'

I turn to see her backing away from me, rubbing her hands on her trousers.

'Fucking hell, Vicks! You've got some sort of ecosystem living in there! Jesus. This is bad. It's not just those little white nits, either. You've got like black things in there!'

Both of us start scratching furiously at our heads.

'I don't get it. We had a shower a few days ago, didn't we?' I can't remember. Oh God. I've completely lost track of time. When did we last shower? A week ago? Longer?

'They like clean hair, though, Vicks. Weren't you paying attention when the nit nurse came to your school?'

'Bloody buggering hell. How the fuck am I going to get out of this mess?' I take a handful of matted hair and tug it.

The colour drains out of Sage's face. 'Check mine.'

'Eh? Your hair's so short I'm sure—'

'Check mine, Vicks!' Her voice is shrill and unSage-like. Panicky.

'Okay, okay. Calm down.'

She sits on the bench and bends her head. Even though it should be greasy from lack of washing, Sage's hair is as thick and silky as the pelt of an animal. It's only about two inches long, so it's not difficult to search through it. A couple of tourists clutching guide books and maps peer at us in bewilderment as they pass. I can't see any nits. There's not even a dusting of dandruff. 'Nope. You're clean.'

'Thank fuck!' she breathes. 'Hang on – have you checked for body lice?'

'Just because I've got a few nits doesn't mean we've got the other kind. Anyway, I haven't been itching. Have you?'

There's a pause before she says: 'You go first.'

I turn over the top seam of my dress, which is where Bob said they like to nest. Apart from a light smattering of fag ash and a smudge of chocolate from a hastily scoffed *pain au chocolat*, it looks clean to me. I also check the straps of my one remaining – and very grubby – bra. Nothing. Thank God. Nits I can just about handle, but the other kind ... Ugh. 'Looks fine to me.'

'Phew,' she breathes. 'My turn.'

'We were lost in France, with some nits and some lice in our pants,' I sing half-heartedly.

'Very fucking funny, Vicks.' Sage gingerly investigates her sweatshirt's collar.

'I can't see anything,' she sighs with relief and looks up at me and smiles. 'Here, you have a look.'

Careful not to let my head touch hers, I look down at the seam. 'Looks okay. Hang on ... wait ... Oh my *fuck*!' There's a little transparent insect stuck to the fabric's ragged edge. And it's not the only one.

Sage's eyes fill with undiluted horror. She backs away from me, rips off her waistcoat as if it's on fire and throws it as far as she can. Then she yanks the sweatshirt over her head, drops it onto the grass and kicks it away with her boot. 'Oh God, oh God!' she mutters over and over again.

'Sage! Calm down!' I try to grab her arm, but she pushes me away. 'Don't touch me, Vicks. Shit, shit, shit! Oh fuck!'

'It'll be okay, Sage,' I say. But there's a nasty part of me that's secretly glad I'm not the one with parasites living off my skin. I dredge up the voice I used on Taffy when he went mental with the axe. 'Come on, Sage, sit down, take a deep breath.'

She hobbles over to the bench and slumps onto it, head in her hands.

It dawns on me that it's the first time I've seen Sage without her waistcoat or long-sleeved sweatshirt. She's still dressed in her baggy trousers, but all she's wearing on top is a grubby old man's vest. As she scrapes her trembling hands through her hair, I spot something else, and have to bite my tongue to stop myself from crying out. The skin inside her forearms is livid with criss-crossing pink scars. Some of the scars are as thick and swollen as earthworms, and snake up as far as her elbows. Whatever caused them must have cut quite deep.

She turns to me, and I drop my eyes before she catches me staring. She crosses her arms over her chest.

'Vicks,' she says, her voice sounding small and lost.

'Yeah?' I answer, still reeling from the sight of the lacerations on her arms. Why hasn't she told me about them before?

'I never thought I'd ask this, but . . . can you lend me some clothes?'

I reach for my rucksack.

Bob's eyes look as if they're finally going to pop out of his sockets as he takes in the spectacle of Sage wearing a dress. 'Sage, my goodness, don't you look a picture. Give us a twirl, love.'

'Don't go there, Bob,' Sage says dangerously. I stifle a snigger. She looks like a little girl playing dress-up. The 1960s gold minidress she finally deigned to wear, after pulling out and discarding every piece of my clothing, sparkles in the sun. The leggings underneath it bag at the knees, and she insisted on wearing one of my spare leather jackets over the outfit. Oddly enough, her hiking boots seem to work with it. It had

taken her ages to get dressed, as each item had to be meticu-
lously checked and re-checked for lice.

'How come I've got them, but you haven't?' Sage demands,
as if the thought has just occurred to her.

I shrug.

'Got what?' asks Bob.

'What do you think?' Sage snaps. 'Fucking lice, Bob.'

'Ah, and here I was thinking you were going on a date or
something.'

'It's not fucking funny!'

'I'm assuming we're not talking about head lice then?'

'Well *yeah.* Vicks has got *them.* But my clothes are full of . . .
the other kind.'

'I see,' Bob says.

'So?' Sage glares at him.

'What?'

'How do we get rid of them?'

'The body lice problem is easily solved. Just boil-wash your
clothes and sleeping bags and take a hot shower. The trick is
keeping them away.'

'Don't worry about that,' Sage snorts. 'I'll be keeping my
distance from everyone from now on, that's for sure.'

'But as for the head lice . . .' He eyes my dreads dubiously.
'I think you'll have to resort to drastic measures.'

My heart sinks. I knew it. There's no way I'd be able to
eradicate them from the tangled mess that falls halfway down
my back.

'But there's a moral to this story, girls.'

'What?' Sage sighs.

'If you lie down with dogs, you get up with fleas.' Bob chor-
tles and wanders away.

Sage gives his back the finger. 'What's his problem?'

'Dunno, but he's obviously pissed again.'

I'm trying to figure out where Sage could have got the lice

from. I suspect my infestation's the result of getting too close to Stefan, but Sage's is a mystery.

'Can we afford a shower and stuff, Vicks?'

Crap. I made fuck all this morning. I shake my head.

'Bob!' Sage yells at his retreating figure. 'Can you lend us some cash? We've got to get rid of these things!'

Bob weaves back towards us.

'Well? We'll pay you back. It's an emergency after all,' Sage pleads.

'Sorry, girls. Haven't been working for the last couple of days.' He nods at the crowds of tourists flooding past our bench. 'There's your answer if you're in a hurry.'

Ugh. Panhandling: it's the bottom of the barrel as far as begging goes. I hate actually *asking* people for money. It's not like doing it with a sign. You really get the full force of the punters' disgust when you approach them with your hand out and a *s'il vous plait* whine.

'C'mon, Chuck,' Sage says. 'Let's get to it.'

We head towards the chemist, pockets bulging with coins. Surprisingly it was Sage who made most of the cash. Mind you, the desperation on her face was clearly genuine, and almost everyone she approached handed over something. Within an hour, we'd made enough for a shower each and a trip to the laundromat and the chemist.

'Oh great, look who it is,' Sage says as we walk past the arty-farty cinema near the Quartier de l'Horloge. It's Taffy. He's kept a relatively low profile since the Axe Attack Experience.

'All right?' I nod at him.

'You stay away from me!' he shrieks, his voice as high as a little girl's. 'I don't want your fucking nits and lice!'

'Thanks, Bob,' I mutter. Mind you, to be fair it might not have been him who'd spread the word. There'd been a fair few *clochards* lurking around the bench when Sage blabbed to him, and she hadn't exactly been discreet.

Sage's face ripples with fury. 'Fuck off, then, you Welsh tosser. I'd rather be crawling with nits than have anything more to do with a piece of shit like you!'

'Piss off, lesbian!' Taffy spits back.

'Oh yeah?' Sage snarls. 'Is that the best you can do? *Lesbian?* At least I'm not a fucking ginger-haired git who also happens to be a stumpy arsehole!'

Taffy turns bright red, opens his mouth, but obviously can't come up with a retort that will rival Sage's venomous swipe. 'Bitch,' he mutters as he clatters past us.

'Stumpy?' I whisper to her, and both of us burst out laughing.

'Christ, Vicks,' she says loudly before Taffy has time to scoot out of earshot. 'I would've got lice ages ago if I'd have known it was that easy to get rid of the prick.'

Without the weight of the dreadlocks my head feels squeamishly light, as if it's about to float off my neck. I keep forgetting that they're no longer there, and every time I try to run my fingers through their non-existent lengths, my stomach twists in shock. I haven't had short hair since I was a child. I hate it – my head now resembles a rotten grapefruit on a stick, and it makes my nose look as bloody huge as Barbra Streisand's. Sage suggested that I bleach the lice out of my hair instead of trying to explain in French that we needed nit shampoo. I'd agreed, and we'd bought peroxide and nail scissors – the proper hair-cutting ones were too expensive – at the chemist. Then, at the shower block, Sage had gingerly snipped off my dreads (making sure she didn't actually touch them), leaving me with a cap of raggedy tufts. We left the dreads where they lay – scattered sadly on the white tiles like giant hairy worms. Sage jumped in the shower while I attempted the next stage.

The peroxide stung like buggery and turned my once black locks into an orangey-yellow mess that feels like dried sheep's wool.

Thank God we're the only people in the laundromat. Our clothes and sleeping bags toss and turn in a colourful mass and the frothy white water soon turns a muddy brown. Our stuff's on boil wash so I don't hold out much hope for most of my dresses. A couple of them are as old as my nan, and are dry clean or hand-wash only.

Ralphie nudges my leg.

'I'll just take him for a quick walk, okay? Back in a sec.'

'Sure,' Sage says without tearing her eyes away from the tumbling mass. As I leave, I catch her mumbling, 'Die, little lice fuckers, die . . .'

Head down, I walk through Les Halles and stop at a fountain so that Ralphie can drink. I hope I don't see anyone we know. Would they recognise me anyway? I sit down and pull out a cigarette. It's getting late and the tourists are thinning out. Out of the corner of my eye I spot a guy with a Mohican leaning against a bank of phone booths. I used to look like that. Fuck it. I get up and wander over to him. He doesn't give me a second glance. I check my pockets. There are still a few silver coins left.

Sage will never know.

I push the coins into the slot and dial the number.

It rings and rings and then I hear my brother's voice: 'Yeah?'

'Kev, it's me, Vicki.'

There's a pause. 'Fuuuuck, sis! You have no idea how much shit you're in!'

'I need to talk to Dad, just get him, will you?'

'Not here.' I can hear The The in the background.

'Hey! Is that my LP?'

'No.'

'You've been in my room!'

'Duh, you've been gone for ever, sis, of course I've been in your fucking room.'

'Just get Mum for me then. Quick, I'm going to run out of money soon.'

'Mum's not here either.'

'Well where are they?'

'Don't you know?'

'How would I know anything?'

'They're with Nan. They're staying in London while she's in hospital.'

My heart plummets. '*What*? What's wrong with her?'

'You what?'

'Why's she in hospital?'

'She's had a stroke.'

'Shit, is she okay?'

'Yeah – look, just hold on.' There's a clunk as he drops the receiver, and I hear him shouting: 'Don't smoke that in here, my folks'll freak out. No . . . no . . . *you* fuck off!' The phone is picked up again. 'Sorry, sis. Look, I've gotta go, Wal's lit a fucking J in the lounge.

'Kevin!' My voice is shrill. 'Is she going to be okay?'

'Yeah, they think she'll—'

The money runs out and the line peep-peep-peeps before it goes dead.

Oh *fuck*.

As if sensing my mood, Ralphie throws back his head and howls.

SAGE

Sitting on a park bench
    Have nits and head lice
    Nothing to eat that's nice
    Fuck it, AYE??

VICKI:

The Death Experience

'Let's go spy on Bobby!' Sage says, knocking back the dregs of our second bottle of wine.

'You what? Why?'

'No reason. Come on, we haven't been back to Opera for ages.'

'Nah.'

'Oh, come on, Vicks. It'll be cool. What else we going to do?'

'I dunno. Hang out at the Pompidou, listen to music?'

'Boring! Anyway, we have to celebrate.'

'We are celebrating, aren't we?'

'Yeah, but I feel like *doing* something.'

Sage scratches her neck. The skin there is beginning to look raw; since the Lice Experience she hasn't been able to leave it alone. Spying on Bobby is the last thing I feel like doing, especially as the day is going so well. This morning, Ralphie and I made almost two hundred francs in less than an hour – a new record. It was as if people were queuing up to chuck their cash at us. It was just what Sage and I needed, especially after all the shite we've been through recently.

I'm even beginning to like my new hair. Yesterday Sage and I splurged on one of those posh L'Oreal packets of hair dye, and my head's no longer the colour of rotten egg-yolk.

I haven't mentioned going home again, and Sage has been

in a terrific mood for days. After I'd shown off my record-breaking cash haul, she suggested we buy a couple of bottles of wine and have a picnic next to the river. But it looks like the alcohol has gone to her head. She's not slurring her words, but she's been twitchy since we made inroads into the second bottle.

'Seriously though, Sage. Why do you want to go back to Opera anyway?'

'Who cares, Vicks? Where's your fucking sense of adventure? C'mon, we're going.' She picks up Ralphie's lead and I have no choice but to follow her. I don't want to risk spoiling her good mood.

I'm sick with trepidation as we exit the Opera station. The chicken baguette I ate for lunch is threatening to come back up, and the sunlight is making my head ache. What if I bump into Jules? Sage is craning her neck, trying to catch a glimpse of Bobby.

'What will you do if Bobby's there?'

Sage shrugs. 'Fuck knows. Just want to look him in the eye, is all.'

But it doesn't look as if she's going to get her chance. As we cross the intersection, there's no sign of his bustling blue figure.

'Bummer,' I lie, trying to keep the relief out of my voice.

'How about we go and say hi to Hervé then?'

'No way!'

'Ah, come on, Vicks. It'll be a laugh. We can't come all this way and not visit the old perv.'

'We can't, remember? You nicked all his dope.'

'So? Potato Head didn't say anything about that when we saw him that time, did he? I reckon they thought they'd lost it or something.'

'I don't want to, Sage.'

'Don't be such a wimp, Vicks. Look, we'll just go look at the building. Come on. I just want to check it out.'

I sigh, but follow her all the same.

Hervé's road looks exactly as it did when we left it. Even the restaurant at the end of the street smells the same. How long has it been since we lived here? Two months? Three? Six? The only difference is the exterior of the Irish pub. Rows of bright balloons are strung across the top of it. Maybe it's celebrating our return. As *if*.

Sage waves me into the alcove in front of the battered green door. 'Do you remember the code, Vicks? Shit . . . What was it? 4768? Nah, that was the Mrs Danvers dump. You?'

'Can't remember,' I lie. We'd left Hervé, Potato Head and Dracula behind us, as far as I'm concerned. I don't want to come face to face with any of them.

'Hey, shall we pop into the Irish pub for one?' Sage suggests.

'Can't. We've got Ralphie.'

She sighs. 'Yeah. You're right. Oh well. Funny we never went in there, eh?'

'Yeah.'

'What *was* that code?'

Ralphie crouches down outside Hervé's door and makes a deposit. Sage laughs.

'Nice one, Ralphie,' she says, bending down to pat him. For once, he doesn't snarl at her. '*Finally* he likes me.'

'What do you want to do now?'

She pulls a joint out of her pocket and waves it in my face.

'Where'd you get that?'

She taps the side of her nose. 'Ask no questions, lassie,' she says in a perfect imitation of Alex. 'And I'll tell yer no lies. Come on, let's go back to the Opera steps and smoke this for old times' sake. See if we can spot any carpet legs.'

★   ★   ★

Maybe this wasn't such a bad idea after all. It's comforting to be surrounded by the familiar curvy opera house sculptures again. We climb to the top of the steps and sit down. Ralphie jumps onto my lap and nudges the crook of my arm. I let go of his lead the he leaps off my lap and scampers away.

Sage fires up the joint, takes a couple of hits and passes it to me. 'It's weird being back here.'

'I know.' I pretend to take a drag and pass it back.

'The last time we sat here it was fucking freezing, remember?'

'Yeah.'

The knot of worry in my tummy loosens. No Jules, no Bobby, no Hervé. Thank God. 'What do you think they're all up to, Sage?'

'Who?'

'You know, Hervé, Potato Head and Dracula. Think Hervé eventually got together with Genevieve?'

'Doubt it.'

'Hey – remember when we convinced Hervé to pretend to be a spy? Totally freaked Natalie out.'

'Oh fuck her. She's probably back home at a second-rate polytechnic right now.'

'Yeah.'

We're quiet for a few seconds.

'Sage? Do you ever wonder what we'd be doing now if we'd stayed at fart college?'

'No. Not really. Well, sometimes I s'pose. What's the point, though?'

'You don't, like, wonder where we'd be if we hadn't burned down the pottery shed?'

'Nah. No point.' Sage stares straight ahead, a faraway expression in her eyes.

'Sage, can I ask you something?'

'Sure.' I still can't get over this new positive and cheerful

Sage, but I may as well take advantage of it. It might not last much longer.

'Promise you won't get mad?'

'Course I won't. It's me! You can ask me anything. What's up?'

I have to ask, it's been festering at the back of my mind since the lice experience. 'You know when you took your sweatshirt off during the lice thing?'

'So?'

The words tumble out: 'Your arms. Were you involved in a car accident or something? Those scars.'

'*Fuck*, Vicks.'

'Sorry, you don't have to tell me. It's—'

'No. It's cool.' She stares off into the distance again. 'I did it to myself.'

'How come?'

'It's not a big deal or anything. Look. There's a whole ton of stuff you don't know about me, Vicks.'

'Has it got to do with the tablets?'

Her eyes widen. 'How did you . . . ?'

'That time you had the bad trip. You mentioned something about tablets.'

'Yeah. I wondered about that, actually. I hoped you thought I was just talking shit.'

We sit in silence for a while again. Sage takes another drag on the joint. Damn. I wish I hadn't brought it up. Her good mood has evaporated. I rack my brain for something to say.

The nagging Jules worry is no longer even a slight issue.

'Something happened to me a while ago,' she says quietly but matter-of-factly. 'And it kind of fucked me up for a while.'

I don't want to hear any more. 'It's all right, Sage, you don't have to—'

'Nah. Fuck it, Vicks. Just listen, okay?'

I nod. The saliva in my mouth has dried up.

'The tablets helped me through a bad patch. I've run out of them now, though, Vicks, and I'm fine, aren't I?'

'Yeah, course.'

'When I was twelve . . . Look, Vicks, I haven't told anyone about this, so don't freak out, okay?'

'Of course I won't.'

An electric tension sizzles between us. The background noise fades; nothing else exists. Nothing else matters. It's just the two of us, sitting here, in our own bubble, alone. I don't dare look at her.

'I was walking my dog in Wombourne. The wood there. You know where I mean?'

'Yeah. But hang on – you had a dog? I thought you hated them?'

'Yeah. Well, it didn't last long. House was too small to keep it, so we had to give it away. You know what the place is like.'

I nod. I've only been to Sage's house once. It had taken me ages and some serious manipulation to get her to invite me there. She never spoke about her folks, even when we were pissed, and I'd been curious (more than curious – desperate, really) to see where she lived. Eventually, she ran out of excuses. I wish I hadn't pushed it. Her parents – a grey, elderly-looking couple – barely said a word to me, and their house looked far too small for the three of them. Sage's room was roughly the size of one of the spare loos in my house, and backed on to her parents' room. The house was furnished like my nan's flat – clashing carpet and wallpaper and dark old-fashioned square furniture. Old people decor.

I wait for her to continue, dread building in my gut.

'So me and Cassie – the dog – were walking in the woods, and I bumped into this bloke, a friend of my sister's. He was much older than me, obviously. She'd just got married to vile Pete at this stage, and this guy'd asked me to dance with him at their shite wedding. I hadn't wanted to. So he's like, "How are you?" and at first I thought he was just being friendly. And he goes, "Do you feel like walking with me for a bit?" And I thought, "Okay, why the fuck not?" Although I didn't say "fuck" in those days, Vicks.'

She pauses to relight the stub of the joint. 'So we walk a bit deeper into the woods and he tries to hold my hand, but I'm trying hard not to let him grab it.' Now she sounds detatched, her voice leached of emotion. 'But I'm starting to feel really weird now, as if something's not quite right, but I couldn't put my finger on what it was. And I was like, "I have to get back home now," and I'm pulling Cassie away, so we can scarper, when he grabbed me and said something like, "You know you want to, I've seen you looking at me," or something shite like that. And then he pushes me down on the ground, onto the leaves and sticks and shit and then . . .'

I take her hand and squeeze it. 'Fuck, Sage. I'm so sorry.'

Sage snatches her hand away from mine and seems to shake herself. She lights two cigarettes and hands one to me. 'Yeah. Whatever. Don't worry about it, Vicks. I'm over it now.'

'And you were how old?' I hadn't meant to speak again, but the question pops out before I can swallow it.

'Twelve.'

'Jesus!' I think of that photograph on the poster. Twelve-year-old Sage. Chubby cheeks and huge grin. *Fuck*.

'What did your parents do? Did they call the cops?'

'Never told them.'

'What?'

'How could I? You know what they're like.' I don't, but I nod as if I know exactly what she means. 'They'd never have believed me,' she continues. 'They knew the guy and everything. My word against his.'

'And your sister?'

'Nah. The guy was practically Pete's best mate.'

'So you must have seen him around and stuff? You know . . . after.'

'Yeah. That was the worst. Bastard.'

'So that's why you . . . hurt yourself?'

'Yeah.' She shrugs. ''Spose. Who knows? All that matters is that things are fine now, aren't they, Vicks? I mean, we're doing okay, aren't we?'

'Yeah.' I'm still trying to get my head round what she's just told me. I'm not sure if I want to cry or throw up.

'Vicks?'

'Yeah?'

'There's something else I have to tell you.'

Oh shit, I think, what now?

'I—'

There's a screech of tyres, the crunch of metal on metal, and the high keening sound of a scream. I stand up and stumble down the first step. My limbs are leaden – it's like trying to run underwater – *move move, move* . . . A part of me knows exactly what's just happened and doesn't want to confront it.

'Vicks!' Sage is yelling. 'Don't look! Don't go down there, Vicks!'

I force myself to head down to the road in front of us, but Sage is gripping my arm and doing her best to hold me back. It takes all my strength to pull myself away from her, but I only make it down two or three steps before my legs buckle.

A moped lies skewed on its side, the confetti scatterings of broken glass streaming behind it on the tarmac. A small van with a mangled bonnet stands ticking like a time bomb and facing in the wrong direction. A man in a motorcycle helmet and a brightly coloured anorak is struggling to get to his feet. And there's Ralphie. Body flung across the kerb, his lead still trailing from his neck. There's no blood, but he's not moving.

Even from here, I can see that it's too late. His neck is skewed at an angle that's just ... *wrong*. As if from miles away I can hear a small child crying.

It's me. The crying is coming from me.

'Come, Vicks,' Sage says quietly.

I turn away. I don't look back.

SAGE

No poem today, Gladys. I've lost it. Keep trying to write them, but they don't work.

Notre Dame is much quieter than usual today, and one of the priest blokes nodded at me as he was passing my pew and said 'hello'. Ironic or what, right? Normally they look at me as if I'm a piece of shite. Maybe he's psychic or something and can tell I'm going away and won't be dirtying up his precious church for a while.

Big news of the day: We've decided to go home, Gladys. We've decided to throw in the towel and accept the consequences. Vicks keeps saying that we'll just go back home for a bit, get cleaned up and sorted out, and then come back with new sleeping bags and better rucksacks etc. I know she wants to check up on her nan, but fuck it. I don't believe her about coming back, Gladys. Look, I know a lot of shit has gone down with Ralphie dying etc, etc, but she doesn't seem to realise that unlike her I don't have anything to fall back on. Fart college was my last chance, and I can't very well go back there, can I?

It was actually dead easy to get tickets home, worse luck. We went to see that priest guy Hippy told me about, the one who helps out tramps and street kids and all-round fuck-ups like me and Vicks. His name was Father Paul, and he was young and boring-looking in a mannequin type of way. He was a bit suspicious of us at first, but then Vicks started crying and I could see he was buying into our story about being teenage runaways who'd seen the error of our ways. Before he agreed to stump up for the tickets though, he said: 'Now, girls. The church does try to help where we can, but can I ask first, are you Catholic?'

Both of us looked him in the eye and nodded, although my stupid family are Church of England, and most of Vicki's relatives are lapsed Jews or something. Turns out lying to a priest is easy.

Wait – fag break.

Been having a think about you, Gladys. Who'd have thought I'd be spouting all this bullshit? I mean, I've gone back and read what I've written at other times, and it sounds like I really hate the Frogs and Paris and shite, and now I'm the one who wants to stay!!! Good old irony. Never lets you down, eh?

I haven't told Vicks what Karen said during the Phone Call to the Parents Experience. I suppose I never thought it would come to this. Karen says the parents have 'washed their hands of me', or some such shite. That they don't 'want anything more to do with me'. That I've 'let them down too often and this is the last straw'. So, when we go back home, I've got no home to go to. I'll only be able to stay with Karen and vile Pete for a few days before all of us go mental. I'm screwed, Gladys. I can't stay with Vicks. The last time I visited her house her folks looked at me as if I was a slug on their posh fucking rose bushes or something. And I don't have any other friends. I'll be forced to live in a crap council flat in Tipton or wherever and basically become one of the living dead.

As much as I hated little Ralphie fuck-wit dog, having him around meant that we had to stay. I knew Vicks wouldn't leave him, as she's soft as shite when it comes to animals. But him dying now is so typical of my life. I'd just managed to talk her out of leaving when it happened. And as Vicks is always saying, it was so fucking freaky that the accident happened at the very spot 'where it all began', ie where me and Vicks met vile Bobby.

Fuck knows why I told her about the you-know-what when I did. If I'd kept my fucking trap shut, maybe she wouldn't have let go of Ralphie's lead and he wouldn't have run across the road to get to another dog, or whatever he was after. But maybe he'd just had enough as well? Just when you think things are going okay, they all turn to shite, Gladys. WHY?????

Should I just stay here? Maybe I fit in best with the tramps. Yeah. Maybe I won't go after all. I haven't decided yet.

I keep wondering what would have happened if me and Vicks hadn't met. If I hadn't seen her at fart college that day. Such a freaky feeling, Gladys. It was like I knew all about her and could look right inside her even before we'd said a single word to each other. I'll never forget it. She was walking up the stairs with this dead snotty-looking bitch and I'd thought, 'what is someone like that doing with someone like her?' It was later on that day that we first got talking. It was easy, effortless, like she also knew how important it was that we got to know each other. Vicki was playing Top Trumps with a couple of tossers from the sculpture class in the crappy canteen, and she asked me if I wanted to join in. Of course I did. From that moment on, no one else seemed to matter at all. It was like all those other fucking tossers just disappeared out of the room. Then, every day we'd meet on the bus and sit next to each other. We'd go to class for a bit and at lunchtime bunk off and buy a half jack of whisky and just get pissed. And the rest is history.

I would never have come here if it wasn't for Vicks, Gladys. I would still be doing stupid sculptures of exploding televisions and stuff. I don't know if that would be better.

Hippy's the only one who knows we're going. He owes us after what happened with Vicks at the squat, so I don't think he'll grass us up. Anyway, I think he's glad we're going. Even though Taffy is no longer one of the posse, I reckon Hippy's still happy we'll be out of the way. Taffy will be all his again, even though Taffy bullies him and cramps his style. Vicks doesn't want anyone else to know we're going. She wants to just disappear one day. Why, though?? I think I'm going to tell Bob.

It's not fair otherwise, is it, Gladys? Maybe Vicks is scared Bob will try and talk us out of it, but I don't think he will. In fact, I know he won't. Because I know Bob's secret. I know why he was in prison and why he gets so sad and why he can't go back to England. I figured it out, Gladys. I asked him about it and he didn't deny it. Another fucked-up thing to add to the list of mind-fuck shit.

Bob was arrested for being a nonce. I hope it wasn't little boys, Gladys. He wouldn't tell me that much. I reckon he just got done for like messing with a rent boy or something. It's so typical, so ironic. Vicks and me are always calling everyone perverts, but it looks like the one guy we actually trusted really is one.

I haven't told this to Vicks. If Bob is sorry for what he's done, does that make it all right?

I have to talk to Vicks and tell her how important it is that she doesn't dump me, although I know it will be tempting.

I'd dump me if I could.

FUCKFUCKFUCK

VICKI:

The Sage Experience

I didn't think we were going to make it. Father Paul had only bought us tickets for the ferry from Calais and our train from Dover to Birmingham. We had to make our own way to the harbour, and we were thrown off at practically every stop. But at least we're travelling light. I gave away all the stuff I'll never need again – including my frayed sleeping bag – to the scammy toothless tramps at the Gare du Nord. And we won't go hungry before we catch the ferry. One of the stops we were dumped at was next to one of those hypermarket places, and we decided to do a spot of begging before we caught the next train. Almost everyone who'd walked past me chucked something in the hat and I'd made an amazing haul. The pocket of Scully Jack is still heavy and distended with a mass of silver francs.

When we reached Calais we still had a bit of time to kill, and Sage decided it would be best spent getting pissed, 'To say "cheers" to Frogland for now,' she said.

It's weird being in a pub again. It's almost like the old fart college days. And this one, although French, is more like an English bar, thank God. Sage and I are huddled at a corner booth on comfy padded benches. The place is dark and smoky and we're the only customers in here. The ashtray in front of us is already overflowing with butts and ash.

'Let's have a whisky,' Sage says. Her voice doesn't sound

too slurry, although both of us have downed three beers.

'You sure?' I check the watch. 'The ferry leaves in about an hour. Shouldn't we head over there? We don't know exactly where to go.'

'C'mon. We've got loads of time. And how hard can it be to find it? Just look for the big fuck-off boat,' she sniggers.

'Don't you think we've had enough?'

'Hello? Can the real Vicki Evans please come back? Since when have you turned into Mother Grundy?' She nods at the bar. 'Make mine a double.'

Of course it's me who has to go up to the bar and order the drinks, even though the barman speaks perfect English. I smother a surge of irritation. Even after all these months of living here it's still up to me to do the dirty work: get the job, beg for cash, buy the fucking drinks. I'm glad we had a shower before we left Paris, and that the barman, although taciturn, doesn't look at me as if I'm a stinky *clochard*. I catch a glimpse of myself in the mirror behind the bar. Little pin-headed Vicki. I don't look anywhere as knackered as I feel though. I wonder what people will think of us when we get back. Will they think we've changed? Do we look different? Thinner? Older? Harder? Damaged? I glance down at my feet and wince – I still feel a nasty lurch of panic whenever I realise Ralphie isn't there. It's not just the painful images of Ralphie's death scene that are doing my head in. As I stood staring down at the accident, there was another part of me, a vile, *twisted* part that was relieved. Relieved that the only thing that was keeping me here was gone. Was dead.

I hate myself for this.

I shake my head to clear it, and take a sip of whisky as I carry the drinks back to Sage.

'So,' Sage says, after downing her double in one go and taking a follow-up sip of beer. 'What happens next?'

'What do you mean?'

'When we get home, of course.'

'I dunno.'

'We'll be coming back here, right?'

I want to say: *what for*? But I don't. Sage has got it into her head that we're only going back to England for a week or so. I've played along with it. Maybe it's time for me to put the record straight. 'What would happen if we *didn't* come back here, Sage?'

'What the fuck do you mean, Vicks?'

'Well . . . we could always get ourselves a job, maybe go back to college for a bit . . .' I let my voice trail away.

'You don't understand, do you?' she snaps.

'What?'

'I haven't got any fucking 'A' levels like you have.'

'So?'

'I've got fuck all to fall back on, Vicks. And you think the college will have me back after what happened? Not fucking likely!'

'So try and get into the Wolverhampton one or something.'

Sage looks at me as if I'm mad. 'I tried, Vicks. Stourbridge only just let me in and I was on probation there for most of the fucking time.'

'But why? Your art was awesome.'

'Yeah, whatever. Try telling that to the stupid tossers who teach there.'

We drink in silence. I can sense the crackle of a potential fight in the air.

'Think we'll have a criminal record?' I say, trying to diffuse the tension.

'God knows,' she sighs. 'Hopefully it'll all have blown over by the time we get back home.' She thumps the table and I jump. 'The plan was, you check on your nan and then we come back here, only more sorted this time, and really try and start something up with the art. We can't just leave Bob and everyone, can we? He just thinks we're going away for a couple of days.'

'Yeah . . . course.'

'Then after we've come back here for a bit and earned a fair whack of cash, we could go travelling for a bit.'

'Sounds like a plan.' Even to my ears it sounds like a lie.

'Another drink?' she asks.

'Sure,' I say. But I don't want one. Again she looks at me meaningfully and I get up and go to the bar. She's getting quite pissed. We both are.

Again she downs the whisky in one go. She looks me dead in the eye. 'Cheers', she says.

'Cheers,' I say. 'Shall we toast to—'

'I love you, Vicki.'

I can't have heard her properly. 'I – you what?'

'I love you.'

Assuming she's taking the piss, I snort with laughter. 'Nice one, Sage. I lurve you too,' I say in a fake French accent.

She smiles at me as if she's just tasted something sharply acidic. 'I mean it, Vicks.' She picks up my left hand, which is lying like a dead fish on the table. She starts stroking my palm. 'I *mean* it, Vicks.'

I struggle to swallow. 'I'm not sure I know what you're saying.'

'You know,' she says, letting my hand drop onto the table. I don't move it. I don't dare.

'Sage? Is that what you wanted to tell me? That day? When Ralphie . . . you know?'

'Doesn't matter now, Vicks,' she says, her voice dead.

I have absolutely no idea what to do or say right now. How can I possibly make this right? I think again about the scars on her arms. How well do I actually know her? *Really* know her? 'Maybe we could go travelling when we get back,' I say.

'I've always fancied going to Israel. Maybe we could go on a kibbutz or something?' God, could I sound any more insincere?

Sage smiles again in that forced way. 'There's something else,' she says. 'Something I haven't told you.'

Oh God. 'What now?'

'You know Rat Girl?'

'Yeah, course. What about her?' I'm relieved she's changed the subject. Maybe things will be all right after all.

'She has AIDS.'

'*What?* No way. How come you know?'

There's something in her eyes that's making me feel more than just uneasy.

'Taffy told me.'

'Blimey. Poor old Rat Girl.'

'Don't you get it?'

'Eh?'

'You know you can get it from sharing needles, don't you? It's not just gays who catch it.'

The floor dips, and the walls begin to spin. 'Oh fuck.'

'Yeah. Sorry to have to tell you that. Sorry to fuck up your life and all.' Her voice is still lifeless, but now there are tears rolling down her cheeks.

Water floods into my mouth and my guts twist. I'm going to be sick. I jump up and race to the loos, knocking my knee on a bar stool as I push my way into the ladies.

When I get back to our table, Sage and her bag are gone. I race outside and look up and down the street. I can't see her anywhere. I walk back inside. There's a sketch book on the table. I pick it up. Pages flutter out from inside it and drift onto the damp carpet. I recognise them instantly. It's the story I wrote for Sage's birthday.

I flick through the rest of the pages in the book. It's full of slanting angry writing. In some areas the biro looks to have gone through the page.

I put it in my bag.

The waiting room for foot passengers at Calais reeks of old vomit and spilled beer, or maybe it doesn't and I'm just smelling the stink wafting off my sweaty skin.

It had taken a lifetime to walk to the ferry station. I wandered down to the harbour like a sleepwalker, my bag hanging like a dead thing from my shoulder. For once it had barely bothered me. What the fuck am I going to do? Shall I get on the ferry? I can't see her anywhere.

We've only got one ticket each. One chance to get home today.

I have to decide.

I take out the book and read the last entry again.

I make my decision.

SAGE

Dear Victoria Evans, what I just told you I told you from the heart.

I know you're not planning on coming back here. I know it and you know it.

Best you get yourself tested for HIV when you get back.

Don't try and find me. You won't be able to.

You are a coward and stupid fucking selfish CABBAGE SLUT.

I meant what I said and you never believed it.

Goodbye, Gladys. Looks like you were my only fucking friend after all.

SHARON

Backstory and acknowledgements

Pompidou Posse was first published in South Africa almost a decade ago. When it came out, several people said to me that they'd been shocked by the behaviour and naivety of the two main characters. I secretly enjoyed the looks on their faces when I told them the book is based on true events and at least one of the characters is based on me (they were right though – I was exceptionally stupid when I was a teenager). I chose not to write the novel as a straight memoir, partly because I prefer writing fiction, and partly because I took too many drugs in the eighties and there are gaping holes in my memory. Some of the events in the novel happened, some of them might have happened, and some of them are made up.

Years after it was first published, Anne Perry at Hodder & Stoughton managed to get her hands on a copy via her partner, Jared Shurin, who is a generous and valiant supporter of South African fiction. Anne offered to publish it in the UK, and I was given a chance very few writers get, not only to see an orphan novel rehomed, but to re-edit a piece of writing that is already in print. I never re-read anything after it's published because I'm a massive coward, and the temptation to rewrite it from scratch was huge. In the end I decided I didn't want to completely erase the rawness of it, as for some reason I thought this would be cheating. This version has had some nips and tucks, but nothing major (a nose job rather than full-on plastic surgery).

It was disconcerting not only rereading and revisiting the book, but revisiting the memory of writing of it as well (it was written as part of an MA through the University of Cape Town), as the lines between the factual events and the made up bits are blurred for me now. It's a real struggle to unpick the fictional from the autobiographical, but I'm not sure that really matters anyway.

Despite evidence to the contrary in Sage's furious Franco-bashing sections, I love Paris – it's my favourite city – but I'm not sure Vicki and Sage would get away with their antics these days. Like me, they are very much products of the eighties (I do like to think of them using Google maps to find the soup kitchen though, or starting a 'me & my dog are hungry' Kickstarter or Twitter campaign).

All mistakes in both versions are, of course, all mine.

Many thanks are due to the following wonderful people:

Anne Perry, who loved the novel enough to revive it from the place where first books go to die. Kelwyn Sole, my MA supervisor, who put up with reams of awful writing with grace and humour. Mike Nicol, who read the manuscript, and then – amazingly – stood up at the Cape Town Book Fair and dared a room full of publishers to publish it (I don't think it would have ever have been published if it wasn't for him). Jane Bowman of Penguin SA who took up Mike's challenge and bravely published a novel set entirely in France in South Africa. My best friend Charlie, who was with me when I returned to Paris to write the first draft in 2006 – together we scoured the city looking for any of the characters and clochards who might still be alive. My daughter Savannah who is not only my most trusted reader but is thankfully far smarter than I am and has never run away from home and developed a drug habit. My mum, Carol Walters, whose help with the re-edit was invaluable and who somehow managed to hide her horror when she first read the details of what her daughter *actually* got up to when she went missing in the eighties. Everyone who kindly read or reviewed the book, especially Jared Shurin, Naomi Wicks, Nig, Si, Paige Nick, Sally Partridge, Karina Szczurek, Natasha Himmelman, Tania van Schalkwyk, Terry Westby-Nunn, Deji Olukotun, Helen Moffett, Lauren Beukes, Louis Greenberg and Sam Wilson.

Thanks and appreciation also goes to my agent Oli Munson, Conrad Williams at Blake Friedmann, Vero Norton and Fleur Clarke, and all at A.M Heath and Hodder & Stoughton.

The novel is dedicated to Savannah, but it's also for Parsley, who was a great and true friend.

Do you wish this wasn't the end?

Join us at www.hodder.co.uk, or follow us on
Twitter @hodderbooks to be a part of our community
of people who love the very best in books and reading.

Whether you want to discover more about a book
or an author, watch trailers and interviews, have the
chance to win early limited editions, or simply browse
our expert readers' selection of the very best books,
we think you'll find what you're looking for.

And if you don't,
that's the place to tell us what's missing.

We love what we do, and we'd love you to be part of it.

www.hodder.co.uk

 @hodderbooks

 HodderBooks

 HodderBooks

Enjoyed this book?
Want more?

Head over to

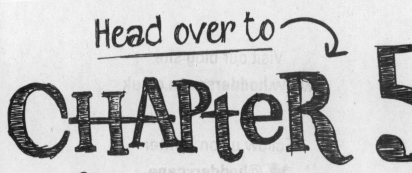
CHAPteR 5

for extra author content,
exclusives, competitions – and lots
and lots of book talk!

Our motto is
Proud to be bookish,
because, well, we are ☺

See you there...

f Chapter5Books 🐦 @Chapter5Books

WANT MORE?

If you enjoyed this and would like to find out about similar
books we publish, we'd love you to join our online SF,
Fantasy and Horror community, Hodderscape.

Visit our blog site
www.hodderscape.co.uk

Follow us on Twitter
🐦 **@hodderscape**

Like our Facebook page
f **Hodderscape**

You'll find exclusive content from our authors,
news, competitions and general musings, so feel
free to comment, contribute or just keep an eye on
what we are up to. See you there!